PRAISE FOR
ALL THE LITTLE HOUSES

"Nobody does explosive and twisted like May Cobb does it. She's in a league of her own."

—Lisa Jewell, #1 *New York Times* bestselling
author of *Don't Let Him In*

"All the Little Houses is May Cobb's most explosive book yet. And trust me, that's saying a lot."

—Jeneva Rose, #1 *New York Times* bestselling author

"Addictive and wildly satisfying."

—Karin Slaughter, *New York Times* and #1 international
bestselling author

"May Cobb does it again—*All the Little Houses* is a deliciously sharp and unflinching dissection of ambition, legacy, and the brutal politics of small-town status. Set against the sweltering backdrop of 1980s East Texas, Cobb weaves a tale as seductive as it is sinister. With the formidable Charleigh Andersen at its center—a woman who built her kingdom from scratch and will burn it all down before she gives it up—this novel grabs you by the throat and doesn't let go. If you love your thrillers laced with danger and dripping in secrets, this one's for you."

—Julie Clark, *New York Times* bestselling
author of *The Ghostwriter*

"A spicy cocktail of mean girls, bad boys, and secrets bigger than the prairie sky. It goes down easy but packs a punch."

—Riley Sager, *New York Times* bestselling author of *With a Vengeance*

"Deliciously twisted! May Cobb does it again! *All the Little Houses* goes down as easy as a cold margarita on a scorching summer day. I devoured it!"

—Elle Cosimano, *New York Times* bestselling author of *Finlay Donovan Is Killing It*

"Big money, big hair, and even bigger secrets will keep the pages flying in *All the Little Houses*, with May Cobb's signature rich bitch characters that shock and enthrall. *All the Little Houses* is locked and loaded for fans of *The Hunting Wives*!"

—Vanessa Lillie, bestselling author of *Blood Sisters*

"Crisp and delicious and devious as a strong cocktail, vivid and atmospheric and steamy as a hot summer day. Reading May Cobb is like happy hour with your most fun frenemy dishing out the juiciest gossip you've ever heard in your life, and *All the Little Houses* is her best novel yet."

—Rachel Harrison, *USA Today* bestselling author of *Play Nice* and *So Thirsty*

"Get ready for next year's obsession: *All the Little Houses* is a dynamic, multilayered powerhouse of a book from an author who writes the inner lives of complicated women with uncanny depth. May Cobb perfectly captures the intensity and precariousness of female relationships, rivalry, jealousy, and obsession, set against the sultry backdrop of an 1980s Texas summer. Timely, twisty, and utterly explosive."

—Laurie Elizabeth Flynn, *USA Today* bestselling author of *Till Death Do Us Part* and *The Girls Are All So Nice Here*

ALL

THE

LITTLE

HOUSES

MAY COBB

Copyright © 2026 by May Cobb
Cover and internal design © 2026 by Sourcebooks
Cover design by Claire Sullivan
Cover images © Silvijo Selman/Arcangel, Jose A. Bernat Bacete/Getty
Images, RapidEye/Getty Images, the_burtons/Getty Images
Internal design by Tara Jaggers/Sourcebooks
Internal image © Peter Dazeley/Getty Images

Published by Sourcebooks Landmark, an imprint of Sourcebooks
1935 Brookdale RD, Naperville, IL 60563-2773
(630) 961-3900
sourcebooks.com

Cataloging-in-Publication Data is on file with the Library of Congress.

Printed and bound in the United States of America.
MA 10 9 8 7 6 5 4 3 2 1

This is dedicated to the beloved memory of Tanda Tashjian,
cherished teacher,
friend,
and guide.
You told me I'd write many, many books, and kept on telling me until
I believed you. Thank you, thank you for always being the light.

They were howling in the moonlight—enormous, and
so close Laura could almost see their glittering eyes.

"Pa," she whispered, turning from the window,
"the wolves have made a circle around the
whole house. What will we do?"

—Laura Ingalls Wilder,
Little House on the Prairie

PROLOGUE

Later

The water claps along the marshy shoreline, its calming ticktock like the clicking hands of a metronome.

Under the spotlight of the full moon, though, the normally placid lake roils, its metallic surface disturbed by both the torching summer breeze and the body recently thrust there.

It's not sinking fast enough. Not as fast as I imagined it would.

And from the car speakers twenty feet away, I can just make out the lyrics to the song the local station has been playing on repeat all summer, a song that seems perfectly summoned for this moment:

Michael Hutchence singing about every one of us having the devil inside.

PART I

I

NELLIE

Now

twist the knob on my car stereo, silencing it.

Just moments before, I was blasting Prince while cruising out here, driving too fast on the backcountry roads, sun bleaching the wild grass a pale yellow, searing the top of my head, the wind whipping my hair into a knotted mess. But I don't care. It's summer. I *have* to drive with the top down. Why else would I have this cherry-red Beamer convertible?

Mom thinks I like fluffy music like Madonna, and her songs are *okay*, but Prince is the tasty little secret I keep from her. Well, one of many. She thinks she knows everything about me; she practically does, but I keep a few things to myself. And Prince is one of them. When I listen to his music, I don't feel like the little rich bitch who lives in Longview's biggest mansion, whose mommy buys her every crisp new Esprit and Guess outfit she wants, and also buys her friends.

I feel free. Wild. Capable of anything.

I kill the engine. It crackles as it cools, little pings of noise, bacon popping in a skillet. I don't want them to notice me, the crowd that's gathered down on the dock. No one turned in my direction when I pulled into the dirt lot, so no one has spotted me yet, thank freaking God. I'm too stirred up, not ready to face them.

I planned on springing from the car, making my way down there with a freshly lit cigarette wedged between my lips, when the crowd parted and I glimpsed her, hands above her head, dancing like she's some freaky hippie from Woodstock. She was showing off some move, and when she finished, she threw her head back, laughed that rough laugh of hers.

Jane Swift.

What the fuck is she doing *here*?

This is *our* spot. Miller's Swimming Hole. Only the rich kids come here.

Who the fuck invited *her*?

Rage builds in the back of my throat, and I want to scream, but instead, I take a nice, long pull of my drink, a cherry limeade from Sonic, packed with their pellet ice, spiked with vodka—lots of it. The alcohol feels good as it slides down, burning away the rage. Or at least numbing it.

She and her weird family moved here a few weeks ago, right before school let out. Who does that? Moves at the end of the school year? We're both juniors, about to be seniors, and there she was in my trig class, the cute new girl soaking up all the attention.

I don't have any friends—not any real friends—but I'm used to it. It's been this way my whole life. I'm a bully, a mean girl, people say, and Mom's always had to bribe my way into acceptable society. People basically *have* to be friends with me. So I'm in with the rich bitches, even if they don't like it. Even if they try and exclude me. Even if they're distant.

It doesn't bug me much—most everyone in town is an idiot anyway—but watching Jane just now, parading in the spotlight, makes it glaringly obvious what an outcast I truly am.

When they first got here, Mom and I were downtown, shopping at Ritz's, the high-end clothing store. We spotted her and her mother on the sidewalk, heading toward Smithy's—basically the feed store. I snickered as they passed us, both of them wearing sad little homemade dresses. But Jane walked with this strut of confidence that pissed me off.

Who the fuck does she think she is? I thought to myself.

As soon as they disappeared inside a store, I said in a low voice to Mom, "I don't like her." Meaning Jane.

"I don't like her either," Mom said.

That's just how we are with each other. She knows to always agree with me.

I take another scorching sip of my drink now, letting the liquor trickle through my veins, dull my thoughts.

Behind the group, the river sparkles, catching the sunlight. It's beautiful out here. It's always been one of my favorite places; everyone is more carefree by the water. Drinking, smoking, swimming. Diving off the roof of the old metal boathouse. And it's just understood that we'll show up at sunset most summer nights. You don't need, like, a formal invitation or anything; you just have to be in with the in crowd, which I guess Jane now officially is. *Ugh.*

She's ruining the beauty of it all. Everyone thinks she's so pure and innocent in her homemade fucking bikini. But I see what she's doing as she casually tugs the thong out of her crack, drawing all eyes to her.

Her own eyes are almond shaped and green—wholesome eyes—but she saves this wicked, evil glare just for me. Shoots it at me when no one's looking. Everyone else, it seems, thinks she hung the fucking moon.

As fucking if.

I don't get it. And normally, one would get skewered in town for having those buck teeth of hers. All our smiles have been trained to perfection with braces, followed by headgear and retainers to maintain, but on her, wild teeth are somehow sexy?

Dustin joked right out of earshot—I saw him make the blow job gesture to his friends—that he bets she's good at going down. I knew he was just doing it to get a rise out of me. It's his main goal in life. Not that she'd ever go after *him*. His family is among the richest in town, second only to mine, so we've lived in the same neighborhood all our lives, but, like me, he's not all that good-looking. I'm with him only because no one else will go out with me, and Mom made it good and goddamn clear that I would have a boyfriend, even if it were a fake arrangement.

I like Dustin okay, but I won't let him do anything other than take off my bra, get to second base. But that doesn't mean he stops trying to go further, every single time. We're stuck together, at least until we graduate, which can't happen one goddamn second too soon.

I suck the rest of my drink from my Styrofoam cup, getting a large hit of the alcohol that's settled at the bottom. I yank down my visor to study my face. My cheeks are flushed, my lips are cherry red to match the car, and my cobalt-blue eyes are swimming. Normally, I'd be satisfied enough with how I look to bolt down there, drop into the crowd, but now I snap the visor back up and drill my eyes into Jane's form, wishing I had super-powers to set things on fire just by looking at them, like Drew Barrymore in *Firestarter*.

I flinch when the icy liquid hits my hot thigh. Without even realizing it, I drilled a hole in the bottom of my cup while staring at Jane.

Jane, who has nothing and is nothing. Who lives on a farm on the outskirts of town. Her dad's a fucking carpenter—but they all act like he's Jesus or something.

Now she's twirling, arms above her head again, before she climbs the rickety ladder to the top of the boathouse, then dives off. Everyone cheers her on.

Everyone seems to already love her.

Whatever.

I'm a rat, and I know another rat when I see one.

2

CHARLEIGH

The waiting is hard. No, excruciating.

Charleigh swishes past the open curtains for the third time this morning, checking for Jackson's convertible in the circular drive, a lavish river of concrete gushing through the turf-green lawn. One of the many extravagant touches she commissioned for this place.

So unlike the dirt drive of her childhood. Forlorn, pitted, and weed-pocked. An actual river of glassy mud when the springtime rains came. The hemline of Charleigh's clothes splattered with muck as she trudged each morning to catch the school bus.

Now she peers around at her manse, watching as morning sunlight splashes across the marble floors, filling the house with light. Freshly squeezed lemonade being poured into a clean, empty glass.

She chews a nail as she stands at the window.

Lettie, her long-suffering housekeeper, could just let him in when he rings the bell, but Charleigh always likes to be the one to greet Jackson. Prying open the hulking pair of doors, folding his taut, tanned form into her arms. The two of them squealing like it's been forever, even though they see each other nearly every damn day.

It's part of their schtick, their special bond.

A signal to anyone looking on (and Charleigh *does* love an audience) that they are the most important people in the world to each other.

Twin bitches, she likes to joke. Charleigh calls him Jackson, but in serious moments, she'll draw out his full name, Jackson Lee Ford, the only person to do so other than his estranged mother, Willamena.

Her stomach continues to churn. She *hates* this feeling, the almost agonizing pinch in her gut. It's not desperation, exactly, but rather anticipation, and she wishes she didn't still get this excited—no, needy—at seeing her best friend.

Her only friend?

At least, her only true one.

He's coming over today to help her decorate for her weekly Bunco night.

In just eight short hours, this room will be buzzing with the sound of a dozen women. Women she claims as friends and women who, in turn, claim her. And technically, they *are* friends, but not in the same way as she and Jackson.

Soon, this space will be filled with the feral clatter of gossip, the clinking of glasses—first champagne, and later, for dessert, grasshoppers—voices climbing higher in octave to match the surging of blood-alcohol levels.

Charleigh's nerves will be muted by then, her own blood-alcohol ratio at peak level as she sweeps her gaze across the room, satisfaction trickling over her when she registers that—once again—she's successfully hosted this klatch of women in her home. They're having fun! Skin flushed, eyes swimming with booze—lost in the dice game and chatter.

But until then, she's hell on wheels, annoying even herself.

"I don't know why you throw these things," Alexander purred into her ear last night as he unclasped the front of her bra. "They make you crazy. And not the good kind of crazy that I'm about to make you."

"Ha!" That familiar rush of attraction zipped over her that she always feels when Alexander makes his moves.

But she also felt a flash of annoyance.

Because he doesn't understand.

He doesn't get it; he's not from here.

Doesn't know what it was like to grow up in this town. Judged by these very women who now hustle into her house, lapping up proximity to the richest family in Longview.

Charleigh grew up here poor, outcast, even made fun of and bullied until she fled to Dallas for community college, then returned triumphant just three years later, engaged to handsome Alexander Andersen, oil heir from Highland Park.

Six foot two with pale golden hair, lean but muscular, with intense eyes the slate color of fjords from his great-grandparents' homeland of Sweden, Alexander was—and continues to be—the answer to Charleigh's prayers. Their attraction was instant, their bond magnetic.

"You seriously should do something else with your energy." He continued undressing her.

But before her lips could form an answer, he was already pecking at her breasts, thoughts of the upcoming Bunco night sliding away as he hoisted her onto the edge of their bed.

3

JANE

Everyone loves a good girl. Especially a poor one, stuck in her station in life, who knows her lowly place yet manages to plaster on a smile.

Here's an underdog they can all root for, but not be threatened by.

She will never have what they have; the cards are stacked against her, so: *Bless her heart.*

But look at how she smiles, curtsies, all gratitude and light, repeating her father's down-home parables about honesty and self-worth.

I don't mind being that girl. Been her my whole life. Teeth bared, yet lips curved into a grin. A warm sensation spreads across my chest when I first meet someone, win them over. It's so easy.

Too easy, in this one-pony town.

Here, they are hungry for someone like me. Ready to feed off me in order to feel better about themselves.

Had a nice chat with that Jane girl today; she sure is sweet!

She doesn't have a stitch of new clothing, but it doesn't seem to bother her, poor thing!

Wonder if we should bring her family a meal? Add them to the church meal chain?

"I have a good feeling about this place, Sunshine," Pa said to me the night we first arrived.

And I do, too. Honestly, despite my complaints.

As soon as I stepped from the truck, the tangy night air suckled my skin. In the deep pines, it's way more humid than in Dallas, and the heat—coupled with the wild honeysuckle strangling our fence, stamping the air with its reckless scent—felt embryonic.

I circled the path around the pond, the grass high and dewy, licking my calves, and gazed up at the belt of stars pulsing in the sky.

I hadn't glimpsed a single star in Dallas.

Then there was the impromptu swim in the pond with Pa that first night after we got the horses settled. The water felt as warm as the stack of pennies baking in the ashtray of our truck.

I hated Dallas. Hated the big city and the fact that we had to let go of most of our livestock. Hated the filthy air and the bland strip malls.

Hated it all except for Luke.

Just thinking of him now sends shivers over me. I miss him so much.

Even though Dallas wasn't for me, that's where he is, and I was torn up—still am—over our sudden departure.

But it couldn't be helped.

"We gotta get back to the land. To what we know," Pa told our neighbor, an elderly gentleman named Mr. Baxter, who was always in his front yard tinkering with a vehicle sitting on cinder blocks.

"Sure gonna miss y'all," Mr. Baxter said, then packed a wedge of Skoal in his gums.

I won't miss seeing that, I thought, but just grinned back.

What we know is homesteading. Our rowdy pigs. Chickens. Farm-fresh eggs so natural, the yolks are the color of tangerines. Not the store-bought, watery mass-produced stuff.

Mom's little wooden shed filled with her drying herbs. Her oils.

The land. Our luscious gardens with tomatoes so heavy, the vines threaten to snap.

Pa's woodworking shop.

The land is in my blood. It's who I am.

I'll never get sick of an open night sky, so pitch-black that it looks like I'm gazing into a bottomless well. I'll never get sick of riding Cookie, my thoroughbred, legs clamped around her strong back as she ferries me through the pasture.

But now that I'm seventeen, I *am* getting tired of some aspects of country living. Of being poor. Wearing handsewn rags, for one, and Mom's hippie-dippie projects. When I was little, dyeing my own clothes and canning fruit was fun. Now it's just humiliating.

Pa tells me we won't always have to live like this. That he's saving.

But peering down at Mom just now from the loft (she can't tell I'm looking at her) as she hums to herself, stirring a pot of figs to make jelly with, I think she *likes* living this way. Likes all this wholesome bullshit.

She circles the kitchen table, then folds her arms around Pa, who's sitting in his chair, whittling a new pipe from a pine log, curls of blond bark spilling onto the packed-dirt floor.

This all is enough for her.

One of the cross-stitches she made when I was a baby hangs above the stove in the kitchen:

A truly good wife is the most precious treasure a man can find! She is good to him every day of her life, and with her own hands she gladly makes clothes. She is like a sailing ship that brings food from across the sea. Charm is deceptive, and beauty is fleeting; but a woman who fears the Lord is to be praised.

—Proverbs 31: 10–31

She and Pa trade Bible verses all the time, sing hymnals back and forth. The family Bible stays parked on our kitchen table, Pa's ancestors' names jotted in the front pages with jarringly short life spans.

Every Sunday night, Julia, little Molly, and I are all expected around the campfire for Vespers, to listen to Pa strum on his guitar and belt out gospel songs for us to sing.

But I narrow my eyes while looking down at Mom's plain face: hair tied back with a bandanna, sweat beading on her upper lip, skin free of makeup, clothes smelling of apple cider; it all makes me seethe. I don't want to be anything like her when I'm older. Pacing in a kitchen to please some man. Pretending to love constant manual labor.

Not that Pa is just some man. He's my everything. But not in that gross way you're thinking; I don't have some messed-up Electra complex. It's just that Mom and I, we've never seen eye to eye. She doesn't like me. It's Pa who has the easy grin for me, the spare quarter he slips me when she's not looking.

Julia's always been her favorite, and now baby Molly is her entire world. I'm the middle child, overlooked, even scorned by her.

I have my own mind, and she knows it, can't stand it.

And I don't care how many shirts she sews, how much bread she bakes and homemade butter she churns, she's not enough to keep a man like Pa interested.

CHARLEIGH

The pot of Folgers she brewed at dawn is now cooked down to a layer of quicksand in the bottom of the carafe; the three giant mugs she nursed all morning aren't helping her jumpy feeling either.

But it's not just the coffee jitters, nor Jackson's impending arrival that's got her on edge.

It's Nellie.

Of course it is.

She's in another one of her bad moods, has been since she hit the back door last night from the swimming hole.

And now it's up to Charleigh to fix it.

Before Nellie even made it inside, the screech of her brakes announced her presence in the drive.

Charleigh sighed. She was at the stove, stirring a pot of Hamburger Helper for Nellie's dinner (she and Alexander having already dined on a sumptuous supper of shrimp linguine prepared by Lettie, knowing Nellie would be out) when she heard the tires shriek.

The back door flung open, then thwacked shut. Nellie's feet thumped as she raced up the stairs.

"Dinner is ready, honey!" Charleigh trilled.

Another door slamming.

Shoulders sagging, Charleigh set the wooden spoon down, steeling herself. Plodded upstairs.

She raised her hand to knock on Nellie's door, but before her knuckles ever grazed the surface, Nellie barked out, "Don't wanna eat right now, *Mom*!" The word *mom* speared out of her mouth.

Charleigh eased the door open.

Nellie sat cross-legged on her bed, tugging her knees into her chest. Her face was beet red and shiny with tears.

Charleigh placed a tentative foot on the white carpet.

A sharp shake of Nellie's head. "Not in the mood…to talk…" she said, her words coming out jagged, like she was trying to stifle more tears, "to *you*."

Charleigh inwardly winced and froze in place, hand still on the knob.

But she knew she had to pry.

Nellie keeping things bottled up was a powder keg waiting to blow.

"Trouble with Dustin?"

Nellie exhaled, blowing her bangs skyward. "God, no. As if I give a *shit* about him."

"Nellie—"

"What?"

"Language."

"Oh, please. Learned it all from you." An eye roll.

"What is it, then?" Charleigh crossed the room, sank to her knees in front of the bed.

Another eye roll, another puffed-out sigh, before Nellie lowered herself to talk to Charleigh. "It's that *new* girl. Jane. She's just like"—Nellie's hands flailed around her face—"already the center of attention and everything. I didn't even get into the water tonight. Left before anyone could even see me."

"Well, that's *ridiculous*," Charleigh offered. "She's not even in your same league, honey. You shouldn't let it bother you so much."

Nellie wrenched her knees closer to her body, began rocking. Eyed Charleigh warily, as though to ask, *Why should I trust you?*

"That's the thing: She has *nothing*, so why is she so popular?" Nellie's voice was a live wire sparking through the air. She hopped up then, bounded from the bed, started prowling around the spacious room. A balloon with the air just let out of it. At least she was talking to Charleigh. "She's already *ruining* my summer! She's, like, all free-spirited and slutty and gross, but everyone's obsessed with her!" Nellie was nearly shouting.

Charleigh rose and clapped her hands down on her daughter's shoulders. Combed her brain for the exact right words, the only words that would work magic on Nellie. "Now, you listen to me. Calm down. Whoever this little Jane bitch is, I'll take care of her."

NELLIE

've been awake for an hour, but I'm still in bed, under the covers, stewing over the scene at the swimming hole last night.

Jane fucking Swift.

Ugh.

The sun smolders behind my thick curtains, the latest from Laura Ashley.

My whole room is done in this print—a cream-colored pattern with vines climbing vertically, green stalks dotted with red poppies.

Mom just had my whole room remodeled. By Jackson, of course.

There she was, dressed in overalls, hair twisted in a high ponytail, actually helping Jackson's crew strip the old, yellowing wallpaper, her bright voice bouncing off my walls as they worked, grating in my ears.

I swear she did it just so she could look cute in those overalls, impress Jackson—and Dad. Remind them she comes from tough stock, because she sure as shit doesn't dirty her perfectly manicured hands that often anymore. Also, to burn off some of that manic, demonic energy.

Sigh. She's *exhausting.*

They worked in there all day, her fingernails chipped and shredded as she peeled off the husks of paper. That flawless face dusted with a fine coat of powder from the drywall.

I yank back the curtains, lift my window, the aluminum frame screeching as I do.

From the pocket of my robe, I dig out my pack of Marlboro 100s. Light one, take a stinging drag, spew the smoke down toward the pool.

Mom's laugh assaults my ears, barking out of her, loud and needy. She's such a sight, holding on to Jackson by his elbow, her actual lipstick prints on his butt cheeks, I'm sure of it.

But he needs her, too.

Needs our money.

She disgusts me. Embarrasses me. She's embarrassing *herself* the way she throws herself at him, at others.

I smoke and watch them, eavesdropping on their gag-me-with-a-spoon conversation about how to decorate the house for Mom's Bunco night. It's hideous.

But I'm the pathetic one, really, because I don't have anything better to do. Not now and not all day. Everyone is probably already at Blair Chambers's house. It's not as expensive or huge as mine, but it's *hers.* She runs everything in this town; she's my lifelong nemesis. She's everything I'm not: tall, beautiful, a platinum blond with sheet-straight hair. Popular.

She was at the dock last night, too. Of *course* she was. She's probably the one who invited Jane out there to the swimming hole. And I'm sure Jane has already been invited over to her pool, that she's there today, lying out with the others, flipping through *Teen* magazine.

Blair and I started out as friends in kindergarten, but when we got to elementary, she turned on me, dumped me. Or tried to, anyway. Like I said, Mom's always made sure I'm part of the group, still invited to everything.

"You're not cool enough anymore, Nellie," Blair said to me one day at recess, her switchblade eyes cutting me as she gave me a once-over. A few feet away, the gang of rich bitches who had up until then been my friends, too, laughed.

I was sitting cross-legged on the ground, building mud forts. Blair and I had just been doing that yesterday, when I guess it was still cool. Not anymore, apparently.

"You're just...*so weird*," Blair added with a snort before tromping off with the others.

It wasn't the first time I'd heard that out of her snotty mouth. I've always been the weird one, out of step with everyone else.

Six months later, at Blair's sixth birthday party, I gave her a shoulder when no one was looking. She tumbled down the concrete stairs near her pool and broke her leg.

"What did you do *now*, Nellie?" Blair's mom, Monica, shrieked, stomping over to us.

I knew I was supposed to feel bad; I didn't. A searing feeling oozed over me from watching Blair on the ground, wet blond hair sticking to the grass: vindication.

But I faked a fountain of tears. "I am so, so sorry, Mrs. Chambers! It was an accident—"

By then, Mom was by my side, pulling me into her, shooting daggers at her. "It clearly wasn't on purpose, Monica. Good *God*," Mom hissed.

Later, on the drive home, in the toasty heat of Mom's Cadillac, she scolded me. "You *didn't* bump into her. I saw you. Jesus, Nellie, you don't know your own strength sometimes. Or maybe you *do*. You have *got* to learn how to play nice." She was shaking, fingernails clicking on the steering wheel as she drove, taking corners too fast, her nerves completely shot.

But she taught me then, as she'd taught me even earlier, that she would take my side, smooth things over, come to my rescue. She taught me that I could do whatever the hell I wanted, that she'd cover for me.

It's not just for my benefit, though, that Mom does that, makes sure I'm still part of the clique. God forbid Charleigh Andersen's daughter is excluded from anything; Mom's *way* too much of a social climber to let that happen. It's really all about how it makes *her* look. And her desperate need for approval. From her friends and also from her own child. I have her eating out of my hand. *Fetch, Mom, fetch*, I'm tempted to say to her sometimes.

So yeah, I'll just sit here smoking, festering today, wondering about Jane and what she's doing. Who she's with.

And this is so pitiful to admit, but Mom's the only one I can talk to about it since I don't have any real friends. Not that it made me feel all that great, baring my soul to Mom last night when I got home. I'm well aware you're not supposed to be best friends with your mom, not when you're a teenager. But it's better than talking to the wall. And when she said that *whoever this little Jane bitch is, I'll take care of her*, well, yeah, that made me feel a tiny bit better. Because I know she means it.

But still, it's pathetic I have to confide in Mom. I mean, she doesn't even really know me anymore. How could she? She's only familiar with the little monster she's tried to shape and mold and control into something presentable. She's incapable of understanding me.

She's simple in her thinking, while I'm complex. And I resent her for it. Even as I cling to her, spill some of my secrets like this bullshit over Jane, I'm repelled by her. And grossed out with myself for confiding in her.

I suck in another drag that burns my throat, then grin as my fog of smoke descends upon them. Taunting Mom to say something. To look up here. Catch me.

She won't dare.

It's our sick little game. I know she can smell it, but she acts like she can't, cutting a wide berth because she doesn't want to set me off, get into it with me.

She's weak like that.

Because she's afraid of what I'm capable of.

I grind the cigarette out in the window seal, leaving the

cherry burning, watching it roll in the wind against the screen like a trapped roly-poly. Another dare of mine: seeing if the universe will see fit to burn this whole house down.

6

JACKSON

eat wafts out in waves when Jackson cracks open the door to his blue-green Mercedes. He slides in.

He should've left the top down; the little two-seater gets as hot as a smoking pistol, the tan leather like glue against his skin, but the Andersens' drive is canopied with towering pecan trees that thud their shells, making a big mess.

As he wheels away, he twists around, flicks another wave toward Charleigh.

She looks almost sad, wistful, as she shrinks in his rearview, her perfect figure silhouetted against her monstrously large neocolonial.

Had he known her before she and Alexander had the house built, he would've advised her differently. More Frank Lloyd Wright, less V. C. Andrews. But alas, he's doing all he can now to make the house—at least the inside of it—as tasteful as possible.

The drive meanders down the sloping hill, the tunnel of trees overhead tossing speckled sunlight across Jackson's dash. Finally exiting and pulling onto the street, his bumper grates against Charleigh's too-steep incline as it always does, releasing a gruff, barking sound, no matter how he angles the car.

Whatever.

He's now free for the day.

Not that visiting Charleigh is some chore.

Not that it's not.

He cruises down the mansion-dotted street with a familiar unease. So happy to have seen her—she *is* his best friend and confidant, the only person he's openly out to in Longview—but also, as with his mother, there are strings attached.

He knows deep in his gut that his love for Charleigh is pure; he loves her, he tells himself, but it's complicated by the fact that she's his biggest client. And she if had it her way, she'd be his only client. She sometimes acts like she is.

But he needs to take a chill pill, be grateful that the Andersens are nearly bankrolling his entire one-man operation, Ford Design.

All he had to do today was lounge by the gurgling pool as Lettie splashed more mimosas into their wineglasses, assuring Charleigh that yes, a Hawaiian theme was perfect for tonight's affair.

He trailed her out to their four-car garage, before digging through bins to find the Tiki torches, plastic palm trees, rope lights, pineapple tablecloth, and armful of rainbow-colored leis.

Charleigh's supply closet is infinite.

And yes, he'll get paid for his time today, but sometimes it makes him uncomfortable how what would normally be typical hangout time in other friendships turns into him being on the clock. The boundaries are fuzzy.

Unless he and Charleigh are out at lunch, or at the Boat House, sipping daiquiris by the lake, he always feels like he's on, like he's working.

Plus, there's the whole Nellie drama. Charleigh was all in a tizzy this morning, chirping about how her daughter is having a hard time. Something about some new girl in town.

Sometimes Jackson wants to slap Charleigh, knock some sense into her. Here she is, married to one of the richest, hottest men in town—a serious catch—living a life of endless privilege, yet she's never content, never satisfied, never at peace.

Yes, Nellie is a handful, to put it nicely, but Jackson sometimes wonders if it's not all Charleigh's fault. He's convinced the girl has never heard the word no, and he has to stifle the urge to say as much to Charleigh. He also stifles the urge to tell his friend to relax, to quit being so up in her kid's business. To quit trying to control her. That child has had everything thrown at her, from rhinoplasty to lavish shopping trips at the Galleria in Dallas, as if any of those things really matter. As if they can fix anything or replace real parenting.

No wonder Nellie's a mess.

But, as Jackson's sister, Katelyn, likes to snidely remind him, he has no children of his own, so can he shut the hell up with his snarky opinions whenever he feels like it, please?

Driving down the main road through the quaint town square,

which will lead him to the tidy bungalow he bought for a song and renovated himself, Jackson tries to shake off thoughts of Charleigh and Nellie. He picks up a cassette, warm as a brick pulled out of a kiln, and slides it into the tape deck.

Duran Duran's *Seven and the Ragged Tiger* thumps through the speakers. Even though it's an older album of theirs, he loves it, loves Simon Le Bon's voice, especially on "Union of the Snake." Loves the way it reminds him of his junior year at SMU and his nights with Brad, a jock type who wasn't out, but most certainly should've been. Jackson still thinks about him from time to time, pines for him, remembering the taste of warm beer on Brad's lips, the sharp tang of Benetton on his skin.

As he grooves to the music, Charleigh pops, unbidden, back in his brain. He's annoyed by the intrusion.

But then, *he loves her*, as he reminds himself again.

She accepts Jackson. And she of all people knows what it's like not to be accepted. Poor as mud when she was growing up. She drove Jackson by her childhood home one afternoon while they were out day drinking, buzzed on margaritas.

He shuddered when she pointed to the depressing lean-to, seemingly plopped down in the middle of an unkempt, marshy pasture on the edge of town. Couldn't fathom that this same woman sitting next to him, mountains of exquisitely primped blond hair spilling over her shoulders, steering her black Jaguar expertly over the blacktop road, once existed there.

But, Jackson muses, the ghost of that insecure inner child still haunts Charleigh, still lurks within her, and that's what draws him to her while simultaneously repelling him. Her bottomless need makes him confident, secure in their bond, while sometimes threatening to engulf him, drown him altogether. Makes him want to run for his life.

Later

The body still bobs on the surface of the lake, a marsh-mallow floating in hot chocolate.

Why am I thinking of hot chocolate right now?

And *why* is it not sinking?

It's not like I thought any of this through beforehand, though. I didn't know this was gonna happen. It wasn't premeditated.

I just *snapped*.

And now I have to figure out what the hell I'm gonna do, how to clean all this up.

Fuck. Shit. What did I do?

7

CHARLEIGH

Now

Charleigh twists her diamond studs from her ears, plunks them down on her vanity, then studies herself in the mirror. *Not too shabby*, she thinks, flipping a curled sheet of hair over her shoulder, the reflection of her ice-blue eyes made even more startling by the thick black liner she applied before the party.

The house is now quiet, empty, the last guests gone, though she can still hear the clapping of car doors in her long drive.

Nellie is sleeping, as far as Charleigh can tell; she's not about to creep down the hall to check.

Alexander is still at men's poker night—they play the same night as Bunco—but their evenings stretch out longer, past midnight, at a local club called the Pig Trail Inn. It's all men bullshitting over cigars dwindling in the ashtray and endless glasses of Jack and Coke.

By 1:00 a.m., Charleigh will be awakened by Alexander's

hands stirring over her belly, sliding down the front of her panties. He will take her then, Charleigh suspended between the dream state and this one.

She loves it, their lovemaking, which has remained as intact and incendiary as when they first met. She was in her fifth semester of community college—her half-hearted attempt at higher education while waitressing. Alexander, though, was a senior at SMU, ready to graduate, and also a brother at the coveted Gamma Phi fraternity. But he wasn't like other frat boys she'd slept with, all drunken fumblers pawing at her. For one, Alexander had his own place, a carriage house his parents had purchased so he could have his own space during senior year. *His own lair*, she thought, after she learned just how good he was in the sack. She'll never forget their first time, how he bent her over the side of his neatly made bed, fingers expertly working her over until she was in such a frenzy that by the time he entered her, she came instantly.

There's no way he hadn't been with several girls before her—he knew *exactly* what he was doing, and he was so criminally hot—but since then, he's been all hers, doesn't have eyes for anyone else.

Charleigh is criminally hot herself.

And tonight, she knows she won't even be sleeping when he gets home.

She's too riled.

Fucking Monica and Kathleen. Well, Monica anyway. Kathleen is too dumb to be that mean, that manipulative, but her chiming in didn't help matters.

After the third round of Bunco, they took their usual break. Lettie trotted out the tray of grasshoppers, frothy green liquid wobbling in crystal glasses.

"So," Charleigh ventured, her voice slurry with booze, "anyone know anything about the new family in town? The Swifts, or whatever they call themselves?"

She was standing while everyone else was seated, scattered around on the plush sectionals. Charleigh's elbow was hitched on the mantel, drawing all eyes her way; she knew full well how her new Bill Blass jeans flattered her, the way they hugged her ass. *I got Bill Blass on my ass*, she joked earlier to Jackson when she called him right before the party.

"Uh, yeah. You seen the husband? He's *so* dishy," Peggy Beckworth piped up, her pitch-black hair swooped to one side as she took a stinging drag off her Virgina Slim. "Saw the whole family at the farmers market last weekend. They look poor, but he's rich in the looks department." Her red-stained lips curved into a grin.

"He's totally smokin'." The sound of Monica's throaty voice weighing in made Charleigh's stomach clench. "I was getting the car filled yesterday, and he pulled into the gas station. Knew it was him because *Swift Custom*—guess it's his business—was painted on the side of his truck."

"Okaaaay," Charleigh drawled. "So, the husband's hot?" She tossed up her hand to say, *So what?*

"And Blair likes the daughter. Jane or something." Monica's eyes gripped Charleigh's with her own, clearly seeking a reaction.

Monica knows that Nellie having no friends and being all but shut out by Blair years ago is Charleigh's Achilles' heel.

Like mother, like daughter.

Monica Chambers, the queen bee of Longview. Always has been. And even though Charleigh and Alexander's wealth unseated the Chambers years ago as one of the town's richest families, Monica is still in charge. Of everything. And everyone. They all think she's some kind of goddess, but Charleigh doesn't even find her particularly attractive. One might describe her as a classic beauty—all fine bones and refined angles, a frosty blond with just enough hairspray to lock in her hot-rollered hair—but the rich-bitch look makes Charleigh's skin crawl.

Anger made Charleigh's throat close up; she shot Monica a tight smile.

"Said she's going out with Jane tomorrow night. Picking her up. And Charleigh," she said, her voice tinged with haughtiness, going in for the kill, "they live out on some farm, out by where *you* grew up." She crinkled her nose at the mention of Charleigh's childhood home.

Monica never passes up an opportunity to bring up Charleigh's impoverished past, reminding her that she's not one of them, not really. No matter how much money she has, she never will be.

Charleigh lifted her drink, then swirled the mint-green cocktail around in the glass before downing the rest. Damn it was good, tasted like candy. But more than that, drinking it gave her mouth something to do other than respond to Monica's taunts.

From across the room, Kathleen sat perched on an ottoman, her slender figure encased in a flattering, flowing red silk gown.

"I didn't want to tell anyone," Kathleen started, her eyes roving around the room conspiratorially, "but I went out to their place and bought one of her potions. And…it's working?"

"*Whose* potions? What are you talking about?" Charleigh's words streamed out of her, high and reedy, desperate; she wished she could vacuum them back up.

"The wife. Name's Abigail. She's kinda pretty but in a down-home way?"

Kathleen has this annoying way of turning plain statements into questions. She is by far the flightiest of the bunch, and also the most fragile, a quality that both ingratiated her to Charleigh— because Charleigh could manipulate her blindfolded—*and* shredded her nerves.

Kathleen choked on her drink, her voice sputtering out of her as her face burned red. "Like I said, I didn't want to tell anyone. But she has this little stand out there, like a…what do you call it, an apothecary or something?" Kathleen looked genuinely confused. "With all these homemade essential oil blends. One of them is called Love Potion, and it's supposed to make your husband want to sleep with you again. Ever since I started wearing it, I can't keep Kyle off me."

A few "hmms," "mmms," and nods rippled across the room.

A mix of both intrigue and of knowing, as if the others were in on it already.

Why hadn't anyone told Charleigh about this? Why was she the last one to know?

"Well, Alexander and I don't need any help in that department." A scoff barked out of her.

"Of *course* you guys don't," Monica said, giving her fake-lashed eyes a roll. "I mean, Chip and I don't need anything like that either, but I *have* been wanting to go out and sample her other offerings, like the one for weight loss. Have another peek at that sexy hubby."

Her other offerings? Again, why was she the last to know?

And weight loss? As if. Monica obsesses constantly about her size, even though she's thin as a bird. Always talking about the latest diet craze in *Cosmo*, punishing herself at the gym at the Boat House multiple times a week. Charleigh possesses too much manic energy to keep weight on her; she's never not in motion, but she drags herself to the weekly classes—Jazzercise and aerobics, Richard Simmons style—just to stay in with the group. After class, the women all gather in the upstairs lounge, bodies sheathed in leotards, skin lacquered with sweat, and gossip while they nurse strawberry daiquiris.

"Weight loss, huh?" Charleigh shot back at Monica.

Another roll of Monica's eyes, a brittle smile that said to Charleigh, *Got ya, made you bite.* And also: *Is that all you got?*

Charleigh's fingernails were digging into her skin, she realized, rage making her ball her fists into tight boxing gloves.

Sometimes, she fantasized about clutching her hands around Monica's neck, squeezing hard until her eyes bulged and the breath left her. This fantasy went back all the way to junior high when Monica, at a slumber party, had chosen Charleigh's bra to be the one placed in the freezer. It wouldn't have been a big deal to any other girl at the party, but Charleigh, of course, had the most cheaply made bra, and Monica led the rest of the gang in a long taunt about it.

Charleigh's bra is from Kmart! Can you imagine?

Charleigh's eyes had glossed with tears as she stormed from the room, then locked herself in the bathroom until Monica finally relented.

Now she forced her hands to go soft, unclench. "Who wants another grasshopper?" she asked the women, eager to change subjects.

Later that evening, as everyone began to trickle out, Charleigh tugged Kathleen by the elbow, pulling her into the empty parlor. "Where is the Swifts' place, exactly?"

"Oh, you heard Monica. It's out by your mama and daddy's place—" Kathleen belted out, her voice as loud as a dinner bell.

"Shhhh!"

"Oops, sorry, I know I get loud when I drink." Kathleen's shoulders shrank into themselves. She was always apologizing for everything. "But their place is out on Seven Pines Road. Near the highway. You can't miss it. Little house on the hill with a red mailbox."

8

JANE

Summer for us isn't like summer for other teens. Ours are filled with chores, with work.

Right now it's not even nine in the morning, and already my hands are stained purple, my arms slashed with scratches from the wild blackberry vines. It's picking season for both the blackberries and blueberries, just one of the things I'm in charge of.

I'll rinse my harvest later, piling the berries high on a cotton towel to let them dry before Mom turns them into preserves. If there's extra, Pa aims to make batches of homemade wine from the fruit. He's been sneaking me his homemade wine since I was thirteen. Just little nips in the evening when he thinks Mom's not looking.

I drag my wooden bucket to the next aisle, kneel on the soggy ground. This work, I don't mind so much. I'm at the edge of our land, high on a ridge behind the pond, far from the house.

Far from Mom, far from Julia.

Ugh. Why is my sister so harsh?

Just yesterday she ripped my head off out of nowhere. It was dusk, and I'd just gotten back from the swimming hole; she and I were watering the gardens. Our vegetable and herb garden, plus the adjoining one, Mom's poison garden. It's fenced off with chicken wire to keep baby Molly out, as well as the livestock, because the plants there can both heal and kill you. Mom is highly skilled at dosing, knowing the right combos to use in her potions.

Anyway, during summer, we water at night so that the sun can't burn off the moisture, robbing the plants of what they need. We watered in silence, except for the fact that I started whistling, happy and sunbaked from the river. Which seemed to irritate Julia. She didn't say anything, just got huffy, so, as usual, I tried to placate her.

My bikini was hanging next to us, drip-drying, when the thought came to me. "Hey, you should totally come with me sometime to Miller's. The swimming hole. Lotsa cute boys. And you can borrow my suit!" I eyed it, adding, "It'd look so cute on you!"

I looked up at her and grinned, trying to break through her moody silent treatment.

She just laughed to herself, a sad, wicked little sound, then said, "You just don't get it, do you? You think you're so cute. Little Miss Hot Thing with your skimpy bikini. You think you look so good in it. But you don't. You just look slutty. And desperate. Which is all you'll ever be."

Tears stung my eyes, which made Julia smile even wider, and I dropped the hose, then ran into the house. I hate that she can still get to me. That I haven't grown a thick enough skin to not care. But despite her nastiness, I miss her. I do. I miss the sister who used to be my one and only best friend. The one I used to race through fields with, prairies tall with grass, covered in wildflowers. She was my confidant, before she turned on me, became a stranger.

So yeah, I like it here where I can be alone, where I can let my thoughts run wild and free as a river, especially when I think about Luke, my stomach pinching with longing.

It's him I really miss. Our fingers laced together as he sped through West End in Dallas in his Camaro, taking me to the clubs. Our kisses tasting of the clove cigarettes we'd smoke. His hand on my thigh as he shifted gears, the car bucking with each change, then taking off like a rocket through the sooty underpasses.

My hair is wringing with sweat as I twist the blackberries off the vines, but I put the headphones on anyway, press Play on my Walkman. A gift from Luke, as is the mixtape that begins to whir in my ears.

"Fall on Me" by R.E.M. starts and I spread out my thin blanket, lie in the shade of the orchard. It's a broody song, but Luke can be broody. It's the side of him I like most, the romantic side.

When we get out of this place, he often said, his voice low and rough in my ear, *there'll be nothing holding us back.*

This place meant Dallas. Meant school. Meant his lousy homelife with parents who were too hardworking and who judged him too harshly.

New York City, that's where I'm taking ya, he'd promise as his hands roved down my sides. I've never been to New York.

Dallas is one of the biggest cities we've ever lived in.

I was born in Walnut Grove, Minnesota, but we moved right after, when I was just a few weeks old, so I don't even remember it. My entire childhood, my whole life, really, has been us picking up from one small town in the Midwest and moving to another, migrating south as we went.

It's Pa's business. He makes custom furniture for the wealthy, and small towns only have so many of those. So we have to move, sometimes hit the cities. I don't usually mind, except now I miss Luke. I'm gonna quit early today, fix my usual ham-and-cheese sandwich for lunch, then ride Cookie to the general store so I can call him from the pay phone.

We have a phone, of course, but I like to call him in private.

9

NELLIE

can hear the shower running—Mom's morning ritual—so I creep along the hall, head downstairs.

I want to eat my Pop-Tarts in private, without having to get into any bullshit "little chat" with her. But when I round the corner to the kitchen, I hear Dad's laughter; he's sitting at the eat-in, the small TV set tuned to *The Price is Right*.

Bob Barker is *not* funny, it's so *not* a funny show, but Dad's a goofball, so between spoonfuls of Frosted Flakes, he laughs.

"Morning, dollface!"

He's called me *dollface* since I was born.

"Morning." I open the pantry, slit open a foil pack of apple cinnamons, drop two in the toaster.

Dad's sitting on a barstool, leaning over his cereal bowl. Still in his pj's, with bedhead, he looks like a little boy. Make that a little boy with a hangover.

I'm crazy about Dad, mainly because his love for me has always felt real, with no strings attached.

No mind games, no control.

So freaking different from Mom.

Some of my happiest times have been with Dad. When I was little, I'd trail him around his great-grandparents' land in Kilgore, the next town over. Just the two of us tromping around the hundred acres of woods and streams, the land that had made our family filthy rich when oil was struck on it in the '20s. Black gold, they call it. Dad's family was already wealthy, descended from some kind of land barons back in Sweden, but the oil money is a different kind of rich. Unlimited.

Mom hates anything that has to do with being outside—probably because she spent her own trashy childhood poor and depressed out on that hideous farm—so she'd stay behind, get pedicures with her friends, or spend some money.

But on Dad's family's land, crunching golden maple leaves under our feet, he taught me to shoot a rifle, use a bow and arrow. Shit I'm actually interested in.

He doesn't care about all the social bullshit that Mom does. Doesn't watch my every move. He lets me just be me. I think he actually would've preferred to have a son, so when I was little, I did my best to play the part, not that I had to pretend that much: not flinching when the rifle kicked my shoulder, keeping a straight face as we skinned the deer we'd hunted, begging him to drive his Jeep Wagoneer faster and faster down the back roads.

Sure, I had Barbies when I was younger—because everyone

else did—but I liked to play with them differently. *Perversely*, is what Blair's mom said.

When the other little girls—like Blair—came over, instead of nice pretend play—picking out clothes, dressing them up—I'd *undress* them. Have Ken and Barbie make out, put him on top of her, and make them grind. Tear off a limb. Strike a match so I could smell their plastic body parts burning. Which was way more fun. But it freaked the other kids out.

I've always been like this.

Darker. Different. Meaner. Rougher.

I blame it on being an only child. No brothers or sisters to check me, to bounce things off of. And Mom, of course, has done nothing but spoil me. When my kindergarten teacher suggested I might need to possibly be evaluated by a shrink, because of *certain signs*—drawing a stick figure of a girl peeing, making little Billy Peters cry when I hit him in the face during recess because he wouldn't share his Christmas cookies with me—Mom shot back at her: *There's nothing wrong with my daughter.*

So yeah, I can sometimes take things too far, but I actually *like* taking things too far. Shocking people.

When Denise Ward had me over to play hide-and-seek—I think I was five or something—I locked her little sister, Sara, in a cupboard in the upstairs laundry room, far away enough that no one could hear her crying. I made sure to shut the door to the room to muffle it even more. Pretended to look for Sara outside, as if she were out there. Kept it up for an hour. When I finally let her out, she was shaking, wet and stinking of pee, her eyes red and puffy, her face covered in tears. The little brat told on me.

Mom, of course, made her excuses when she came to pick me up. "Nellie didn't mean it; she just doesn't know how to act sometimes. We're so sorry. Would y'all like to come swimming tomorrow at our place? I'll have ice cream for the kids."

But in private, she grabbed me by the shoulders, shook me. "You could at least *try* to act like a little lady sometimes."

I wanted to kick her shin with my patent leather shoe.

Next thing I knew, she threw me into etiquette class, a sad little joke I was forced to attend every Saturday morning in the basement of the local museum. I learned the absolutely useless skills of wearing white gloves, how to properly hold a teacup, and lay out silverware in the correct order. *Kill me now.*

The toaster pops, and my Pop-Tarts shoot up. I take a seat next to Dad, burning my hands as I tear one in half to eat it.

"Whaddya say, kiddo? I'm about to head out to the rifle range. Wanna come?"

We don't really go to the land anymore, but we do still hit the rifle range sometimes. Dad is really sweet, but him asking me is a bit depressing. Because he knows I have nothing better to do. Which makes me not want to do it.

"Maybe next time," I answer, staring past him out the window while still chewing my breakfast.

"What? Scared I'll beat your score this time?"

"Ha! Fat chance."

He taught me well, so well that I shoot better than him now, outscore him every time. I'm a marksman. And I like it. Being really, really good at something. No, *great* at it. Something none of the other prissy bitches can do. But I'm in no mood to go today; I'm too keyed up about Jane.

Dad walks his bowl over to the sink, leaves it for Lettie to rinse. He messes up my hair before leaving the room, like I'm still a little girl. "Next time, okay?"

"You got it," I answer, hot tears forming. *No, no, no.* I shake my head, flick them away with the back of my hand. It's kind of pathetic how much Dad showing his feelings really gets to me.

After he exits, I twist the knob on the television, tuning it to another station. *Little House on the Prairie* is on. Great. I walk to the fridge, take out the jug of milk, pour myself a cold glass, then settle back down on the barstool to watch it. It's a rerun, the episode where Johnny Cash plays a preacher coming through town, but we find out he's up to no good. I like the newer ones, where Laura and Nellie are teenagers, and Nellie is even meaner.

Mom named me Nellie for two reasons. First, Nellie was my great-grandmother's name, on Dad's side, supposedly a take-no-bullshit Swede. And second, Mom grew up reading the books the show was based on. God knows she didn't have anything better to do out on that wasteland. She wanted, she told me when I was younger, to name her daughter something strong, something brave.

And for some moronic reason—I think to try and somehow please her mean-ass mother—she gave me the middle name Jo, which is her own middle name and Gran's middle name as well.

I wouldn't hate it, except when Blair found out, she used to taunt me with it when we were little, call me by it. *Jo! How perfect! A boy's name to match your flat chest!*

But I love the name Nellie, love being named after someone on TV, someone tough. I used to have Mom try and fix my hair like Nellie's. Instead of the ringlets, she'd do French braids, with glossy red ribbon on the bottoms.

I'm pretty freaking sure that Mom now regrets ever naming me that.

"Nellie!" Her voice cuts through the air, instantly irritating me.

I spin around. "What?"

"I'm running a little errand. Be back later. There's leftover lasagna from the party last night and—"

"Got it, Mom," I say, cutting her off, spinning back around, and twisting up the volume until it's so loud, she won't dare try to talk over it.

Sometimes I think my darkness comes from *her*. That beneath all her beauty and high-society bullshit, the scrawny girl who grew up with my mean grandparents is still there, lurking, readying to pounce. No one else knows that sometimes Mom drops the act. Snaps. Strikes out. With a cuss word or three. With a slap. She grew up rough. She can hide who she truly is only for so long.

10

JANE

On the thin blanket I've spread out, I roll over on my back.

A heavy cloud the shape of cotton drags through the sky, blotting out the sun, so I gaze up at it, my fingers threaded over my eyes. When Luke comes to visit, I'll bring him to this very spot, deep into the night.

He's already eighteen. I'm seventeen, but my birthday's in two weeks. June 13. I'm hoping he'll come see me then. Now that it's warm out, he could sleep out here at night, and no one would be the wiser.

I'll wrap up chores out here soon so I can call him. Do it under the guise of needing to get Indy, the baby lamb named after Indiana Jones, some more socks.

Luke and I talk at least twice a week. I'll usually call around noon when I know he'll be home on his lunch break from working at his father's body shop, his long, lean body stretched out on the sofa while he flips through a book. Usually poetry.

Ezra Pound, E. E. Cummings, Sylvia Plath. Like I said, broody. But he's who got me into more modern poetry and also music, the alternative stuff, the good stuff that woulda never seeped through the local stations in the cowpoke towns where I've lived.

When we get to New York, he'd promise, *we can focus on our art.*

Luke loves to draw, to sketch, and is amazing at it. My art is more nebulous. That's the word Luke used to describe it, a new word to me but one I like rolling around in my mouth.

I love words, and every time I come across a new one—especially something exotic like *nebulous*—I jot it down in my little black leather notebook. The definition, how to use it in a sentence. Dad gave it to me on my fifth birthday for this very purpose. He'd made a trade, building a workbench for a leathersmith in exchange for a new saddle, reins, and my notebook.

"Words are knowledge, and knowledge is power," Pa said that evening as he pressed it into my hands, a grave look shadowing his handsome face.

Now the book is lined with hundreds of words, my handwriting changing over the years from simple print letters to the more elaborate cursive I've been able to master.

Because we've moved so much, Pa and Mom weren't always able to keep us in school. So Pa homeschooled us. Mom did, too, but I swear to God, no pun intended, she's only ever read one book: the King James Bible. Her teaching thus far has been life skills: Churning butter, making candles, sewing clothes. Being a good wife. Being a good Christian lady.

But my mind is thirstier than that, something Pa has always seen in me. So he's done his best to expand my library all these years, picking up used books in junk shops and estate sales, and now I have a trunkful at the foot of my bed.

He's had me stick to the classics: Shakespeare, Faulkner, Hemingway, etc. For poetry, the Romantics: Wordsworth, Shelley, Coleridge.

I love the poetry most, the way the words lock together, the way a whole story can be told in a single stanza. I lie in bed at night and read by my gas lantern, memorizing and reciting the words until Mom has enough and shushes me, orders me to sleep.

When we were still little, Julia and I put on little plays for Mom and Pa. We've never had a television. First off, we can't afford one, but also, Pa has forbidden them. He thinks they're the stuff of mind control, and anytime Julia or I protested and begged, desperate to be like the other kids, he'd shoot back with a quote from one of his favorite thinkers, Marshall McLuhan: *The medium is the message.*

So we've had to make our own entertainment. Julia used to like stories, just like I do. But once we hit puberty, all that became childish to her. Anything artsy. The stuff of useless daydreams. And in her defense, she *is* more book smart than me. She aces math, science, history—all the things that are outside my grasp and bore me to tears.

You better start thinking about what you're gonna do with yourself when you grow up. If you ever grow up, she'd warn me with a bitter shake of her head.

But I don't want to grow up. Not in that responsible, dead-inside way she's talking about. And Julia herself doesn't exactly share what *her* plans are. She may act all stern and religious like Mom (though I can't tell if she *actually* buys into the religious stuff or just pretends to), but I know her well enough to know she damn sure doesn't want to wind up barefoot and pregnant like Mom. She's too independent to rely on some man. Even still, I know she'd love to finally fall in love. But, like the talk of cute guys at the swimming hole, that topic is off-limits, which is why she tore my head off for daring to mention it.

The little I've been able to pry out of her is that she's gunning for community college next fall now that she's out of high school. Somewhere local. Maybe get on her way to earning a biology degree, become a teacher. I'm sure it's the money that's the barrier. Finances have always been a stressor for us, which is why we've learned to not bring it up to Mom and Pa very often.

But one day before Christmas last year, I heard her arguing with Mom, telling her that since she's the beekeeper, she should be able to keep all the profits from the sale of honey. Guess what happened next? Mom had to dig bills out of the register after our open houses and days at the farmers markets to pay her, while all my labor goes unpaid—gets funneled back into the family, as Pa says.

Hitting puberty tore us apart in another way, too. I personally think my sister is so beautiful, with her straw-blond hair and clear blue eyes, but as soon as we hit adolescence, the boys flocked to me while all but ignoring her. Doesn't help that she insists on wearing Coke-bottle glasses when she could have contacts. And that she doesn't seem to want to even try with fashion. So boys taking notice of me and not her makes Julia downright hate me. She's hostile to me every chance she gets.

And I'm not gonna lie, it breaks my heart. Because we moved so much, she was my only true, constant friend, and I've lost her.

Which is probably why I'm clinging to Luke so hard. And that dream of his to get us away from our sad little nothing lives.

You're still forming; it's the most important time for an artist, Luke says to me. And he's right. I know I like to sing backup for Pa when we sit around the campfire. I know my voice is good. And lately—maybe because of the poetry—I've started to think about songwriting. Snatches of melody with words will come to me, usually when I'm out here working. But I'm still finding my voice.

I can see myself fronting my own all-girl band, something neo-punk and edgy that would drive Mom completely out of her skull. A smile tugs across my face just thinking about it, the way she would run shrieking from the room if she saw me up there, my eyes streaked with heavy black eyeliner, my lanky legs in fishnets, snaking out of a leather miniskirt. Luke standing in the front row, cheering me on.

Luke turned me on to a whole world I didn't know was out there. He feeds not only my body but my mind.

A warm breeze thrashes through the orchard, rattling the

vines. I screw open my canteen, take a long pull. It's the freshest-tasting water I've ever had, another advantage of living here.

When Pa bought this land, it came with everything we could lay eyes on: a pair of tawny mustangs, a rust-red tractor, and the well, built from limestone, which is where I got the water.

Also, a pile of lumber. Even metal patio furniture.

But the big selling point for Pa was the outbuildings. A tiny toolshed so ancient, the slats of its tin roof are warped, like bacon shrinking in a skillet. Pry open the door, though, and you'll find it's filled with a shallow row of gleaming tools, far more than we've ever had before.

Kitty-corner from the shed is another structure, the small wooden room Mom has already set up shop in, twisting her herbs into bundles to hang from the rafters to dry, lining her shelves—newly built by Pa—with amber glass bottles that hold her oils and potions. And Julia's jars of honey.

And the final building is an open-air lean-to, Pa's woodworking station. He's there now, his circular saw vibrating through the air, but so far away, the sound is faint, a mosquito buzzing in my ear.

Pa wouldn't care that I'm with Luke; he actually took to him when he befriended Luke's dad to work on our truck.

But I still keep it a secret.

I can't risk the others knowing.

11

CHARLEIGH

Rolling down the highway, Charleigh's hands clench the steering wheel, feathery pines shimmying past her window as she drifts onto the shoulder.

Her stomach seizes like it always does when she turns down Seven Pines Road. So she rarely does. She likes to keep her past firmly there. Including her mother and father.

Years ago, soon after her wedding, she and Alexander bought her parents' land for them, freeing them from their harsh landlord, Mr. Greer. The transaction was sort of an unspoken agreement that the Millers wouldn't be bothering Charleigh and Alexander much after that. That they'd keep to themselves.

Not that they minded. Ever since Charleigh had left home, they took to calling her *highfalutin, too big for her britches, stuck-up*.

"You just don't know how to act no more," her mother, Ruthlynn, said as she thumped her tin of Skoal, packing down the tobacco.

Charleigh had come home from Dallas one Christmas to visit.

It would be the last time she made that mistake, coming home from school on winter break to see them.

Once she and Alexander moved to Longview and had Nellie, though, they'd bring their daughter out to visit her grandparents on occasion. But Ruthlynn and Hank were no more tender with little Nellie than they had been with Charleigh.

"What is wrong with that child? She's already a little heathen," Ruthlynn remarked, loudly, one time, a sour smile creeping across her thin lips. "And her nose is bigger than Dallas."

As if she were one to talk about manners. That woman has no more class than a drunken hobo.

Charleigh presses on the gas with her Cole Haan moccasins, accelerating so fast that her childhood home blurs past. Which is exactly the goal.

But still, the brutal memories flock back.

Charleigh rising at dawn as young as five years old to go and milk the cows, stomach grumbling with hunger that would be only momentarily satisfied by stale toast and one scrambled egg. They never had enough of anything. Food. Money. Patience. Kindness.

Charleigh feeding the pigs, stepping around their muck.

Cleaning the chicken coop when she got home from school, even when freezing sleet stung her little hands.

And when shit went wrong—and it was always going wrong, like the pasteurizer breaking just as they were getting ready to process the milk—her parents' already-foul moods would spiral. Charleigh learned early on to scatter, lest she get the stinging wrath of Ruthlynn's switch or Joe's belt.

Both her parents drank. And not in the fun, casual way that she does when she's socializing. To revel. To celebrate.

No, they did it to escape. The cheap alcohol—Old Crow whiskey or Schlitz beer—turned her parents into even more bitter caricatures of their miserable sober selves.

Just driving by the old homestead, Charleigh can summon the smell of her father's cheap, filthy cigarettes, feel the scorch mark on the top of her thigh where he extinguished one, drunk and cursing her for spilling the carton of Tropicana, a luxury at their home. Can hear their endless bickering.

She can't believe she's out here now, but she has no choice.

Nellie.

Just as Kathleen had said, Charleigh couldn't miss the Swifts. Before she's even to the end of the road, she spots the red mailbox, slows the Jag to a crawl. Right next to the mailbox is a barn-red sign with lettering:

Swift's Custom Furniture & Swift's Apothecary.

Kathleen could have just told her to look for the signs, but that would've been too simple.

Charleigh sucks in a breath, turns into the drive. As she crosses the cattle guard, her leather seat thrums beneath her. She doesn't miss this feeling, of being sucked back into farm life.

But this land is different. Majestic. Their little wooden house is perched back far from the road, the drive a long, meandering lane that slopes over the rolling hills. The meadow is so green, it's almost emerald, so much more vibrant than the mud-caked pasture of her childhood. And the land is dotted with chubby pecan trees so ancient, they look prehistoric. This homestead is well tended to, cared for, a row of paperwhites lining the drive like little flags.

She eases into the small gravel parking lot, the pebbles crackling under her brand-new tires.

Charleigh steps from the car, peers up at the house.

It's small but tidy. A homey cabin with what appears to be an upstairs loft. A pair of crystal-clear windows on the second floor wink down at her in the crisp morning light.

The porch, which hugs the front and sides of the house, is wooden, unfinished, but immaculate, without a particle of dust on its threadbare boards. A basket of pecans rests next to a rocker, their caramel-colored shells waiting to be shucked.

Another pair of signs, these smaller but carbon copies of the ones at the entrance, are planted at the front left corner of the house, arrows directing her down a crushed-granite path.

Other than the tractor parked out in the glistening pasture, there's no other vehicle, no sign of life, so Charleigh is not even certain that anyone's home.

She treads down the path, rounds the house.

A small wooden shed with the insignia *Swift's Apothecary* stands about thirty paces away. There is no door, only an open-air entryway where a door should be.

What the hell, Charleigh thinks, as she strides over.

She mounts the wooden steps—also threadbare but immaculate—pauses at the threshold. Clears her throat.

"Oh! Come on in!" The merry voice chirps, sounding like it's coming from beneath the baseboards.

Charleigh steps inside. From behind the counter, a woman pops up. She has a bandanna fixed to the top of her head, a dusting rag lolling in her hand.

"Don't mind me, I was just cleaning the display case." The woman beams at Charleigh.

Charleigh grins back. Studies her. It's the same woman she and Nellie spotted downtown soon after the Swifts arrived. The wife, Abigail.

And like that afternoon, Abigail is dressed in what Charleigh, having grown up herself in handsewn clothes, can easily see is a homemade dress. All of the woman's attire today is made from gingham, blue and white, and honest to God, it looks like something one of those back-to-basics religious women might wear.

Her face is tanned. Well, maybe it's just dirt. Charleigh can't tell. She's plain, that's for sure, verging on homely, but there *is* an appeal there. Her voice, for one, is warm, smooth like honey. Her hair is natural blond—but straw colored, more like dishwater blond. And even though she's slender, she seems...*capable*. Her blue eyes shine as if the sun is setting behind them, and her demeanor is cheery, but one of forced cheer, Charleigh thinks, as if Abigail has seen hard times but stepped right over them, just kept on going.

She also looks young. Charleigh pegs her for early thirties. Wonders how she has a seventeen-year-old.

"How may I help you?" she asks, tilting her head to one side, placing the rag down. "I'm Abigail, by the way." Dimples pucker her cheeks as she grins again at Charleigh. She reaches out her hand for Charleigh to shake it.

"Charleigh. Charleigh Andersen." When Charleigh offers her own hand back, she's acutely aware of the gold Rolex dangling from her wrist, the clash of their vastly different classes.

"Pleased to meet you, Charleigh. And I like your name. "It's"—Abigail knits her eyebrows together—"*different*."

Charleigh's used to hearing this. Sometimes it bothers her, but coming from Abigail, she senses it's a compliment.

Why *is* she here? What is she supposed to say? *I'm looking for your brat daughter because my own brat child already hates her?*

"I heard from a friend about your products, so thought I'd drop by, have a look—"

"Ah! Great to hear that word of mouth is spreading!" Abigail clasps her hands together. "It usually does, but it can take a while, so I'm grateful it's catching on quickly here." She waves her arm around, gesturing to her shelves of amber-colored bottles. "I bet you're here for the love potion." She steps on her tiptoes, pulls down a dropper bottle, slides it across the counter to Charleigh. "It's my most popular botanical."

The cream-colored paper label reads, *Love Potion Number #9, made with care (and love!) and all-natural oils. Ingredients: ylang-ylang, lavender, jasmine, and amber. Jojoba oil and arnica oil.*

Charleigh studies the fine print, which is truly so fine that she has to squint: *Proverbs 31 Woman*.

Huh? Charleigh would have to look that up later. *Whatever.*

"Here, take a whiff." Abigail plucks the bottle from Charleigh, twists it open. "Mmmmm..." she sighs. "Keeps your man happy." A self-satisfied smirk creeps across her face.

Charleigh begrudgingly takes a shallow sniff. "It's nice. But honestly, I don't need any help with *that*."

Abigail screws the bottle shut. That same cheery grin is fixed on her face. "Yeah, well," she says, turning, placing the bottle back atop the shelf, "we *all* think that." She murmurs this last part in a hushed tone, as if she's saying it to herself.

"Excuse me?" Irritation ripples across Charleigh's chest.

Unsmiling, she murmurs this last part in a hushed tone, as if she's saying it to herself. The cheery grin is back, this time with a vengeance. Another tilt of the head as if Abigail feels pity for Charleigh. "Nothing." She shakes her head like she's removing unsavory thoughts. "Perhaps...you are looking for something else, then?"

Okay, Charleigh doesn't like her. Doesn't like how she carries herself. Her audacity, acting like she's above her lot in life, unbothered by it. And, if Charleigh's honest, what annoys her most is Abigail's cheeriness, even if it's the forced kind.

Charleigh looks past the woman to the rear entrance that, like the front, doesn't have a door, just an open entryway. She hears sparkling laughter dancing across the field.

"Wanna see the rest of the place?" Abigail asks.

"Sure."

Charleigh couldn't give two shits about *the rest of the place*, but she's gathering intel, so she trails this woman to the little wooden back porch.

"I like to take my breaks out here. Have a rest, drink a cold glass of tea," Abigail says, staring straight ahead. "In fact, I have some brewed. Would you like—"

Charleigh bats her hand in the air, declining. "No. Just drank a whole Coke in the car. But thanks."

Charleigh follows the sound of laughter to a little toddler who is in a high wooden swing that hangs from one of the branches of the fat pecan trees. The child can't be more than two, but she kicks her legs out and tucks them back underneath her as if she's been swinging this way for years.

"I know what you're thinking." Abigail's maple syrup voice reaches Charleigh's ears. "Who in their right mind would leave their toddler out here alone? But that's how I've raised them all. And they've come out just fine. Plus, Julia, my eldest, is back over there. So she keeps a watch on her."

Abigail hitches her chin to the far southeast corner, where a teenager is outfitted, head to toe, in full beekeeper attire, hands rhythmically moving over pastel-colored bee boxes as bees spin and pirouette through the air.

"So, you have other kids, then?" Charleigh asks, trying not to make her inquiry about Jane so obvious.

A sigh seeps out of Abigail, as if she's weary. "Yes, Julia over there's my oldest, like I said. Eighteen going on thirty."

Charleigh snickers.

"Oh, not in *that* way. Thank God she's not boy crazy. No, she's my responsible one. Can't wait to get out on her own, though. It's Jane I'm worried about."

Yeah, well me, too, Charleigh thinks but doesn't say. "How so?"

"You got kids, Mrs. Andersen?"

"Just the one. Nellie. Seventeen. Turning eighteen next month. But going on thirty. And *in* that way you're thinking."

"Ha! Well, my Jane's not here. The middle one. She's off on her horse somewhere." Abigail shakes her head again; a strand of her pale hair escapes the bandanna.

Dammit. Charleigh really wanted to lay eyes on her.

"She must be in the same class as my Nellie, or was, before school let out."

A wistful look passes over Abigail's face. "Can't say I recall her mentioning your daughter. But we did just get here only a month ago."

Charleigh can't decide if this is a good or bad thing, Jane not bringing Nellie's name up.

"You must've gotten started early? You look so young to have an eighteen-year-old." There's a bite to Charleigh's voice; she can't help it. Doesn't want to help it.

Abigail's face flushes. "I credit my skin-care oils for my youthful looks." A smug sneer tugs across her face. "How old are *you?*" she asks in a tone that implies she thinks Charleigh is very old.

"Forty-one. You?"

"Thirty-six. So yeah, I got pregnant early; I'd just turned eighteen. But that's part of our purpose as women, right? I didn't mind it at all. I love being a mommy more than anything. Well, I love being a wife, too."

Who *is* this woman?

The toddler gives her legs another powerful kick, then lofts herself from the swing. She flies through the air before landing on all fours.

"Honey! Be careful!" Abigail glances over at Charleigh with a look of alarm, but it feels fake, like she wants to look flustered so that Charleigh won't judge her, even though she's not ruffled at all. Abigail, for instance, doesn't rush over to the child.

The little girl claps the dirt off her knees, toddles over to a garden.

"And that's baby Molly. She's eighteen months old, definitely going on thirty," Abigail hoots.

Molly walks up to a strawberry plant, starts twisting the garnet-colored fruit off the vine. Charleigh is amazed. The girl uses her dress—also obviously handmade—as a vessel in which to carry the fruit.

She waddles over. "Mama, hungryy! Hungryy!"

"Okay, my sweet girl!" Abigail gathers up the strawberries, rinses them off with the hose that's attached to the rear of the apothecary. Steps inside, then returns with a cereal bowl and baby spoon. She pops a clean berry in her mouth, chews it, spits it inside the bowl. Repeats.

What in the hell?

"Here, baby." Abigail spoons the chewed-up mixture into Molly's mouth.

"All disease begins in the gut," Abigail says solemnly to Charleigh, whose own gut churns with disgust. "I don't want to just feed her rice cereal and all that other processed garbage off the shelves. I want to introduce her stomach to all the flora it needs. So this is my method."

Then, to Charleigh's horror, Abigail lowers the strap on her dress and pulls out a breast, which is plump. *Capable.* Molly climbs in her mother's lap and begins suckling.

No one, and she means *no one*, whom she knows breastfeeds. Especially in front of someone else. And the strawberries. Jesus H. Christ.

Repugnance overtakes Charleigh. Abigail flicks a glance her way, lifts an eyebrow as if to ask, *Are you woman enough to handle all this?* Charleigh's positive that her expression betrays her repulsion, so she turns her head. She will *not* give this woman the satisfaction of acting bothered. It's as if Abigail is *daring* her to say something. But no way she's taking the bait.

Her gaze falls on a clothesline, and instead of watching the toddler breastfeed, for God's sake, she keeps her eyes trained on the cotton dresses and baby clothes that flutter in the breeze.

"You breastfeed your girl when she was a baby?" Abigail asks, taunting.

Great. How is she supposed to avoid this trap?

Of course she didn't breastfeed Nellie. How ghastly. But maybe that's to blame for how Nellie turned out.

Charleigh pretends, though, that she doesn't hear Abigail, keeping her face stone-still, her eyes glued to the action on the clothesline. After an awkward beat, Abigail doubles down.

"It's one of God's many blessings that he bestows upon us as women. It's one of the ways we can serve our families."

At this, Charleigh twists back around. Confronts the woman head-on. A sly smile creeps across Abigail's face.

Charleigh smiles back at her, but it's a smile that says, *Keep up this banter, and I'll kill you.*

Abigail stares down at her toddler, coos baby talk in her ear. Lifts her eyes back up to Charleigh, as if to say, *This act is making me more powerful than you, no matter how much money you have.*

Bile rises in the back of Charleigh's throat, but her thoughts are cut in half by the noise of a truck rumbling through the field, approaching the house.

It's a vintage red truck, a Chevy, Charleigh notices as it draws closer, with the lettering *Swift's Custom Furniture* stenciled down the side, just as Monica described.

At the sound of the truck, Molly unlatches herself, hops up, and starts clapping. "Papa! Papa!"

Abigail leaves her breast exposed, cuts her eyes back to Charleigh.

It's a beautiful breast, a *perfect* breast, and Abigail knows it, evidently wants Charleigh to know it, too.

Charleigh can't help it; she rises from the porch, and a loud sigh escapes her. She thinks she can hear a snort of laughter from Abigail.

As the man climbs from the truck, Abigail strides across the field to greet him, breast tucked back inside her dress, Molly running at her heels.

Even from twenty feet away, Charleigh can tell that the ladies were right: He's drop-dead handsome. Tall, lean, dressed in a Henley shirt with the buttons undone, exposing a tanned chest. His hair is honey colored and swooped to one side, licked by sweat.

Abigail leaps into his arms, and he lifts her, spinning her around as though he's been away at war for years and is just returning. The two kiss, first a peck, then a full-on make-out session as baby Molly tugs on her father's pants leg. When they unlatch, he lifts the child to his hip and spins her around, and Abigail shoots Charleigh another self-satisfied look.

Every nerve in Charleigh's body is rankled. She *hates* this woman for everything she stands for—all the corny religious bullshit—and again, hates her for everything she has and for the fact that she seems unbothered by all that she doesn't have. Plus, she's provocative, haughty. Thinks she's better than Charleigh. *As if.*

And if Jane is anything like her mother, Charleigh can see why Nellie hates her, too.

"Hey, there!" The man is now striding toward Charleigh. "Ethan. Ethan Swift. Pleasure to meet you—"

"I'm Charleigh. Andersen."

Ethan clasps Charleigh's hand in his own, squeezes it, pumps her arm with his very ripped forearm.

Charleigh's previous distaste dissipates as her eyes lock on his, which are a light brown, so light that they almost look amber. Ethan fixes her with a crooked smile, flicks those eyes over her, grins back with what appears to be approval.

Abigail clears her throat. "Charleigh here was just leaving! Seems we don't have anything she's looking for."

Charleigh's mouth hangs open; she wasn't exactly on her way out but it's clear that Abigail wants her to be.

"Unless, that is," Abigail adds, moving in for the kill, "you *do* want to try some of my skin-care botanicals. For antiaging and all."

This little bitch. Charleigh could punch her right now.

A humph barks out of Charleigh. "No, no thank you. I'm not really comfortable using anything on my face that hasn't been approved or professionally tested."

An answering humph shoots out of Abigail.

"Well," Ethan says, his voice low and sweet, the strings of a cello being bowed, "maybe you're interested in a custom piece, then? It's what I do. I make custom furniture."

As beguiled as she is by Ethan, she will *not* be doing any dealings with this weird family. The line in the sand has been drawn.

"Maybe you'd like to see some of my work?" Ethan hitches a brow, and wait, did he just *wink* at Charleigh?

"Thank you, honestly, but…I really only have antiques, and I use a decorator and everything, so I really don't need anything—"

"Oh, who's your decorator?" Ethan asks.

It's none of his business, that's who, but what can she say?

"Um, Ford Design. Jackson Ford's the owner."

"Well, it was *so* nice of you to pop by," Abigail pipes up, scooping Molly into her arms and moving quickly away from Charleigh, whom she's clearly giving the heave-ho.

"Well, see you around, then?" Ethan grins at her. A slightly crooked grin that makes him even sexier. Wickedly so.

"Yes." Charleigh walks around him, neck flushing, keys balled in her fist. She reaches her car, crams herself in as quickly as possible. She's totally spun around. *Why does Ethan have to be so hot, and also, what the fuck kind of freak show was all that with the woman?*

12

JANE

give Cookie a gentle squeeze with my right leg so that she'll make the turn.

We haven't taken this route home from the general store before, but I know that this particular oil road cuts over to the highway. From there, we can follow along the shoulder until we hit Seven Pines.

The sun is a laser overhead, but on this grassy lane, the pine trees are so tall, so thick, that Cookie and I ride in a blanket of shadow.

Mom hates it when I ride bareback, but I know Cookie prefers not to be weighed down by a saddle, especially under the blistering sun. And I prefer it, too. This free-falling, wild feeling I get when it's just me and Cookie galloping across the field, no barrier between us, Cookie's strawberry-blond mane loosely latticed through my hands.

It's bonding, like I'm telling Cookie that I trust her, and she, in turn, trusts me.

Under the cloak of the piney shadows, the air rushing by feels almost cool, electric. Like my whole body's being bathed in the clean, sharp scent of the forest.

When we get to the store, I step inside, letting the cold from the AC blast me. I head for the lamb socks, but take my time roaming the aisles, pining for things I can't afford, like the cute lime-green watering can with daisies painted on it. It's not that I care much for material things, but sometimes I wish I could be like Blair, a normal teen with an actual allowance.

I finally get to the socks, pluck them from the shelf, head for the counter. It's Denny who is at the register today. Son of the shopkeeper, Mr. Oldham, and they only boy in a long time who's had eyes for Julia. He's tall with a freckled face and short red hair. Kinda cute but in a nerdy, gawky way.

I can tell straightaway my sister is at once happy that he's taken a shine to her but also mad that he's not one of the gorgeous ones. So she's frosty with him, but flirts back just enough to keep him on the hook.

After the first time I saw them flirting, I asked her about it later that night while we were doing laundry.

"So, Denny is kinda cute. And he seems to think you are, too."

The corners of her lips lifted into a grin, but her face turned right back into a stone. "You're just jealous that he's taken notice of me and not you for a change."

Such a bitch.

There I was, trying to be nice to her, trying to encourage her to maybe date him or something, but she had to cut me down.

Whatever. As I reach the counter now, Denny's grinning at me.

"Julia with you today? Outside maybe?" Red streaks his neck as he asks me this.

"Nah, she's back at the farm. Working with the bees."

He takes my money, makes change. "Tell her I said hi, will ya?"

Man, I wish he'd work up the nerve to ask her out. Turn her back into an earlier, kinder, and much less cruel version of herself. If that's possible.

I'm about to leave when he adds, "And hey, wait, lemme get you a free Dr. Pepper. On the house."

I'm not sure if I should accept it; he's only ever offered this to Julia, and I wouldn't want her to think I'm betraying her somehow. But before I can say no, he's handing me an icy cold bottle that I can't resist.

After slamming it, I slip back outside onto the porch, plunk a quarter in the pay phone, and call Luke.

He answers on the first ring. "Heeeey," he says with a lazy drawl.

I can picture him pasted along the sofa, top button of his jeans undone, dragging a hand through his hair.

"How'd you know it was me?" I smile into the receiver.

"I'm psychic," Luke teases.

"Well, if you're psychic, then tell me, when are we gonna see each other?"

"Mmmm… Not sure. Let me ask my Magic 8 Ball."

He actually has one.

"Hold on." The sound of the ball being shaken fills the line. "It says, *You may rely on it.*"

"*That's* not a good answer. I wanna know when. Like, my birthday's in two weeks—"

"June thirteenth, I remember. Only you would be born on the thirteenth, you wicked thing."

This makes me laugh. "So…what do ya say? Seriously, you gonna come for my birthday?"

"Well, I wanted to keep it a surprise, but I actually think I'm gonna be there before then."

I squeal so loudly, Cookie turns and looks at me. "Really? I miss you so much, babe."

"Ah, not as much as I miss you." Luke's voice gets lower; I can picture his hand moving down to his zipper.

The thought sends shivers zinging over me.

Not that we've gone all the way. We haven't. I may be wicked in my own way, but I still want to wait until I'm truly eighteen to take that step. If I even want to make it then.

But I love kissing Luke, doing other things with him I shouldn't be doing, like taking off my shirt, letting him kiss me all over, and kissing him all over right back.

"You just gonna show up, then? Unannounced?"

"Don't spoil the surprise any more than you already have."

I can hear the grin in his voice.

After the call, I cluck at Cookie, who sidles up to the porch so I can mount her.

We trot down the lane, and then I nudge her with the heels of my boots, signaling for her to canter. Once we reach the highway, she breaks into a gallop again, the wind blasting my hair, cooling the sweat from it.

I want to ride all the way to Dallas. I *can*, I think; this road would eventually spill onto the freeway that leads there, but there'd be too many cars for Cookie, too much commotion.

I could hop a train like a bum the way I did that one time in Missouri. We lived in a small depressing town, and one Friday, I hopped the freight train to St. Louis. But once I got off, meandered around, I became intimidated by all the busyness of the big city—I was only thirteen—so I called Pa to come pick me up. He was *so* disappointed in me, but maybe also kind of proud?

No, I should wait for Luke to come visit *me*.

The ground on the shoulder beneath Cookie's feet is marshy, the thundering of her hooves muted by the boggy soil. Only the sound of cars whizzing past fills my ears.

When Cookie descends into a basin, I lean down into her spine even more. I hear a car buzz up behind us. Instead of soaring past, like the other vehicles, this one slows until it's keeping pace with me and Cookie.

What the hell?

I twist my neck to the left, very slightly, to avoid changing Cookie's course. It's an apple-red Beamer. A convertible, but the cream-colored top is up.

I can't make out who the driver is. All I see is a blur of blond hair, and I wonder, *Is this person lost, looking for directions?*

But they're not rolling their window down, so I bring my attention back to Cookie. "You're a good girl," I say, stroking her neck, trying to keep her calm, keep *myself* calm, because the car is sticking right next to us. Inching closer. I feel as if I'm being squeezed between the bimmer and the wooden fence line that runs along the highway, even though there's still plenty of space.

But alarm seeps over me; the taste of metal fills my mouth.

I shoot another look at the driver, who revs the engine loudly before peeling away.

At the commotion, Cookie spooks, gallops toward the fence line.

I try to guide her back, but by now she's in full-blown panic mode. She races farther off the road until my leg explodes in pain, dragging alongside the barky fence, which soon claws me off Cookie's back.

13

NELLIE

couldn't stay cooped up in the house for one second longer, so I bolted, went to buy some smokes.

I get them on the edge of town at a little mom-and-pop gas station, where they don't card me for alcohol. I'm sure it helps that I always slap an extra twenty in the old man's hand, but he's at least a hundred, so he's not giving a fuck about anything anymore.

I got a carton of Marlboros and a six-pack of Coors Light, then took off driving the back roads, chain-smoking, sipping beer.

On my way back home, as I was driving down the highway, I spotted someone riding a horse. Which you never see. Sure, there are horses everywhere, but not on the goddamn side of the road.

As I got closer, my pulse started to race when I realized it was *her*.

Jane.

Her hair was loose, flowing down her back as she galloped between the shoulder and the fence line. I cackled. I mean, I've never seen her drive before because I'm pretty sure she's too poor to own a car, but a *horse*? How funny! How sad. Also, thank *God* she wasn't actually hanging out at Blair's house as I had imagined.

But then, watching her coast down the road, head held high, riding as if she were Anne of Green Gables or something made my blood boil. So I pressed on the gas, veered a little closer. Hung right beside her.

She looked over at me like she was confused, and I couldn't stand the sight of her one second longer, so I revved the engine at her, then sped away.

14

JACKSON

Jackson hates when Charleigh does this to him, leaves him hanging, waiting for her.

Not thirty minutes earlier, he was in his home office, iced tea in hand, the crossword puzzle from Sunday's *Times* stretched out before him. He likes to linger over it, make it stretch out into the week. It's one of the things he does on break to shut off his mind: unlock a solution to something that's been eluding him.

Then Charleigh called, all in a huff. "What are you doing right now?"

Jackson's head spun with different excuses. He set his ballpoint down, sighed. "Working on a bid, actually," he lied. "Why?"

"For who?" she demanded.

None of your business.

"Just a small deal; it's nothing really." *I promise you're still my biggest client.* "Why, what's going on?"

A groaned wheezed out of Charleigh. "Nothing."

He pinched the bridge of his nose. "What is it?" *Nothing* always meant *something*, usually something big with Charleigh.

"Can you sneak away? Meet me at the Boat House for a daiquiri? I just met that new family, the Swifts, and am *dying* to talk to you about it."

So now this is happening. Jackson's sitting outside on the deck, stabbing his frozen drink with his straw. He feels like a spectacle here. In Longview, yes, but especially at this chichi members-only club.

Dressed in dusty-rose IZOD khakis and loafers, Jackson subtly tries to signal that he's gay (no other man in this town would dress in any shade of pink), even though he's only out to Charleigh.

But it always fails. One of the old guard here, a woman in her late fifties, hair piled into a shellacked beehive, will spy him sitting alone and approach, usually with a not-so-attractive young woman in tow. The young'un is still single for a reason.

Jackson, who was raised with manners and is a people-pleasing middle child, thank you very much, will usually diplomatically extricate himself from these desperate attempts at setups by referring vaguely to a love interest back in Dallas.

The gorgeous women in town, on the other hand, are mostly all taken. Not that he has an appetite for them, nor they for him, once they get a clue. But it somehow doesn't stop them—when they've had enough to drink—from pawing at him.

One thing he learned a long time ago: wealthy women think they own *everything, everyone.*

Charleigh included. To her credit, she's never drunkenly groped or hit on him; she's too in love with Alexander, for starters, and who wouldn't be? But her thirsty possessiveness is insatiable.

He takes a long, icy pull from the strawberry daiquiri and is immediately punished with brain freeze. But it's smoldering out. Even with the fans whirring, Jackson feels like he's hovering over a steaming pot of gumbo, and the afternoon sun spackling the lake only makes it feel hotter.

Where is that woman?

He tugs his Ray-Bans down, another attempt to ward off anybody who feels the need to approach him.

Ugh, this town. Jackson isn't used to this, this fishbowl-like existence. He was raised in a metropolis—Houston, for Christ's sake—then went to college in Dallas. The only reason he's here? His smothering mother, Willamena, refused to hand over any of her massive inheritance from his late father to help Jackson kickstart his design business.

"Find you a nice wife to marry, settle down with, and you can have all the money you need," she said to him the last time he saw her, her coral-colored lips pressed into a smirk.

So he worked for a year in Dallas as a bartender at a club on Greenville Avenue, lived in a cheap studio apartment, and stashed away as much cash as possible. He hoped to find an affordable place to set up shop. But when he went looking, he was dismayed. He wanted to stay in Dallas, live in a city with thriving gay bars and nightlife, but he had to cast his net wider.

The drab suburbs didn't appeal to him, but when he went

just a few hours east, he landed in the lush piney woods and was enchanted. The moment he laid eyes on the craftsman-style home for just $5,000, he was sold.

His long-term goal is to get to San Francisco. And he's determined to make that happen, to keep his overhead low, funnel as much of his earnings into savings as he can bear.

But that doesn't mean that this town doesn't get to him sometimes, doesn't drive him bonkers. There actually used to be a lone gay bar here on the outskirts called the Rainbow Room, but there were too many assaults in the parking lot, too many closet-case rednecks making it a sport to beat the hell out of the handful of gay guys brave enough to patronize the place.

That was before Jackson's time here. So now there's *really* no place to find a potential boyfriend. He goes back to Dallas as much as he can, crashing on friends' sofas over the weekend, but for now, he's stuck here.

It's not all bad. He *loves* his home, loves his yard. Has trained a row of wild muscadines that grow along his back fence into a thriving orchard. Not that he makes wine with them, not yet anyway. Just preserves. But he adores puttering around his back patio, watering his potted plants, taking his coffee out there in the early mornings with a book, sitting in the shade of the giant magnolia, whose blossoms are so fragrant, they smell like gardenias.

Charleigh's laugh barks through the air. He looks up to see that she's trapped talking to someone, raising her eyebrows at Jackson as if to say, *Save me?*

She looks impeccable; nothing new there. Hair in a sleek ponytail underneath a broad sun hat. Bronzed shoulders bare in her strapless jumpsuit. She must've taken her sweet time getting ready.

Jackson raises his hand in a wave, which gives Charleigh all the ammo she needs to launch herself away from the woman.

"Hiiii!" she trills.

"Hey!" He stands to hug her. "So, what's the big emergency?"

Half of Jackson's daiquiri is now gone; he's actually buzzed enough to want to hear the dirt.

But Charleigh's eyes scramble for the waitress. She flicks her hand up in the air until the server comes over.

"What are you having?"

"One of these"—Charleigh motions to Jackson's drink—"and another for him. Also some mozzarella sticks. That sound good?" she asks Jackson.

He nods.

She grabs his drink, sucks in a large sip through the straw. "Sorry, I *need* this. Can I have the rest? Pretty please?"

Jackson grins at his friend. "By all means, my lady."

"Okay, so I went out to see the Swifts. Like I told you last night, all the girls are already using the wife's potions or whatever, so I had to see for myself, and for Nellie. The new girl, Jane, wasn't there. She was on her *horse*, if you can imagine it, but when I say that family is *weird*, I'm talking total freak show. Plus, they're super religious, like *too* religious if you know what I mean."

Nobody can skewer like Charleigh Andersen, and Jackson would be lying if he said he didn't enjoy the gossip. What the hell else is he supposed to do for entertainment in this godforsaken, small-minded town?

The waitress places the basket of fried cheese between them, sets down their drinks.

"How so?" he asks.

"The woman *breastfed* in front of me!" Charleigh nearly shouted, causing all heads to swivel in their direction.

"Yikes. Really?" Jackson has his act of mock horror down to an art. "Like, covered with a blanket in front of you or—"

"No! She just flopped her big knocker out for all to see, smashed her daughter's face into it!"

"Gross! I mean, boobs are already gross but yuck." He dipped a mozzarella stick into the ramekin of marinara, then took a bite.

"That's not even the *gross* part," Charleigh hissed, nearly spraying him with daiquiri. "She chewed up a strawberry, spit it into a bowl, then spoon-fed her daughter the mix!"

"Ewwww! Maybe don't tell me this while we're drinking frozen strawberry daiquiris?"

Charleigh cackled, took a criminally long pull of her own drink. "So, I can see why Nellie already can't stand the daughter. Like, that wasn't the worst of it. The worst of it? That woman. Abigail's her name. There's something about her that irritates. She just has this...*audacity* about her. Like whyyyy?" Charleigh's eyes are swimming with booze. "She literally has nothing. Lives on a farm. Wears homemade dresses. Is okay-looking but nothing great. Of course, I didn't buy a thing. And I really can't see why the others are already so up on her."

Bingo. *This* is what's actually bothering Charleigh, Jackson thinks, but keeps it to himself. The fact that her friends are into this woman.

The hum of a boat approaching makes them both turn to look. It's a ski boat, with a teenage blond at the helm, filled with other teenage girls. The driver of the boat waves to the crowd on the dock like she's the queen of England.

"Fucking Blair," Charleigh spits.

"Ah, yes, Nellie's friend—"

"Nemesis. Little brat."

Blair lowers the lever on the boat, causing it to speed, sending a powerful wake toward the deck. Lake water tides over the boards, soaking the edge of the deck.

"I hate her."

"I know you do," Jackson says. "And I know you secretly hate the woman who spawned her, even though you still insist on hanging out with her, but back to the Waltons."

Charleigh laughs again. Jackson loves making her laugh.

"I just left without buying any of her bullshit products. Didn't buy anything from the husband either."

"Husband?" Jackson lowers his shades, eyes grinning at Charleigh. "Do tell. Details, please."

Charleigh rolls her shoulders, heaves out a sigh that blows her bangs skyward. "He's smoking hot. Like ridiculously good-lookin'." She shakes her head, stirs her drink. "Too good-lookin' for that woman, I'll tell you that."

Jackson picks up a cheese stick, passes it over to Charleigh. "Eat. At least one."

"Fine." Charleigh pulls it apart; hot cheese strings downward over her plate. She devours it. "Guess he makes custom furniture or something."

"Really?"

"Yep. But I turned him down, too. We don't wanna have anything to do with that family."

15

JANE

My leg feels like it's on fire. I look down, see blood seeping through my jeans.

I grasp the top of my thigh and try to move the whole leg. It hurts, but it obeys. Thank God. Next, I try to bend it. I'm able to do this as well.

Whew.

But when I go to stand, searing pain shoots through it, and I collapse.

In the distance, Cookie's orange coat is just a blur as she gallops farther and farther away from me.

Shit.

Will she know to turn on Seven Pines? Will she find her way home? Will I ever see her again?

Hot tears cloud my vision, but I blot them away with the back of my hand. I don't have time to cry. I have to think.

I probably shouldn't have ridden her bareback; maybe mean old Mom is right.

That damn beamer. I wonder who the hell it was.

Cookie's never spooked like that before, but then again, no one's ever driven right up on us.

Cars race past me, but I can't even think about trying to hitchhike—Pa told me never to do it. Under any circumstance.

But I can't just sit here, boiling to death.

I grab hold of the fence, hoist myself up.

I hobble forward, able to put a little pressure on my right leg while holding on to the fence.

This truly sucks. Blair and her friend Stacy are supposed to pick me up tonight, take me out to the Circles. It's the first time she's ever come over, given me a ride, and I was really looking forward to it. I've only hung out with them at school and at the swimming hole because I could ride Cookie there, tie her up where no one could see her.

Not that I'm ashamed to ride a horse; I'm just embarrassed that I don't have a car like everyone else my age around here. As cool as Pa is, he doesn't want me driving his work truck at night, especially if he knows I'm gonna be drinking. Not that we actually discuss all that, but because he's been letting me have nips of his wine since I was thirteen, he's no dummy.

Pa could drop me off places, but that would be even more embarrassing than being seen on Cookie.

Tonight was also gonna be my first time to ever go to the

Circles, which is basically a clearing in the middle of woods where the teens here party.

After about half an hour of limping, to my massive relief, I see a shiny red truck cruising toward me. It's vintage, unmistakably Pa's.

I wave my arms wildly, shout at him even though I know he can't hear me.

He sees me, though, and slows, crossing the median of the highway, and eases onto the shoulder next to me.

"What in the world, Sunshine?" His shirt is puckered to his skin, wringing with sweat. He looks concerned.

I burst out in tears; I can't help it.

"How did you even know where to find me?" My voice comes out mangled.

"The horse *knows*."

That's one of Pa's favorite sayings.

Massive relief. "Cookie? She came home? She okay?"

"She's like a boomerang. Yeah, she's fine, only some scrapes. I drove the usual way to the store, and when I didn't find you, I decided to look down here. What happened?"

"This asshole—sorry, this jerk—sped up to us in a red BMW, rode right next to us. Revved the gas. And Cookie took off and swerved toward the fence, which dragged me off her."

"Lemme see."

I stick out my right leg.

"Jesus."

"Can you stand on it?"

"Yeah, but it hurts."

"But how bad? One to ten."

I grit my teeth, put my weight on it. "Five."

Pa nods briskly. "Okay, okay, lotsa blood, but hopefully it's not broken." He scoops me up in his arms, carries me into the passenger seat.

Back home, he pulls right up to the front porch, yells for Mom.

She steps out the door, a scowl stamped across her face, hands on her hips. She narrows her eyes at me.

"Come down from there and help us!" Pa yelps at her.

I wrap an arm around each of their necks so they can guide me up the steps, get me inside.

The cabin feels dark and cool, almost cave-like, after being out in the summer sun. It takes my eyes a few minutes to adjust.

We have a few windows, but they're small. Pa told me it helps keep the place from being like an oven in the summer. Guess he's right. We do have AC, but it's just a window unit, wheezing in the corner.

I spy baby Molly asleep in her crib in the far corner, her chubby thumb plugged into her little mouth.

Mom and Pa lower me into a chair at the dining table. Julia's sitting across from me, knitting a scarf. She's always engrossed in some kind of activity. Overachiever, busy bee. When our eyes meet, she smirks.

Cold bitch.

"Ethan, leave us. I'm gonna get these jeans off her," Mom says. "Julia, put that away and help me, would ya?"

Pa bends down, kisses my cheek. "You'll be all right. I'm gonna get back to work." He gestures with his head to the backyard, to his woodshop.

Before he goes, he tucks my hair behind my ear, smooths the top of my head. As he does it, I shoot Julia a satisfied smile. She knows I'm Pa's favorite and can't stand it. It's just another reason why she hates me.

A huff barks out of her. Followed by the sound of her chair scraping against the dirt floor.

"Stand up, lean into me," Mom orders me.

I unbutton my pants, ease them off my hips, then sink back down into the chair.

Kneeling, Julia slowly peels them off me.

"Ouch!" I yelp.

"Sorry! I'm trying to take it easy."

It feels like razor blades are digging into my skin with each tug.

Finally, they're off.

Mom examines me. "Tsk."

The whole outside of my leg looks mauled, a huge scrape running from my ankle to the top of my knee.

Mom wrenches my leg, moving it into different positions.

"Ouch!" I yell this time.

"Hold steady, I need to see if there's a fracture." Mom's mouth is a flat line. It's as if she's put out, even though *I'm* the one who's injured.

"Or I could just go to a doctor like a normal—"

"You know we don't use doctors. At least until we find one who understands our values." Mom jerks my leg again, sending a fresh hell of pain through it.

"And what are those values, exactly?" I ask, angry at how she's manhandling me. Punishing me. "That if you have a broken bone, God can fix it?"

"Watch your mouth!"

"It's not like this was my fault—" I screech.

"Tell me again, *why* did you have to ride today?"

"Indy needed new socks..." I stop. Those fucking socks must be along the highway somewhere.

"Well, if you didn't insist on riding bareback, maybe this all wouldn't have happened. But at least your leg's not broken, far as I can tell."

I don't have to look over at Julia to tell that she's grinning, lapping this up.

"Well, if I had my driver's license, like a normal teen—"

"That's enough outta you, young lady. You know we can't afford another car. You trying to stress your father out even more?" Her voice is shrill, hideous.

"I know how to drive the truck. If I had my license, he'd let me. I could be added to the insurance—"

"Julia," Mom says sharply, cutting me off. "Get me a bottle of tea tree oil from the shed, the washbasin, and a couple of clean rags."

But Julia lingers, her eyes darting between me and Mom. She loves it when we argue, when I get in trouble.

"Julia! Now!"

My sister slowly rises, takes her sweet-ass time exiting.

"Don't hurry or anything, I'm just in danger of losing my leg." I cut my eyes at her.

She pauses, shakes her head, but finally heads out the back door.

Mom grips my wrists, squeezes them. *"For where you have envy and selfish ambition, there you find disorder and every evil practice."*

She stares me down, her eyes steely.

"James 3:16," I shoot back. "I know this verse very well, Mother."

"Humph. I'm surprised you remembered. Seems to me like you've forgotten it. Carrying on about what other teens, so-called 'normal teens,' might have—"

I yank my wrists from her grip, but literally bite my tongue. If my leg's not broken, I'm going out tonight, and I don't want to push it.

We sit in silence, glaring at each other. Her eyes taunt me, wanting to provoke me, push me. I keep my trap shut.

Baby Molly stirs in her crib, her golden curls damp with sweat against her forehead.

Julia toes the back door open, supplies in hand.

Mom pours the tea tree oil on a rag, then applies it to my leg.

I nearly jump from the chair; it feels like she's sticking me with a fire poker.

A snicker bubbles out of Julia, and I notice the corners of Mom's lips slightly lifting, too, as if she's trying to hide her smile.

"Jesus, Mom, you could've diluted it!"

"Not with these wounds! I have to get it clean. Now settle back down."

At least this time she dips the rag in the washbasin first, then dots it again with the oil. It stings less this way, but still, I can't get away from these two soon enough.

16

JANE

 few hours later, while Mom is busy in the kitchen cooking dinner, I slip into the bathroom to do my makeup.

I called Blair earlier. She'll be here in ten minutes.

To spite Mom, I put my black eyeliner on extra thick, swipe on my darkest red lipstick. And because my leg's wrapped in a bandage, I'm wearing a miniskirt. Well, sort of a mini. It's something Pa bought me in a secondhand shop in Dallas, only because I begged him. It comes down to my knees—that's the only reason Mom allows me to wear it—but I'm able to roll the waist up, make it shorter when I'm out.

I step out of the bathroom.

Everyone's now sitting around the dining table.

Mom eyes me. "Where do you think you're going, dressed up like that?"

"There's this party tonight, out in the woods. And Blair and her friends are giving me a ride."

Now that I'm almost eighteen, I don't have to ask their permission to go out. But I do have to be home by midnight.

Mom stirs the pot of potatoes, thwacks the side of it with a wooden spoon. "Well," she starts, running her eyes up and down me, "you look like a whore. All that makeup on."

"Abigail, please!" Pa barks at her. "She's had a hard enough time today already."

Mom rolls her eyes. But she doesn't argue with Pa. That never happens.

Julia's bouncing baby Molly on her knee, fingers twined through Molly's hair, but she's listening, pressing her lips together like she's saying, *I better keep my trap shut; I might say something funny, something mean.*

"Julia, wanna come with me?" I ask. Of course I don't want her to. Not after she was so nasty to me earlier. And if I'm being honest, she always makes things awkward because she basically has no social skills—except around adults, that is. I ask only to make a good show in front of Mom and Pa. Plus, what if she *could* actually meet a guy? I've never seen Denny hanging around this crew, but what if there's someone else? It would be such a massive relief.

Julia tsk-tsks. "Um, no thanks. I'll pass."

"Who is this Blair girl?" Pa asks warmly.

"Blair Chambers. She's only, like, the most popular girl in school." My face flushes from boasting. But I wanna give it back to Mom, to Julia. And I know Pa will like hearing this. He likes it when I make new friends.

"That's good, honey," Pa says, then winks at me. "Just be careful out there, okay?"

"Always." I wink back. "I'm just gonna wait outside—"

"You are *not*," Mom says. "I wanna meet this girl. You ashamed of us or something?"

Um, yes. I'm ashamed of Mom in her dowdy dress, looking like some housemaid. And if I'm honest, I'm embarrassed of our simple home. A cabin with one big open room downstairs, Mom and Pa's bedroom down a shallow hall. My and Julia's loft upstairs, reachable by a ladder. Baby Molly's crib in the corner, five steps from the kitchen table.

"'Course not. Just nervous," I lie, "and wanted to go sit out on the porch in the rocker."

Blair's headlights shine through the window. My stomach feels like a fist is squeezing it. I hear her car door open, then slam shut. Then her feet drum the steps up to our porch. She knocks.

I make sure I'm the one to answer. "Heeey! Thanks for giving me a lift."

"Of course!" She smells like heaven—she's wearing real perfume, not that crap Mom makes—and her blond hair has so much Aqua Net in it, it practically glistens. "Can I come in? Jesus, what happened to your leg?"

"Horse accident. Tell you about it later." I step aside, let her through. "Everyone, this is Blair! Blair, this is my mom and dad, my sister Julia, and my baby sister, Molly."

"Oh my god, she's so *cute!*" Blair practically sings, and I realize she's tipsy. I can smell the alcohol on her breath. "And this place, it's so..." Her bloodshot blue eyes scan the room as she tries to find the right word... "Well, it's *so* cute, too!"

Julia gives her a weak half wave, but Pa steps forward, shakes her hand. "Mr. Swift. Ethan. Pleasure to meet you." He beams at her.

Blair beams back, and I know what she's thinking: *He's cute, too.*

Everyone *always* has the hots for Pa. Doesn't hurt that he looks ten years younger than he actually is.

Mom wipes her hands on her apron. "And I'm Mrs. Swift. Please, call me *Abigail*." Mom's voice is bright, cheery. Like she's about to present us with a tray of freshly baked cookies. Like she wasn't just cutting me down two seconds ago.

She can turn on the charm when she needs to.

But I see her looking at Blair, judging her. Mom hates anything that smacks of material wealth. Or, at least, outwardly showing it.

I loop my arm through Blair's, guide her out the door. "Bye!" I say, trying to sound to Blair as if my family annoys me, trying to sound cool. When we're on the porch, I even close the door harder than normal, a middle finger to Mom.

17

JACKSON

J ackson picks at the label of his icy Michelob, wads the gummy paper into a tight ball. A compulsive habit of his. Some folks smoke, while Jackson fidgets with paper: napkins, beer-bottle labels, receipts.

The Texas Rangers flicker on the screen above him, and for not the first time tonight, he wishes he were in Dallas, watching the game live with his friends.

But at least he's at his favorite watering hole in town, Sullivan's, perched at the bar with a decent view of the TV. Nolan Ryan's on the mound, winding up, preparing to strike out another Astro.

Sullivan's is just a dive bar, really, a sawdust-on-the-floor beer joint on the outskirts of town, but that's precisely why he likes it so much. He can come here to unwind. It's blue-collar types who frequent the place—farmers and oil-field workers, who mainly keep to themselves. None of his ritzy clients would come here; Charleigh and her ilk wouldn't dare cross the threshold, so, for the hours he spends here, it's as if Jackson gets to escape Longview for a bit.

"I don't know *why* you insist on going to that shithole," Charleigh said to him once.

It's near her childhood home, right off the highway by Seven Pines. "It feels like real Texas to me, I guess."

"Whatever that means." Charleigh rolled her eyes.

Jackson does *not* wear his pink IZOD shirts in here, though. He's careful to dress in a button-down and jeans, even going so far as to don a pair of cowboy boots.

So far, no one has fucked with him.

But Ginny, the owner and barkeep, wouldn't allow that anyway. She's tough as old leather and doesn't suffer any rough play in Sullivan's. Even though she's married, Jackson has always suspected that she's gay. And he feels like she can sense that he is, too, and that's why she keeps extra watch on him.

"You want another, cowboy?" Ginny asks, tilting her cowgirl hat toward him.

"Sure, why not?"

Ginny fishes a cold one from the cooler—an amber bottle flecked with ice flakes—and sets it on a fresh coaster. Fills a paper tray with roasted peanuts, placing it next to Jackson's beer. His heart melts; this is more of Ginny's mothering him, making sure he has something in his stomach to help sop up the alcohol.

He digs his wallet from his back pocket, peels out an extra five, slides it over to her.

"Thanks, hon." She winks at him, then slams the cash register drawer shut with her hip.

He pries open a peanut, pops one in his mouth. Then another.

A man saunters over to the bar, eyes the empty barstool next to Jackson.

He's dressed like he's from another time, like the 1800s or something, in a button-down Henley, a pair of leather suspenders snapped to his pants. The top trio of buttons on his shirt are undone, exposing a triangle of tanned flesh.

"Do you mind?" He gestures to the barstool, flashing a gleaming lopsided grin at Jackson. The man's hair is honey blond, his eyes pools of caramel.

Jackson's stomach capsizes. "Be my guest!" he replies awkwardly, hoping the man doesn't think he meant that literally.

"What're ya havin'?" Ginny asks him.

"Whiskey. On the rocks, please."

Jackson tries to train his gaze back toward the Rangers game, but all he can sense is this person in his periphery. He risks a glance. This man is gorgeous. Hot buttered rum in a glass. Tall, lean, but muscular. His sleeves are cuffed above his forearms, which are whittled, sculpted.

A man who works with his hands, Jackson thinks with approval.

He watches as he downs half his drink in one swallow and wipes his mouth with the back of his hand.

He swivels in his barstool toward Jackson. Beams that smile at him again. A smile that oozes mischief.

"Come here often?" he asks Jackson.

Jackson gulps. It almost feels like a come-on, but he spies a gold wedding band on the man's ring finger. "Yeah, actually I do."

Thank God I'm on my fourth beer, Jackson thinks, so his nerves aren't in overdrive.

"It's the only place in this town where I feel like I can clear my head, ya know?"

The man laughs. "Yeah, I hear ya."

"And you?" Jackson asks. "Come here often?"

"Nope. First time."

"I mean, th-there's fancier places downtown, of course," Jackson stammers, wanting to keep the conversation going, "and then there's the strip clubs, but I don't have much of an appetite for titty bars—" Jackson pauses. He can't believe he just blurted that out.

But the man holds Jackson's gaze with his toffee-brown eyes, cocks his head to the side. "Yeah. Neither do I."

Jackson doesn't know if he's saying this because he's clearly married…or if it's some kind of code. The thought is almost too delicious to think.

"Ethan. Ethan Swift." He offers his hand to Jackson.

Damn it.

In his tipsy state, it hadn't dawned on Jackson that this must be exactly who this man is.

The enemy.

He takes Ethan's hand, shakes it. "Jackson Ford. Pleasure to meet you." He tries to steer his tone to cold, professional.

"Pleasure's all mine." Ethan slings back the rest of his drink, lifts his glass at Ginny.

She pours him another.

"I'll have one, too," Jackson tells her. He needs something stronger than beer in this moment. But what he really needs is to get the hell out of here. He can't, though. He's mesmerized by Ethan.

A grin forms across Ginny's lips, but she bites it back, fixes Jackson's drink.

The whiskey scorches the back of Jackson's throat, making him shake his head.

Ethan chuckles. "Not used to the strong stuff?"

"If I'm being honest, no. I usually cut it with Coke."

"Will you get my new friend here a Jack and Coke?" Ethan asks Ginny.

"Here, allow me." He grabs Jackson's drink, tilts his head back, empties the rest down his throat. Smiles that crooked smile at Jackson.

Jackson feels overheated, as if his clothes are suddenly too tight.

When Ginny passes him his drink, he takes a long pull, tries to cool himself off.

What the hell am I doing? Jackson thinks. Followed by *Fuck it*.

"That better?" Ethan asks, his voice cutting over the clacking of pool balls and bar noise, smooth as maple syrup.

"Much!" Jackson manages to reply.

Ethan drums his hands along the bar. Long, elegant fingers.

The kind Jackson can imagine nibbling on. But that wedding band.

Like Jackson, Ethan seems fidgety. A live wire. Jackson wishes he could say something smart, clever, but his tongue feels like a brick in his mouth.

Perhaps because of the awkward silence, Ethan fishes something out of his leather satchel.

Jackson nearly gasps when he sees what it is.

A palm-sized Bible.

What the...?

But Charleigh did tell him they were religious nuts.

Jackson divorced himself long ago from any ties with the church. Aside from the handful of Methodist churches in Dallas and Houston that openly welcome gays, Christianity is a foe to his community.

But he can't pry his eyes off Ethan as he leans over the bar, that lock of golden hair now dangling across his forehead, luscious fingers paging through the battered-looking Bible.

Through his straw, Jackson sucks in more Jack and Coke, savoring the sweetness of the soda mixed with the bite of the whiskey. He flicks his eyes back to the Rangers game, but then they rove—of their own accord—back over to Ethan.

As if sensing this, Ethan closes his Bible, turns to Jackson. "I know it might seem odd, but I like to take this wherever I go."

Jackson nods, his brain incapable of forming a reply.

"I know religion isn't for *everybody*." Ethan says this in a low voice, almost conspiratorially, as if he's all but saying he's well aware that Jackson is gay. "And organized religion isn't really for me. But this," Ethan adds, tapping the Bible, "the pure word, meant to be read in both churches and places of ill repute, by everyday men, is almost poetic to me. Especially the Psalms."

Ethan licks a finger, flips through the tissue-like pages. "*I waited patiently for the Lord. He drew me up from the pit. I delight to do your will, O God. My heart fails me, but you are my help.*" He closes the book, slips it back in his bag. "It's almost like a country song, you know?"

Jackson nods again. *Say something clever*, he thinks for the second time this evening. "Yeah, I don't go in much for the church—"

"I bet you don't." Ethan's eyes move over him. Trickling down his chest, to his jeans. Jackson feels like he's being lit on fire. "And hey, I'm not trying to convert you—there's nothing worse than a man pushing his own beliefs on another. I just wanted to explain why I take my Bible to the bar. Helps keep me on the right path."

But the way Ethan's looking at Jackson, it's as if he wants to be led right *off* that right path.

"Gotcha." Jackson takes a nip of his cocktail. "So, what line of work are you in?"

Jackson knows the answer to this, of course, but the time has long passed for Jackson to admit that he's already heard all the dirt on the Swifts from his catty best friend.

"Woodworking," Ethan says, winking at him.

The double entendre isn't lost on Jackson; he chokes on his drink. "What kind of...woodworking?" Jackson can play this game, too.

"Mmmm..." Ethan moans. "Custom stuff. High-end furniture. One-of-a-kind pieces. Like, really, anything a client wants. Credenzas, tallboy dressers, sideboards. You name it. But I really only like to work with the choicest woods."

"That's really fascinating!" Jackson says too brightly. But it is. Finally something they can talk about. "I'm a designer. Interior design. So I'm genuinely interested."

"I knew I liked you for a reason." Ethan's voice is husky. He inches his barstool closer to Jackson's. "What's your specialty?"

"Kind of like yours. I work with high-end clients. Scouting for everything from antiques to the latest pieces from the showrooms in Dallas. That sort of thing."

"Wanna come see my stuff sometime?" Ethan combs his bangs back into place with his hands. "I mean, no pressure. But my shop's out on my land." Ethan juts his head toward the exit. "Not far from here."

Don't say yes, don't say yes, Jackson thinks. Cut this off right here. Nothing good can come from this. The man is married, and Charleigh will skin him if she finds out he talked to Ethan even this much.

Jackson's mouth hangs open, trying to form words. "I'd love to," he finally says, stomach spinning.

"I'm about to head out. Wanna come outside, exchange cards? Mine are in the glove box."

Jackson's boots crunch over the white gravel as he trails Ethan through the parking lot. Above, the sky is clear, the moon a pale quarter dangling above them.

Ethan's truck is parked next to Jackson's convertible.

"Nice signage," Ethan remarks about Jackson's magnetic sign on the side of his car that reads, *Ford Design*.

"Yours, too," Jackson says. And it *is* nice. A vintage-looking font, perfectly painted in white, that reads, *Swift's Custom Furniture*.

"Thanks. Painted it myself."

Of course you did, Jackson thinks. As if he needs another reason to have a crush on this man.

As they swap cards, Ethan's hand brushes Jackson's, sending electricity zipping up his arm. Jackson turns to leave, cracks open his car door, lowers himself inside. Before he closes it, Ethan says, "Hope to see you soon. I bet we have a lot more in common than you think." Ethan winks at him again.

18

JANE

The clock in the dash of Blair's Mercedes reads five past midnight.

Great.

One thing I always try to do is make curfew, even though I break each and every other one of Mom's rules: no smoking, no drinking, no fooling around with boys, etc. But I do my best to meet curfew so she can't have one obvious thing to hold against me.

I'm praying she's already asleep.

I have Blair drop me a little ways from the house, to keep the noise to a minimum.

Pa's truck is nowhere in sight. *Humph.*

I creep up the steps, tiptoe across the porch. Creak open the front door.

My shoulders sag.

Mom's sitting at the kitchen table, reading the *Farmers' Almanac.*

In the light of the lone bulb hanging above her, her face looks older, solemn. I almost feel a pang of pity for her, there all alone with that dreary book, but then her expression sours at the sight of me.

It's like she can smell the booze from there. The cigarettes, the weed, the cologne of the boys who got close enough to me to flirt.

Her eyes skewer me, giving me the same once-over she gave me before I left.

I tug my skirt down.

"You're late." She shakes her head, trains her gaze back to the pages now in her lap.

"Not my fault. I tried to get Blair to leave earlier, but—"

"I was starting to get worried."

"It's only five minutes, Mom."

She whistles out a sigh.

"Where's Pa?" I ask, trying to change the subject. And to provoke her. "Why isn't he home?"

She closes the book, narrows her eyes at me. "Your father is out. You know he needs to find new clients."

Ah, so that's what she's calling it.

I can't help it—it's the alcohol and my own spitefulness—but the corners of my lips lift into a grin.

"*What?*" Mom spits out, her voice strained.

I recompose my face, turning it into a blank mask. "Nothing." I drop my eyes to the floor, then head for the ladder that leads to the loft, swerving around her on my way.

I can feel her stare lighting into the back of me.

I wince in pain as I mount the bottom rung of the ladder—my leg is still a mess—but I force myself to climb.

I'm halfway up when her voice slithers across the room, icy cold, mean. "I can smell tobacco smoke on you. I don't know who you think you're foolin'; I can also smell boy all over you."

I pause, then keep pulling myself up.

If only Mom knew half the shit I've done with Luke.

She, of course, thinks you need to be married before you give yourself away, but I often wonder: For her, was it the chicken or the egg with Pa? She was eighteen when she got pregnant with Julia. They've always told us they were already married, but other than a single photo of Mom and Pa in church clothes, standing outside a small chapel in Minnesota, there are no wedding pictures, no documentation. No actual wedding date on the back of the photo.

I slide under my quilt.

Julia's in her bed, across the loft, asleep. Or pretending to be. I'm sure she heard everything that just went down with Mom.

Whatever.

Moonlight trickles through the high window, streaking shadows across the quilt.

Other than dealing with Mom just now, I had fun tonight.

As soon as Blair pulled out of our drive, Stacy lit up a joint in the back seat, passed it up to me. "You smoke?"

I'd smoked weed a few times with Luke, but I don't really like how fuzzy-headed and paranoid it makes me feel.

"Absolutely," I said, pinching the hot paper between my fingers, taking a stinging drag, wanting to look cool.

"Woo-hoo!" Blair hooted in approval, slapping me a high five.

The Circles, she explained as she drove us there, are a cluster of empty streets in the middle of a forest. A developer intended to build a subdivision out there but lost funding, so now it's party central for teens. Even though there are streetlights, it's tucked so far back into the woods, no one from the highway can see in, tell what we're up to.

We poured out of the car, pot smoke trailing after us. About a dozen kids from school were already there. A boom box sitting on Tommy Fields's truck bed was blaring Guns N' Roses, "Sweet Child O' Mine."

Blair sauntered over, and the two made out, right in front of everyone. Tommy is Blair's boyfriend. Tall, dark hair, strong. Star quarterback.

Stacy handed me a Solo cup filled with something red.

"It's *so* good," she gushed. "But strong. It's Hunch Punch. Basically Hawaiian Punch with Everclear."

I took a sip; it tasted like a cherry Jolly Rancher. I gulped it down.

Even though it's summer, a bonfire was burning in a trash can, throwing out sparks.

Then, from across the flames, I felt her stare. Noticed her eyeing me with a wicked grin.

Nellie.

I never actually met her in school. We were in the same trig class, but no one ever introduced us, and each time I tried to catch her eye, she'd be glaring at me.

So I'd started to glare back.

And tonight, she was giving me the same dirty look she always does.

What the hell?

I'd always thought it was because she's the richest girl in town and probably the most stuck-up. I thought she was looking down on me.

What I learned tonight, though, is that that's not it at all; she's just *strange*.

But what made my head spin even more as she shot daggers into me with her bizarro stare is that she was leaning against the hood of her red bimmer.

A red bimmer that could've been the one that ran me and Cookie off the road.

I actually lifted my hand, tried to give her a wave across the bonfire, but she rolled her eyes, then pulled a long drag off her cigarette.

I couldn't help it—getting people to like me is my superpower, and I just had to find out if it was her who'd caused my accident—so I walked over to her. "Hey, so you're Nellie, right?"

She laughed. "Duh."

Okay.

I felt Stacy and Blair's eyes on us, felt them drawing closer.

"Well, I'm Jane." I stuck out my hand for her to shake it.

But her arms stayed lashed to her chest as she studied me coolly with her swimming pool–blue eyes. She worked the cigarette between her fingers, which were sticking out of black lace Madonna gloves. Her eyes popped when they got to my bandage.

"What's wrong with your leg?" she asked. Not with concern. Almost mocking me.

"I got thrown from my horse—"

"Oh my god! So that *was* actually you? You actually like, ride…a horse?" That same wicked grin curdled across her mouth.

"Yeah, I *actually* do," I replied, my pulse throbbing in my temples. "But hey, nice car." I jerked my chin at her bimmer. "Thanks a lot for running me off the road earlier, nearly killing me."

"What?" she sneered. "Like it's *my* fault you can't control your horse."

Unbelievable.

"*You* caused this?" Blair said to Nellie. She and Stacy were standing next to me by then.

Nellie just scoffed.

"Well, *of course* you did. Little psycho."

"Yeah, like sorry, whatever." Nellie snickered. "Maybe you should get a car instead. I don't know where you're from, but this is an actual modern town."

"Shut up, Nellie!" Blair shot back. "Jane's awesome, and her farm is also supercool. I just picked her up out there, and there's all this amazing stuff—"

"Oh, Blair, you're so full of shit!" Nellie practically shrieked. "You hate the outdoors unless it's Miller's Hole or waterskiing," she said, her hands flailing around her, "or this. You were the biggest scaredy cat at summer camp, jumping at every bug—"

"Okaaaay." Blair rolled her eyes, turned to me. "Don't worry about Nellie." She flipped her blond hair over her shoulder. "She's just jealous."

She looped her arm through mine and turned to walk away, so I followed. After a few steps, she said, loud enough for Nellie to hear, "And...*weird*."

After my second cup of Hunch Punch, I ducked into the woods to pee. I heard a loud rumble, looked up to see a Ford Bronco crawling toward the party.

A guy hopped out of the driver's seat. Seeing him up close, I recognized him right away as Dustin Reeves. Nellie's boyfriend. I'd met him at the swimming hole night before last. He kind of gave me the creeps.

He spotted me and staggered over, clearly already drunk. Unlike Tommy, or Luke, Dustin is not exactly handsome. He's oafish. Tall. A rich mama's boy, kinda pudgy, with teeth like a shark's. But trying desperately to look cool in his Metallica T-shirt.

My heart drummed in my chest. We weren't out of sight of the rest of the party but far enough away to make me feel uncomfortable.

"Damn, girl, how'd that happen?" he asked, pointing at my leg. Laughing. His eyes moving over me as if they were devouring me. I felt squeamish.

"An accident," I said, keeping my tone neutral, not wanting to bring Nellie's name up, get into it with him.

"Looks bad. Seriously, what happened, huh?" His alligator grin grew wider, uglier.

But I kept my face as still as a stone.

From across the bonfire, I could feel Nellie's stare again.

Great, I thought. *Now she thinks I'm hitting on her hideous boyfriend.*

"Later," I said to Dustin, then stomped off.

In the car ride home, I asked Blair and Stacy what they thought Nellie has against me.

"Against *you*?" Blair scoffed. "More like against the whole world. Don't take that shit personally; she's just a bitch."

"Total bitch."

"But she almost ran me off the road today."

"She'd do that to any of us. She's a monster."

But a tiny part of me felt sorry for her for some reason. Probably because she seems like such a misfit, even though she's the richest girl in town.

Blair steered with one hand, hotboxed a joint with the other. "She's, like, a freak. But because her family has all this money, we have to hang out with her. But she's just…"

"Twisted!" Stacy chimed in, leaning in from the back between mine and Blair's seats. "Should I tell her about the playhouse incident?"

"Totally!" Blair laughed.

"So get this. And this is just one example of Nellie's weird-ness. When we were like seven or something, my parents had this brand-new playhouse built for me. Like, it was awesome. Almost as big, no offense, as your house."

My face burned with embarrassment.

"And Nellie comes over one day to play and brings this Easy-Bake Oven thingy she just got. Like, her parents spoil her rotten. Even more than mine and Blair's do. Anyway, I kind of fell in love with the toy. And she accidentally left it behind. I know this was mean of me, but when she came over the next day to get it, I told her it was mine and that she couldn't have it back."

"Boom!" Blair shouted. "That was enough to make her explode."

"But the thing is, she didn't. Not right away. When I wouldn't give it back, she gave me the most evil stare and stormed out. That night, my parents shook me awake. There were all these red lights outside and sirens blaring because my playhouse had caught fire and was burning down! The little bitch set my playhouse on fire!"

"They could never prove it, of course," Blair said, shaking her head dramatically, "but we *all* knew it was Nellie. So, like, just don't mess with her. Like I said, we *have* to be friends with her, because that's how this town works, but...fuck..."

I slunk down in my seat, feeling unsettled, and watched as the pine trees pulsed past by window.

Later

How the hell did it come to this?

I hear a twig snap and whip my head around, terrified that someone is watching me, or even worse, that someone saw me. Saw what I did.

But then I see a rabbit jolt from the forest, and breathe a huge sigh of relief.

I never imagined in a million years that when I woke up this morning, I would *kill* someone today. I was just going about my ordinary life.

But that's not really true, is it? Nothing about my life has been ordinary these past few weeks.

19

NELLIE

Now

cannot wait to get out of this shithole town. I hate it here!

I'm home from the Circles, locked in my bathroom, scrubbing off my makeup and smoking as many cigarettes as possible.

Why do I even give two shits about Jane? I know I shouldn't care, but it burns me up. Fucking Blair giving her a ride there? Rushing to her defense about the stupid horse thing? Are you kidding me?

I just wanted to spook her a little, had no idea I'd cause her to fall. And now even that has backfired on me, made Jane even more popular with Blair and her crew.

Then, after she left, Dustin dragged me over to his Bronco to make out. He's gross, but it's better than being with no one. But while he was fumbling with my bra, he started to laugh.

"What?" I asked, embarrassed, my buzz killed.

"Nothing. Nothing about you anyway."

I smacked his hands down, pulled away from him. "Tell me right fucking now."

He shook his head, then looked down at his lap, almost sheepishly. "That Jane girl." His voice was rubbery from too much Hunch Punch.

"What *about* her?" I asked, striking up a fresh smoke.

"She's just...*somethin'*." He shook his head again, smiling.

Fuck me. I couldn't give two shits about Dustin, but it's not like I need him having a crush on her.

"You've gotta be kidding me," I said.

"What?" He twisted in his seat to face me, tilted his head.

"You like her?"

He grunted. "Um, no."

But I could tell from the way his face became splotchy and red that he was lying his ass off.

I opened the door.

"Hey! Where you goin', baby?"

"Oh, fuck off, loser!"

Dustin was gross enough to me before, but at least we had each other. Now he's gonna be dead to me if he doesn't watch it. Jane doesn't need any more attention than what she's already been getting.

All the guys tonight were mooning over her. Making asses of themselves. Even Tommy had a chubby when he was talking to her.

I've never had the hot guys pay me any attention, other than to make fun of me. Push my buttons. I learned real early, like in elementary school, that I wasn't cute. Not like the other girls, who already had boys asking them to "go" with them. And not like Mom and Dad, who are freakishly good-looking.

Other than my light-blond hair and blue eyes, I don't resemble them. My eyes are just ordinary, dull, not the crystal shade they both have, which mesmerizes people. One day at church when I was little—and we never go to church except for the big holidays— some old lady with a loud voice stopped me in the hall and dug her bony hand into my shoulder. "You're the Andersen girl?" she asked. "You don't *look* like your mother. Humph! That's unusual!"

I tried to step away from her, but she kept her grip on me. "You must look more like your father," she said, as Dad was walking toward us. She stared him down quickly before adding, "Come to think of it, you don't really look like him that much either!"

Even though I was only six, I knew exactly what she was talking about. But I'd never really thought of it like that before. That not looking like them meant something bad.

But the worst of it? That came when I was ten. Mom and Dad were out at some charity ball, and when they stumbled inside—no doubt drunk off too many martinis—they sent the sitter home.

They thought I was in my bedroom, asleep, but I was sitting at the top of the stairs, waiting up for them.

I heard Mom say to Dad, laughing, "How do we even know she's really ours?"

"Hey," Dad replied. "She's beautiful."

My heart swelled for him just then. But, after a second, he added, "In her own way."

In her own way.

I didn't know what to make of that. Was it a good thing? To be different? Dad made it sound like it was, but I wasn't sure.

But I damn sure used all this to my advantage. The next morning, I demanded Mom take me on a shopping spree in Dallas. If I didn't have the looks the other rich bitches did, then I needed to have more. Of everything. More makeup, more clothes, the latest, biggest TV set, the best Apple computer.

I waited for hungover Mom to say she wasn't in the mood for the drive—then I was gonna tell her that I heard that nasty thing she'd said about me. But she just said yes, and off we went. So I never told her, but her evil words have been growing inside me ever since, festering.

I'm not enough of a pussy to let anyone get me down, though. Not Mom, not Blair, and for shit sure not fucking Dustin. And not Jane.

Even with all my makeup wiped off, I no longer hate the girl in the mirror and the way she looks. I'm seventeen; I've grown into myself. My lips are fuller, my face is just *better*—sure, the nose job Mom made me get in seventh grade helped—but I've also just matured. I'm not the pathetic little thing I used to be. My body's developed now: I have curves, and I'm taller. And I go to the best hairstylist in town.

But even with all this, nobody in town can see past who I once was, the ugly duckling. The freak.

No matter what I do, I'll never look like Blair, with her heart-shaped face, model bone structure, perfect figure. Or Jane, who, despite her buckteeth, is pretty, though I hate to even admit it.

The only time *I've* felt pretty is when I went to Dad's family's place in Stockholm. I was fifteen, and my parents sent me over there for the summer.

I was in heaven. I was accepted. They don't have the same bullshit beauty standards over there in Europe that they have over here. My cousins took me skinny-dipping in the lakes, clubbing at the underage spots in the city. Boys actually wanted to dance with me, actually hit on me. Made out with me. I got felt up in the bathroom at one of those clubs by a tall blond boy named Sven, who was hotter than any boy in Longview.

And because they're not so uptight over there, my big clan of cousins and aunts and uncles thought my darker side was funny.

To a point.

Until I got sent home.

I had developed a severe crush on a distant cousin, another tall blond named Thor. He came and spent weekends at my aunt and uncle's massive house, and I was always flirting with him. And I thought he was flirting back, because he was always nice to me. I thought he liked me, too.

One night, when we went skinny-dipping, all of us, he was dog-paddling in the water right in front of me, like a foot away. I thought he wanted to kiss me, so I leaned in, but he looked confused, shook his head, then swam away.

I was enraged.

And then I had an idea. I knew he had a peanut allergy. Could die from it.

So, the next weekend, I ground some up into powder and mixed it into my trail mix. Begged him to go hiking with me. To show me a new trail.

Once we were about a mile into the forest, I sat down on a rock and pulled out the trail mix. Offered him some.

He ate a fistful.

Happiness spread through me.

Not one minute later, he was gasping for air. Pointing at his backpack, motioning for me to unzip it, locate his EpiPen.

I just glared at him.

His hands started flailing around wildly, his face pleading with me to help.

I bit my bottom lip, careful not to smile.

And didn't budge.

I glanced at my Swatch.

One minute had passed.

His face was now red as a Christmas sweater.

His choking sounds were getting louder, but we were all alone, the noises muffled in the grand forest.

Two minutes.

I gave him another nasty stare.

Then I unzipped his backpack. Found his EpiPen and slapped it in his shaky hand.

On the way home, I walked ahead of him on the trail.

"You just tried to kill me!" he shouted after me.

"I don't know what you're talking about." I lifted my shoulders in a shrug.

When we got back to the house, he told my aunt Elsa what had happened. I know because I was eavesdropping from the next room.

Next thing I know, Mom's calling, telling me she's on her way to come and get me.

I was furious. Not only did I not want to have my summer cut short, I'd actually been planning on begging her and Dad to let me stay, to finish out high school there.

"Not after the stunt you just pulled! Have you lost your mind?" Mom shrieked across the line.

I could picture her clasping the wall phone in the kitchen, frantic.

"I'm telling you, he's lying," I hissed over the phone. "He's been sneaking into my room at night and..." My voice shook with fake tears.

"And *what*?"

"He's tried to touch me."

Mom sucked in a quick breath. It was almost like a sound of relief, like she wanted to believe me, was happy that there might be some alternate spin on this whole disaster. Someone else at fault.

"And, well, I threatened to tell on him. So now he's made up this giant story about me, to cover his own ass."

"Nellie, if you're lying to me, I swear to God—"

"Mother!" I squealed, loud as I could. "I'm not! I'm totally mortified! This is so embarrassing!"

Aunt Elsa sent me home anyway.

I don't think any of the Swedes bought my little story, but it kept me out of trouble with Mom and Dad at least.

And I plan to go back there. Maybe even instead of college. Surely they've all forgiven me by now?

The door handle rattles, snapping me out of my thoughts. That's followed by a fist rapping against the door.

"Nellie, what are you doing in there?"

Sigh. Mom.

Why can't she just grow a pair and ask me if I'm smoking?

I stub out my cigarette, empty the ashtray into the toilet, douse the air with perfume.

Yank open the door.

Mom jumps back.

"What? What's the big emergency?" I snap.

Mom shrinks a little, combs her French-manicured finger-nails through her feathered bangs. "Just wanted to see how your night went."

I exhale loudly, lean against the doorframe. "Shitty. Okay?"

"Is this about Jane?"

"Yeah. So?"

Just having to talk to Mom makes me want to light up another Marlboro.

"Well," she says, a tiny smile spreading across her lips, "I think you can stop worrying about her. They are weird. The whole family is cuckoo. I went out there earlier today—"

What the fuck.

"You did?" I practically shout at her. "Without telling me first, asking me? Was Jane—"

"No, calm down. She wasn't there. Her mom sells"—she bats her hand around in the air"—potions or whatever, and some of the women have been out to her little shop, which is just a lean-to, really, to buy 'em, and so I went to investigate. For you, for me."

I hate it when Mom meddles. Sure, I like for her to fix things, get me out of deep shit, do things for me, make shit happen, but sometimes…sometimes she takes it too far. Like hauling ass out to the Swift farm.

God, they must think we're such freaks!

"Did you tell them you were my mother?"

Mom flinches, as if I raised a hand to her. Her eyelids are shaded in emerald-green eyeshadow; she blinks her fake long lashes so quickly, it seems like she's trying not to cry.

"'Course I did. But the lady—excuse me, the *very strange woman*—couldn't have cared less. Seems like she doesn't have a handle on Jane, like she doesn't even like her. But I'm telling you, they are *low-rent*. Beneath us. They can't shine our shoes. *So* not worth worrying about."

She's talking so fast, I can't tell whether she's trying to convince herself or me.

"Don't worry, I didn't even say anything about you. Just mentioned to the woman that you were the same age as Jane. Nada more. Got it?"

I blow out a sigh. Roll my eyes. "Okaaay. So, like how *was* their place? Tonight Blair was saying how cool it is, which is so annoying—"

"It's a real dump, sweetie." She steps forward, tucks a lock of hair behind my ears. Her wrist smells like Giorgio, the perfume she's worn for as long as I can remember.

I can tell she's just saying that for my benefit. I'm sure Blair was right; I'm sure it is cool.

"Their house is basically a shack, and the shop is basically a shed. The woman was wearing this ugly dress, breastfeeding her baby in front of me, exposing herself—"

"Ewww!"

"Not a good scene. So chin up, young lady. The novelty will wear off soon. I promise."

20

JACKSON

Jackson switches off the Weed eater and thuds it to the ground. Sweat streams from his head, dousing his bare neck and shoulders.

He's shirtless, wanting the sun to scorch his skin, turn it from pasty to the golden-chestnut color of Ethan's. He's been out here for two hours, head full of that man, edging the grass and pruning his muscadine vines. Working his biceps and triceps, which are not as sculpted as they once were.

When he lived in Dallas, Jackson hit the gym nearly every day, but here, well, he doesn't want to work out with the upper elite. So he hits his home gym in his garage, pumping iron once a week—though, if he's being honest, it's dwindled to once a month.

He hasn't been motivated. But now all he can think about is Ethan. His husky voice, his chiseled forearms, those butterscotch eyes.

I bet we have a lot more in common than you think.

Though it's blazing out, the memory of those words sends a shiver over Jackson.

Ethan hasn't called him yet. And he hasn't dared to call Ethan. But he is *dying* to. Is one day too soon to follow up?

A feverish chorus of cicadas swells all around him, a million violins being played tremolo, a term he remembers from high school orchestra, which describes fast bowing. Their vibration is so thick, it almost feels like he's being ensnared by it, a physical membrane encasing him.

His backyard is paradise. Just half an acre, but he's trained every square inch into something verdant: the organic garden in the southeast corner dappled with enough sun to grow pudgy tomatoes, pumpkin-colored habanero peppers, and leafy cilantro, which Jackson blends into jars of fresh salsa.

A gang of spindly pines rims the edge of his property just beyond his fence line, casting pools of shade over his lawn. The Saint Augustine grass that carpets this section is so lush—out of the sun's reach—it almost looks like a green lagoon.

In a slash of direct sunlight, his wild muscadine orchard flourishes, the tendrils of the vines gripping the metal chain-link fence, its vines pregnant with green orbs of grapes that will bloat and turn a fleshy pink in late summer, when they're ready to be harvested.

Jackson's never made wine with them before; last summer was the first time the grapes were mature enough to be pressed for that purpose. Instead, he froze them in Ziplocs, made jam over the holidays.

He staggers inside through the back door, pries open the fridge, and pours himself a tall glass of cold iced tea. After gulping it down, he notices his answering machine blinking at him. Five new voicemails.

His heart raps against his rib cage.

Let it be Ethan.

With shaky hands, he presses the Play button.

Charleigh's voice thunders through the kitchen. "Hey! Just me! Call me when you get a sec."

He sighs, hits Delete.

"Heeeey! So, I need to talk, call me. 'K, bye!"

His shoulders sag; he groans. Charleigh again. Delete.

"Where are you? I thought you were going to be home today?" Delete.

"I know it's only been ten minutes, but I really need to talk!" Delete.

"Jackson Lee Ford! Call your best friend! She's going out of her skull!" Her voice is almost a screech at this point. "Seriously! Call a bitch back, or I'm comin' over to make sure you're not dead or something!"

Ugh. This woman. Damn!

21

CHARLEIGH

Where the hell is he?

Charleigh is still shaking inside from what just went down. All she wants is to dish to Jackson, who is not answering his damn phone.

After she called a second time and he still didn't pick up, she actually went into Alexander's home office to talk to him about it, not that he'd care.

She was still dressed in her purple leotard, and when she slunk into his room, his eyes carved her up. "Come here, baby. What is it?"

She crossed the room, circling his desk.

He leaned back in his leather chair, gesturing for her to sit in his lap.

"That *woman*, Abigail Swift, was at the freaking Boat House today! Can you believe it?"

Alexander swept her ponytail to one side, stroked her neck.

"And...so?" he purred in her ear. She could feel him stiffen underneath her.

She was *not* in the mood.

Of course, she didn't say that out loud.

"And...well, it's members only! We don't pay five hundred bucks a month for them to let just anybody in!"

A laugh yapped out of him. Charleigh gave him an elbow, sprang to her feet.

"What's the big deal? Why do you care so much if she was there?" His eyes crinkled with mirth.

"You don't get it!"

He blew out air, folded his arms across his chest. Pouted, obviously, because he wasn't going to get any from her right then. "I honestly don't. We have more money than God. You're at the top of the food chain. For Christ's sake, Charleigh, you're getting all wound up over nothing."

People advising Charleigh with any version of *calm down* has always had the opposite effect on her. That phrase is gasoline being poured on a campfire. Frustration surged through her veins; she stomped from the room.

She plodded into the kitchen and tried Jackson yet again. Slammed the phone into the receiver when he didn't answer.

She had gone to the club for her weekly Jazzercise class but arrived late. She was planning to catch the last of the class, then hit the upstairs lounge for daiquiris with the ladies right after, like they always did.

As she neared the exercise room, she heard the final bars of Olivia Newton-John's "Physical," the song the instructor plays at the end. Charleigh was going to pull the door open and step inside, but just as her fingers curled around the handle, she noticed something through the glass.

All her friends were clumped in a circle. Just as the song ended, they pulled apart, revealing who was in the middle: Abigail.

Charleigh's ears literally began to ring at the sight of her. She opened the door but didn't enter, just stood staring at the unbelievable scene.

She wasn't in a leotard, of course, but another one of her handsewn getups, a prairie dress. But her fawny hair was slick with sweat, so it was obvious she'd been a part of the class.

Emily, the perky instructor, trilled, "And a special thanks to Abigail, for joining us today!" Her hair was twisted up in a high ponytail, which swung as she continued. "And thanks for your potion! I've been having the best sex of my life!"

What the…fuck.

Charleigh let the door close, turned around, and galloped over to the front desk. "Excuse me, Lucy."

Lucy, the receptionist, petite with a mousy-brown bob and cat-eye glasses, looks demure but loves gossiping, shooting the shit with everyone.

She folded her newspaper, glancing up at Charleigh. "Heeeey! What's up?"

"What is *she* doing here?" Charleigh jerked her head toward the exercise class. "That lady in the dress."

"Oh," Lucy said, grinning. "Abigail?"

"Mm-hmm…she a member?"

"No, but she brought by these samples." Lucy ducked under the desk, ostensibly to retrieve them.

"Oh, I don't need to see!" Charleigh squeaked.

"Okaaay." Lucy slunk back up to sitting. "Well, I've gotta okay this with management, but I think we're going to start carrying them!" Her eyes glittered with excitement. "So I gave her a friend's pass today. I mean, *of course*, she'd need to join to keep coming, but I just thought—"

"Got it." Charleigh cut her off, then, biting into her tongue, tromped away.

Where the fuck is Jackson?

22

JANE

The sound of Pa's circular saw convulses across the pasture.

It's two o'clock, and I'm still out here working, aerating a new patch of red clay soil in order to plant purple hull peas and okra. We've never grown these before, but Mr. Oldham at the general store swore they'll thrive here.

Finished with the last row, I walk over to Pa, who's slapping freshly cut two-by-fours to the ground, laying out the frame for something.

"Whatcha building?" I ask.

He tugs off his mustard-colored leather gloves before tossing them to the ground. "It's a surprise. You'll see soon enough."

Sweat leaks off him. He looks haggard today. That makes sense, after his late night.

He didn't drag his ass in until one in the morning. Mom was pissed.

I was still awake, tossing in my bed when I heard them arguing.

"Don't touch me," Mom rasped at him.

"What? Sorry I'm late, but we need more accounts. Can't make it on your oils alone." There was a bite to his words.

Mom spewed out a bitter laugh.

"I found some good leads," Pa added.

I twisted in my comforter, pulled my pillow on top of my head to block out their bickering.

I've long suspected Pa of fooling around on Mom. I mean, first of all, he's crazy handsome; I see the way women look at him. How they take to him, throw themselves at him without even realizing or seeming to care that other people might notice. Hell, they might not even be aware of it themselves. He's *so* charming, *so* good-looking, and it's not that Mom is ugly or anything. She's just fine in that department, but kind of plain. Kind of boring. And definitely uptight.

Pa's in another class. By himself.

I wouldn't exactly blame him if he were cheating.

"Have fun last night?" I ask him, teasing.

"I could ask you the same thing." His face cracks into a grin.

"You got me."

He swipes a stream of sweat off his forehead. "Hey, listen. You think you could cozy up to that Andersen girl? Make friends?"

Dread sweeps over me. I never turn Pa down for these types of requests, but dammit. *Nellie? Really?*

"How do you even know about her?"

"Her mom came out here yesterday. They seem like good prospects—"

"She did?" My stomach grinds. "Mom didn't say anything about it to me."

"She probably didn't think anything of it."

"Yeah, well, they *are* the richest family in town. But she's a real piece of work, Pa. A real bitch to me—"

"C'mon, Sunshine. Please? Just try?" His graham cracker-colored eyes are pleading.

"Pa, she's the one who tried to run me off the road!"

"She *is?*"

"Yep, we talked about it last night and everything. She's real screwed up in the head. She's *so* weird. Said she didn't mean to, didn't even realize she'd done it—"

He claps his hand on my shoulder, gives it a squeeze. "Baby, I'm sorry, but I'm sure it *was* just an accident. People who don't know about horses, well…"

I sigh. I mean, he's not *wrong*. But still.

"And you can sell ice water to the devil, remember?" He squeezes my shoulder again. Bends down to retrieve his gloves.

I turn away, heading inside.

I'm so fucking sick of being poor.

And of being the one in this role. Sometimes I wish I were more like Julia. Homely, unlikable. She doesn't get put into these kinds of positions. She wouldn't allow it anyway.

Even though she's the family beekeeper, I've learned a lot about beekeeping from her through the years. Enough to know this: She's kind of like the guard bee. Not that she is actively protecting us, more that she's protecting herself. She's the one out front, separate from the hive. Shutting out this part of our lives from her. Keeping herself at a distance. Silently judging us for what we do.

Me? I'm the scout bee. The one in charge of buzzing around, searching, always on the lookout.

Mom fancies herself the queen bee, of course, keeper of us all, but everything in me feels that her reign is going to end at some point.

Because Pa? Classic drone bee. The one most likely at risk of flying off to mate with other queens. To form a new colony.

23

JACKSON

Against the early-evening sun, the lake is a shimmering cape of a thousand shiny pennies.

Jackson has to squint when he gazes out over the water. It's so humid, so torrid out; he wishes they were gathered inside, but, same as last year, the annual summer fish fry at the Boat House is being held out on the massive dock.

The ancient wooden posts groan against the deck as waves lick the surface of the lake.

He didn't want to come tonight. He'd much rather have gone to Sullivan's, hoping to catch sight of Ethan again. But since he missed all of Charleigh's calls yesterday, she's been extra clingy; he knew there was no getting out of this thing.

Sigh.

The Andersens even picked him up in Alexander's Jeep Wagoneer. He rode in the back seat with Nellie, feeling like her sibling, a child being driven to a dance by his parents.

When he slid into the sumptuous leather seat, Nellie appraised him.

"Nice shirt," she said, then twisted her frame toward the window, chewing a fingernail, as if she were too cool to say another word.

Normally, he would think she was being a smart-ass with her comment, as was her way, but he could tell she was sincere this time, real respect registering, if not in her tone, at least in her cornflower-blue eyes. He *is* wearing the latest Tommy Hilfiger, a button-down rugby.

Charleigh passed him an icy wine cooler, peach flavored, which went down like candy.

Studying Nellie's profile, Jackson felt a pang of pity wash over him. She looked fine, hair done in a single French braid down her back, tight and rigid bangs hair-sprayed to the heavens, flawless makeup. Dare he say she looked attractive? But so fidgety. The nail biting, the sighing, the angst radiating off her like a fragrance. As he watched her, it hit him: They're both outcasts.

Now he sits next to her at the wrought iron table, steam rising off their baskets of catfish, skins fried to a golden brown.

Alexander and Charleigh gave Jackson and Nellie the best seats—the ones facing the lake. And while Jackson likes to think this was altruistic, he knows it's only because Charleigh must have her eyes glued to the front, to the action.

He drags a hush puppy through the cup of tangy tartar sauce. It's so hot, it scorches his tongue, but then melts in his mouth. Alexander follows suit but grabs two, devouring both at the same time.

The man is six-two, and his appetite is insatiable. In more ways than one, according to Charleigh. Jackson's always liked Alexander. He's easy to look at, yes, but, *so* not Jackson's type. He's too clean-cut. Like Charleigh, he's almost too perfect, gleaming in his crisp white button-down, blond hair trimmed in a preppy style. Frat boy.

He's chill, though, not stuck-up at all, despite his bottom-less wealth, and, ever since Jackson first met him, Alexander has been welcoming. When the Andersens travel, Alexander will suggest that they invite Jackson. Just last year, he accompanied them to Paris, visiting the most famous antique showrooms with Charleigh, selecting pieces to be shipped back home.

He suspects that Alexander appreciates Jackson basically being Charleigh's chaperone because a) he's male and can ward off other men while—because he's gay—not being a threat to their marriage and b) because Jackson soaks up so much of Charleigh's high-maintenance energy.

Jackson shudders to think what Charleigh will be like once Nellie flies the coop. She'll be completely bonkers; he imagines he really *will* feel like one of their children then.

The waitress appears with a tray of margaritas on the rocks for the adults and a glass of iced tea for Nellie. Charleigh licks the salt-crusted rim of hers, before slinging half of it down in one gulp. She, as ever, is gleaming tonight, in a low-cut white halter top with red shorts, her bronzed skin and toned shoulders on full display. She lifts her glass again, grins at Jackson.

Then he watches her face contort, her eyes narrow. "Fuck *me*," she spits.

Jackson and Nellie both turn their gazes away from the lake, toward the restaurant.

The Chambers—Chip, Monica, and Blair—are spilling out of the dining room onto the deck, looking like some polished Barbie family. At their side are the Swifts. Ethan, and someone Jackson assumes to be the wife, and one of the daughters.

"Mom!" Nellie's voice sounds discordant, like a piano key out of tune. "What the fuck is she doing here?"

"Shhh...keep your voice down," Alexander admonishes her.

Jackson has never liked Monica. Doesn't really see why Charleigh constantly twists herself into knots to keep up with her. I mean, he *gets* it—she is the queen bee—but he can't stand her. She always makes him feel like a caricature, *the gay man in town.* Her voice gets higher, brighter, more over the top when she addresses him, like when someone screams at a deaf or foreign-born person.

She's a dead ringer for Morgan Fairchild, and her daughter is her carbon copy. Rich bitches personified.

But his attention is trained on Ethan, who's dressed much like he was the other night, in a simple button-down Henley. This one is white, dressier, though, and his hair looks freshly shampooed, his honey-colored locks glistening in the dying sunlight.

Jackson's stomach twirls.

Like Charleigh did, he lifts his cocktail to his lips, slams half of it.

Both families are heading over, Blair's eyes lasering them, a wicked red-lipped grin slashing her angular face.

Fuck me, Jackson thinks.

"Heeeeey!" Monica trills as they approach the table, looping Ethan's wife's arm through her own.

Jackson sizes her up. Humph. She's *okay*, but rather plain, if you ask him. Dressed in a floral-patterned dress—homemade, by the looks of it—as Charleigh warned him about. Unlike the other ladies at the Boat House, her hair is devoid of any product, but rather than looking natural, it just looks sad and lifeless. She has a nice rack, though, he'll give her that, but otherwise, she's very ordinary, the kind of blank-canvas beauty that certain men are attracted to, the kind that can be molded into anything they want.

"Well, hey, Andersens!" Monica is clearly already soused, her sky-blue eyes bloodshot and swimming. "I wanted to introduce you to the Swifts! Though Abigail here has told me y'all've already met." She all but sneers at Charleigh.

Ever the gentleman, Alexander rises, pumps Ethan's hand. "Alexander Andersen, pleasure to meet you."

"And you as well. Ethan Swift."

Jackson can't pry his eyes off Ethan, but so far, Ethan hasn't even glanced his way.

Monica plants a claw on Ethan's shoulder, a possessive gesture. "Ethan here is a *master* carpenter. He's building Chip a custom desk for the home office!" She lowers her voice to a whisper, cups a flat palm against her lips, like she's telling us a secret. "Costs five grand!"

Chip, who has his back turned to us, is busy checking out all the ladies on the deck, seemingly oblivious to Monica's chatter.

Charleigh's face has turned scarlet; she looks as though her skin is on fire.

"Amazing!" Alexander offers.

"And this is Abigail, his wife!" Monica gives her a nudge, as if she's presenting a show pony.

"I've already had the pleasure. Good to see you again, though," Charleigh manages to say through clenched teeth.

It just lasts a second—and Jackson's pretty sure he's the only one who clocks this—but he catches Alexander's eyes flick over Abigail's chest, sees them crimp into a smile.

"Charleigh here tells me that y'all live out on some land?" Alexander asks.

Abigail giggles nervously, schoolgirlish. "Yeah, over off Seven Pines Road. We like it out there. Like to live off the land, grow our own food—"

Charleigh snorts into her glass.

If Abigail notices, she doesn't show it, her dewy face still brimming with that schoolgirl smile.

"I myself like the land, too. My family, my ancestors, have a real nice piece out in Kilgore. Lots of woods. But we don't get out there all that much anymore, do we, babe?"

Charleigh places her drink down, skewers Alexander with her cold glance, obviously for being cordial to the enemy. "Nope. This is about as outdoorsy as I like to get." A dark laugh slithers out of her.

"And this is?" Alexander asks, motioning to the girl. No doubt trying to steer the conversation back to calmer waters.

"I'm Jane. Jane Swift." She beams at each of them. Now it's Blair's turn to sneer at Nellie, flaunting Jane in front of her.

A flash of anger zings through Jackson; he feels oddly protective over Nellie.

He peers at Jane. There's an elegance there that she clearly gets from her father. Same golden hair, same easy grin. Same copper-colored skin. A true natural beauty doesn't need a lick of makeup, though she wears it, her cat-green eyes rimmed with black eyeliner.

"Skank," Nellie says, under her breath, but loud enough for them all to hear.

Jackson squirms. *Damn, that Nellie can be horrid. But also, the girl can handle herself.*

Alexander's face reddens, and he clears his throat. "You'll have to forgive my daughter here—" He shoots Nellie a withering stare.

But again, Abigail pastes on her wholesome smile, as if she didn't just hear Nellie calling her daughter a slut. "Well," she says, shaking her limp hair around her shoulders. "And you must be Nellie," she says, still wearing the same sunny grin, though her tone has an undercurrent to it.

Nellie just stares her down.

Then Ethan steps forward, smiles at Jackson.

Jackson's pulse ricochets. Is he about to out him in front of Charleigh, make it known that they've met before?

"I'm Ethan. And you are?" His caramel eyes dance over Jackson. Knowing.

144

"Jackson. Jackson Ford." He takes Ethan's outstretched hand and squeeze-shakes it, wanting never to let go.

"Oh, forgive me!" Monica bubbles, this time draping her arm around Ethan's neck. "I forgot *all* about you!"

Bitch. And also, bitch, get your hands off him. He's my crush.

"This is Jackson Ford." She draws out the *Ford*, making Jackson sound like some kind of big deal, even though he knows she's just being sarcastic. "The local decorator."

Cunt.

"And my best friend," Charleigh says, snaking her hand across the table to clasp Jackson's.

Touché.

Jackson's eyes veer back toward Ethan, who is openly staring at him. A sly grin tugs at the corner of his lips, and Jackson's insides melt. After a second, Ethan hitches his chin toward the restaurant. A signal to Jackson.

"Excuse me, please. I'm in need of the men's room." Ethan pivots away.

Jackson drains the rest of his drink, wipes his mouth with the back of his hand. After what he hopes is an inconspicuous amount of time, he pushes his chair from the table. "Nature's calling me, too. Be right back."

24

JACKSON

Jackson's hands shake as he clasps the bathroom doorknob, opens it.

Ethan's standing over the sink, soaping his hands. His eyes find Jackson's in the mirror. "I didn't even really need to go, just wanted to talk to you. In private."

Jackson gulps. "Me, too. I mean, I don't actually need use the restroom." *How awkward.*

Ethan lifts a thick linen cloth from a stack atop a silver tray, dries his hands, twists toward Jackson.

He's even handsomer than Jackson remembered from the other night. If that's possible. And he can smell him, a clean, woodsy scent that somehow also smells like sex. This man reeks of it.

"Sorry I acted out there like we'd never met before." He cocks his head to one side, drinks Jackson in with his eyes. His long lashes flutter as they trace over Jackson.

"I...I—" Jackson mutters. His mouth has gone dry, his tongue immobile. How is he supposed to respond? *Yeah, me, too. Sorry, my best friend, Charleigh, hates your family, so she can't know that we've already met because I kept it a secret from her?*

"It's just that I didn't exactly tell my wife about you." Ethan takes a slight step toward Jackson. "She knew I was at the bar, trying to drum up clients, meet people, but I didn't mention we were hanging out all night. Together."

He tilts his head again, smiles that crooked grin.

Heat washes over Jackson. If they were in a bar right now, or at a party, this would *definitely* be a moment where a kiss might happen. And he's tempted. So tempted to lean in, grab the back of Ethan's head, graze his lips with his own.

But...what if this is all in my head? All one-sided?

They stand there, staring at each other. Blood whooshes so heavily through Jackson's ears, he's confident Ethan can hear it, detect his attraction.

"I also wanted to see if you'd like to come out tomorrow?" Ethan's voice, like the other night, is molasses sweet. "To my place? You know, to look at my stuff. Wife's gonna be in town."

Jackson swallows and tries to steady his voice. "I'd love to. Is ten a.m. good?" *Why is he putting a specific time on it? What if ten is not good? God, he sounds like such a dork.*

"I can make that work."

Whew.

The door cracks open, and Charleigh's voice peals through the room. "Jackson! I can't stand to sit there one second longer, so I'm heading to the bar to get a drink. Or several. Want anything?"

Heat scrapes up Jackson's neck. He's both embarrassed that his *mommy* is shouting at him—at least she had the good sense not to poke her head in—and angry that she's intruded on this moment.

Jackson rolls his eyes, which Ethan catches, then rewards him with a playful grin.

"Get me another 'rita!" He tries to sound authoritative, bossy. Then immediately backpedals. "Be right out!"

Charleigh finally releases the freaking door.

"Guess that's our cue," Ethan says.

Dammit, Charleigh. I wanted one more second alone with him.

Ethan inches around him, his hip lightly brushing Jackson's as he moves.

Trembling, his breath catching, Jackson nearly jumps.

"See ya tomorrow, huh?" Ethan asks, lifting an eyebrow.

"You bet."

You bet? Kill me now.

He trails Ethan, stepping back out onto the deck. And while logically he knows this is not the case, he feels as though there's a spotlight above them, dousing them with light, broadcasting their flirtation for the whole crowd to see.

"*There* you are!" Monica's voice bounds toward them. She's now seated with her family at a table, which, thank God, is far away from the Andersens. She waves her hands wildly at Ethan, as if she owns him, gold bangles jingling down her stick-thin arms.

If Jackson could shove her off the deck into the lake right now without getting in deep shit, he'd do it. Instead, he turns and heads toward the bar, toward Charleigh, whose head is cast back as she shoots a jigger of tequila.

25

NELLIE

That fucking ho. Walking in with Blair, dressed up in her pathetic, raggedy sundress, like she's all that. That pattern can only be found at a fabric shop. I'd almost feel sorry for her if I didn't hate everything about her so freaking much.

I was just gonna ignore her, but she narrowed her eyes at me, gave me the dirtiest look. So I called her a skank. I'm happy everyone heard me. After Mom bolted from the table, I did, too.

It's just understood that the teens will escape their parents at these things as soon as possible. They're really just excuses for the adults to see and be seen and get plastered.

I stomped off and found Dustin by the side of the Boat House, smoking. I bummed one off him, then took a drag so hard, my lungs burned, and I couldn't stop coughing.

"Everyone's going over to Miller's to skinny-dip. Wanna go? I have wine coolers stashed."

I squirmed.

I only skinny-dip if it's pitch-dark out; I'm way too self-conscious otherwise. "Um, *no*," I said, looking at him if he just asked me the dumbest question ever. "But is your Jet Ski here?"

"Yeah, but I wasn't gonna take it out tonight—"

I flicked my eyes up to his, batted my lashes. "If you let me drive it, I'll give you a hand job in the thicket."

The thicket is a little forest between Miller's Swimming Hole and the Boat House. It's where teens stash their liquor, weed. It's where the ones who go all the way do it.

I had a plan.

The swimming hole is really part of the Blanca River, the part where's there's a slight bend, forming a pool. Part of it feeds into the lake where the Boat House is. It's a private lake with these fancy houses. When I was little, I used to wanna live on it, but Mom told me our grotesquely big house is too big for the lots out there.

Five minutes later, Dustin and I were mounting his Jet Ski, me up front, hands on the throttle. The sun was just starting to set behind the tree line, so the lake still glittered. I eased away from the dock slowly, not wanting to cause a scene.

But when we rounded the bend and reached the river, I squeezed the throttle, picked up a little speed.

Even though they were still about a hundred feet away, I could see them, their heads bobbing, wet hair stringy and glued to their scalps. They were clutching red Solo cups, hoisting them above the water.

Blair swam to the shore and climbed out topless, with only her bikini bottom on. I couldn't hear her over the noise of the motor, but I could tell she was laughing. Her perky boobs bouncing, her head tossed back. Her body is sick. I mean, *perfect*. Skinny but with just the right amount of curvy, and she knows it. Tommy and the rest of the boys who were treading water were cheering her on.

She grabbed the rickety ladder, then climbed to the top of the old boathouse to dive.

It's like this unspoken rule that whenever we're all out here, Blair dives first. How fucking stupid is that? That she even gets dibs on diving? It's bullshit.

She stood on the roof, hands over her head, showing off her crazy body even more. Then she dove.

When she broke the surface, I could see everyone clapping for her.

I killed the gas, letting the Jet Ski rock against the wake.

"What are you doing?" Dustin asked.

"Don't worry about it."

Jane was next.

Her skinny ass climbed out of the water and started moving up the ladder. Very slowly because her leg was still a bit wrecked from the horse accident, but she didn't let that stop her. Lean but curvy, her homemade bathing suit bottom riding up her crack. Tits out, like Blair.

Dustin whistled through his teeth in approval. I gave him a sharp elbow.

"Heeeey! Ouch!" he whined.

"You watch your ass."

After she plunged into the river—more of a thunk, a cannon-ball, and not the graceful dive of Blair, who is captain of the diving team—her head popped out of the water, grinning that toothy grin of hers. Everyone cheered as Blair passed her a fresh Solo cup.

Anger shredded through me. I was furious, so I squeezed the throttle, accelerating so fast, the thing jerked and almost threw Dustin off. The motor buzzed in my ear like a bumblebee, but so loud that it made them all look up, glance our way.

I kept roaring toward them. At first, everyone was smiling, laughing at us, almost sneering, but as we got closer, I sped up even more, aiming at them.

Their faces turned scared; that's when glee overtook me.

"What are you *doing*?" Dustin asked, horrified.

I didn't *want* to run them over. Well, if I'm being honest, for a few seconds, I *did*.

There wasn't time for them to swim away, so they started shouting at me to slow down, to move.

At the last possible second, I cut a sharp left, spraying water over the group, soaking their precious drinks, filling them with river water. Then I steered away from them.

"Fucking psycho!" Blair yelled after me.

"Yeah! Crazy bitch! You coulda killed us!" Tommy screamed.

Laughing, I gave them the finger.

26

CHARLEIGH

f Charleigh grits her teeth any harder, they'll grind to dust.

She shifts in her seat, tries to settle, when all she wants do is crawl out of her skin.

They're in the car, heading home from the fish fry.

Alexander's behind the wheel, as usual. Not only because he's *always* at the helm, but because Charleigh's good and hammered

Again.

She's pissed, of course, that fucking Monica brought the Swifts to *their* private club, parading them around like some prized jewels. Like she obtained the latest, most sought-after designer handbag and had to flaunt it.

He's making Chip a desk for the home office. Costs five grand!

Ugh! Who talks like that? Like, who gives a shit?

And the way she had her paws on Ethan. So disgusting! Charleigh bets she wants to *really* have her paws all over him, because Chip is just a big doofus, not the smoldering sex object that her Alexander is. That Ethan is.

But she's equally pissed at Alexander.

She gets that he was raised right, with manners, unlike her. That he's effusive and that it's usually all just an act, a way to keep things nice and oiled and smooth. He *knows* how in a twist she is about the Swifts. And forget about her—he knows how very upsetting all this has been to *Nellie*.

I mean, should she have uttered the word *skank* about Jane, barely under her breath, in front of Jane's parents? Hell no. But Charleigh's proud of her daughter for sticking up for herself. Blair was being a snot-nosed bitch, as usual, and Charleigh saw the way Jane was glaring at Nellie. Like Nellie's beneath her.

Charleigh gets why Nellie hates Jane. She's *just* like the mother: audacious when she shouldn't be. But the difference is Jane's actually a looker, dammit, unlike the mother, so she does kind of have a right to the airs she's putting on. And Nellie can't compete with that. With Jane's poise, her gemstone-green eyes, her whole *vibe*.

She let Nellie leave the table, ride home with Dustin. Last time she saw her, she was driving away on his Jet Ski. Dustin is like Chip. Oafish, not exactly handsome. But rich. And the Reeves are a tolerable enough family. Nearly as rich as the Andersens are, but Sherry Reeves doesn't flaunt it, doesn't even hang out with the rest of the ladies very much. Like Alexander's family, she comes from *old* money, which Charleigh always pictures to be like ancient gold coins stashed away in some cave a thousand years ago, passed greedily down from one generation to the next.

Sherry has class, and she would rather lounge about in her crisp mansion by herself all day, gaze at the fine art on her walls, flit off to the Met in New York.

So, yeah, truth is, Charleigh sort of pushed Nellie and Dustin together. Arranged a few "convenient" run-ins with the Reeves, hoping those two would attach, pair off: buying season tickets to the local theater, inviting the Reeves to join them for a night out, having them over for burgers, that sort of thing.

This was last year, when Nellie was a junior, because Charleigh couldn't bear the thought of her daughter entering senior year with no one to take her to homecoming, no one to go to prom with. And let's face it, no one was going to ask her without Charleigh intervening.

Sherry was down with all of it, also looking for a partner for her bratty, spoiled rich boy who is all thumbs.

Charleigh doesn't intend for Nellie to stay attached to him forever, just until college, when her prospects open up and she can land someone better. More suitable husband material. But she'd never had a boyfriend, the poor thing, and needed a starter relationship.

As far as Charleigh can tell, she hasn't had sex with him. She's not 100 percent sure on this, but one night recently, she eavesdropped outside Nellie's door. Dustin was trying for it, and she heard her daughter say, "Ewww, no. Get off me, Dustin. You know I'm not doing *that*."

She skulked away, tiptoed back down the hall, thinking, *I wouldn't give it up for him either, Nellie. Good girl.*

Now she squirms in the passenger seat again, lets out a ragged sigh.

Alexander has just finished snapping at her.

She wasn't even talking to *him*, she was twisted around, addressing Jackson.

"Can you believe the nerve of Monica? And don't get me started on that weird-ass family—"

"I don't see what you're so worked up about," Alexander spat at her, his white fingers clenching the steering wheel. "Why can't you ever just let things be? And I was so embarrassed by Nellie, the way she talked to that poor girl—"

"Oh, fuck off, Alex! You are so oblivious. You didn't catch the way *sweet* little Jane was glowering at her?"

"No, I—"

"Exactly!" Her voice was jumping up in register; she felt slightly ridiculous, but once she gets on a roll, she can't stop. "We didn't *raise* our daughter to roll over, to let people shit all over her—"

She flicked a glance at Jackson, whose eyes were wide as saucers. He hates confrontation, shuts down when he's witness to her and Alexander's battles. Which are rare, but they do tend to happen when she's tied on one too many.

"God damn it, Charleigh, I'm not saying that." He hissed out a whole-body sigh.

She knew she was pushing it.

"You never see my side in all this. I wasn't raised in some fancy family like you. I don't have the *privilege* of letting things slide off me—"

"But that's precisely my point!" Alexander shouted. "You *do*! I've given you everything—"

He loves to toss that in her face, failing to grasp just how deep her scars run. That yes, she knows they're on top now, but she also damn well knows how fast and far one can fall. How precarious everything is. He doesn't understand what it feels like to grow up like she did—never accepted, always pitied or shunned. Forever on the outside, desperate for access and approval. He doesn't know the depths of ruthlessness in people like Monica and her little spawn, Blair.

He wheels up in front of Jackson's bungalow, tires screeching as he pumps the brakes too hard. "Sorry about all this, man," he says over his shoulder to Jackson.

That's it.

Charleigh flings open the door, hops out. "I'm gonna have a nightcap with Jackson," she spews. "He'll bring me home later."

She slams the door so hard, the window shakes.

27

JANE

t's almost midnight. I'm staring at the antique wall clock in our loft, watching as the second hand goes by.

Trying not to throw up, I'm focusing on the ticking, taking in long, calming breaths. I had too much to drink tonight. I'm not even sure what was in those cups—more Hunch Punch or just vodka-spiked Kool-Aid?—but they went down smooth and fast, and before I knew it, I was shit-faced.

Oh, well! I had fun. I mean, I don't usually go in for rich girls, but Blair is actually interesting. Like, she's been to Europe, seen the famous castles, loves to tell me all about it in vivid detail and not in a show-offy way. Plus, she pays for everything. My drinks, my smokes. She gives me new lipsticks. She thinks I'm this cool, exotic girl because I lived in Dallas and other places, too. Outside of here.

I dunno. It's slim pickings in this town, so I'm just going with it. Being part of the in crowd has never been my thing, but it does have its perks, like yes, Blair buying my stuff, but also like Mom and Pa and I getting to go to the Boat House, me getting to swim at Miller's.

But Nellie...

Shit. I'm not one to back down from playing chicken, but for a split second, I thought she was going to tear our heads off with that Jet Ski. I seriously did. My plan was to dive down and swim as hard as I could to the bottom before she got to us, but thankfully, the lunatic swerved at the last possible sec, barely missing us.

She's demonic.

Her eyes were almost glazed over as she sped toward us with that monster of a boyfriend sitting hunched behind her.

"Fucking psycho!" Blair yelled at her, an earsplitting scream that was full of real terror and fear.

"You crazy bitch! You coulda killed us!" Tommy hollered.

"What the fuck was that about?" I asked.

"She basically wants to off us all, I guess?" Blair said, laughing, though she sounded nervous, a giggle being stretched on a tightrope. "You know she's jealous. She *hates* that we all love you, I just know it."

But at least Pa got to see how *nasty* she is to me, calling me a skank. But what he didn't see—what I made sure to do in the slyest way possible—was me provoking her. I gave her the biggest death stare ever. Then I dropped it instantly, changing my face back into its usual sunny, good-girl expression. Just to fuck with her.

There's no way he'll ask me about her again after that.

I even had fun skinny-dipping. I mean, yes, I could feel *all* the boys had their eyes on me, even Tommy, Blair's boyfriend, but Luke is a free spirit, always flirty-flirty with everyone, so I just kind of assumed he'd be cool with it. It's not like I let anyone kiss or touch me.

And honestly? *I'm* cool with it, Luke coming on to others and me doing the same. I don't want to wind up being one of those controlled, under-the-thumb women like Mom.

So I took off my dress, keeping my bottoms on like the other girls (not the boys—they went full commando), unlaced my bikini top and let it flop on the grass, then let the hot wind kiss my chest. It felt *great*; I felt *free*. And everything was fine until Nellie tried to mow us down. It was even fine after that, except for how much I drank.

The room's tilting around me now, but I keep my eyes focused on the clock. *Tick, tock, tick.*

The back door creaks open.

Mom and Pa.

They've been outside, sitting around the campfire.

From the sounds of it, he's had as much to drink as I have.

I know they think I'm asleep, so I sit up, lean toward the railing, cock my ear.

"All's I'm sayin' is to think about it—"

"Ethan. I've never done anything like this and am ashamed you're asking—"

"We need more *money! M-O-N-E-Y!*" Pa actually spells the

whole word out, his lips tripping on some of the letters. "And that man took a shine to you—"

"Wha—"

"Don't deny it! I caught it. His wife may have a stick up her ass, and their daughter is bizarre. Nellie. The balls on her... But the man—"

"You seriously want me to—"

I sit up all the way now, my tipsiness fading fast.

"I'm just saying you could butter him up. They could be our biggest account! Just...you know, take the truck into town tomorrow. Load it up with a box of your oils. Take Jane with you—"

Ugh.

Forever the scout bee.

The very last thing I wanna do is spend my Saturday trapped with Mom and all this madness Pa's pushing on her.

"And bump into the man. We'll look 'em up in the phone book. Park outside their house, wait and see if he leaves, and follow him."

28

JACKSON

Mmmm, this coffee is the *best*!" Charleigh trills from Jackson's kitchen table, her legs tucked beneath her. She's wearing one of his old SMU T-shirts and a pair of his sweats. Bedhead and all, she still looks resplendent in the morning sunlight that gushes through the windows—casement windows that are original to the bungalow and that Jackson painstakingly stripped and repainted a deep gray, all by himself, thank you very much.

"Seriously, this isn't some Folgers BS. How do you even make this?" Last night's makeup is smudged around her eyes; she clutches the mug as if holding on to a life raft.

"I *am* fancy with my coffee. Like I am with everything," Jackson says, then winks at her. "I get the beans at this natural grocery store in Dallas and grind them myself before each brew. Glad you approve."

"Approve?" Charleigh guffaws. "You're never getting rid

of me! Been here a thousand times but forget each time how *adorable* this place is."

Jackson eyes the clock on the stove: It's nine. It's at least a twenty-minute drive out to Ethan's; he *better* be getting rid of her ASAP. But, of course, he can't tell her that.

"Speaking of which," he says, clearing his throat in an exaggerated, playful way. "I *do* have a ten-o'clock appointment."

"Yeah, yeah." Charleigh bats her hand through the air. "I heard you grousing about that last night. With *whom* again?"

Annoyance grips his throat. As always, she's being territorial.

"The Johnsons," he lies. "They want me to consult with them about their dining room. But they probably won't ever even follow through."

He's picked that particular family because they're ancient. Because Charleigh doesn't have any direct communication with them, so the chances of her busting him are nil.

"Fine," she says. "Wanna hang out tonight, though? I'm still mad at Alexander, so it'd be good if I have other plans."

"For real?" Jackson's voice practically squeaks. "Leave that good man alone. And no, I'm not on his side, like I told you last night, over and over, but you need to let this one go."

Last night, their *one drink* turned into two bottles of wine, Charleigh sloppy on his couch, monologuing about the Swifts, about Nellie.

Jackson squirmed. He pretty much tells Charleigh *everything*— what he had for breakfast, how he's avoiding his mother's phone calls, what he had for lunch, if he kissed a guy in Dallas—so not being able to tell her, make that *gush* to her, about his heart-throb, Ethan, is excruciating. Excruciating because he can't tell his person anything about it, and excruciating because he knows she'd mangle him for it.

After a certain point, when the pinot noir turned his mind to jelly, he considered testing the waters, perhaps mentioning how attractive Ethan is, gauging her response, but…he couldn't bring himself to blurt out the words, fearing that she'd be able to see the real reason behind them.

Just go out there today and see if there really is any there, there first, he told himself last night.

"Okay, whatever," Charleigh says now. "I'll forgive him for being nice to the enemy, but—"

"You know I'm on Team Charleigh here, and Team Nellie, for that matter, and that Swift woman *is* off-putting—"

Charleigh snorts, nearly spitting out her coffee.

"But don't torture your pretty husband over it, okay? He honestly just wants you to be above it all. So be above it all!" Jackson himself has had three mugs of coffee to saw through his hangover, so he's aware that is voice is too loud, bouncing off the walls.

"O-*kaaay*! You better take me home now. You're starting to sound like *him*." Charleigh rolls her makeup-smudged eyes, but a teasing grin inches across her face.

Jackson's entire Mercedes shudders as he crosses over the cattle guard. Once he's on the dirt-paved drive, he eases off the gas even more, careful to avoid the ruts and potholes.

It's exactly 10:00 a.m.

Should I have arrived fashionably late? he wonders. Will he look needy, being so prompt? No, Ethan mentioned his wife will be away, and who knows how long she'll actually be gone.

God, he's nervous, hands slick on the wheel, sweat biting his armpits even though his AC is blasting.

Is he wearing too much cologne?

The sweating makes him feel like he is, that it's oversaturating the air around him.

He slows down even more, cranks his window, hoping the fresh air will dissipate the strong scent.

Calm the fuck down, he tells himself. *Play it cool. Look at the man's furniture, praise him, and see what happens.*

But what do you think *is going to happen, Jackson?* He can't stop the hamster wheel of his brain from running through all the different scenarios.

God, he shouldn't have had all that wine last night. And all this coffee on top of it. Fucking Charleigh and her drama. But let's get real, he was probably going to drink his fair share all on his own anyway, to steel his nerves for this morning.

Ethan comes into view. Standing at the head of his drive, hand resting on a shovel that's planted in the earth, head slanted to one side. As he pulls closer, Jackson sees his grin: crooked, mischievous, inviting. Almost as if Ethan can read his careening thoughts.

Whew. Here we go.

Fuck, did he just say that out loud? With the window down? Surely not.

Jackson twists the keys, kills the engine.

He climbs from the car.

"Sorry, I shoulda warned you about our drive. Your shiny Benz is gonna get all dirty out here." Ethan's still grinning that sly grin at him, and even though he's talking about Jackson's car, it feels fraught, like he's really hinting at something else.

"I'm not one to mind a little dirt," Jackson replies, going for flirty but instead just sounding awkward.

Ethan bites back his smile, locks his eyes onto Jackson's.

"It's so lovely out here," Jackson offers.

And it is. Rolling hills, jewel-green pasture, pastoral house. Plain but charming. The Swifts are evidently of modest means. This isn't the rich side of town, where acreage fetches a lot of coin; it's the jagged outskirts where real farmers live. People living hand to mouth.

"Thank you. Got a deal on it, and I know it needs work, but it's home. For now."

"Do you intend to stay a while?" *God, please don't let this fine man hear the neediness in my voice.*

"We usually move around a lot. My business calls for it. Only so much need for furniture, especially the custom kind. But I really like it here and would love to settle in one place for a while. Throw down some roots for the baby." Ethan flicks his chin to the house. "She's inside napping. Older sister's keepin' an eye on her. But she's probably napping, too." His eyes clasp onto Jackson's again, as if to convey, *We are pretty much alone.*

Heat creeps up Jackson's neck. The sky above them is

swollen with clouds, threatening rain, the air thick as pancake batter.

Jackson eyes a structure in progress next to what appears to be Ethan's woodworking shop—an open-air structure with a table saw and scraps of lumber.

"What's that going to be?" he asks.

"It's what I'm working on today. A shed. Digging postholes for the framing. Gonna be a guesthouse. I'll rig a window unit, run plumbing, too."

"All on your own?" Jackson thinks about his crew and how quickly, efficiently they could knock this project out. But he bites his tongue from saying another word about it, realizing that Ethan most likely can't afford their labor.

"Yep! Should be done by the end of the week. At least with the shell. I work fast." Again, that crooked, mischievous, wickedly hot grin slides across his face. "Wanna see the shop?"

"I wanna see it all," Jackson says pointedly.

"Hm." Ethan continues smiling at him. Then peels off his glove and drapes it over the handle of the shovel. "Allow me."

Jackson follows him up the stairs to the modest house.

"You can see the inside another time. I don't wanna disturb the baby." Ethan leads him around the back via the wraparound porch. On the back side, the land slopes up, cresting into a ridge. Jackson sees a glimmering pond and, behind that, some kind of orchard.

"That's the blueberry crop. Jane tends to it. I intend to make wine from the berries if we have enough—"

"I grow wild muscadines!" Jackson chirps. "Never made wine, but if you know how, you're welcome to my grapes." *My grapes? Did I just really freaking say that?*

"You serious? I'd love 'em. I have all the equipment and everything. And I'll share the finished product."

The air presses down on Jackson, causing him to sweat even more. That, and standing on the back porch next to Ethan, whose amber eyes are basically caressing him.

Ethan hops off the porch, and Jackson follows. Trails him around to a neat little shed with a *Swift's Apothecary* sign hanging above the entryway.

It's tiny, but open-air, with rows of twinkling glass bottles lining built-ins. From the ceiling, bundles of herbs are twined, hanging upside down to dry. The little room smells piney, like a spruce tree. "This space is incredible!"

"Yeah, it's the wife's shop. She's really heavy into botanicals. All-natural stuff. Using Mother Earth to heal us…"

Jackson, of course, doesn't let on that Charleigh already told him all about it.

"God, that must sound so dopey to you," Ethan says, leaning against the counter.

"Not at all. There's something to it—"

"Yeah, we just prefer to try and live as close to the land as possible. Not going in for pesticides, man-made chemicals, prescriptions—"

Jackson nods vehemently, his neck almost aching from how hard he keeps bending it. Naturally, he doesn't agree with all this—he pops antibiotics when he has an infection—but he wants Ethan to believe he understands him, believe that he's open-minded to an alternative way of thinking.

Jackson traces the row of bottles with his finger, stops when he reads a label that says, *Love Potion*. The skin on his face burns.

"And that right there? Her biggest seller. The ladies really go in for it."

"Does it work?" Jesus, did he really just ask that?

Ethan shakes his head quickly, the kind of jerky motion one makes when they've swallowed a bitter pill, then casts his gaze to the floor. His mischievous smile has been replaced with a sheepish one.

Is he embarrassed?

"Well?" Jackson presses.

"I'm sure you understand," Ethan says, lancing Jackson with his eyes, "we've been married for nearly two decades. I love my wife, but—"

He doesn't need to finish his thought; everyone knows about the seven-year-itch, the sparks dying down, the humdrum of marriage.

Jackson can feel his pulse threading through his neck. The thought of Ethan being unsatisfied is an enormously overwhelming one. *So much opportunity.*

A bolt of sunshine slashes through the clouds, spilling golden light across Ethan's perfect cheekbones. As in the men's room at the Boat House, Jackson yearns to lean over, kiss him right now.

"Lemme show you the rest," Ethan says, tromping from the room.

Wordlessly, Jackson follows, his eyes tracing Ethan: the small of his back, where his shirt is damp with sweat; the delicious sliver of a gap between his beltline and skin, exposed where his shirt creeps up above his hips; leather suspenders clasping his pants, holding them up.

Jackson imagines snapping those off, tugging Ethan's pants down.

He's drunk with these thoughts as they walk the few paces to the woodworking shop. When Jackson follows him inside the open-air structure, he sees Ethan has more than just a table saw; he has a proper workbench glittering with tools, a circular saw, and assorted pieces of furniture in various stages of production.

Sitting on one of the worktables, a thick Bible is splayed open.

Jesus Christ. Literally.

"This will be the top of the desk I'm making for Chip Chambers." Ethan glides his hand across a slab of wood that rests on a pair of sawhorses.

"Nice wood!"

"Yep. Solid piece of maple. As you can imagine, the Chambers are *very* particular." Ethan rolls his neck, rolls his eyes.

Charleigh may be territorial, but she's not all that particular; she pretty much leaves all design decisions up to Jackson, which he loves. It's because, unlike the other wealthy people in this town, Charleigh comes from nothing. And even though she actually possesses better taste than most, she's modest about it. The other wealthy folks here, though, can be downright *astonishing* in how demanding they are, how full of their own opinions and importance.

"Believe me, I know," Jackson replies. "What are you thinking of for the legs?"

"Ah, they, of course, wanted something tacky. Spindly legs with feet like a dragon's, but I talked them out of that. Convinced them that mid-century was the way to go. Timeless, clean lines, dovetailed joints—"

"Love it. That's *so* to my taste, too."

Ethan walks toward something. "But this—this is what I really wanted to show off to you." His hands palm a gorgeous piece of wood; his playful smile is back.

Jackson practically floats across the space.

It's an oval-shaped piece, the color of honey, with intricate scallops cut out at the edges.

"This is absolutely *divine*," Jackson gushes. "Maple?"

"Close. Alder. I've been saving this piece of wood ever since we lived in Minnesota. Here, come closer."

Jackson moves right next to him.

Ethan circles so that he's standing behind Jackson. Reaching around him, he lifts the wood from the bench, angles it to make the sun hits it just right.

Jackson gasps.

"Ha!" Ethan laughs into the back of his neck. "It's hard to see unless the light hits it just right, but I knew you'd appreciate it."

Rimming the edge of the wood is a thin border of inlaid walnut. It's gorgeous. Jackson has only seen this type of handiwork in the small old showrooms in Europe. This is old-world-level craftsmanship.

"Inlaid walnut."

"Bam."

"This is truly exquisite. How in the world—"

Ethan moves in closer, presses him ever so slightly.

Taking Jackson's hands in his own, Ethan traces their fingers over the river of the inlaid wood. "See how smooth it is? Like it's always been there? If you can believe it, *that's* the hard part. Not the actual scoring. Which is no picnic either, but—"

Jackson can barely breathe. Ethan's ropy arms are clasped around him; his hands are still in Ethan's; he feels Ethan's hot breath on his neck. He doesn't want to move a muscle, break this spell.

"Where in the world did you learn how to do this?"

Ethan keeps running Jackson's hands over the wood like he's guiding the planchette across a Ouija board.

"My father. One of the only good things he taught me." Ethan's tone darkens.

"This is seriously showroom quality. If you'd like, I could introduce you to some connections I have in Dallas—"

Ethan presses in even closer; his hip bone juts right up against Jackson's butt. His vision swims from the contact.

"I appreciate the offer. But, if you haven't figured it out, I prefer to cut the middleman out." Ethan's voice is low, rough, in Jackson's ear. "Be my own man."

Jackson literally gulps, positive that Ethan can hear him.

He feels himself stiffen, is afraid that Ethan can sense that as well.

"No, I get that. And respect it." His mouth is dry, like it's filled with dust.

"We just moved here from Dallas. And I know those showrooms, but yeah—"

"Where in Dallas?"

"Tiny house, *decrepit* house, in lower Greenville—"

"I know that area well—" Jackson thinks about the gay bars there, wonders if Ethan ever wandered into one. Is considering asking him.

"Hated it. I'm a land man, but it was close to Highland Park, to the wealthy, so lotsa clients. Speaking of which, if you know of anyone in town who might be interested, I'm still trying to build my business here. Like your friend Charleigh?"

Jackson freezes. He can't exactly explain to Ethan that *hell no*, Charleigh Andersen is not interested, that she out and out hates his entire family, so instead of replying, he chews the inside of his cheek.

"I mean, no pressure, but…" Ethan's breath pants along the back of Jackson's neck.

Even though his head is full of Charleigh right now, his body is full of Ethan, of being this close to him; his groin feels like it's on fire.

"No big deal. I can put in a word with her," he lies. "But it's tough here right now. I know everybody seems like they're dripping with it, but the recession has made people tighten their purse strings. I've lost clients lately—"

"Sorry to hear it."

"But we'll come out of it," Jackson hurriedly adds, not wanting to scare Ethan away from town. "And in the meantime, I'll brainstorm, get some referrals for you."

Jackson hears footsteps; Ethan releases his arms, twists around.

"Pa, what are you *doing*?" A girl's voice, bewildered, accusatory, slices through the air.

Jackson clears his throat, turns around, too.

She's tall. Taller than Jane. Must be the older sister. She's dressed head to toe in beekeeper wear.

"We're talking *business*." Ethan's voice is scalpel sharp, slicing back, cutting through the air, which has instantly thickened with tension. "*Julia*, where is your baby sister?"

"In her swing. Right by the bee boxes, so I can keep watch."

Her tone is one of a martyr, and though a fine mesh of net clouds her face, Jackson feels as if her expression is hardened, mouth twisted into a snarl.

"Honey, this is Mr. Ford, Jackson Ford. A well-acclaimed interior designer here in town." Ethan's voice is level, but prodding. "He's doing me the honor of looking at some of my pieces."

When Julia doesn't speak or budge, Ethan crosses the room, takes her by the wrists, jerks her forward. Gives a sharp cough.

She raises her hood, bores her sky-blue eyes, framed with a pair of cheap, dime-store glasses, into Jackson's.

She's not near as pretty as Jane, Jackson thinks. She more favors the mother. Her eyes aren't the almond shape of Ethan's and Jane's; they're round, the blue dull. Her face, too, is round, her mouth small.

And it's not just her homeliness—her vibe is flat, too. Stoic, laced with disdain, as if she can sense the gay on Jackson, as if she knows how close he and Ethan were to getting it on.

"Pleasure to meet you." She sticks out her hand for Jackson to shake.

His hand is drenched, so Jackson drags it across his jeans first, then accepts hers. "Pleasure is all mine! Your father here is quite the craftsman! I'm so impressed!" He's overdoing it, trying to cover up their near indiscretion, but he can't help himself. "Truly amazing work!"

She stares back at him coolly, calculating. Remains icily silent.

"So, you'll be in touch?" Ethan asks Jackson, clapping him on the back as if they're old pals and not almost fuck buddies.

"You bet!" Jackson clambers away, sneakers clawing the dirt floor, adrenaline slinging through his veins as he moves as quickly as he can back toward his car.

29

JANE

Sweat trickles down my chest; I pluck the front of my dress, trying to cool off.

Mom and I are parked outside the Andersens' house. Well, not *right* outside. We don't want them to see us. But if they do, Mom has a whole story cooked up about how we're going door to door in the neighborhood, taking around her samples.

The windows are down, but the air is still. Fat clouds hang over us, threatening rain, but it seems like it's all gonna be a big tease. That we'll never get a drop, and the whole day will have this muggy, weighty feel to it.

I take a long pull of my Coke, then drag another greasy Tater Tot through ketchup and devour it.

Mom wrinkles her nose at me. She hates fast food, never lets us eat it. Calls it the devil's food, the devil being big corporate America.

But this morning I went to Pa with my palm held out and shook him down for a five-dollar bill, my payment for agreeing to do this. He handed it over, then told Mom to *take her wherever she wants to go.*

I swear that even more than the drinking or smoking, when I snuck around with Luke, the fast food was what I loved most. Crunchy tacos from Taco Bell, salty fries from McDonald's, gooey cheeseburgers from Whataburger. After mainly eating homemade meals and organic vegetables from our garden, this stuff felt *sinful*, tasted like heaven.

Thinking of Luke just now, a lump burns in my throat. I miss him. Haven't talked to him since the accident with Cookie. Obviously, I'm not riding her anytime soon to the general store again, so I've been waiting for a moment at home when I'm alone so I can call him.

"Put that mess away," Mom orders. "I see 'em."

I stuff the carton back in the paper bag, crimp the edges down. Peering up at their house—no, their *mansion*, which could easily swallow a dozen of our homes—I see the Andersens striding across the lawn.

Mrs. Andersen's drop-dead gorgeous, her natural beauty made all the better by things Mom hates: makeup, jewelry, fine clothes. And Mr. Andersen is like some kind of Viking god. I thought this at the fish fry when I saw them with Nellie, and now the thought pops back up again: I can't believe she's *theirs.* She's not ugly but she's not *them.*

Mr. Andersen's got his hand on her lower back. He swings

open the passenger door to his sleek black Jeep Wagoneer before tucking her inside.

Our own engine grumbles to life, and Mom hand cranks her window shut, motions for me to do the same. She twists the knob on the AC, and it gasps like it normally does before spitting out air that smells like an old leather shop.

Oh, to ride in that Jeep Wagoneer, a chariot being driven by a prince.

As they glide out of their drive, Mom inches forward, careful to wait until they've almost made it to the end of their street before falling in behind them.

Their castle is on a giant hilltop, and my stomach turns as we coast down the street.

Pine cones the size of footballs crunch under our tires; I feel like I'm at the arcade playing *Ms. Pacman*, trying to see how many pellets we can eat before getting gobbled up by ghosts. The ghosts, of course, are our missions. Always are. I won't say I feel *skittish* exactly—I'm too used to it for that. But before each one, I do feel kinda sick in my gut. Never know what's gonna happen.

We're on the main road to town now, trailing them.

Mr. Andersen puts their left blinker on and turns into the shopping center.

Mom pulls into the parking lot, still keeping her distance.

They're in front of a place called Talk of the Town Salon. Mrs. Andersen hops out, then disappears inside the beauty shop.

Mr. Anderson climbs out, too, but he walks a few doors down to Smithy's Goods. I've been in there once so far with Mom and Pa; it's like a general store but with *everything*. Hunting and fishing gear, a sandwich counter, deer feed, you name it.

"What's our plan?" I ask.

"I don't know!" Mom snaps. I can tell her nerves are frayed, too. "Let's just go," she adds, her voice stern but shaky.

I grab the cardboard box of oils from the floorboard as I exit, then kick the door shut with my foot.

A bell clangs against the glass door as we enter. It feels like all eyes in the place land on us.

Of course, we *are* a sight, me and Mom in our handmade dresses, out of step with the times.

I spot the top of Mr. Andersen's head right away. He's down a few aisles over. "Mom," I whisper, jerking my head in his direction.

She tugs at my elbow, and I follow her, sweat stinging my eyes, my nerves heading into overdrive.

He stops at the end of Aisle Three, his hand tracing a row of boxed ammo.

Mom pauses, then grabs my elbow again, pulls me down Aisle Two, moving fast toward the end. She grabs the box from me, races around the corner, and—what do you know?—bumps into Mr. Andersen.

"Oh! I'm sorry! Didn't see you there!" Her voice is full of sunshine. "I blame it on this," she says, smiling down at her oils.

"No worries!" Mr. Andersen says, grinning at both of us, but especially Mom. "Hey, we met the other night—" He cocks his head to one side, runs his eyes over her chest.

She usually dresses very modestly, very *biblically*, but I saw that before she approached him, she tugged down the top of her dress, putting her serious cleavage on full display.

He's kind enough not to say, *Hey, we met the other night, and my daughter called your daughter here a skank.*

Mom hitches the box onto her hip, sticks out her hand. "Yes, we did. I'm Abigail. Abigail Swift. And this here's Jane, my middle one." Dimples pucker her cheeks, and she's beaming so hard at him, her face might crack.

"Pleased to see you again, Mr. Andersen," I say, giving him my warmest smile. "I'm Nellie's age," I add, not sure why I just brought her up. Mom shoots me a look that says, *Shut it.*

"Hey, honey," Mom says, as if she always uses this pleasant tone with me (never happens), "could you go find the twine? The mason jars?"

I don't want to budge, but I mind her. I head to the far end of the store, where the goods are. But instead of staying there, I creep back toward Mom and Mr. Andersen. Walking up Aisle Two, I keep my steps as quiet as possible.

I hear laughter.

Shifting a can of dog food to one side, I peer through the opening.

Mom's got her hip jutted out even more, head tossed back as she laughs, throat bared, and she's let the shoulder slip down on her dress so that her bra strap is showing.

Mr. Andersen's hungry eyes are moving all over her body. I'm close enough to see that they're deep blue, electric. He's even handsomer this close up. Pa's handsome, too, but this man could be a print model.

I'm kinda shocked by the attention he's paying Mom. *Mom?* Especially when he has *that* wife? But I guess Pa is right: he did take a shine to Mom after all. Humph. I don't get it. But whatever.

"Yeah, I love the outdoors, love going out to my land," Mr. Andersen says.

"You a hunter?" Mom asks, twisting a lock of her hair with her free hand.

"I am. Or…I was. I mean, I still hunt sometimes, still go out there and camp, too, but…not as much as I'd like." His voice low, he takes a step toward Mom. "Like I said the other night, the family's not so into it. These," he says, rattling the box of bullets at Mom, "are for the shooting range."

"Well, I for one can't get enough of it," Mom says, locking her eyes onto his.

I blush at her brazenness. Other than with Pa, I've never seen her like this. She's always the dutiful wife, devoted, faithful. This flirty side is…jarring.

"I love sleeping under an open sky, out in the fresh air, beneath the stars. Sometimes without even a tent. Or a sleeping bag." A wicked grin creeps across Mom's lips.

It may be creepy but I gotta hand it to her, she's hooking him. A verse from Bible study, which she leads us in, flashes across my brain: *For the lips of the adulterous woman drip honey, and her speech is smoother than oil.*

Mr. Andersen inches even closer to her, leans in. "Whaddya have here?" His fingers edge the lip of the box. Their heads are nearly touching. His crown of golden hair, perfectly held in place with light product, glistens in the light streaming down from the skylights.

There's something about him; he's not only gorgeous; he's magnetic. Can't say I blame Mom for fully getting into character here.

"Oh," she says, tapping a finger to her cheek, blushing, "these are just my samples. I make my own oils and botanicals."

"That's amazing," Mr. Andersen says.

He pries one from the box.

His lips crinkle into a smile. "Love Potion?"

Red streaks claw up Mom's neck. "Yep. It's my most popular one. Your wife—"

"Charleigh—"

"Yeah, she came out to visit us but said y'all weren't in any need of it—" Now it's Mom who leans in closer, tilting her chest down so that we can both see down the top of her dress.

"Did she now?" Mr. Andersen replies, sounding like he's got a frog in his throat.

"She also said y'all weren't interested in my husband's customs, but," Mom says, licking her lips, "you seem to be a man of exquisite taste. So maybe *you'd* like to look at some of my husband's work, see for yourself?"

I feel overheated just spying on them, my breath hitching in my lungs, wondering how long this will go on.

At this, Mr. Andersen is silent. He scratches the back of his neck, and as he does, his shirt crawls up, revealing his tanned, toned abs.

Mom lowers the box to the floor; his eyes feast on her boobs.

She nearly knocks her head into his face when she stands back up. In her hand, a business card. She flicks it toward him.

He accepts, gripping it in his fingers.

"Shop's out at our place, on our land. Come see us sometime. Number's on the back. I'm almost always there."

She heaves back down again, collects the box.

Mr. Andersen's eyes are crimped into a smile; his mouth is dangling open.

Hook. Line. And sinker.

Later

The scorching wind rattles through the pines, scrapes the surface of the lake.

It's the kind of lashing wind that kicks up before a summer thunderstorm, which I wish would erupt right freaking now so the pelting rain could help sink the body.

I'm shaking, I realize, and have to hug myself in order to keep from quaking.

Calm. I need to calm the fuck down.

Come up with a plan.

Fix this.

PART 2

30

NELLIE

Now

can't believe it; I have a crush.

A *real* one, not the pretend thing with Dustin, but the kind that makes my heart feel like it's gonna burst out of my chest. I feel almost dizzy, almost sick. I haven't actually felt this way since Thor, back in Sweden. Poor Thor.

But also *fuck* Thor.

Enough about him. Every inch of my body feels like it's lit up, electrified, but in a good way.

It's weird, but *everyone* in this house seems to be in a good mood. When I stumbled in, Mom and Dad were still up, even though it's long after midnight. I was dreading Mom barreling down the stairs, needling me about my curfew, but instead, I was greeted by Dad shooting a Nerf ball from the Nerf gun straight at my butt, hopping around the room like he was some special-ops person.

He's such a lovable dork—the only man in town who still

aims a Nerf gun at his teenage daughter. But anyway, I thought to myself, *What's gotten into you?*

Then Mom slunk around the corner, wineglass in her hand, laughing at us, at me dodging Dad's shots. Saying nothing about me being late. A miracle. One that makes me suspicious.

It's Friday night, and it's now one a.m., and I'm dancing around my bedroom, blaring the single that he gave me tonight. "Kiss Off" by the Violent Femmes.

It's a rough song, loud and crazy. A few secs ago, Mom poked her head in, looked like she was worried about me. But I think even *she* could see the change in me, tell that something good has happened. She finally just shrugged, smiled, and shut the door.

No way I'm telling her about this. Not yet anyway. This is all mine, delicious hard candy in my mouth that I never want to dissolve.

Luke. Luke Napolitano.

That's his name.

How *sexy* is that?

Never mind that he's connected to Jane, to the Swifts. Even that can't change the way he made me feel.

It was just a normal night at the Circles. I drove myself, not wanting to get roped into anything with Dustin. Not in the mood to put out.

So I was leaning against my beamer, alone, chain-smoking, sipping on a spiked cherry limeade, when they got there, pulling up in Luke's red Camaro, windows down, the new INXS album blasting out of the car.

Everyone looked at each other because no one recognized the car.

And then he stepped out.

Tall, lean, *foxy*, his coal-black hair licking his shoulders, his face telling everyone he doesn't give a fuck, his torso squeezed into a faded Ramones T-shirt. With his black biker boot, he stubbed out his cigarette, flung his bangs back.

I couldn't breathe.

We don't make boys like that in Longview.

And then *she* crawled out of the passenger side. Jane. With her weird-ass sister, Julia, whom I'd just met for the first time.

Almost made me feel sorry for Jane, to have to have a sister like *that* tag along. Jane at least makes an effort to look cool, to wear makeup, to dress a little more like a normal teenager, but Julia just stared at us all from behind her thick glasses, her flat, bony body lost in one of those hideous prairie dresses.

My heart sank; I figured he was Jane's boyfriend or on the way to being. Then, as they walked over to everyone, she introduced him to Blair as her friend: "He's a friend of our family from Dallas. His dad shipped him here for the summer to apprentice under Pa. He's staying with us."

And they didn't hold hands or act affectionate to each other at all. But I did see the way Julia was looking at him all night, with big puppy-dog eyes.

"Gay rod." Dustin coughed these words into his fist, loud enough for all of us to hear.

I wanted to punch him in his flabby stomach, kick him in

the balls, but I just rolled my eyes, took another drag off my smoke.

If Luke heard him, he pretended like he didn't. Didn't act bothered at all.

Blair, of course, pranced over to him, all flirty, basically throwing herself at him even though Tommy was standing right there.

Luke was all smiles with her, and they talked for a while, so long that I felt like I didn't stand a chance.

But when he started heading over to the keg, I raced there.

It was just the two of us.

He was squeezing the nozzle, filling a cup with beer, and when I walked up, almost out of breath, he looked up, flipped his bangs out of his eyes, and smiled at me. "Need one?"

His tone was scratchy, a heavy smoker's voice, and sweet. Made me melt.

"Sure," I said coolly.

When he passed me the plastic cup, his fingers touched mine.

"Got a name?" he asked, grinning at me. "I'm Luke."

"Nellie."

"For real? Like from *Little House*—"

"*On the Prairie*, yes."

I was bracing for him to tease me, like everyone else over the years, but he flipped his bangs back again, his eyes smiling. "That's awesome. She's a total badass. Must mean you are, too."

"Not if you ask *them*," I blurted before I could stop myself. My face burned. But there was something about Luke that made me trust him, made me wanna open up to him.

"Humph," he scoffed, scanning the crowd. "Fuck 'em, right? I can tell you're different. I'm—" He scratched the back of his neck. "Let's just say that I'm different, too. So I get ya."

Now my face was on fire, and I was positive he could see my skin glowing beet red. I sucked down half the beer. Then the other half. Which made him snort.

"Damn, Nellie!"

Good, I thought. *I've impressed him.* I stuck out my empty cup for him to refill.

"I like a girl who can hold her liquor."

He worked a cig between his lips as he filled my cup.

I studied his fucking gorgeous eyes: dark, mysterious, deep brown, but somehow also lit up.

"So, tell me, what's everybody got against ya?" He tugged down his T-shirt, which had crept up, showing off his tan stomach.

"They all think I'm a freak."

He laughed. "Well, are ya?"

"Maybe?" I said in my flirtiest voice.

Behind him, the bonfire was sparking.

I could feel everyone's eyes on us, and it made me feel so good, so powerful.

"Ha!" He smirked. "Not afraid to tell it like it is, are ya?"

He hotboxed his cigarette. Like him, it was different. Rolled in brown paper, smelling kinda funny, like flowers or something.

"What are you smokin'?" I stuck my hip out, tried to act even flirtier.

"It's a clove. Ever had one?"

I shook my head.

"Well, let me give you your first." He dug a pack from his back pocket, shook one out. "Better yet, I've got something even more fun to smoke. Follow me."

As I walked with him, I felt like I was floating, a balloon that had been released, in danger of drifting into the sky.

I followed him to the line of the woods, where his Camaro was parked.

"Climb in."

The inside of his car smelled like his cigarettes, sweet and smoky. He rummaged through his console, then came up with a joint. "This cool with you?"

"Shit, yeah!"

Pot usually makes me feel silly, giddy, a little paranoid, but it gives me the giggles.

He fired it up, took a long drag, passed it to me.

The paper was still wet from his mouth; it tasted like how I imagined kissing him might.

I took an equally long drag, to show him I was cool.

He reached up, slid back his sunroof. "If we lean our seats all the way back, you can see the stars."

I did exactly what he said, pulling the lever, pushing the weight of the seat down with my back.

I glanced over at him. His shoulder-length hair looked like silk. I wanted to reach across and touch it. Run my fingers through it. He was staring straight up at the sky. I kept looking at him, hoping he'd look back at me, working up the courage to lean over and kiss him. But he took another pull off the joint, then blew the smoke upward through the roof. He pointed. "I swear that's Jupiter. You see it?"

I peeled my eyes off him, looked through the opening at the red dot he was pointing at. "Yeah, I do. That's so cool."

"It's the planet of good luck."

"Is that so?" I asked, teasing. "Are you an astronomer?"

"Ha. No, more like an astrologer. Jupiter's my ruling planet. I'm a Sagittarius. You?"

"Scorpio. Through and through."

"Coulda guessed it, Nellie." He said my name like it was a naughty thing, a playful thing, a beautiful thing, and my stomach turned to butter. "All darkness and passion."

He turned to me then, his brown eyes twinkling. I fought the urge, again, to lean over, kiss him, maybe crawl on top of him.

He would have to make the first move.

Instead, he popped the lever on his seat, springing it back up. Dug around in his console again, this time fishing out a single, waving it around.

I came up to sitting, too.

"Ever heard of them?"

On the paper cover was the band name, Violent Femmes, and a photo of a barefoot little girl dressed in a dress, peering through a window. Edgy.

"No. We only get the Top Forty songs here on the radio." I rolled my eyes, pretending to be put out by that.

"Well, Nellie, you're in for a treat. I have *so* many songs to teach you about."

He jammed the cassette into the deck, then twisted the knob so that it wasn't as loud as when they pulled up. The guitar sounded jangly, the singer's voice all raw, and the lyrics dark… but funny? It was about a loner, but a badass loner. I swayed in my seat to the music, acted like I was *so* into it, that I understood it.

"But this one, 'Kiss Off,' this song could be your theme song," Luke said after he turned it off. "Better yet—here, it's yours." He popped it out of the tape deck, slapped it in my hands.

And now I'm listening to it over and over, not quite believing that this boy sent from heaven gave it to me. Not that I really believe in heaven. I mean, let's get real. But that he could look inside my black heart and see me so clearly… I will never get rid of it; I'll sleep with it next to me because he touched it and it's a gift from him to *me*.

When we climbed out of the car, everyone was looking at us.

Blair especially, her arms crossed across her chest like she was sulking. I nearly peed my pants, I was so happy.

But there was Julia. She was glaring at me with those eyes of hers. Whatever.

Also Dustin. *Ugh*.

Luke high-fived me, and I wobbled back to my car, fuzzy from the weed. *Delirious* from Luke.

Drunk, Dustin shouted after me, "Hey, Nellie, what the fuck? You aren't leaving yet, are you?"

I'll pay for it later, but I couldn't help myself, especially after he called Luke a gay rod. I didn't stop and turn around, just raised my arm and gave him the finger in front of everyone. Burned him.

31

CHARLEIGH

Charleigh peels Alexander's arm off her as stealthily as she can, then slips from the bed.

Pale morning light nudges through the curtains.

It's dawn; she needs to pee but doesn't want to wake him, so she tiptoes to the bathroom, practically floating across the carpet.

Alexander's been all over her since their spat after the fish fry.

Feral.

Wanting it all the time.

Not that she doesn't, and she loves his hunger for her, but, whew, the man needs to give it a rest. Give *her* a rest.

The day after the fish fry, when she stumbled in hungover from Jackson's, she rode with Alexander downtown, not a word exchanged between them.

He dropped her at the salon so she could get her hair done while he stocked up on ammo at Smithy's.

They were barely home and through the back door when he came up behind her, lacing his arm around her belly, lifting her skirt.

"What are you doing?" she asked.

"Nellie's not home." He panted in her ear.

With his foot, he toed the back door shut, then marched them a few feet over to the eat-in dining table. He tugged Charleigh's panties to one side and traced his fingers over her until she could barely breathe.

Bent over the table, they had frantic sex.

Afterward, she turned around, wrapped her arms around his neck. "What was that all about?"

"I don't like fighting with you," Alexander said, his slate-blue eyes spearing hers.

She slid her hands down to the tops of his shoulders, guided him into a chair. Straddled him. "I don't like it either. Not one bit."

"So," he said, his voice low, "let's not fight, then."

His lips grazed her neck, and before she knew it, they were at it again, Alexander holding her up by her hips as she bucked against him.

Charleigh creeps from the bathroom now, down the hall to Nellie's room.

She cracks open the door, peers inside.

The air smells like a combo of cigarettes and Jean Nate, and Nellie is curled on top of her Laura Ashley comforter into a tight ball, still dressed in last night's clothes: a black miniskirt with fishnet tights and a Bangles sweatshirt with the neck cut out.

Charleigh grins, remembering poking her head in last night, catching Nellie dancing, actually smiling.

Has to be over a boy, Charleigh thought.

She knows these things.

And that it's probably not Dustin.

Charleigh closes the door, her mouth still curled upward.

She'll take a happy Nellie any day. It's a rarity.

32

JACKSON

The night—heavy and panting, black as a panther—oozes into the cabin of Jackson's car. With his windows lowered, forest-scented air swirls through his tiny Mercedes, lifting his thick hair.

Duran Duran's *Seven and the Ragged Tiger* cassette is still in his tape deck, and as he veers onto the highway, the very one that will take him back to Ethan's land, he twists the volume, willing Simon Le Bon's voice to replace the one in his own head, the voice that says, *Jackson Lee Ford, what are you doing?*

Because he knows *exactly* what he's doing, and he doesn't want nerves, or the thought of Charleigh screeching at him if she ever finds out, to stop what he thinks is about to happen.

Exactly thirty minutes ago, he was slouching on his sofa, thumbing his clicker between the Rangers game (a bore; they were up from the first inning) and *Fantasy Island*, the only show on Saturday night worth watching, when the sound of his telephone ringing punctured the air.

His whole body sighed at the sound of it. It could be only one of two people: Charleigh or his mother. Not that he wouldn't want to hear from Charleigh, but at this hour on a Saturday, she'd be tipsy and bitching about something or someone, in an endless loop.

Plus, he was salty at not having been invited to wherever she most likely still is, only getting asked, plucked from his house, when it suits *her*.

But after the third ring, he stripped himself off the couch to answer it and spoke in a slightly annoyed tone (because he's never outwardly confrontational). "Hello."

A pause.

A man chuckling?

"Hellooo—" Jackson said a third time, this time with more pointed irritation in his tone.

He was about to plunge the phone back down on the receiver when he heard Ethan's voice, throaty and saccharine, over the line. *Buzzed*. "This a bad time?" Ethan asked, but not in a concerned way, more mischievous.

Jackson's heart battered against his rib cage. He gripped the back of a chair, steadied himself. "Uh, no, not at all. I was actually just watching—"

"Good," Ethan said, striding over him, "because I was *actually* just calling to see if you wanted to come out."

His mouth dangled open. Then words surfaced, floated out. "You mean tonight?"

"Yes, right now."

The chirping of night birds filled the line.

He imagined Ethan standing on his porch, the front door shut, strangling the phone line so that he could talk in private.

"Wife's just about asleep, kids are in bed, so I thought you could come over, have a drink with me—"

"I'll leave in ten," Jackson rushed to say, suddenly afraid Ethan might change his mind.

"Park just inside the gate, and kill your headlights, too. Meet me out back, up by the pond."

The thought of a rendezvous, of Ethan not even pretending that this meeting was about anything else—woodworking, scoring clients—made Jackson nearly asphyxiate.

And now as he's edging off the blacktop road, rumbling over the Swifts' cattle guard, killing the engine, he feels once again like he might pass out.

Before he steps from the car, he hand cranks the windows back up, then drags his fingers through his hair to put it back into place.

He creeps along the drive on foot, like a burglar, ears attuned to everything: the ensemble of night birds that warbled over the phone earlier, the glow of fireflies whose amber light bites at the darkness swelling around him, the sound of his cowboy boots gnawing on the crushed-gravel path.

Despite his effort to remain cool, the damp heat causes his shirt to stick to him, leaving sweat to ring his armpits.

The lone front porch light winks at him, but other than that, the house is asleep. Curtains drawn, lights extinguished.

Jackson circles the house, cutting a wide berth, his breath hitching as he spies Ethan's form silhouetted against the night sky, whiskey bottle tilted to his lips.

The ground beneath his feet turns marshy as he crests the hill, nears the pond.

Ethan spots him and waves the bottle.

They are far enough away from the house, where their voices won't carry. But still, Ethan talks in a hushed tone. "Glad you could make it. On such short notice."

A crescent moon, its surface marbled with pewter, droops just above the tree line, casting snowy light over the water, over the sharp features of Ethan's delectable face.

"Well," Jackson mutters, tongue fumbling in his mouth.

Ethan palms him the bottle. "Want a swig? Sorry I don't have cups, but I was trying to be quiet, not wake the wifey." He winks at Jackson.

Jackson's stomach stirs. The bourbon scalds the inside of his mouth, but he takes a nice long pull anyway, tries to steady himself.

The air near the pond is tropical, briny. Ethan walks over to a tiny dock, the wood slats so old, they bark in protest under his weight, and jerks his chin skyward, inviting Jackson to join him.

They sink, cross-legged, down on the slats.

"Nice night like this, I'd say we could go for a swim, but"— Ethan stretches his legs out, supporting his weight with his elbows—"had a little too much." He wiggles the bottle at Jackson.

"Then I've got some catchin' up to do," Jackson says, lifting the bottle from him.

He takes another long drink, reclines back like Ethan.

"Like I said, glad you could make it. I figured," he starts, a lock of hair dangling over his forehead as he leans forward and takes the bottle from Jackson, "we could pick up where we left off."

"Ha!" The laugh chokes out of Jackson's throat, unbidden, but he's caught off guard by Ethan's directness, his amber eyes probing Jackson's, glazed over with alcohol.

"On second thought—" Ethan says, rising to his feet.

Panic seizes Jackson's chest. Did he just kill the moment with his stupid, nervous laugh?

But then Ethan peels off his Henley, undoes his belt. Kicks off his boots, steps out of his pants. In the cold moonlight, Ethan's tighty-whities glow fluorescent.

Every vein in Jackson's body throbs with want. His eyes linger over Ethan's almost-bare body. Lean muscles taut and rippled, skin velvety smooth, those eyes glinting down at Jackson.

"Join me?" Ethan lowers himself into the water from a ladder attached to the dock. "It's not deep here, so I shouldn't drown. But you can hold me up if I look like I'm in danger." He winks.

Jackson's hands claw at his shirt, paw at his jeans; he's never undressed so fast in his life. Standing on the dock, he feels exposed in his thin boxers, his body offered up for Ethan's approval. Damn his lame home gym and lackluster exercise regimen. Why has he let himself go? But as he flicks his gaze down to Ethan's, he sees he has nothing to worry about. A grin as wide as a crocodile's cracks Ethan's face, his eyes roving hungrily over Jackson's body.

He climbs down the ladder, pond water like a warm bath enveloping him into a hug.

Standing, their chests peek over the surface.

"Feels amazing, right?" Ethan asks, dipping his head into the water, shaking it off like a wet dog.

"Yes, it's refreshing," Jackson says dumbly.

"I'd stay out here all night if I could. Sometimes I feel trapped, sleeping in there—"

The house is so far away, it looks like a miniature of itself, a dollhouse shrouded in shadows.

"I hear ya," Jackson replies, even though he doesn't understand. He doesn't feel trapped in his own house, just lonely.

A hot breeze blasts over them, puckering the surface of the pond, shredding the stand of fuzzy pines that sit off to one side. Between his toes, the ground is squishy.

Ethan takes a deep breath, closes his eyes, exhales as though he's releasing the weight of the world off his toned shoulders. When he opens them again, that mischievous grin is back, smeared across his lips.

He takes a step forward to Jackson.

They are so close, their skin is almost touching.

He leans in even farther as he stretches to reach the whiskey bottle resting behind Jackson on the dock. As he retrieves it, his arm grazes Jackson's neck. Ethan tips the bottle up to his lips, takes a shot. Still clasping it, he tilts it to Jackson's lips, inching even closer as he does.

Thump, thump, thump, Jackson's heartbeat gongs in his ears. He accepts a sip.

As soon as the glass leaves his lips, Ethan's mouth is on him, the bottle thudding against the dock.

Ethan teases at first, his lips only brushing against Jackson's, nothing more.

Jackson stands in the water, stock-still, not wanting to mess this up. And wanting to make sure that what is happening is actually happening.

Ethan's tongue parts Jackson's lips.

Holy hell, this is actually happening.

His fingers crawl to the back of Jackson's neck as he kisses him full on, sending shivers skittering down Jackson's spine.

This man can kiss.

Good grief, can he kiss.

And Jackson kisses him back, wrapping his arms around him.

Ethan unlatches his lips, sways like he's swooning. Locks his copper eyes onto Jackson's. "I've thought about doing this since the first time I bumped into you at that bar."

Language is drained from Jackson's system. He can respond only in kisses. He pulls Ethan's face to his, then drags his hand down Ethan's chest, which smolders. Ethan moans. Shaky, Jackson slides his hand inside the waistband of Ethan's underwear, begins touching him.

"My God," Ethan utters, then nibbles on Jackson's shoulder.

Waves ripple out around them, small halos of water that seem to echo the pulsing between them.

Jackson tugs Ethan's underwear off completely. Slaps it up on the dock. Continues caressing him until Ethan's nibble nearly turns into a bite, his voice strained in Jackson's ear: "Jesus, you *really* know what you're doing."

After he finishes, Ethan fumbles with Jackson's boxers, wrenches them down. "My turn."

Jackson shudders at the touch, his whole being nearly convulsing.

"Will you climb on the dock for me, sit on the edge?" Ethan asks.

The slats are warm against Jackson's ass, reminding him of the wood at the sauna at his old gym in Dallas. He's leaning back, resting on his forearms, and Ethan is still in the pond, his face between Jackson's legs. Jackson groans as Ethan takes him in his mouth.

Talk about someone who really knows what they're doing.

Jackson can't help it; his hips buck slightly as Ethan continues, his fingers clutching Ethan's luscious hair. Above him, stars streak across the sky, but he knows that's not what's really happening. His vision is blurring from *this*, and before he can help it, he hears himself shouting Ethan's name. Then Ethan's mouth is on his, shushing him, making far better use of his tongue.

The men loll on their backs, hands laced together.

"That was…really something." Ethan's sugary voice drifts into Jackson's ear. "Come out again anytime. *Please.*"

Jackson still struggles with vocabulary, with speaking, with words, so he lifts Ethan's fingers to his mouth, begins to nibble.

Jackson coughs as he enters Sullivan's, the air in the bar smoke-choked milky-white smog from the cigarettes churning above everyone's heads.

"Evenin', darlin'!" Ginny calls out while wiping the bar down in front of Jackson. "What'll it be?"

"Jack and Coke." He's grinning so hard at Ginny, he feels like his face is going to split.

He couldn't go straight home, not after *that*. He needs a drink, needs time to process it, to relive it, to luxuriate. Plus, he's dying to tell somebody—it's too delicious to keep to himself—and Ginny's the only person he can spill it to.

"Never seen you so happy," she says as she fills his glass with ice.

Jackson tilts his head, shrugs. Coy, bashful.

"Oh, Lord. Please tell me it's not about that man!" She sprays the glass with Coke, pours a shot of Jack on top. "Jackson—"

"What? And shhh, keep your voice down."

Ginny leans across the bar, her blue eyes wide as biscuits. "Tell me."

Jackson takes a pull of his drink, sets it down. He's relishing this. "Well, let's just say, I just left his place—"

"And?"

"Well, we…ya know…"

She grins, then bites it down. "Man's got a wife, saw his wedding ring—"

"So?"

"Okay, yeah, whatever about that." She flings her hands into the space between them, says, "But—"

"But what?" Jackson shakes the ice around in his drink. "That man is *divine*. And you know it."

"That man is *trouble*. Anyone who brings a Bible into a bar and who looks like *that*..." Ginny whistles out a sigh, shakes her head, places her hand on top of Jackson's, then warns, "Watch out."

33

JANE

The sound of Pa strumming his guitar tickles my eardrums.

It's Sunday, early evening, and we're all gathered on the wooden dock of the pond for Vespers.

And by all of us, I mean *all* of us.

Luke is here! I can't believe it. He wasn't lying about surprising me.

He's only been here two days, but everything is already so much better.

Not that we can show it.

He knows—especially after what went down in Dallas—that we must keep us a secret.

So now he sits cross-legged, baby Molly in his lap, her sweat-soaked hair glued to her forehead, head rolling on Luke's angular shoulder. She took to him like a long-lost sibling, toddling toward him, chubby arms open, babbling, "Wuke, Wuke."

Pa sings the last words to John Denver's "Take Me Home, Country Roads"—sometimes he mixes in a folk song with hymnals—plucking the final notes, the sound pealing out over the water.

"Tonight we celebrate the arrival of Luke, good son of Antonio and Rose, sent here to learn how to be an even better servant of the Lord." Pa's voice rings out over the pond.

He coulda been a preacher. I swear to God, he loves the attention, loves the air of authority. So now he's a pretend preacher.

"Amen!" Mom adds, beaming at Luke.

Luke smiles, dips his head in reverence. Damn, he's good at playing his role, too.

"And tonight, we also celebrate Jane's birthday. My Sunshine is eighteen! As of yesterday. I can't believe it!" Pa says, his eyes glassy with tears, his voice thick. He's also tipsy; I note an open bottle of whiskey sitting next to his guitar case. "Shall we?"

My cheeks flame. "No, Pa, that's not really necessary—"

But before I can protest anymore, the birthday song belts out of all of them, even baby Molly. Mom mouths the words, though her lips are a tight line, as if she hates the very fact of my birth.

But I flick my eyes away from her, land them on Luke.

Delicious Luke, whose deep-brown eyes kill me, who sings the birthday song as if he's serenading me, like it's just the two of us out here.

When he arrived Friday night, it was late, the sky already the color of river silt.

I was doing my nightly dousing of the gardens.

Water was dribbling from the mouth of the garden hose, turning the crumbly soil silky when I heard the rumbling of Luke's Camaro, a sound I have memorized as well as any lyrics to a favorite song.

I jerked my head up, saw the beams of his headlights moving over the pasture as his tires dipped in and out of potholes.

What the…?

Pa came striding out of the house, roped his arm around my shoulder.

"He's coming to live here for the summer. Apprentice under me. Get outta trouble in Dallas, get a taste of good old clean country living. I know y'all are friendly, so I thought you'd be happy—"

I swiveled my gaze toward Pa's face, scanned to see if he meant something more by *friendly*. He didn't seem to. But I decided I didn't care if *he* was on to us. Long as he kept his trap shut in front of the others.

"Luke's great. I *am* excited. Someone other than Julia to talk to."

At this, Pa chuckled. "And I figured we could use the extra help around here."

My stomach clenched. What exactly was Pa gonna make Luke do?

But then he squeezed my shoulder, set me at ease. "And Mr. Napolitano specifically said he wants him to learn the trade—"

"Woodworking—" I rushed in. As if to cement it.

"Yep, exactly. So he'll be staying out here in the shed I just built. Working side by side with me, learning the different saws and such. Like my pa showed me."

Deep into the night, well past midnight, when I was certain everyone else was asleep, I crawled down the ladder from the loft, slipped out across the pasture to Luke's shed.

Creaked open the door.

He was on a mattress, leaning his upper body against the wall where a headboard should be, reading by lantern light. A crumbling copy of a collection of Rumi's poetry.

"Thought you'd never come." He grinned up at me, patting the spot next to him for me to take.

On the floor, a single candle burned in a votive, and a bottle of red wine stood ready, waiting to be uncorked.

After we each had a glass, I slipped under his thin bedspread with him, let him spoon me, keeping my ears pricked for any sounds, any signs that we were being watched.

We kept all our clothes on, just in case, Luke's voice in my ear, growling, "Happy early birthday, Jane."

All the next day, he was at Pa's side at the sawing table, sweat streaming off him, his gorgeous skin glistening.

I noticed that Julia made a lot more trips by Pa's shed than normal.

He was a sight: Smooth, tanned. Tall, lean, but with muscles rippling. Moppy hair made even sexier by the work, the sweat, the messiness.

Of course, we had to invite her to the Circles with us. And, *sigh*, *ugh*, of course she said yes. I swear she somehow knows about us, wants to drive me crazy by not letting me be alone with Luke.

I even let her ride shotgun, mainly because I didn't want me and Luke to slip up, to somehow forget and hold hands over the console as we always do.

Though we couldn't act like we were together, pride still crackled through me when I introduced him to everyone. I thought Blair was gonna pass out from flirting with him so much.

And Nellie. Whew.

I still can't believe he let her inside his Camaro, hung out with her like that. Like I said, we aren't the jealous types, but it definitely bugged me. Because it was *Nellie*.

When I snuck into his cabin later that night, I brought it up, carefully choosing my words so I didn't sound clingy.

"Be careful with that Nellie girl. She's...*weird*."

Luke laughed. "That's judgy. And not like you at all."

I socked him in the arm. "No, it's just"—I shifted in his bed and sat up—"she's been mean to me. Ever since we moved here."

Luke's fingers tickled the top of my hand. "Really? You ever wonder why?"

I shook my head. "No, but Blair said it's because she's just jealous."

"Bingo. I mean, look at you." His fingers were now in my hair, twisting a strand. "And that girl's twisted up. I can relate to that. She needs a friend—"

"But does it have to be you?"

215

"Ha, no. But I mean, yeah, maybe? Like, no, I'm not gonna be her new best friend, but I will be nice to her. You should try it, too. She's not a bad person—"

"Ha, fat chance."

"Jane Swift." His lips brushed against mine. "You're a devil."

34

NELLIE

t's dusk when I arrive at the swimming hole.

As I pull into the parking lot, my heart leaps when I spot Luke's orange Camaro.

My top is down, so I can hear splashing, giggling. Everyone is already here.

My flip-flops smack against the ground; I'm walking so fast down the hill, I feel like I could trip, but I'm anxious to see him. So anxious, my insides feel like they're gonna burst into flames.

"Ready, set, goooo!" I hear Tommy yell up at Blair, who's standing on top of the boathouse, getting ready to dive.

Sigh.

She's topless, and as she raises her arms above her, glancing down at the dock to make sure everyone is watching, I see the profile of her perfect tit.

Then I see Luke grinning, treading water right near where she'll land.

My stomach balls into knots. I feel like I'm gonna be sick.

Everyone, it seems—including Jane—is skinny-dipping.

Fuck it. Luke and I have a connection, and I'm going for it.

As Blair flies through the air, plunges into the river, I mount the dock.

All eyes land on me, but I just stick my hip out, paste a fuck-you look on my face.

I may not be naked, but I wore my skimpiest Daisy Dukes and my red string bikini. Revealing enough to be hot but with just enough fabric to cover my scar.

Dustin's not here for some reason; I am so fucking glad he's not. We haven't talked since I shot him the finger at the Circles the other night.

When Luke catches sight of me, his eyes land on mine, and he flicks his chin up, smiles. Waves at me with his dry hand, which is holding one of his clove cigarettes. "Yo!"

"Yo!" I say back, trying to sound cool, but my voice comes out shaky.

I plop down on the deck, screw open the bottle of Mad Dog 20/20 I brought with me, take a huge gulp.

Jane's back is to me, and she's holding on to the dock with her arms, head tilted, like she's high. Her chest is underwater, but I can tell she doesn't have a top on either. Whatever.

Her creepy sister is sitting on the shoreline, under a big Cypress tree, dressed in one of her hideous prairie dresses, scowling. Why the hell is she even here if she's not in a swimsuit? Doesn't seem like she parties. I guess anything's better than sitting at the fucking farm all day.

"Got a sip for me?" Luke's voice lands in my ears. My whole body heats up.

I scoot to the edge of the dock, dangle my feet in the water. Undo the top button on my shorts, zip them down. "If you think you can handle it." I wink at him.

He winks back.

I want to jump in, wrap my whole body around his, and never let go.

But I gotta play it cool.

Even though the sun is starting to set, turning the sky a blazing red orange, it's still smoking hot out here, the heat roasting me.

He takes three long glugs, shakes his head as if he's just tasted nasty medicine.

"Jesus, Nellie, that stuff'll put hair on your tits." His grin grows even wider.

"Gross," I say, but smile back at him.

As if she can't stand me getting attention from Luke for even one second, Blair swims over, splashes him.

"Hey!" He spins around, douses her back.

She squeals so loud—like a little girl—I feel like my ears are gonna split.

She also makes sure to bob up and down as she treads water in front him so that her chest peeks over the surface.

I'm furious.

I take another scorching sip of Mad Dog, then thunk it down on the pier.

Loud enough so that Luke peels his eyes from Blair for a sec and glances back at me. I lift my eyebrows at him as if to say, *Be my guest. Go ahead and flirt with the boring rich bitch.*

But he doesn't take the bait, just turns back to Blair, who continues her bob-and-titty show. Then she paddles toward him until she's only inches away, her bare titties almost touching his chest.

He clears his throat, red marks staining his neck. He looks like he's under a spell. And why wouldn't he be?

Fucking Blair. Get the hell off my man.

"Hey, Nellie," Jane says, twisting around and fixing me with a sarcastic stare.

"Greetings," I say in my snidest voice. "Care for a snort?" I shake the bottle at her, daring her to say no.

"Suuuure," she purrs, taking it from me. She cocks her head back, downs more than even Luke. Passes it back. "Needed that. Thanks."

It's not, like, super noticeable, probably to anyone but me, yet she, too, seems annoyed by Luke and Blair, coolly watching them.

"Do it one more time!" Blair shrieks.

Luke takes a long drag; then his cheeks inflate and deflate as he blows smoke rings.

Gag. She's acting like she's never seen this before. I fucking hate her so much right now.

"Let me try," Jane says, lifting the smoke from Luke's fingers.

"Hey, that was mine!" he says, but in a playful way.

Jane sucks in the biggest drag ever, flips her head back, then puffs out the longest trail of smoke rings I've ever seen.

"Dayum, girl," Luke says.

Instead of passing him back the cig, though, Jane flicks it far into the river with an angry snap of her fingers.

Luke hangs his head. Turns back to me. "Hey, can I have another swig?"

I lean over, making sure my boobs are pressed together to show off my cleavage, then hand him the bottle back.

His eyes are finally on me. I feel like I'm going to pass out with how fast my head is spinning.

Taking a drink from the bottle, he keeps staring at me.

I'm pushing my hair out of my face when I feel a tug at my back, feel my top slithering down.

What the fuck?

Blair's evil cackle fills my ears.

That heifer snuck up behind me, undid my bikini top! I'm gonna fucking kill her!

My boobs dangle out for everyone to see; Luke's eyes are pasted onto them. Shame fills every pore on my body. I know he can see my scar, dark and wormy, just under my left nipple. He's definitely disgusted. Has to be.

But, if he is, he doesn't show it. He's still staring at me, his mouth hanging open.

I cup myself, covering them, snatch my top off the deck.

Then I scramble to my feet, elbowing Blair as hard as can when I pass her on the way back to my car.

"*Fucking bitch*," I hiss at her.

"Oh, come *on*, Nellie! I was just messing around!" she squeaks after me, no sincerity in her voice.

"Nice rack, though!" I hear Tommy say, which actually makes me grin.

"More like too good to be true!" Blair shouts. "Her daddy bought her those titties. It's why she has that scar. From the surgery. Isn't that right, Nellie Jo?"

I freeze, spin around. "You're such a fucking *liar*, Blair!"

But I know nothing I can say will make anyone believe me. When my tits came in, they were the one perfect thing about me. So perfect that Blair had to concoct a story about them. Whisper to everyone that I'd had a boob job, that the scar I got from hunting with Dad was proof of it. I was holstering a shotgun when it kicked me hard in the chest, the scope cutting into my skin.

"You wish, Nellie Jo! Just like your nose, they're fake."

Wicked bitch. And now she's using my middle name, which she hasn't in years. Just to fuck with me. Try and push me over the edge. I'm so filled with rage right now, I've never wanted to seriously kick someone in the face as much as I'd like to kick her.

Everyone is quiet, waiting for me to explode. But I don't have a good comeback because my breasts *are* so perfect that they do look fucking fake.

My face burning, I turn around and keep heading to the car.

My arms are still across my chest when I reach the door and lean down, trying to pry it open with my fingers while still covering myself.

"Need a hand?"

I can't breathe. It's Luke.

"Uh, kind of?"

He pops open the door, and I hop in the driver's seat. He looks the other way while I get my top back on.

"You don't have to leave, just because—"

"Just because the whole world just saw my tits?"

"Hey, it's not that big a deal. C'mon, don't let her get you riled. She just had too much to drink."

I hate that he's defending her. But I love that he chased after me.

"Plus," he says, tossing back his wet hair, which sticks again to his tanned shoulders, "they look pretty real to me." He winks at me.

I gulp.

"Tell ya what, wanna get high?"

Minutes later we're sitting in his Camaro, same as the other night, the leather seats cracked and baking the backs of my thighs.

He fishes out a joint from the console, fires it up, sucks in a drag, and passes it over to me.

I inhale as much as I'm able, then go into a coughing fit. But after that, my mind is numb. I loll my head over on the back of the headrest so I'm looking at him. "Why are you nice to me?"

He laughs. "Why wouldn't I be?"

"Everybody else hates me—"

"Yeah, yeah, we've been over that, remember?"

The cherry on the joint burns orange as he takes another drag. "I like you; you're...different...like me."

Through the cloud of smoke, I study his perfect face. His petal-like lips, his intense dark eyes, his kissable neck.

Fuck it. What am I waiting for?

I lean over the console, gently grab the back of his neck. Put my lips on his and kiss him. His lips feel so good, but he doesn't kiss me back, just sits there, still as a stone.

A nervous laugh chokes out of him. "Ummm..."

Absolutely mortified, I shrink away, slink back into my seat. I want to throw up. I want to *die*.

I cross my arms in front of my chest again, suddenly feeling naked. Dirty. *Dumb.*

"Hey, heeeey." Luke's voice grumbles across the console. "I'm sorry if I gave you the wrong idea. And I *do* like you, Nellie, just—"

"Just not like *that*?" I spit out. "I get it, heard it my whole life."

"No, no, no, that's not it."

Huh?

A pair of fireflies dance right in front of his windshield. I know I'm stoned, but they look like they're about to make out, just like I wanted to do with Luke ten seconds ago.

"Well, what is it, then?"

He fiddles with his visor, slides out a clove cigarette. Lights it. Then passes it to me, lights himself another one.

"I'm seein' someone."

Huh.

"Someone, like, back in Dallas?"

He shakes his head.

"Here?" The word screeches out of me.

He nods. "But we're kinda keeping it under wraps, like low-key."

"Jane?" I ask.

Luke sighs, but shakes his head. "Nah, she's a family friend. That'd be, like, weird..."

It's Blair, then. It's gotta be. The way she is around him, the way he is around her. And, of course, they have to keep it a secret—she's Tommy's girlfriend.

"Got it," I say, cracking open the door, stepping out.

"Nellie, wait, you don't have to—"

I pause, not wanting him to think I'm mad at him. Because I'm not. I'm mad at *Blair*. "What? It's no big deal. But, like, I just wanna get outta here, ya know?" I say, trying to keep calm.

"We cool? Can we still be friends?"

I lean back into the car, lowering myself so that my not-fake perfect tits will swing in his face again. The tits he was obsessed with minutes ago by the river. I can beat Blair at this. Luke and I are soulmates; we are so fucking alike. He will grow tired of her stupid, silly bullshit.

Again, he stares at my chest, can't take his eyes off it.

"You bet." I wink at him, flash him a devilish smile, and shut the door.

35

CHARLEIGH

Charleigh twists her hair into a ponytail, then drags a hand towel across the back of her neck.

The sound of sneakers squeaking chirps all around her; she and Kathleen just finished up a match of racquetball at the Boat House. Charleigh won every game, of course; she's ruthless on the court.

They stumble from the glass container, paw their keys out of the rectangle box outside the court.

"Daiquiri?" Kathleen lifts an eyebrow at Charleigh.

"Sure, why not."

They head upstairs to the lounge, pry open the door. On the TV set hanging above the bar, MTV plays a Paula Abdul video, "Straight Up," and Charleigh, who, just an hour before was admiring her own figure in the locker room mirror, eyes Abdul's body with jealousy.

"Strawberry daiquiri for me," she says.

"And I'll have a piña colada," Kathleen tweets.

As the blender whirs, Charleigh's eyes land on a flyer taped to the far wall. Pressure builds in her chest as she squints to read it. It says SWIFT'S APOTHECARY across the top. She can't make out the rest.

"Be right back." She hops from her barstool, saunters over to scrutinize.

SWIFT'S APOTHECARY
HAVE YOU LOST THAT LOVIN' FEELIN'?
Join us for an afternoon workshop on fertility,
femininity, attraction, and more! Learn how natural
botanicals can help put the spice back in your marriage!
$10/person. Organic sack lunch included.
This Saturday, July 7, 3 p.m.
123 Seven Pines Road
903-555-1212

All the tabs but one are torn from the bottom of the sheet. Charleigh leans in, rips it from the flyer, jams it in her pocket. She doesn't know why she took it; she has no interest in going to it, *obviously*, but then, if everyone else is going, she doesn't want to be left out.

Ugh, that family, and ugh, that woman.

"Charleigh! Drinks are up!" Kathleen raises her piña colada, shakes it.

"You going to this hootenanny?" Charleigh asks, fishing the wad of paper out.

"Yeah. It's this Saturday. We're *all* going. Didn't Monica tell you?" Kathleen's eyes shine with innocence. She can be so naive sometimes.

Of course, Monica didn't fucking tell me, Charleigh thinks to herself but doesn't say out loud. "Nah, she didn't. Probably because she knows I'm not interested. That family is weird as hell. I mean, I get that," she says, scooting her stool closer to Kathleen's and lowering her voice (Kathleen loves a good dish session), "she wants to bang the husband and all—"

Kathleen snorts, sweeping a sheet of her glossy hair over her shoulder. "She does not."

"Does, too. You see the way she was pawing at him at the fish fry."

"I mean, he is *so sexy*. I'd do 'im." Kathleen smirks.

"You'd never cheat on Kyle—"

"Ha! You don't think he cheats on me?"

"I didn't say that...but—"

"Well, that's why I wanna go to this thing. I've been using her oils, and they *work*. Kyle is frisky as he's ever been. But Abigail told Monica that she wants to introduce even more stuff, something called a jade egg—"

In that instant, Paula Abdul's video ends, and the words *yoni egg* ring out across the room, prompting stares.

"That's so fucking gross."

"No it's not. And she's gonna go into all the Kegel stuff, how to make your, you know"—Kathleen motions down to her pelvic area—"tighten back up after childbirth."

"You're gonna make me choke to death on my daiquiri if you keep this nasty talk up."

"Don't act like you're above it, Charleigh. We all need to do what we can to keep our men happy. And this goes beyond our men. She's promising to wake the divine feminine in all of us."

"What does that even *mean*?" Charleigh howls.

This clearly stumps Kathleen. She gazes down in her glass, stirs her straw through her frozen drink. "I don't know," she says, her voice small. "But I'm going to find out."

36

JANE

twist in my sheets, can't get comfortable. We got to the river early today—Luke, Julia, and I—before everyone else showed up, and after being out there for so long, the sun torched my skin.

I'm pink all over, hot but covered with chills at the same time, and a little steamed inside.

Luke. Mom.

At least my sunburn's bad enough that I told him not to expect me in his shed tonight.

I get the whole free-spirit thing. And *I'm* a free spirit, too, but he got a little too close to Blair for my comfort. Or rather, he let *her* get a little too close to him.

How would he feel if I let Tommy or one of the other boys creep on me like that?

I'm mad at Blair, too, which is irrational because she doesn't know we're really together.

And I'm pissed about that, pissed that we have to keep this a secret.

But we do.

From Mom, from Julia.

Of course, Julia wanted to join us again today. I swear she somehow figured out that Luke and I are in love, and of course, she wants to tear that down, so there we were, Julia riding shotgun, me squeezed in the back, hot wind lashing my hair as we weaved through the backcountry roads.

When we got to the swimming hole, I dove in first, the icy water jolting me out of my heat stupor.

Julia just sat on the banks, watching me and Luke swim. He was real careful not to get near me, acting instead like we're brother and sister, or best buds, when all I wanted to do was wrap my legs around his waist, have him devour me.

Then the rest of the teens trickled in, bringing a boom box and a cooler full of beer. Tommy even brought his bong, the sides of the glass thick with resin.

I could have ignored Julia, pretended she wasn't watching—and grading my every move. Like how when Blair removed her bikini top, I did as well, flinging it on the deck while Tommy hooted at us.

The boys shimmied out of their bottoms, letting their parts dangle in front of us like it was no big deal. Luke took his trunks off, too, but stayed in the water. I prolly woulda strangled him if he had actually shown himself like that to Blair.

Boobs are one thing, in my mind, but private parts are a whole other.

All the more reason that I got so angry when I saw how close he was letting Blair get to him, her tits on full display, inches from him.

I hate that this is making me feel like one of those possessive girls. We might have to say *fuck it* and just be together, let everyone know.

But I know what a bad idea that is.

Shit.

And Nellie. Why the hell did he have to go after her, get back in his car with her? That totally grates on my nerves.

"It's not like we did anything," he said when I asked him about it.

We were alone by the garden, him standing there with his hands dug in the pockets of his cutoffs, looking guilty.

"Whatever," I said, twisting away from him to water Mom's poison garden. "But you could just, like, think about how all this makes me feel."

"I felt sorry for her! That's all there is to it! And I do like her, as a friend. But this is impossible. Hiding from everyone—"

"Shhh, keep your voice down. You know Julia's always lurking—"

He moved closer so that he could talk in a whisper. "You know you're the only girl for me, Jane Swift. And I want you so bad—I wanna do so many things to you right now—"

My anger turned to jelly. I'm always putty in his hands. The thought of us actually *doing it*—especially now that I'm eighteen—makes me feel like I'm a giant Ferris wheel, spinning in the sky, about to drop eighteen floors.

I love this boy so much, can't wait for us to get the hell outta here, hop a train to New York with our suitcases and nothing else. We don't belong here. It's starting to make us crazy. It's too much pressure, this hiding.

"I love you, Jane Swift," he murmured in my ear, his breath tickling my neck, before Mom came out on the front porch, calling us in for dinner. Splitting us apart.

After we ate an embarrassingly simple meal of black beans and corn bread with a salad I made from tearing a hunk of romaine from the garden (Pa *does* need more clients), I stood side by side with Mom at the sink.

Soap bubbles tickled my arm as I washed dishes while she dried and put them away.

Everybody else was on the back porch, listening to Pa play his guitar.

Mom twisted the faucet, making the water hotter.

"Ouch! That's too hot."

"If you don't get the temp up, you don't kill the bacteria," Mom said, her lips in a tense line.

Normally I would relent, but it hurt with my sunburn, so I twisted it back down.

Mom sighed.

"I'm sunburned!"

"And whose fault is that?" She gave her head a sharp shake. "Saw you being real friendly with Luke earlier in the garden."

The hairs on the back of my neck pricked up.

"We are just *friends*. Just cause he's a boy doesn't mean there's somethin' going on."

"Well, Julia said you were whoring it up down at the swimming hole earlier." She slapped her drying rag on the counter, jammed her hands on her hips while staring me down, daring me to say something.

I laughed. "I don't even know what that means. I didn't even kiss anyone—" I was scrubbing a teacup with so much force, I thought it might shatter in my hands.

Mom's palm flew across my cheek, stinging my sunburn. Felt like she held a match to my skin. *What the…?*

"You're not foolin' me, young lady. I did *not* raise you to behave like this!" She was shouting now, her words ringing through the cabin.

"Mom, what are you talking about?" I said, holding my cheek, which still throbbed.

"Julia! She told me that you were parading around out there *topless*! Like some kind of stripper or something! If you're not careful, you're gonna wind up like—"

Fury rose behind my eyes; I wanted to strangle Julia for tattling on me, wanted to strangle Mom for acting like such a controlling bitch. "Like *what*?"

A sharp laugh barked out of her. "Nothing. Forget it."

"Like you? Pregnant at eighteen? Then again at nineteen."

Another slap flew across my face. Hot tears bubbled in my eyes, but I stormed away from her, out the front door.

And now I'm fighting sleep. Or my body is. Mom can fuck right off. I forgave Luke to his face—and part of me knows I won't hold a grudge, since it's just not who I am—but another part of me is still hurt, thinking about him and Blair. And Nellie.

37

CHARLEIGH

Sunlight pulses through the kitchen window. It's late afternoon, and Charleigh is just home from racquetball, her veins fizzing with alcohol.

Alexander's out on his land today, dove hunting; he said he was likely going to tent camp, spend the night. Which is fine with her. She needs a break from him, from all the sex, even though she loves it, is grateful for it. Is grateful that she's not in a position like Kathleen, trying to use potions and whatnot to keep her husband by her side. How pathetic.

Through the window, she spies Nellie lounging on a chair in her red string bikini, flicking through *Seventeen* magazine. She's wearing heart-shaped sunglasses, her blond hair pulled into a high ponytail.

Charleigh sighs at the sight of her, at how *normal*—no, *happy*, *content* her daughter actually looks.

Usually, she'd be locked in her room, chain-smoking, feet

thudding the floor in angry steps. She never lies out by the pool anymore. This is because of that boy, Charleigh thinks, whoever he is. She's tanning herself, spritzing her hair with Sun-In, and yes, smoking a cigarette, but doing so in a calm manner, delicately ashing in a Sprite can.

Charleigh strides outside, springs herself on Nellie.

Nellie flinches.

"You don't have to put that out because of me. I know you smoke."

Nellie lowers her sunglasses, rolls her eyes. But there's also a smile playing on her lips. *Thank God.* "I know you know." She takes a long pull, then drops the butt into the soda.

Charleigh walks toward her, two glasses of iced lemonade in her hands. Spiked with a little rum. An offering.

"Beverage?" she asks.

"Sure. Lemonade. Great."

"No, this is *adult* lemonade."

Nellie eyes her suspiciously. Charleigh never drinks with Nellie, but she's on a mission to find out who Nellie's mystery man is.

"Okaaay." Nellie accepts the drink. "What's in it for you?"

"Ha! You can't just have a drink with your dear old ma?"

"Cut the shit."

Charleigh sinks into the chair next to Nellie's.

The pool gurgles next to them, and Charleigh, buzzed off her daiquiri, almost feels like a teenager again. Except she never had this experience as a teen, only wished she had. A surge of emotion washes over her as she thinks about all she's managed to give Nellie. She may not be a perfect mother, but just look at all this. When she was Nellie's age, she'd be in the barn scrubbing dairy equipment right now.

And, for once, Nellie seems *okay*.

Nellie sucks down half her spiked lemonade through the straw, grins at Charleigh. "Well, this is actually kinda nice." She licks a finger, pages through the magazine. "But what's the deal?"

"Well," Charleigh starts, her voice quaky, "you seem…I don't know…*happy* or something." She flips her free hand through the air, as if asking a question.

Nellie peers at her over the top of the chlorine-crinkled magazine.

"You're acting…like a girl in love."

A laugh sprays out of Nellie. "God, Mom, you sound like you're in a movie from the thirties or something. But yeah, I met a new boy I like."

"And…tell me…what's his name?"

"Oh, fuck it. Okay. His name is Luke. And he's bad, Mom. A bad boy like I'm a bad girl. He's so hot, too." Nellie shivers.

Charleigh's insides clench. *A bad boy, bad like her?* "What do you mean, *bad*?"

"Well, he's covered in tattoos for one thing, has longish hair, drives a Camaro. I don't know, he's *cool*. From Dallas—"

"Nellie, how old is this boy?"

"Eighteen, Mom. *God*."

Charleigh takes in a deep breath, resets herself. Getting info from Nellie is like trying to herd a scared cat. She must tread lightly. "But what else do you mean about him being bad? Like bad-bad? Or just…?" She keeps her voice neutral, like a middle school shrink.

"Like, he didn't graduate from high school. He's here for the summer trying to better himself or whatever."

"Where does he live? What part of town?" Charleigh takes a long gulp of her drink.

"You're not gonna like it."

"Try me."

"He lives out with the Swifts, and he's learning how to woodwork under Mr. Swift." She sucks the remainder of the lemonade through the straw.

Dread swamps Charleigh. *Not that fucking family again.* They are literally everywhere, closing in on her. She lets out a forceful breath.

"What?!" Nellie stabs her with her tone, jolting her back.

"The Swifts? We hate them, remember?"

"Well, like, whatever!" Nellie practically shrieks.

Keep calm, Charleigh, keep calm.

But it's too late, Nellie's face has already darkened. "Don't have a hissy fit, *Mom*." She says *Mom* as if it's the most disgusting word in the whole world. "It's not like we're *together*. I'm pretty sure he's with Blair. But…I'm gonna work on him because he's, like, everything I've ever wanted. I have to have him."

Charleigh feels like she's going to have a heart attack. She's never heard Nellie gush about a boy like this. This could end so badly. It could end like…well…Thor over in Sweden. Not being able to get Nellie exactly what she wants is a source of excruciating pain for Charleigh.

"Well, what can we do?" she asks.

Nellie recoils. "Nothing. Like, don't do *anything*. I got this." Her chair scrapes against the concrete as she stands up and storms inside, slamming the door shut behind her.

Great.

Charleigh pokes at the ice in her glass with her straw, wonders how she can so quickly go from confidant to shit for brains with Nellie, faster than Alexander can go from zero to sixty in his Wagoneer.

38

JACKSON

The pile of discarded clothes on Jackson's bed keeps growing. He yanks shirts off the hanger, holds them up to his chest, then studies his reflection in the full-length mirror he picked up in Italy one summer with Charleigh.

Florentine, ornate with a gold rim, it looks like it belongs in a king's chambers. He loves it. It cost her one thousand bucks. Jackson balked, but they were at an auction house, and the Andersens' bill was already over $20K.

"It's nothing," Charleigh insisted. "Plus, you deserve it."

With that, he could not argue. That morning alone, she'd dragged him for hours over cobblestoned paths in search of the perfect entryway piece. Something grand to announce their wealth the second folks stepped inside their home. A piece they wouldn't find until the following winter in Paris, where they scored a dazzling marble-topped table, the legs carved with intricate scrolls.

And this afternoon it felt like it would take at least that long for Jackson to land on the perfect shirt.

Sigh.

He can't believe Charleigh roped him into this, but he's elated to be going. And nervous. And excited. And delirious.

Last night, over margaritas by her pool, she trotted out the ask.

"Darling, you don't have plans tomorrow, do you?"

Jackson didn't, but he *had* planned on calling Ethan. Seeing if he could sneak out there again. But that was for later, in the evening.

"Umm, no, why? What are you—"

Charleigh licked the rim of her salt-crusted glass, swirled the drink around before taking a generous sip. "Well, this is gonna sound ridiculous, but I'm going to this workshop thingy out at the Swifts tomorrow—"

The blood drained from Jackson's face. He raised his own glass to his mouth, not to drink more, but to hide his expression. "But...you hate them?"

"Obviously. But apparently they've taken in this troubled teen, and...wait for it..." she said, uncrossing her long bronzed legs, and leaning in, "Nellie's got a crush on him. Like big time."

Jackson gulped at his margarita. "So, what does that have to do with *you*?"

She batted him on the arm. "Duh. *Everything*. And you know this."

"And what's this workshop?"

242

Charleigh rolled her eyes so dramatically that Jackson thought they might spring from her head. "It's some freaky bullshit that Abigail's cooked up. And all my other *friends* are going." Her voice was slurry now. "About her *love* potions, Kegel exercises—"

"Ewww, hold it right there—" Jackson laughed.

"And you get a sack lunch for the price of admission. Fuck me. But it's a good excuse to go out there and investigate. Get eyes on this boy. See what we're dealing with."

And not for the first time, gratitude washed over Jackson for the fact that he has no kids. What an absolute nightmare, it seemed. And his sister's children are no different. Well, they aren't *Nellie*, but they *are* spoiled rotten, running roughshod over Katelyn and her husband, Blake.

Blake deserves it, though. Ever since the AIDS crisis exploded, Blake treats Jackson as if he's contaminated, eyeing him when the kids crawl in his lap begging for shoulder rides. Jackson sees them less and less because of this. Now, when he goes to Dallas, he'll make some excuse about how he's short on time and can't swing by the house, begging Katelyn to bring herself and the kids to a restaurant instead.

Charleigh lifted the pitcher, refilled their glasses. "So? You in? Please, *please* God damn it, don't make me go out there all alone!" Her crystal-blue eyes were pleading, desperate.

"But I'm a dude, lest you forgot. Are you sure I'm welcome at this Kegel bash?"

Jackson was horrified about what Ethan would think, him tagging along on this. But he was also antsy to lay eyes on him again. He hadn't called since their rendezvous last Sunday, and Jackson was getting restless.

Fuck it.

"Yes, I'm in. But if it's gets weird, you have to promise me we'll bail."

"Deal!" Charleigh crashed her glass into Jackson's, dumped the rest of her 'rita down her throat.

He settles on a faded graphic tee, a royal-blue shirt he picked up at Amoeba Records in San Francisco years ago. It hugs his chest nicely and shows off his triceps, which he flexes in the mirror, promising to make them even more toned in the coming weeks. Ever since Sunday, he's been pumping iron every day, running laps around his block, punishing himself with push-ups.

He untwists his bottle of Obsession, then dabs the tiniest amount on his neck.

He jumps when he hears Charleigh in his drive, her door clapping shut.

What is he doing, trying to get found out by her? Will it be awkward with Ethan? And also obvious?

As they turn off the blacktop into the Swifts' in Charleigh's Jag, Jackson stifles the urge to tell her to slow down when they approach the cattle guard. She's been here already, of course, and must know to decelerate; also, he cannot let on that *he's* been here.

His hands tremble in his lap; his breath spasms in his throat.

Calm the fuck down, Jackson, he thinks, a pep talk to himself.

"You all right?" Charleigh asks, her own voice quaky. Why is *she* nervous?

"Yes, why? I am *delighted* to be here!" He grins at her like he's lost it.

A sharp elbow to his torso.

"Owww!"

"Shut it. I don't wanna be here either. Trust me," Charleigh grumbles. "Drinks at the Boat House afterward on me, okay? We'll be in and out."

In the pasture in front of them, at least twenty cars are wedged into spots.

In and out, my ass, Jackson thinks. *This shindig will last all goddamn day.*

"Jesus. She drew quite the crowd." Charleigh sucks in a breath, exhales sharply.

"Who knew Vagina Day would be so popular?"

Charleigh snorts. She puts the car in park, shakes her hair over her shoulders, primps her bangs, then snaps her visor shut. "Shall we?"

39

CHARLEIGH

O h, the things a mother will do for her daughter. And, if she's honest, for herself.

Like tromping across a pasture in heels to attend some bizarro workshop. But there are all her "friends" clumped in a row, seated in front of Abigail, who's holding court over them, barefoot in a flowing white dress with an honest-to-God daisy chain resting on top of her head like a crown.

Annoyance blasts through Charleigh. This woman thinks she's the second coming of Christ, and Charleigh's friends are drinking the Kool-Aid. She grips Jackson's arm, grateful that she's dragged him out here with her.

"So, friends, *this* oil," Abigail trills, "you'll want to use it sparingly and"—she motions in a circle over her pelvic region—"down there. Like, not *on* it, but just above the root chakra."

"Chakra Khan," Jackson whispers in Charleigh's ear.

"Stop it, God damn it, don't make me start laughing."

"Oh, *hi*!" Abigail greets Charleigh and Jackson dramatically. "Glad you two could join us!" There's a flash of pity in her voice that Charleigh detests, a note of *I know I've captured all your friends' attention, and I am so sorry.*

"Please find a seat. Anywhere."

They sink into the grass. Monica turns around to face them, shoots Charleigh a smug grin. As soon as she swivels back around, Charleigh gives her the bird. "Bitch," she says to Jackson under her breath.

"And this oil is ylang-ylang blended with lavender and crushed rose quartz. I grind it down to a powder so fine, you won't even feel it. But your *body* will. It's one of the stones used to awaken the divine feminine within us all."

Sweat streams down Abigail's neck, a slow-moving river that trickles down between her full breasts. Her blue eyes dance with mirth; she's grossly lapping up all this attention, even though Charleigh's never seen or heard anything more ridiculous in all her life. She cannot *stand* this woman, has to unclench her fingernails, which are digging into the soles of her palms.

"I want everyone now to take a deep breath. Draw the breath in all the way down to the root chakra, hold it for a few seconds, then release." Abigail shakes her head at the crowd, as if they're dumb schoolchildren. "Let's try that again. This time, close your eyes. Now breathe."

Jackson's eyes are dutifully shut, but Charleigh keeps her cracked open; she's not big on following rules, especially these, here. She peers around at all her brownnoser friends, whose eyes are closed tightly. Their chests rise and fall with the breathing exercise, but Charleigh's own breath is tight, taut. She can't help it—a chuckle bubbles out of her.

Abigail's eyes fly open, narrow at Charleigh.

Charleigh lifts her shoulders into a shrug to express, *What's the big deal?*

From behind Abigail, the sound of a saw buzzes to life. Irritation flashes across her plain, makeup-free face. The instant the buzzing dies down, Abigail barks over her shoulder: "Ethan! Can you cut that out until I'm finished?"

Ah. So all is not well at the Walton house, Charleigh thinks to herself. *Ms. Abigail needs to use some more of her own love potions.*

In the background, Ethan steps from his shed, tanned skin shiny with sweat, buttons on his shirt undone, exposing his delectable chest. A saw dangles from one hand like it's merely a play toy, and he raises his free hand at the crowd. "Sorry, ladies!" he says, his flirty smile across his face.

Charleigh notices Abigail's jaw tensing, untensing, even though she's pretend smiling at him.

All eyes fly open now, drinking in the delicious sight that is Ethan Swift.

Even Charleigh—who is *beyond* irritated by this strange family—feels a stirring of passion in her gut while she gapes at him. Imagines what he can do with those strong arms, the different positions...

Her dirty train of thought is interrupted by Jackson, who clears his throat, gives her a stare that says, *Busted.*

248

"Whatever," she whispers in his ear, "this family is effed up, but that man is fine."

"You're telling me," Jackson whispers back.

"See, there's somethin' in it for you, after all. Eye candy."

"Speaking of which, I'm gonna go talk to the good man, check out his wares. I can't sit here for one second longer and hear about labia."

"Jackson Ford!" she calls out, clutches for his forearm, but he's gone. Standing and striding away.

"Later," he says to her, winking.

Well, shit.

"Now I want everyone to rise! Join hands!"

No fucking way.

Charleigh stands, but doesn't join in on the kumbaya.

"I want us all to feel the feminine divine moving between us, sparking, lighting up. God said that we were made from a rib from Adam, and while that is true, *we*, after the holy father, are the givers of life. Life comes from our wombs. Our sacred wombs!" Abigail thumps her chest like a baboon.

Fuck this. Charleigh stomps off in search of Luke.

As she creeps around the crowd, Abigail daggers her with her icicle-blue eyes.

Standing in the back of the woodworking shop is a rangy teen. Luke, Charleigh surmises. Arms spiderwebbed with tattoos, jet-black hair tickling his shoulders. He's wearing an INXS T-shirt, and everything about him spells *trouble*.

Charleigh sees why Nellie declared him to be her soulmate.

Underneath the bad boy veneer, he's shockingly handsome, with chestnut eyes that smolder and a worldly air about him that makes him seem like he's in his early thirties.

She scoots past Ethan, who, thankfully, is chatting up Jackson.

"Hey there!" she trills at Luke.

He mops his bangs out of his face, flashes her a gleaming smile.

"Charleigh Andersen. And you are?"

"Pleased to meet you, ma'am. I'm Luke. Napolitano. Stayin' with the Swifts this summer. I'm from Dallas."

"Oh, how nice. Luke?" She goes in for the kill. "I think I've heard my daughter mention you."

"Oh, yeah?"

"I'm Nellie's mom."

And that's when she catches it. The slightest ripple across his face, the tell that he might actually like Nellie. His tan skin blooms scarlet, and he swallows hard before he speaks again. "Oh, yeah! Nellie's really somethin'. Hung out with her a few times."

"Awww, that's so sweet of you to say that!"

"Well, it's true. She's cool, ya know? Not like most girls…"

"Well, thing is," Charleigh says, then dips her head toward his and lowers her voice so much that she's certain Ethan and Jackson can't hear her, "I know it *seems* like she has a boyfriend."

Confusions ripples across Luke's face. This is obviously not the turn he expected the conversation to take. Shit, why did she think she could talk to a teenage boy? Why is she even talking to him in the first place? Meddling.

"Uh-huh—" he mumbles, fumbling with his hands.

"Well, forget about all that." Charleigh bats her perfectly manicured hand in front of her as if she's sweeping away a mess. "What I'm trying to say is that you seem like a nice boy—"

Luke shoots her a look that says, *Yeah, right, lady.*

"And so, I dunno, maybe you could take her out sometime?"

He raises his eyebrows at her.

"Like on a date—"

He sinks his hands into his pockets, studies the sawdusted floor. "I didn't mean to give the wrong impression. Nellie's cool and all, but…and, she may or may not have a boyfriend, but…" He practically whispers this next part. "I have a girlfriend."

"Ahhh!" Charleigh says too loudly. "I see!"

Nellie will die if she ever finds out I had this conversation.

"Can you do me a favor?"

Luke nods.

"Can you never say a word about what I just said? I'm just a big old idiot. You see, most people don't like my daughter." By God, she's making this so much worse. "And so, when I come across someone who actually does, I dunno—"

Luke's looking at her as if she needs to be committed. Also, and this is much worse, as if he's wary of her. "This'll stay between us, ma'am."

"Thank you." She twists around to leave but stops. Spins back around. "Your girlfriend local?"

He scoffs, twists his hands inside his pockets. "Yep."

She's crossed the line again. "Well, that's so wonderful!" *Is it that little bitch Blair?* she wants to ask.

"Well, hello, Mrs. Andersen!" Ethan's honeyed voice glides over to her ears.

Grateful for the intrusion, she plods away from Luke.

"Howdy, Ethan."

He gives her that crooked smile like he did the other day when she was out here, a smile that seems to say, *I can tell how you look with your clothes off, and I like what I see.*

"You reconsidered?" He cocks his head to one side.

"Excuse me?"

"Having me design you something. Build you a piece—"

His smell—woodsy, zesty—fills Charleigh's nostrils. Despite how much she hates this family, good Lord, he is sexy. Sexual. Dripping with it. Maybe Abigail's potions are the only reason he hasn't strayed from her, because she's so god-awful by comparison.

"Jackson here," he says, clapping Jackson on the back, "can vouch for how good I am."

Why does everything he say sound filthy? Sexually charged?

Jackson's neck glows red; he shifts his weight from one foot to the other as he looks up at Charleigh sheepishly. "His pieces *are* quite exquisite."

Why is Jackson putting her in this position?

"Sorry, but you know I only like antiques," she says with as much apology in her voice as she can muster. "I'm sure your work is nice, Mr. Swift, but—"

"It's only gonna get nicer with Luke here. C'mere, son." He gestures to Luke. "Saw y'all talking, but proper introductions are in order. Luke, this here's Jackson, finest interior designer in town. And this is Mrs. Andersen, queen of Longview."

"Ha! Hardly—"

"Seems like royalty to me!" Ethan beams at her. Damn, he's good. Smooth. "Luke here is like a son to me. Good kid. Gonna be a damn fine carpenter and woodworker." He claps Luke on the shoulder.

"Pleasure to meet you, Luke," Jackson offers. "Let me know if you need anything."

"And yeah, we met a sec ago," Charleigh says awkwardly. "But hi again." She wants to bite her tongue off.

Luke dips his head, smiles.

"We really gotta get going," Charleigh says. "I dragged poor Jackson out here to see what all the fuss was about." She sounds like such a catty bitch. "And it's incredible, what all she's doin'. But it's really not my bag."

She yanks Jackson by the arm, pulls him into her. Squeezes his bicep, her signal for him to help her out of this mess. "So great to see you again!" he says to Ethan. "And to meet you, Luke! And I'll think about what you said—"

"I'd appreciate it," Ethan replies, and did he just *wink* at Jackson?

With Jackson's toned arm in her fist, Charleigh tugs him away.

40

JACKSON

ell, that was excruciating. Jackson's whole body glistens with sweat as he slides into the passenger seat of Charleigh's car, heart thudding in his throat.

Jackson here can vouch for how good I am.

Could Ethan have outed him any more? Maybe it wasn't obvious to Charleigh at all—his and Ethan's palpable attraction— but whew, he was squirming. Big time. And then for Ethan to bring that up at the end...

"What did you mean when you told him you'd think about what he said?" Charleigh crinkles her nose at him as she drives through the pasture.

Ugh.

"Nothing, really. He just asked me if I could help him find some business. Like contacts and stuff, ya know. They're obviously living hand to mouth—"

"Okay, okay, whatever. As you well know, I don't want him making me any furniture. They are the enemies, 'member?"

Jackson twists in his seat, aims the air vent at his face.

"Even if he *is* cute."

"He's totally cute. C'mon."

"Okay, but what'd you think about Luke?"

Jackson scratches the back of his neck. He wasn't *thinking* about Luke; he was thinking—the entire few minutes they were in the woodshed—about Ethan. Ethan's perfect mouth on his cock. His hands on Ethan's groin. What he wants to do to Ethan next. While Charleigh was nosing about with the kid, the edges of Jackson's vision went fuzzy as he stood, once again, in front of Ethan. Ethan's sly smile was the physical embodiment of a dare if there ever was one. Daring Jackson to kiss him, right then and there, while no one was looking. He took a step forward, causing Jackson to flinch back, giggling under his breath at Jackson's reaction.

But no way he could ever let Charleigh find out what happened between them, what's *still* happening between them, even if he wanted to take Ethan right then and there.

Ethan tipped his head toward Jackson, whispered, "Call me later tonight. I have to see you again. Soon as possible." His voice scratchy in Jackson's ear.

Jackson's heartbeat jangled in his throat so violently that he could only nod dumbly.

And now he's being ferreted away to the Boat House when all he wants to do is sink down on his sofa in the privacy of his own home, daydreaming about Ethan until it's time to call him. Reliving every single second of it.

"Jackson!" Charleigh snaps, thwacks him on the thigh.

"Oh, sorry. Um, yeah, Luke? He seems…nice but edgy?"

"Exactly." Charleigh punches the gas after she turns onto the highway, as if she can't get to her next cocktail fast enough. "So he'd be perfect for Nellie. But I totally fumbled back there. Did you hear us?"

"No, I was playing nice with Ethan, keeping him out of your way. What happened?"

A ragged sigh oozes out of her. "He's got a girlfriend. He said Nellie was cool, though, so there's potential."

"Except that he's already dating someone—"

"Yeah, Nellie thinks it's fucking *Blair*, even though she's with the town football star. But she's a little whore like her mother. I know for a fact Monica wants to mount Ethan. That's the *real* reason she was out there today—"

"A fact, huh?"

"Okay, not a *fact*, just a suspicion."

She best keep her grimy hands off him, Jackson thinks.

She swerves into the parking lot of the Boat House, tires shrieking underneath them.

"You ever thought about getting new friends?" he teases Charleigh.

"Naw, that's what I got you for, honey."

"Lucky me!" Jackson hoots.

"Hey!" she replies, mock hurt.

"So, if Luke *is* seeing Blair, then—" Jackson asks.

"Nellie seems unfazed by it. So—"

"So why did we go out there?"

Charleigh scoffs. "To *investigate*. Gather intel."

"Poke around where you're not wanted."

"But yeah, and if he *is* with Blair, I will find a way to fuck that up. Free him up for Nellie."

"You're just as twisted as she is."

"You're damn right. But don't think for a sec that Monica wants her precious baby dating that punk. So..."

Jackson pops open the door, sticks a leg out. "Enough! Being a parent is a mind fuck. Being a friend to a parent, an even bigger one."

"That's why the drinks are on me."

41

JACKSON

The night heaves around Jackson. The wind is still one minute, gusty the next, nicking his face from different directions, wringing the necks of the pine trees—sooty against the night sky—that line the walk to the pond.

He can't believe he's out here, but he couldn't stand it one second longer.

He tried to call Ethan late last night, as Ethan had requested, but Abigail answered, her voice brittle over the line. "Swifts."

Jackson's tongue fumbled in his mouth. Should he hang up? But what if she pressed *69, dialed him back?

"Yes, hi, is Ethan available?"

"Who's calling?"

"Jackson. Ford. We've met a few times. Hi."

"Yes," she said plainly.

"I'm a local decorator, and I told your husband I'd try and refer some clients his way."

At this, she warmed, her voice whirring like cotton candy spinning in a vat at the county fair. "Oh, hi, Jackson! Forgive me! Long night. Just finished with the dishes. But I'm sorry, Ethan's out."

Jackson's heart plummeted. Had he waited too long to call? Could he be out with Ethan right now if he'd just called half an hour earlier?

"No problem! Just tell him I called. He's got my number. My business card, I mean." *Hang up the phone, Jackson, before you screw this up.*

"Will do! So lovely to talk! He'll be so happy you rang!"

Jackson stirred in his living room for the rest of the night, debating going to Sullivan's to see if Ethan was there. But Ethan could've called him from the pay phone. No, he didn't want to look desperate.

Like he does right now, traipsing through the Swifts' pasture, hunting for signs of life.

Ethan's truck is parked out front, and like the other evening, the house is darkened, curtains drawn, cloaked.

Jackson phoned a few hours ago, but the line just rang and rang.

Call me later tonight. I have to see you again. Soon as possible.

Ethan's words from yesterday are what drew him out here, hoping that, like last Sunday night, he'd be by the pond, sipping whiskey.

Jackson's halfway to the water when a crow caws at him, causing him to start.

He turns back to look at the house, making sure the ruckus hasn't stirred the occupants. But the house lies dormant, asleep. Ethan's probably inside, snoozing next to his wife; Jackson entertains the juvenile thought of sneaking up to their bedroom window, softly pelting it with pebbles, then realizes that might get him shot dead.

It's pitch-black out, only a sliver of moon and a few stars straining from behind the clouds in the crushed-velvet sky, and Jackson can just make out the footpath encircling the pond.

As he crests the hill, the rickety dock comes into view, a postage-stamp-size square from where he's standing.

There's someone on it. Lying on it.

It must be Ethan.

Jackson has to suppress the urge to break out into a sprint.

He's ready to get on that dock, do what they did the other night. And more.

But as he gets closer and it comes into clearer view, it's not Ethan he sees at all.

It's Abigail.

Naked from the waist up, full breasts glowing in the sieved moonlight, her dress pooled around her hips. She arches her back as she grinds over someone underneath her.

Jackson gasps, scoots over to the tree line to take cover.

Fuck. He's just walked up on Ethan having sex with his wife.

Tears bite his eyes; he hates himself for his wishful thinking: that Ethan and Abigail's marriage is a farce, a sexless thing that Ethan is trying to escape.

And now he's gotta find a way to creep back out of here, get away unnoticed.

Abigail is rocking even harder now, her face contorted with pleasure, her moans skidding across the water. Evidently, this woman's *feminine divine* capacities are in full effect.

Jackson is transfixed. He can't stop watching, though he knows he should, even as it cracks his heart, but he needs to watch. Not for pleasure—this is not a turn-on to him; it's torture—but in order to sear this into his brain. That Ethan very much wants to have sex with his wife, is still evidently quite passionate about her. Watching for a sec longer will help him get over it more quickly. This fantasy of him and Ethan.

He's about to pull his eyes off Abigail when she wrenches Ethan up from the dock to kiss him, clasping the nape of his neck so forcefully, it's like she's riding a mechanical bull.

But it's not Ethan who rises from the dock, straddled by Abigail.

It's another man.

Long torso, lean back, a shock of short blond hair.

What the hell?

Jackson gasps for air a second time.

Sticking near the pines whose trunks bray in the breeze, he creeps closer to the dock to get a better view.

The pair is locked into a kiss, Abigail writhing faster, her form enveloped by the ropy arms of the man whose body thrashes against hers.

He can hear the man's grunts, can see his bare ass against the slats, but can't glimpse his face.

Shit.

He's gotta get even closer.

He takes advantage of the swell of sound between them, the fury of the pace they're keeping, and crunches over the carpet of pumpkin-colored pine needles that litter the ground.

As they unlatch their lips, the man turns his head ever so slightly in Jackson's direction.

And Jackson gasps a third time, so audibly that he slaps his hand over his mouth to quiet himself.

Because he knows the man that Abigail is mounted on, is pleasuring with each jolt of her hips.

It's Alexander, whose eyes are thankfully screwed shut, his hips continuing to sway as he jolts Abigail into ecstasy, her moan twisting into a full-throated cry.

Whirling around as fast he can, Jackson staggers along the edge of the forest, all but high-fiving the pine branches.

Dueling emotions swirl in his gut, joust in his mind.

First, elation. Because the man fucking Abigail isn't his Ethan. Because Ethan's wife is having a torrid affair on him, cheating. Their marriage is, indeed, a farce, the sexless thing that Ethan hinted about. Which means that what he and Ethan shared the other night was real.

The other emotion? Pure horror.

His best friend's husband is fucking another woman.

And not just some other woman, but *this* woman—*Abigail.* The very bane of Charleigh's existence.

How could Alexander do this to Charleigh?

42

CHARLEIGH

'm thinking Black Cats, gold sparklers, Roman candles, that sort of thing," Charleigh says to Jackson over the phone. "Just buy as much as they'll sell you. I'll pay you back when you get here."

"You sure this is a good idea? I mean, the Fourth is three days away. Like, *why* are we trying to plan a massive party with zero lead time?"

Charleigh splashes more Folgers into her mug, tears open a packet of Sweet'N Low, then dissolves the crystals into the brew. "Because I *want* to." Cradling the mustard-yellow wall phone with her ear and shoulder, she steps into the butler's pantry, shuts the door. "You *know* why. For Nellie. I wanna get in front of this Luke thing. And fast. Show him who we are, what we have to offer."

A jagged sigh fills the line. "You do know this means you'll have to invite his surrogate parents, your sworn enemies, the Swifts."

"Obviously." She rolls her eyes, wondering why Jackson is being so difficult, so pouty. "Look, I'll cover you the next three days, pay you overtime, whatever—"

"It isn't about *that*." His voice is crisp, shard-like.

"Okay, then tell me—"

"I've already *tried*! You hate those people, and you shouldn't be butting in on whatever Nellie's got going with Luke. It seems like a recipe for disaster to me. Times ten. Plus, we have three days! I'll probably have to drive to Dallas to rent the margarita machine on such short notice. We could do an end-of-summer party instead."

Charleigh sets her mug on a shelf, twists the cord around her index finger so tightly that she might tourniquet it off. She knows he's only trying to talk reason into her, be sensible, which is why they're such a good match. She's hotheaded, impulsive. Wants to pick at every scab, untangle every knot. She wants to have this party, *now*. No wonder Nellie is such an impulsive brat herself; Charleigh is a garbage role model.

"No, I want to go through with this. I know it's ridiculous, but c'mon, everybody's tired of the same old fireworks bullshit at the Boat House. Plus, if this being last-minute means some people can't make it, then all the better."

"How are you certain the Swifts will accept, bring Luke?"

"Because you're gonna talk to them, talk to Ethan. Tell him that I'm interested in possibly commissioning him to make me something after all."

"But you're not, really, are you?" Jackson practically shrieks at her.

She holds the phone out an inch, wonders again why he's being so onerous and challenging, when he's usually as moldable as Silly Putty.

"Of course, I'm not actually *really* interested in any of Ethan's furniture, but if I have to throw a few dollars at him to lure Luke over, who gives a shit?"

Another barbed sigh seeps over the line. "Okay, fine, I just think you're playing with fire."

"So?"

"Okay, fine. Whatever. But I'll only agree to help if we can please rethink the Mexican-food buffet. I am *so* not okay with doing that at the last minute."

"Deal! What are you thinking, then?"

"Barbecue. From Bodacious. We're not making Lettie haul out briskets for everyone. Red-checkered tablecloths, all-American look. Apple pies. Buckets of beer on ice. We'll hire a bartender, *if* I can get one on such short notice. Keep it simple. And I'm nixing the margarita machine."

"Sold." Charleigh cuts the line before Jackson has a chance to change his mind.

She lets out a long sigh, rubs her temples.

Jesus Christ, that was like pulling teeth.

The rational side of her knows that Jackson has a point, that this is dangerous, that it does indeed feel like playing with fire. But that's precisely what excites her about it. Charleigh Andersen is not one who can be bothered with thinking about trivial things like consequences. And her friend should understand that by now. Once a plan hatches in her brain, it can't be stopped; she's like a bitch with a bone.

Walking over to the counter, she snatches her notepad and jots down a reminder to reward Jackson with something special, maybe surprise him with a Caribbean cruise out of Galveston? Anything to keep him from being all huffy, while paying him back for going along with her little plan.

43

JACKSON

Jackson touches the bags under his eyes with the pads of his pinkie finger, delicately dotting moisturizer there to try reducing the puffiness.

He gazes at his reflection in the mirror; he looks like hell. Hasn't slept since Sunday night, since he caught Abigail in the throes of it with Alexander. The secret he's been keeping is acid, burning a hole in his stomach.

How to tell his best friend that her husband is a lying, philandering, asshole son of a bitch? He's heartbroken himself over it, having had Alexander on a pedestal all these years. Jackson truly thought he was one of the good ones. Not that he can't sympathize with how much the man puts up with. Lord knows Charleigh's a handful and a half—but still. He thought they were solid. And if they're not solid, who is?

Their big Fourth of July bash is tomorrow, and earlier today, Alexander helped drag extra lounge chairs across the patio to wedge by the pool, helped Jackson string rope lights from the stately pecan trees.

Alexander whistled while he flitted around the backyard, the whistle of someone who was newly serviced, Jackson thought bitterly.

Every time he thinks he's landed on a way to break the news to Charleigh, his thoughts spiral, the words that he's so carefully prepared in his head starting to feel like glass on his tongue.

Hey, Charleigh, sorry to be the bearer of bad news, but I was out at the enemies' land, trying to have another rendezvous with Ethan— which, sorry, I haven't told you about because I knew you'd go apeshit— and I caught Alexander fucking his wife's brains out.

Charleigh will be devastated, obliterated. Unable to function. The least he can do is let her have her party; then he'll figure out how to handle it. Because what if it was just a one-time thing? Is it worth detonating their marriage over?

Alexander's *always* been one of the good ones; Jackson's certain of it. He has a radar for this kind of thing. And as drop-dead handsome as Alexander is, with women tossing themselves at him, Jackson's never detected a whiff of infidelity. He's seen Alexander in action, turning cool to anyone who comes on to him, and, also, how very hot he is for Charleigh all the time. Almost nauseatingly so. They are one of *those* couples. So hopefully it's just a one and done. A mistake.

Jackson's also been desperate to talk to Ethan but hasn't been able to reach him. And it's not for lack of trying. The very next day, when Charleigh hoisted the Fourth of July party on him, he phoned the Swifts to invite them.

Abigail answered again, but this time, Jackson wasn't nervous. His knowledge of her indiscretion gave him fuel, somehow making him feel like they were on an even playing field.

Ethan was away again, but Abigail greedily accepted the invitation to the party on their family's behalf.

"Can you tell him to call me back, please? I still want to talk to him about some leads I might have."

"Absolutely!"

But so far, Ethan hasn't called, or if he has, it's been while Jackson's out, hustling around town to prep for the party, and Ethan hasn't left a message. Each time Jackson walks in the back door, he treads straight over to his answering machine and presses Play, shoulders sagging in disappointment when he doesn't hear that lusty voice on the tape.

Even though it fills him with trepidation, he can't wait to tell Ethan, holding out hope that this bomb will bulldoze the shell of the Swifts' marriage, clear the way for Jackson and Ethan to continue what they've started.

Obviously, their relationship will still have to be discreet— Ethan has children to think of, and this tin can town is too backward to openly embrace them as a couple—but they'd sure as hell not have to sneak around as much.

Jackson daydreams about Ethan coming over to his place, the two of them tangled together on the sofa...

He sighs, plunging into bed, pulls his cotton duvet, stuffed with a down comforter, right up to his chin. A splurge from Neiman Marcus last time he was in Dallas. As his melatonin kicks in, making him drowsy, he imagines Ethan right next to him, Jackson's head resting on that beautiful chest.

44

JANE

can't believe we're being dragged out to Nellie's house tomorrow for the Fourth of July. Not that I give a shit about the
actual holiday; I just don't *want* to go to her house. With
Luke, Pa, and Mom.

But also, I kind of do? That glimpse I got of it the other day
while we were parked out front made me want to see how those
people actually live. I bet it's like a castle in there.

Mom brought it up at the dinner table tonight, humming
as she passed around the bowl of mashed potatoes. All chipper.
I bet she's chipper; she's gonna get to see Nellie's hunky dad
again.

"That man, Jackson, called for you earlier," Mom said,
thwacking the wooden serving spoon against the salad bowl.

Pa glanced up, cleared his throat. "And? What did he say?"

"Well, he invited us all out to the Andersens' tomorrow
evening. For a Fourth of July party. Said Mrs. Andersen had

reconsidered and wanted to see about you making something for them after all." Mom bit a grin back. "So I think we should go."

"You do?"

"Yes, obviously."

I wondered why Pa was even hesitating, but I was just happy he was.

Then he started in on Luke. "Son, you could do well to work the room, chitchat with everyone. Follow Jane's lead; she's really good at it." Pa winked at me.

My stomach soured. I seriously do not want Luke getting involved in all that. Especially if it means more flirting with Nellie.

"Make sure you really lay it on thick for the Andersens." Pa lifted a slab of ham onto his plate. "And like I said, follow Jane's lead. You need to learn—"

My fork scraped the plate. "I don't know if that's such a good idea. Can't *we* just handle that part of it? Luke is here to learn woodworking, not how to act like a politician—"

Pa cut his eyes over to me, jerked his head to the side. "Stay out of it, Sunshine."

I would have felt better if someone had cold slapped me across my face. "But—" I protested.

"That's part of the business, too. Meeting people, getting clients, building trust—"

Luke's eyes shifted between the two of us. He shrugged at me, as if to say, *It's no big deal; let it go.*

So I did.

"I wanna come—" Julia blurted.

"No," Pa said, dragging his cotton napkin over his lips, "you are to stay here with Molly. I don't need any distractions."

"But..." Her voice cracked, and I thought she might break out into tears. "Why can't *Jane* stay home this time?"

Tension thickened across the table. It was on.

Pa couldn't say, *Because your sister is much more charming.* So he fumbled, twisted his napkin in his lap.

"You know your sister is the face of our operation. You know she can work a room. This is too important! This could land us our biggest client!"

Julia pushed her chair back with such force, it sounded like she scratched the wooden floorboards. She stood and slid it back under the table so violently, the dishes clattered.

Behind her, the back door slammed.

If she were kinder to me, I'd chase her, try to make nice.

Instead, a sly grin crept across my face.

At least I wouldn't have to deal with her prying little eyes at the party.

45

NELLIE

Pine needles crunch under my Keds, looking like tinsel scattered across the ground.

The party is in less than an hour, and I'm racing around, getting things ready. I've picked this particular spot behind the garage, on the far side of our property, because the woods here are thickest.

It's the perfect place to make out, stash beer. Of course, I've been here before with Dustin, but now I'm anxious to bring Luke out here. Away from everyone. I tuck a picnic blanket behind a wide tree trunk, wedging in a six-pack beneath it.

Shivers run all over me as I think about getting Luke all to myself.

Mom said I was allowed to have him up in my room, but I don't trust her not to spy, not to snoop. Plus, my room is so frilly with my Madonna posters and my flowery wallpaper, I'd honestly be embarrassed for him to see it. He'd think I was a teenybopper loser.

It's steaming today; I just got out of the shower, and my hair was still wet when I walked out here, but it's already dried, the sun blazing through the trees, mosquitoes nipping at my skin.

I look back at our house, our mansion, try to imagine it through Luke's eyes. Will he be impressed, like Mom thinks he will? The only reason she talked me into doing this bash was saying she thought it'd be smart to get Luke on our own turf, to let him see what we're all about. And the opportunity to see him again so soon—not at the swimming hole or at the Circles with those losers—was, well, I mean…

But now I'm all twisting myself into knots, thinking about his reaction. Will he just stick me in the rich-bitch category? Not that that seems to bother him as far as Blair is concerned. Will all this nauseate him? Or will he think it's cool? Like maybe Dad's toys—his four-wheeler, his golf cart, his rifle collection, his archery target, all just a few steps from where I am right now.

The house looks like it's dressed up for a wedding: the valets out front in black tuxes, red, white, and blue ribbons tied from our long white columns, the fountain out front bubbling with water. A giddy feeling comes over me—it kinda is like a wedding in a way: mine.

46

JACKSON

The setting sun streaks the sky, leaving fiery-orange claw marks across a navy-blue backdrop.

It's almost showtime.

Jackson stands in the squashy lawn of the Andersens' backyard, surveys, with pride, his handiwork.

He may, by trade, be a decorator, but in addition to bartending his way through college, he picked up the odd catering gig and can now party plan in his sleep.

With the champagne fountain frothing beside him, he dips a crystal glass under a stream, filling it with the pale-gold liquid. He allows himself a sip, the bubbles fizzing down his throat. Perfection.

Around the pool, lanterns pulse with light, continuing in a trail around the side of the house and along the redbrick path, illuminating the way for guests.

In the middle of the courtyard, the brass band from

Shreveport that Jackson found at the eleventh hour does a sound check, their horns catching the last dregs of sunlight.

For a long stretch, the folding tables are laden with barbecue: platters of cognac-colored ribs, the flesh shiny and glistening; mountains of creamy yellow potato salad; and trays of brisket, smoked to charred perfection.

On the desert table: blimp-sized watermelons sliced in half—some of them spiked with vodka—nudge against aluminum trays filled with buttery banana pudding.

And on every other surface, amber-colored bottles of beer nose out of tubs of ice.

Charleigh flits around—wired on coffee and now buzzing from the three glasses of champagne she's already downed (Jackson's counting)—looking resplendent in a red-and-white gingham top tied just below her breast line, flashing her toned abs, matched with a pair of stark-white shorts, feet tucked into a pair of six-inch peekaboo sandals.

Even Nellie looks radiant in a red halter top and cutoffs so short, the fringe barely tickles the tops of her thighs.

Jackson himself went for casual as well, a crisp white button-down with a pair of faded jeans and tan loafers, his black hair glossy with mousse. On his wrist sits his gold Rolex, one of the lone treasures of his late father's that his cruel mother finally bequeathed him.

It's 7:58.

The air fills with car doors slapping shut, the clamor of voices crawling along the path that winds to the backyard. The first of the guests have arrived: Charleigh's mousy friend, Kathleen, being steered along by her husband, Kyle David. Clumps of other familiar faces, men in white polos and khakis, and women in sundresses.

Jackson's heart hitches in his chest as he sees them: the Swifts. The top of Ethan's head sways over the other guests, his lush hair swept to one side.

Jackson lifts the flute to his lips, glugs down the rest. He steels himself to glimpse the rest of Ethan, to tug him away at some point tonight to tell him what he saw.

47

NELLIE

'm trapped in a conversation with Dustin's parents, Sherry and John, next to the pool.

I can feel Dustin's pouty stare from across the water. He's talking to some of the other boys—so thankfully I can avoid him for the moment—but it's as if Mrs. Reeves knows we had a fight; she's being clingy, her bony fingers, covered in chunky gold rings, planted on my shoulder.

"I just think this is such a *wonderful* party, Nellie, don't you!" She smiles at me like a crazy person, her lipsticked mouth like a clown's.

"It's fine," I sigh, forcing myself to smile.

It's sunset, that time of evening when light plays tricks on everything and it's hard to see clearly. But I know I saw the Swifts arrive a few minutes ago, the mom in some flowy white dress, the dad in a simple button-down and jeans, and Jane in some sort of plain tee and long skirt. As they first rounded the corner from the front of the house, I could also see Luke, lanky and tall and brooding.

But now, as I scan the party, I don't see him at all.

"Well, nice talking to ya," I say to Mrs. Reeves, twisting my shoulder out of her grip and walking away.

"Oh, Nellie, do come find me later, dear!" She's actually sweet, but no thanks, lady.

I also can't find Mom or Dad. But squinting up toward the house, I can see people in the back room—the den—moving in front of the floor-to-ceiling windows. I just can't make them out.

On my way up the hill, I swipe a beer from a bucket, pop the top off, Then pour it in a Solo cup. Not that Mom will be policing me tonight, but some of the parents might not like me drinking openly like this.

The dewy grass licks my almost-bare feet—I'm wearing sandals—because I'm on the move through the yard, taking the shortest path, walking as quickly as I can; that's definitely Luke inside my house, talking to Mom and Dad.

Great.

As I get closer, I can hear Mom's rough laugh escape through the open French doors.

"Hi!" I say, loudly announcing my presence, studying Luke's face. He actually looks happy, thank God. Not disgusted.

"Well, hey there, darlin'," Mom says, clearly already tipsy. "We were just taking Luke here on a tour of the house." Her blue eyes are swimming, and she fans her arms out dramatically, like Vanna White.

Dad slings an arm around Luke, beams at me. "Your friend Luke here and I are already fast buds." When he gives Luke a squeeze, I die a little inside.

How humiliating. *Buds*, really?

Jesus, Luke looks so hot in his ratty Echo and the Bunnymen T-shirt, which barely goes down to the top of his jeans.

"We've already made plans to go shooting together sometime." Dad gives Luke another squeeze.

I look at Luke, raising my eyebrows to ask, *Is that for real?* And to my great relief, a gorgeous smile takes over his face, and he nods, says, "Sounds so rad to me. I've never been shooting before. I wanna go all cowboy."

Dad laughs at this, a little too loudly, a nervous, eager-to-please laugh, but whatever. Luke seems to be enjoying himself.

Mom clears her throat. "Honey," she says, addressing Dad, "we should go check on the rest of our guests—"

Damn, she's good sometimes.

"Oh, sure!" Dad clumsily steps away from Luke—seems like he's had his fair share to drink, too—claps me on the back, then pecks my forehead like I'm a small child.

Alone in the big room with Luke, I want to drag him upstairs, throw him down on my bed. Peel all his clothes off. Mine, too.

"What are ya drinkin'?" he asks, his eyes hungry.

"Ah, sorry, a beer. Want some?" I pass it to him.

He downs it. "I need like ten more of those." I swear to God, his fucking perfect eyes are actually twinkling. I could faint.

"Well, I have a stash in the woods, just for us—"

He tilts his head. "Mmmm. Nice work!"

"Wanna go? I could also use a little..." I mimic the act of smoking a jay.

"I do, but I'm supposed to socialize a little. Mr. Swift's orders." He makes the sign of a salute, sarcasm dripping on his face. "So let's go bullshit with everyone, and in an hour, I'll meet you."

I'm totally disappointed that I can't have him all to myself right now, but I know I need to play it cool. I'm also excited, though, that he wants to sneak off with me, even if I have to wait.

He shakes his hair out of his face, drains the rest of my beer. "Sorry, I *really* did need that. So, where is this secret spot?" Again, his eyes do that twinkle thing, and my knees feel like they're gonna buckle.

I twist a lock of hair around my finger and smile at him shyly, trying to look as sexy as possible. It feels weird standing in my den with him instead of outdoors, in the dark at night, or in his Camaro. Like I'm exposed. "Okay, so we have this big-ass garage." I fling my hand in that direction. "On the side of the house."

"I know it; your dad took me out there, showed me the Ping-Pong table, his four-wheeler—"

"My dad *does* like his toys—"

"I think he's cool as shit, actually."

Every vein in my body tingles. "Really? He's kinda dopey—"

"But cool," he insists.

Whew. Maybe this was a good idea of Mom's after all.

"So you go to the garage, then walk about forty feet, and you'll see this, like, clump of trees. That's the spot."

"Well, see you there, Nellie Andersen." That same grin curls across his face, lighting me on fire.

"Deal." I turn and head out the French doors before I fuck this up.

48

CHARLEIGH

The air outside is sticky, sultry. As Charleigh wades through it, down the brick steps leading from the back of the house, veering around the brass band, she's already unsteady on her legs.

Why is she wearing six-inch sandals? A mistake.

And also, the three glasses of bubbly and the beer she's now nursing may prove to be a mistake. She needs food.

Charleigh weaves her way over to the picnic tables boasting sumptuous platters piled high with mouthwatering offerings. She's overcome with pride by the splendor of it all: her giant rolling backyard, now churning with tuxedoed waitstaff, the brass band perched on her brick patio, the champagne fountain sparkling with a teetering tower of crystal flutes. Who could ever have imagined this would be her life? That this would all be hers? There are at least seventy-five people here already, not too shabby for last-minute invites. No one in their right mind turns down a party at the Andersens', last second or not.

Spying Jackson across the lawn, she lifts her beer in a toast. He raises his glass of champagne, winks at her. What a darling he is.

And Luke. Luke showed no sign of being bothered by their awkward conversation the other day, thank *God*.

Charleigh made sure to stand out front with the valets until the Swifts arrived so she could intercept him. That woman, Abigail, still gives her the creeps, and as Charleigh and Alexander walked along the path leading from the front drive to the backyard with them, she taunted Charleigh with her greeting. "So *nice* of you, generous, even, to have us over. What made you change your mind about my hubby's customs?"

Bite your tongue, Charleigh thought, forcing herself to keep her eye on the hot young prize: Luke.

"Well, people can change their minds, right?" she said airily. It was the best she could do.

"They sure can, Charleigh," Ethan piped up, his eyes swimming over her body.

He's damn sexy, but while Charleigh might entertain thoughts of him in the buff, polishing some masterpiece of his in her living room, Alexander is the only one for her.

"We're *really* delighted y'all could make it," Alexander offered, looking like the lord of the house in his starched white button-down, tanned forearms jutting from his cuffed sleeves.

A girlish laugh bubbled out of Abigail. She actually looked

decent, for the first time ever, Charleigh thought, in a long white dress that actually looked store-bought. Her face was still devoid of makeup, but somehow, she was glowing, and she had a swipe of cherry-colored lipstick on her mouth. The dress hugged her in all the right places, especially around her ripe breasts.

Wench.

When they got around the house, Charleigh looped her elbow through Luke's, motioned for Alexander to join them. "Would you like a tour?"

"Umm...sure?" He phrased it as if it were a question.

Ethan shot a glance at him. Luke flipped his bangs out of his eyes, smiled. "I mean, yeah, I'd love it!"

Charleigh and Alexander took him on the *fun* tour. Just the downstairs. The posh living room, the giant kitchen, the butler's pantry. Then Alexander took him into the garage while Charleigh hung back. She didn't want to seem like *too* much of a show-off.

She nestled herself against the laundry room wall that leads to the garage, eavesdropped. Alexander seemed to really woo him, showing off all his fun shit, like the four-wheeler, his rifle cabinet, his camping paraphernalia.

Charleigh grinned to herself, gripped her champagne flute. Exhaled.

Now she grazes on a rib, careful not to stain her top, then spoons a clump of potato salad on her plastic plate.

She'd pounce on Luke at some point tonight, later, after the boy was good and liquored up.

49

JACKSON

The night air hangs on Jackson like a wet cloak. It's breezeless out. Good for fireworks, but bad for vanity and comfort.

He sips at his icy cold beer, mops his hairline with the back of his hand.

They aren't putting on a fireworks show, per se, but as soon as it's pitch-black out, they'll pass around the Black Cats to the kids, and the caterers will shoot off the Roman candles, etc.

The party's been in full swing for an hour now, the band playing, the guests feasting—mainly drinking—and Charleigh seems pleased.

Jackson would call this a success but for the fact that he can't seem to get a second alone with Ethan. The man has not stopped working the crowd, roaming from couple to couple, shaking hands, cracking jokes.

Jackson knows he's desperate for the business, and obviously he wasn't expecting to make out or anything, but damn, a little Ethan attention would help ease the roiling in his jittery stomach.

Instead, he drinks. This is his third beer, on top of that first glass of champagne. His peripheral vision is cloudy, and he can feel his inhibitions loosening, so he knows he needs to slow down, ease off the sauce. He just can't seem to stop himself.

When the Swifts first arrived, he made it a point to greet them. After all, he is the one who invited them here.

Abigail sprung herself on Jackson, surprising him by folding his body into a tight hug. "Thank you for inviting us!"

His face flushed; he awkwardly patted her back, then looked over her shoulder at Ethan, who shot him a smirk.

"Yes, thank you, Jackson," Ethan said, offering his hand to shake.

Jackson never wanted to let go, longed to pull Ethan behind the nearest tree, tug him into a lingering kiss. Instead, they made small talk in front of the rest of the guests, Jackson inhaling Ethan's godlike scent: wood, fir, sex.

Then Ethan was pulled away, almost by an unseen force, to the party.

Jackson now sinks to sit on a brick step, halfway up the rambling lawn, alone. Watches the partygoers below, a tangle of sweaty, intoxicated bodies boiling around the perimeter of the pool, the various stone patios, the gazebo.

Monica—hair starched to the heavens, silk blouse draped off a shoulder, tight shorts squeezing her buns—slinks an arm around Ethan's neck like she owns him. And just like the night at the Boat House, her husband, Chip, doesn't seem to notice, busy as he is flirting with the rest of the women at the party.

Monica's been trailing Ethan all night, Jackson's noticed, but now anger flares within him at this brazen display of affection.

Who the fuck does she think she is?

Because Ethan's making her husband a five-thousand-dollar desk, she thinks he's her property?

But Jackson knows what's really upsetting him is the fact that Ethan seems to be enjoying the attention, snaking his own arm around Monica's thin waist, grinning that roguish grin of his.

Jackson chugs the rest of his beer, sighs. Surely Ethan's just playing the game, he tells himself. He literally just told Jackson the other day that he needed to see him again, as soon as possible.

Jackson's gaze then alights on Abigail, whose head is tossed back in a full-throated laugh at something Alexander is saying to her. They're standing off to the side of the crowd, brazenly flirting.

Charleigh's too soused to notice; she's sitting at the lip of the pool, her toned calves submerged, margarita in one hand while she gestures with her other. She's holding court with Kathleen and Kyle, eyes animated, her throaty voice carrying over the din of drunks.

As soon as Ethan unlatches himself from Monica, Jackson will make his move, tell Ethan that he needs to have a word. Suggest to him that they go up to the house together under the guise of something. No one will care, and no one will notice, especially that hussy Abigail, who's still moon-eyed and preening in front of Charleigh's husband.

Charleigh, meanwhile, must be so satisfied with how the night is going—Jackson has noticed Luke circulating through the crowd like Ethan, charming, happy—that she's failed to notice her man all but drinking Abigail in with his eyes.

Fuck.

He's gonna have to tell her soon. Real soon. But first, he's *got* to tell Ethan.

50

NELLIE

stagger over to a lantern, study my Swatch in the light. Exactly fifty-five minutes have passed since I stood in the bright den with Luke. Time to go meet him in the woods.

I've watched him, from a distance, for the past hour. How he smoothly makes his way through the crowd, cheeks dimpled as he smiles.

I wonder, though, what the guests *really* think of him, with his chain wallet, tattoos.

Blair, of course, has been trailing him like a puppy, and for a while, he stood there talking to her and her nauseating mother. Monica seemed to like him, tossing her phony-ass head back as she laughed, her aqua eyes on him like a target. She must know Blair has a crush—or, she might even know that they are dating, *if* that's who he's really seeing—because Monica Chambers is not just nice to anybody.

Fury boiled inside me watching them together, the way Blair

flipped her hair over her shoulder, the way her neon cutoff tee almost crept up to her tits when she stretched her arms over her head. Her fucking laugh is so loud and hideous; she sounds like a little girl on drugs. Or a helium balloon that someone's stretching the mouth of, letting the air out.

But I watched Luke, too, and he seemed to keep a good space between them. Like, he so could've put his arm around her, leaned in more, *something*, but he kept his hands jammed into his jeans, his arms stick straight by his side.

And he's about to come meet me. Just the two of us.

He must already be headed up because I haven't seen him in a sec; he slipped off when I was busy dumping another bottle of beer into my Solo cup.

I take a sip, start heading up the hill. I'm kind of walking zigzag. I'm not *wasted*, but I'm definitely buzzed and feeling so happy that I actually wave at the band Jackson hired to play for us. *So* not me.

I need to pee because I've had too much to drink, so I hop inside real quick, use the bathroom off the kitchen. Then I check myself in the mirror, wipe off the black liner that's smudged underneath my eyes, fluff out my hair. I like what I see staring back at me, my cleavage all out there just for Luke.

I step into the kitchen and am about to head toward the back door when I hear something. Almost like a grunting. Coming from the garage.

I decide to go that way instead, check it out; I don't want anyone wandering up on me and Luke. Spying on us.

I open the door and walk into the garage. It's completely dark except for the moonlight that comes in through the windows.

The area is huge—it's big enough to hold four cars with a divider in the middle.

The sound gets louder. Definitely grunting.

Whoever is making the noise is on the other side of the divider.

I creep over there, as soft as I can, not daring to breathe.

I reach up and grab the wall before peering around it.

Then I lurch and gasp, immediately slapping my hand to my mouth to stop the scream.

On the Ping-Pong table, Mrs. Swift is bent over, her dress riding up all the way on her hips.

And behind her is Dad.

The room spins. I stumble backward, nearly tripping in my Keds.

What in the actual fuck is happening?

Well, I know what is happening, can see it with my own two eyes: Dad is giving it to Mrs. Swift from behind, his khaki shorts hanging on his ankles, his pale bare ass shining in the moonlight as he bangs Jane's mom.

I feel sick, like I want to retch. And angry tears are burning in my eyes. My throat burns. I'm positive that if I open my mouth, fire will come out.

Mrs. Swift's giant tits are out of the top of her dress, flopped onto the table, and Dad keeps moving his hands over them while grunting.

I want to march over there, pull him off her, slap him, strangle her, and shout, *This is my dad, you fucking whore.* I want to pound his face with punches until he cries. I can't believe he's doing this to Mom. To me. What a nasty pig.

I want to punish Jane with this, grab her out of the crowd and drag her up here so she can see and be as horrified as I am. But I can't. I can't let this get out.

I can't stand this nastiness one second longer. I'm about to leave when Mrs. Swift moans and twists her head. Her eyes are closed, but now her face is pointing in my direction.

I could kill her right now.

I need to get out of here.

I'm about to turn away when she opens her eyes, spots me.

I shoot her the dirtiest look I can manage, pray that she can't see the tears shimmering in my eyes. I'm expecting a look of shock or horror—or even apology.

Instead, her expression freezes for a second, and then the evilest smile I have ever seen creeps across her face.

Like she's telling me she's on top, she's won this.

I snap my head away and bolt from the room.

51

JACKSON

Jackson's not a smoker, but he's having a cig now, with the valet crew.

He stepped around front to take care of the guys, pay them before the night is over, before the mad dash of inebriated partygoers descending to collect their vehicles.

He smokes for the camaraderie and to cool his nerves. He still hasn't gotten a second with Ethan. He made an awkward attempt a few minutes ago to wedge himself between Ethan and Kyle, but Ethan shot him a look that said, *How can I possibly escape right now?*

So Jackson bowed out, let it go. But the more he imbibes, the more desperate he's feeling to blurt their nasty secret out.

He's also been watching Alexander like a hawk. Alexander, who is positively beaming tonight.

Jackson exhales, following the stream of smoke with his gaze, then stubbing the cigarette out on the drive.

He's anxious to get back to Ethan, or at least to watching Ethan, but he wants to slip inside first, freshen up. Wash the smell of smoke from his hands. Maybe gargle if he can find mouthwash.

He's headed to the side door by the garage, the one that leads to the kitchen, when he sees Nellie storming out, her face slick with tears.

What the hell?

"Nellie!" he calls out after her. She's streaking toward the woods.

She freezes, turns around. Wipes her tears away with the backs of her hands. He can see that her body is still quaking.

Boy trouble?

He strides quickly over, filled with the urge to reach out, hug her.

But he knows she's feral on a good day, a wild animal that would flinch at such behavior. No, he must tread lightly.

"Hey," he says softly.

At least he's gotten her to stop.

Her face is pale, sickly, and haunted, as if she's seen a ghost.

Even though Nellie is a nightmare, he still feels that protective impulse over her, and, filled with booze, he'd love to land a punch on Luke, Dustin, whoever has broken her heart.

"What?" she says, tossing her hands up around her face, her nails painted a glossy black. "What do you want?"

"Nellie." He takes another step forward. She doesn't budge. "I know we're not exactly *close*, but you know you can tell me anything." Jackson wishes that *he* had someone to talk to right now about all that's swirling around in his brain. But instead of Nellie feeling the same, she has the opposite reaction.

"You're right," she says, a scowl mauling her face, "we *aren't* close."

She spins on her Keds, then bolts toward the woods.

52

NELLIE

As soon as I turn away from Jackson, get out of his sight, tears start rushing again, soaking my cheeks.

Dammit. I hate crying more than anything. It's pathetic. I've never been a crybaby.

But I feel lost, spun around, like someone sucker punched me.

I can't believe I just saw what I saw.

Dad. What the fuck.

I can't believe he'd do that. Mom and Dad are always so gross—they kiss in front of me, they're always holding hands, they're embarrassing in public with this shit—so I never thought I'd have to worry about *this* kind of thing. It makes me sick.

That was actually nice of Jackson to try and find out what was wrong with me, but bless his little heart, the only person I want to talk to right now is Luke.

As I head toward the woods, my mind spins. Do I tell him

what I just saw? Will he be able to keep his mouth shut? I can't believe she smiled at me like that.

Part of me wants to keep it a secret for now, see how I can use it. I mean, she *knows* I know, so I could, like, bring their whole goddamn family down with this. Jane included. Ruin her daddy's little business. Her mama's, too.

But that might mean hurting Luke. Which is the last thing I wanna do.

I know he got thrown in juvie, hasn't graduated high school yet, and that studying with Mr. Swift could give him a real shot at a trade. So I'm kinda squeamish about blaring this out just yet.

I don't know what the fuck to do.

All I want to think about right now is seeing him, getting obliterated with him, getting down with him on the blanket I stashed, and making out. Hopefully more.

I dry my face, readjust my bra, *breathe*.

Bullfrogs croak all around me—we have a little creek that trickles through the back of the woods where they live—and my heartbeat bangs in my ears.

But on top of these sounds, as I get closer to the spot, I hear laughter.

Specifically fucking Blair's giggles.

What the actual fuck?

"No, *you* stop it—" I hear her saying playfully, all flirty. Followed by more of her hideous squeals of laughter. "Hey! That tickles!"

"Luke!" I holler before I can stop myself. My voice sounds

like a needy screech in my ears, but I can't help it. I'm desperate to see him, not *her*. And what the fuck are they doing in *our* meeting place together?

"Oh, God!" Blair howls. "It's *Nellie*. Good God. Is she, like, your stalker or something?"

New tears threaten to spring, but my rage overtakes the urge to cry. My fists are balled as I continue marching toward them, my breath jagged.

When I'm just about there, Blair stumbles out from behind the clump of trees, her hair sticking up and her T-shirt now turned inside out.

I feel sick all over again.

Luke walks out slowly, stands next to her. Waves at me with a clove cigarette in his hand. "Hey. We were just hangin' out. But there's still some beer left—"

"Ha—" I huff. It rushes out before I can stop it. God damn it, I sound so ridiculous; I hate it. "I'm good. You two enjoy—"

"Hey, sorry, it's not like—" Luke is walking toward me now, but my eyes are dripping again, my nose starting to leak.

I'm a mess, and I don't want him to see, so I put my hands out, wave him off. "Later."

"She's *such* a drama queen." Blair's voice whips my backside.

"I think we should go back to the party now," I hear Luke say in a serious voice before I pound down the hill toward the champagne fountain, which I intend to drink buckets from.

53

CHARLEIGH

Where is Alexander? Charleigh wonders. It's almost time to light the firecrackers, and the man is nowhere to be seen.

He's probably inside, taking a piss, which Charleigh needs to do as well, so she pushes herself up to standing. Her legs are wobbly. How much has she had to drink? She will hate herself tomorrow. She breaks apart from the crowd that's knotted together around the pool.

She feels herself smile.

This has been a huge success, and the night is still young.

That hot little Luke has been the life of the party; she watched as Nellie watched him, enraptured, in love. And she herself feels better about Nellie being with him. Not that she ever felt bad about it, scratching her way out of nothing as she did when she was Luke's age; everyone knows she's not judgy like that.

But still. Good to see the boy can be charming, even effusive.

And where is he now? Come to think of it, where is Nellie? Hope springs through her chest as she imagines them upstairs in Nellie's bedroom, entangled on top of her comforter.

But she's almost to the back patio when her daughter comes charging past her, face streaked with tears.

"Baby! What's wrong?" Charleigh slurs at her.

"Nothing, Mother," Nellie growls, her fists tightly balled by her sides.

Charleigh rushes over, tries to put her arms around her.

Nellie swats them away. "Not now." She darts off down the hill.

But it's *not* nothing; Charleigh can see them: Blair and Luke walking together, touching, coming out of the woods like a single entity. Blair's hair is a rat's nest, her shirt inside out. She's laughing, leaning even more heavily into Luke.

That little fucking shit. I will destroy her.

54

JANE

My voice is hoarse from all the talking. I'm so *sick* of this party, so ready to blow this pop stand.

Luke and I put on quite the show—I honestly didn't think he had it in him, he's such an anarchist—but he played the part well. Too well. My stomach hurts thinking about it.

A little while ago, Pa came over to us and clapped us both on our backs, his eyes dancing. "Well done, you two. Well done!"

Ugh.

I scan the drunken faces for Luke. I haven't seen him in a sec.

I need to find him, beg him to take me home. We rode in the Camaro, Pa and Mom following us in the truck.

I haven't seen Mom lately either, come to think of it. And Nellie's dad is nowhere in sight.

I see Nellie, though, near the champagne fountain, chugging. After downing a full glass, she wipes her mouth with the back of her hand, stomps over to the bar. She snatches a whole bottle of tequila, screws the top open. Seems to swallow it whole before staggering off to the woods.

I actually feel like going with her.

That's when I see them.

Luke and Blair, coming down the hill together.

Everyone sees them. They're a spectacle.

Blair's making sure of that with her loud cackle, her nauseating squealing. The way she walks, knocking into Luke's shoulder, like they're a couple. Which it *totally* looks like they are right now.

He knows I was sensitive about this the other day after the swimming hole, so how dare he? What where they doing in the woods together?

As they get closer, I see that Blair's T-shirt is now inside out.

I'm so angry I could scream, but I just stand here, watching them.

Fuming.

Calculating.

Planning my move.

55

JACKSON

Rattled from his run-in with Nellie, Jackson notes his palms are slick against the knob of the side door.

He cracks it open, heads toward the guest bath.

As he's about to enter, he sees the backside of Abigail, her white dress wrinkled like a wadded-up napkin, slipping out the French doors to the back courtyard.

Hmmm.

He approaches the bathroom, and as he does, he hears water splashing, a man whistling.

Alexander.

Seething, Jackson clenches his jaw.

He's not waiting any longer, he's going to pry Ethan away from the fray, tell him.

Alexander shuffles from the bathroom. "Yo!" he says to Jackson, clearly startled. Alexander's face turns a shade of crimson. "Didn't know you were out here!"

"Your *friend*," Jackson says, simply because he has too much booze surfing through his veins, "just left." He hitches his chin toward the patio door.

"I don't know what, or who, you're talking about. I just came in to take a leak—"

Maybe that's true, Jackson thinks. *Maybe Abigail came in and used the other guest bath underneath the staircase. Maybe I should shut my trap.*

But then, he knows that's not true. He's positive, sure as he's standing here, that Alexander and Abigail just had a quickie in the pantry, in the bathroom, up against the wall.

"Nothing," he mutters to Alexander, pushing past him to enter the restroom.

Alexander claps him on the shoulder as he exits. "Good party, man, thank you." Another clap, that says, *Hey, we're good; all is good between us, right?*

Finally alone, Jackson shuts the door, studies his reflection. Even with the damp night, every hair is still in place. *Thank you, hair mousse.* He doesn't find any mouthwash, but he gargles with water, splashes some on his face. Scrubs his hands with the vanilla-scented pump soap at the sink.

The party could go on all night, but Jackson can't be sure of how much longer the Swifts will stay—they do have a baby at home—so it's now or never.

He steps out the French doors. People are drunk enough that they're now dancing to the band, the trumpet squeaking, the snare drum popping, hips swaying.

Ethan stands by the champagne fountain, chatting with Sherry Reeves, Nellie's boyfriend's mom.

Perfect. He'll be happy to have Jackson rescue him from her clutches.

Jackson dips a glass under the stream of bubbly, then takes a long sip before approaching Ethan. Whose skin gleams in the fluorescent light of the fountain, who has grown even more handsome the drunker he gets. His smile is looser, wickeder, that magnificent body honey glazed with sweat.

Jackson sidles up next to him. "Hey! Can we chat a sec?"

Mrs. Reeves arches her eyebrows at the intrusion.

"Sorry to butt in, Sherry; it's business!" Jackson bats his lashes at her, takes her hand, squeezes it.

She crumples under the attention. "Oh, no bother! I will catch this *darling* man later." She winks at Ethan. Honest to God, *everyone* is under his spell.

They step a few feet away from the crowd.

"What's up?" Ethan asks nonchalantly. Coolly, even.

Jackson's chest tightens. "Well, first, heeey," he says, going for the flirt.

This seems to snap Ethan back to reality, back to the fact that just one week ago, they were going at it on his dock. "Heeey. Sorry we haven't had the chance to hang out more tonight. It's just—" He lifts his hands, gestures to the crowd gesticulating on the makeshift dance floor. "It's been *so* great. Made lots of connections. I think even the Andersens are actually gonna have me—"

"Yeah, about that," Jackson says, stepping closer, lowering his voice. "Let's go somewhere where we can talk. In private."

They walk alongside each other, Jackson steering him away from the crowd, toward the woods. He's leading him to the far side of the property, to the very back—opposite the rear of the house—where a rust-colored creek meanders. Far away from the front, where the valets are gathered, far away from the spot where Nellie staggered out, tear-soaked, and far away from the back, where the babble of the party is starting to fade in Jackson's ears, the deeper they make it into the woods.

All around them, a choir of bullfrogs croaks, their throaty song encircling until it feels like they're in hell and gone from civilization.

"This far enough?" Ethan pants, winded.

"Yes."

Before he drops the bomb, Jackson would like a kiss. He leans in, slips his hand through Ethan's. Tugs him toward him, his mouth on Ethan's in an instant.

Ethan kisses him back, but it's without the same fervor of the other night. His lips are almost still, his tongue timid.

"What's wrong?" Jackson asks.

"Nothing, just—I don't want us to get caught, okay? Like, I've met *so* many people here tonight, and well, we both know—"

Ethan's preoccupation with making connections is starting to gross Jackson out. But he wants to play it smooth.

"No, I get it. You're right, sorry," he says, tongue stumbling in his mouth.

"I mean, we can certainly get together soon, though, like…" Ethan brushes Jackson's lips with his thumb, sending lust surging through his bloodstream. "Like we did the other night. Out at my place—"

"Yeah," Jackson says breathily. "I'd like that. That's actually what I wanted to talk to you about."

"Whaddya mean?" Ethan asks, his breath on Jackson's neck, a hungry thing.

"Well, the other day, when I was out at your place with Charleigh, and you said you wanted to see me again, and soon, so I tried calling. But got your wife. And—" He's not sure now if he wants to continue.

"And what?"

"Well, later that night, I came on out. Thought I might catch you at the pond. Saw your truck, but—"

"But what?"

"Well, I hiked up to the pond. And at first, I thought I'd walked up on you and your wife, well, y-you know—" Jackson stammers, his words on the spin cycle now. "I saw *her*, on top of someone. On the dock. I thought, at first, like I said, that it was you, but—"

Ethan winces, his delectable features darkening.

He knows damn well he wasn't on the dock having sex with his wife, is obviously waiting for the gut punch.

"And I walked a little closer, and that's when I saw it wasn't you."

Ethan drags a hand through his silken hair, clutches at the ends. "What the hell are you saying, man?" His tone is as angry as a startled red hornet.

Jackson's stomach sours. He was so not expecting this reaction. He takes in a breath, recovers. Continues. "She was on top of—and having sex with—another man. Alexander Andersen, to be exact."

"That son of a bitch!" Ethan nearly yells, his amber eyes savage, searching. He bites the back of his hand, apparently deep in thought. "You certain about this? Like a hundred percent sure?"

Jackson gulps. Takes the gun off safety, goes in for the kill. "Yes. Absolutely, no doubt."

As Ethan reels, so does Jackson. The man had all but told him that his marriage is a husk, a shell. Loveless. And Jackson remembers how frantic Ethan was the other night with him, shedding clothes, lips all over each other. So he's slightly dumbfounded by the way Ethan is acting, like he gives a shit about his marriage.

"I'm sorry to be the bearer of bad news." The words trickle out of him because he can't stand this silence, pregnant with fury, for one second longer. "But I thought, ya know," he says, grinning. He doesn't mean to, but it just happens as he slips into his daydream of their future together. "I thought this might mean—" He gropes for Ethan, who slaps his hand away.

Jackson flinches. Inside and out. He feels like his heart has been speared. *What the fuck is going on?*

"Hey," he says, calmly as possible, "I thought—"

"You thought *what?*" Ethan spits at him. "That I wanted my marriage to end? That what happened between us was anything other than being fuck buddies?"

Tears prick Jackson's eyes. But he shakes his head, whisking them away. "Yeah, well, I thought you really liked me. I thought your marriage was, like, on ice. I thought we could be together, like really—"

"Well, you thought *wrong.*" Ethan's eyes surf with rage now. Blind, visceral rage.

But Jackson still can't accept this. He *knows* how it felt being with Ethan. How in sync they were, how hungry their bodies were for each other. Not to mention how much they have in common with their paths, their interests. No, Ethan is just being a coward.

"Look, I get it. It's scary to be out. I was scared even in a big city like Dallas, and I'm not even saying—or suggesting—that we *be* out, but I know you have feelings for me, Ethan. I know what I feel with you is real. And you can't deny it."

The moon sifts through the trees, spangling Ethan's face with strained light. His jaw muscles tense, untense, as if he's working over a problem in his brain. Well, of course he is.

Jackson's breath is suspended in his throat as he awaits Ethan's response. He still has the urge to lean into him, to kiss him again. But he suppresses it. Waits.

When he finally speaks, Ethan's voice is like a circular saw in Jackson's ear. Loud. Erratic. Biting through wood. "If you ever tell anybody, and I mean *anyone*, what happened between us, I will *kill* you." Spit dangles from Ethan's lips, and his index finger shakes as he waves it in Jackson's face.

Jackson feels like Ethan just sawed him open. Disemboweled his guts. Ripped out his heart. "But—"

Just uttering that one word prompts Ethan to put both his palms up, to shove Jackson with such force that he falls backward into the creek.

"What the fuck, man? You didn't have to—" His lower back seizes with pain, but other than that, he's fine. Except for his mangled feelings, that is. Oh, and he's now soaking wet.

"You tell a soul," Ethan warns, now swaying over him, "and you're dead meat."

Later

can't take my eyes off the body. And yet I can't turn away.

But I have to.

I have to figure this out, clean this mess up.

If it doesn't sink, if I can't *get* it to sink, then as soon as the sun comes up, someone will see it.

I need help.

Like right fucking now.

I stagger through the gravel parking lot, almost twisting my ankle in the process. I'm limping a bit, heading through the gravel to go find the only person I can trust to help me get out of this nightmare.

Fuck. Fuck. Fuck.

PART 3

56

JANE

Now

Can I have the keys to the truck?" I ask Pa. Sweat's pouring off me; I wipe my face with the hem of my shirt.

I've been working up at the ridge all morning, picking blackberries off the vines. I could've taken the day off, but I've been trying my best to avoid everyone.

Especially Luke.

"Why? Where you goin?" Pa asks. His shirt is wrinkled, his hair's a mess, and he looks even more hungover than I do.

"Swimming hole. I'd take Cookie, but Julia must've—"

"Yep. She left a while ago. Said she was going on a ride, stopping at the general store."

I sigh. I hate it when Julia takes Cookie. Cookie's mine, and Julia doesn't even like horses that much. She's just doing it to get back at me for getting to go out last night. Oh, well, at least it means she won't be at the river, spying on me.

"Couldn't you just ride with Luke?"

Another sigh huffs out of me. "I *could*, but…we had a fight."

Pa raises an eyebrow. "Anything serious? Anything I need to know about?"

"No, it's fine. But I just don't wanna hang out with him today, ya know?"

"Oh, I know. Believe me," he grumbles, and I wonder what the hell he's talking about.

He digs the keys out of his pocket, slaps them in my hand, then squeezes my shoulder while pecking me on my head. "Have fun, Sunshine."

"Will do! Later!"

I scurry out the front door before Mom rears her ugly, miserable head.

As I'm walking down the steps, I see him leaning against his Camaro. His hands are burrowed in his pockets; his face looks sheepish.

Luke still feels bad.

Good.

He's got his swimming trunks on, towel dangling from his neck, and he points to the car, his way of asking if I'd like a ride.

I want to forgive him. I want to go over and hug him, climb in the car, forget our spat, but I have to make him suffer a little longer. I don't totally trust him. Not just yet.

I shake my head, holding up Pa's car key as if it's a trophy.

Last night, soon after he and Blair stumbled out of the woods, *together*, we left. It's like the whole mood shifted right then and there. Pa rounded us up, his face serious all of a sudden, and angrily told us it was time to leave.

Had he happened to notice that Mom and Nellie's dad had been missing from the party for a little while, at the same time?

"Let's go! We need to get on home. Molly's gonna wake us all up at dawn."

I didn't argue. I was seething, ready to go, teeth gritting every time I glanced over and saw Luke.

I wouldn't even speak to him until we were nearly home, when he raced off the highway onto our blacktop.

"You can't just shut me out, Jane. I said I was sorry. I know it looked bad, but nothing happened between me and Blair—"

"Fuck you," I growled. I'd never spoken like that to him, but I was humiliated and seriously upset. And very drunk.

He took a huge drag off his clove, flicked it out the window. "I don't know what I can say to convince you—"

"Her fucking shirt was turned inside out—" I screeched.

"She must've done that right before she got to me. I swear, I didn't touch her. She did try to touch *me*. Went to kiss me. I just laughed it off, tried to play cool—"

"Why were you even up there?"

I twisted in my seat, my eyes searing into him. At my question, he gulped.

"Nellie wanted me to meet here there, okay? We were gonna, like, get high together."

"And how do you think that makes me *feel*?"

"Seriously? We were just gonna get stoned. Nothing else."

"But that's not how Nellie sees it, and you know it."

He raked a hand through his moppy hair. "I was only doing what your Pa put me up to, working the room, trying to get in good with the Andersens. So, when she asked me, I thought it'd be no big deal. Plus, I was jonesing. You think I liked doing all that shit?"

"Well, don't do it, then! You don't have to do everything Pa says. He's not your master."

"Easy for you to say, Sunshine."

"Go to hell," I said nearly under my breath, even though I knew he was right. I don't have to do everything Pa says, and for now, Luke kinda does. "I'm sick of your flirting."

He placed his hand on my thigh, and I batted it away.

It burned me up that he was prancing around with Blair, going to meet Nellie.

We thundered over the cattle guard, and I sulked in silence as his Camaro poked its way through the pasture.

57

JACKSON

Jackson's compact Mercedes rattles as he flies down the interstate, barreling toward Dallas.

He had to get the hell out of Dodge.

He's a wreck, barely slept. Every time he woke and shot up in his bed, he relived the whole wretched scene with Ethan, and each time, he felt his stomach quake, felt like he was gonna hurl.

It's the middle of the work week, but his clients can wait. *Charleigh* can wait. He called her before he left—just so that someone would know where he's going—and was relieved when she didn't pick up.

She'd be able to read his voice, tell that something's off, *way* off, and he's not yet ready for all that yet. He's still digesting it. Which is the biggest reason he's heading to Dallas.

"Hey, so I'm going away for a few days, to Dallas, to unwind," he said vaguely into her answering machine, "but if you need me, I'm staying at the Galleria."

He splurged on a fancy room, but hell, Charleigh had paid him five grand in cash for throwing the party together at the last minute—and it *was a giant headache to do so*—so he deserves this. Along with a spa treatment and a fine meal at the fancy Italian place there.

Fuck it, bring on the carbs. He's about to blow his whole diet, his whole fitness routine.

Why did he ever think he was good enough for a looker like Ethan? Not that Jackson's *not*, but he's no Ethan; Ethan is godlike.

He should've heeded Ginny's warning: *Anyone who brings a Bible into a bar and who looks like that… Watch out.*

Why did he ever think that a Bible-toting man whose wife looks like she's from the 1800s would actually ever be comfortable being gay? Pursuing anything with Jackson other than a drunken tryst?

But screw that, Jackson knows what he felt was real.

And not just on the physical level. He and Ethan have a very flirty rapport that goes beyond looks or attraction: They speak the same language about design, about craftsmanship. And no way is Jackson the first man Ethan's been with.

He knows Ethan's gay, or at the very least bi. And he also knows that their marriage is a farce. Maybe it hasn't always been—they do have children together—but Abigail is banging Alexander, and Ethan is hooking up with Jackson. Not exactly a storybook romance or family values.

So, what gives?

He still can't believe Ethan's explosive reaction, his threat to kill Jackson if he told a soul. Ethan's just lucky he hadn't blabbed it yet to Charleigh. But, seriously, he hadn't seen that blow coming at all. That cruel, ugly, hateful threat: *You tell anyone, and you're dead meat.*

So, yeah, he's going to Dallas to get out of that bonkers town for a minute, lick his wounds. But also, he's on a mission. He's going to snoop. Sniff around about Ethan.

He mentioned that he lived in Greenville. Jackson's certain Ethan must've hit some of the gay bars there.

And he intends to find out.

It's not that he still wants to be with him, not after that rage he flew into last night; it's more to help process it. To confirm that what he had with Ethan was real. That there are other men he's been with. And if so, how did he end things with them?

58

JANE

When I pull into the dirt parking lot, Luke's Camaro is already there.

I see him on the grassy banks, to the left of the old boathouse, talking to Nellie.

Sigh.

I jerk the gearshift into park, swing open the door, bolt from the truck.

I'm still officially ignoring him, so I head down the hill in the direction of the dock, on the other side of the boathouse.

I'm wearing my skimpiest bikini, the most revealing one I own. I bought it in secret at a thrift shop in West End in Dallas. On the way out here, I pulled over on the side of the road, changed into it.

It's crocheted; you can practically see my nipples through it. Which is the whole point.

I fly down the hill, hair waving behind me, feeling sexy, powerful.

I've got my shades on, so it's easy to ignore Blair's wave, pretend I didn't see it.

Instead of going over to her, I shimmy over to Tommy, who's all but gawking at me. He's such an easy target. He's standing on the dock with everyone else, including Blair, and I rush over to him, throw my arms around his neck, purr in his ear: "Heeey." I press my chest against his.

When I feel him get hard in his swim trunks, a smile tugs the corners of my mouth up. Victory.

"Well, hey, Jane," he says, his words all awkward in his mouth.

I can feel Blair's eyes on me, needling into my back. Still dangling from Tommy's neck, I twist around, and sure enough, Luke, who definitely just heard me, is walking over to us, jaw squared. Blair's got a hand planted on her hip, eyes narrowed.

Good. Serves them both.

Again, Blair doesn't actually know that Luke and I are a thing—we've been so undercover—so it's not even rational that I'm mad at her—but fuck it, I am. I hate her right now, hate the sight of her. Hate her rich-girl prissiness, hate the way she flings herself at him every chance she gets.

So I decide to dig the knife in deeper.

I dive off the dock into the chilly water, which burns my skin; it's so cold after being out in the heat. I paddle out a little ways, call out, "Hey, Tommy, can you bring me a beer?"

I'm treading—where I've swum out to, it's too deep to

stand—and as I'm waiting, I eye the old metal boathouse, watch as the wake from a speedboat that just passed slaps the bottom of it.

I swim back toward the dock, rest my arms on the baking wood, watch as Tommy scrambles to fish two beers out of the cooler, grinning like a loon as he does so. He lowers himself down the ladder, passes me my beer.

"Cheers?" He grins at me expectantly, like I'm gonna kiss him or something. I have half a mind to, and I'm sure he'd appreciate it, especially after Blair's performance at the party last night, but I have no desire to kiss Tommy. I'm just acting. But I do move toward him, so close that our arms on the deck are touching, close enough so that I can feel his hot breath on my neck.

I need to show Luke how it feels to be put in this position. So he'll stop doing it. And Blair.

I love Luke so fiercely, and I'm clinging to the dream of us in New York City together. Not about to let Blair, or anyone for that matter, get in our way.

She's now sitting cross-legged on the dock, smoking a joint. And maybe *pouting*? Behind my glasses, I squint at her, but the sun is so bright, it's hard, from this angle, to make out her expression.

In my periphery, I see—no, *feel*—Luke standing on the far corner of the dock by the boathouse, leaning against it. Now he's the one sulking. Again, good.

As if desperate to reclaim the spotlight, having been out of it for precisely five minutes, Blair springs to her feet. Walks over, begins climbing the ladder to the old tin boathouse. Giggling as she does. *Why is she always giggling?* She's always the first to dive in from the roof; I guess she waits for everyone to arrive before she does so, just so she can have her full audience.

Once she climbs the final step, she clambers on top of the roof, looks down to make sure everyone is watching.

We are.

She raises her arms above her, sways her hips, places her hands together.

Then she jumps off the roof, diving smoothly. It's a good twenty feet to the water, and I have to admit, it's a little too high for me. To jump off, it's fine, I've done that, but to dive, you need to have had real lessons, like rich-bitch Blair has all her spoiled-brat life. Not like me; I learned to tread water, keep my head above it, in swimming holes.

Before she hits the lake, a bloodcurdling scream ripples through the air.

I look over to find Blair diving directly into the tip of an old metal canoe that wasn't there seconds ago.

Her scream is immediately replaced by a booming *thunk*.

59

CHARLEIGH

ate-afternoon light streams through the kitchen window. Charleigh, sunburned—and yes, disgustingly hungover—stands there gazing out over her backyard.

She was just in the pool, trying to get rid of said hangover, but the sun is a torch, and the pool is warm as bathwater; the dip wasn't at all refreshing.

So she's slicing through a dozen lemons, intent on making a fresh batch of lemonade for herself and for when Alexander and Nellie get home.

Alexander from the shooting range, Nellie from the swimming hole.

The citrus fruits, pulled from the fridge, feel cool against her fingers. At least *that's* refreshing.

Whew, this headache, like a vise gripping her temples.

She'd love to have Jackson over right now, mix up some margaritas, a little hair of the dog, but after she toweled off from the pool, she trotted over to her answering machine, which was blinking at her.

He's in Dallas, or on his way there, staying at the Galleria for a bit.

Maybe she'll go surprise him in a day or two. Do some shopping.

Because she sure as shit doesn't want to be around *here*, around *Nellie*.

Her daughter's been moping about all morning, smoldering in her disappointment after seeing Blair together with Luke last night, but unable to be consoled, reasoned with. Every time Charleigh tried to open her mouth this morning, Nellie's responses were biting. Cruel.

She was even caustic with Alexander, and she *never* is.

"Wanna go to the shooting range with me?" he asked her at the breakfast table.

She scraped her chair back, stood to leave. "No, you go. By *yourself*."

Charleigh had no idea what Nellie meant by that, but she was relieved when she yelled at them from the front door, ten minutes later, that she was headed for the swimming hole.

She hopes that whatever happened last night is all smoothed over by the time Nellie gets back. She hopes Luke is out there, gives her plenty of attention. Or at least a little.

Charleigh is chopping up the last lemon when the back door bangs open, causing her to jump. She's not expecting either one of them home for another couple of hours, but when she twists around, Nellie is standing there, her hair damp from the river, water droplets pinging the Spanish tiles.

But that's not the only thing that's dripping onto the iced-tea-colored floor.

Nellie's face is contorted with tears; she holds her hands out in front of her. Charleigh races over to inspect what she's trying to show her, and as she gets closer, droplets of red mix with the river water on the floor. Her white tee is spackled with blood, her cuticles stained red.

"What happened to you?" Charleigh nearly shouts.

Surprising her mother, Nellie wraps her arms around her waist, gives her a hard squeeze. She's shaking. And sobbing.

"Oh, baby, what is it? What happened? Are you all right?"

More sobbing. Then, finally, she speaks. "There was an accident out at the swimming hole—Blair..."

"Blair did this to you?" Charleigh's voice flares like a lit match.

Nellie unlatches herself from her torso. "No, Mom, I'm fine. I'm not hurt at all. This is Blair's blood—"

Alarm bells begin ringing in Charleigh's ears; her throat constricts with dread. "What are you talking about? What happened? What happened to Blair?"

What she really wants to say, to scream is *What have you done now?*

60

NELLIE

lood. There was so much blood and that horrible smacking sound when Blair hit the tip of the canoe.

I was sitting on the shore, in the grass, chain-smoking, on the far side of the old boathouse when it happened. I wanted to be away from everyone else.

I got there first, like an hour before the others.

I couldn't stand to be at home one second longer, couldn't stand Mom's prying, her eyes smeared with black liner from the night before, drilling into me. The endless questions. Then Dad at the breakfast table. The sight of him disgusted me. I had to get the fuck out of there.

A little while before it happened, Luke pulled up, then came down and sat with me for a sec. I couldn't help it; I was still hurt, so I gave him the cold shoulder, would barely look at him.

Then, when Jane came down the hill, he gave up, walked away from me.

Next thing I knew, Blair was climbing the ladder, mounting the roof, ass shimmying before she dove.

And then her hideous scream and that god-awful sound that I can't stop hearing.

I didn't actually see it happen; I couldn't from where I was sitting, but I think the canoe drifted out from the boathouse just as she was diving, and she dove right into the metal tip.

The force of her diving must've pushed the canoe out because after her scream, that's what I saw: the canoe wading out into the middle of the river with Blair left behind to sink in the water.

And the blood.

So much blood clouding the water.

I immediately got up from the shore, dove in. I'm a serious swimmer, so I moved as fast and as hard as I could to get to her. Tommy was frozen but screaming for someone to run to the club and call 911.

By the time I reached Blair, others were behind me, then surrounding us.

She wasn't moving, and the blood was oozing out of her; we dragged her gently to the shore so she wouldn't drown.

We were all scared to move her. They say in the movies *not* to do that, and her chest was rising and falling, so she was at least breathing.

Next thing I knew, the ambulance was there, covering her in blankets, taking her vitals. Asking questions. That's how I heard that her head had cracked against the tip of the canoe, causing the gash that bled through their bandages.

Then the police arrived—I guess that's standard—and started asking us all more questions, scribbling our answers down in their notepads.

Tommy couldn't stop crying, and Luke looked he was going to be sick.

I couldn't read Jane's face. She still had those stupid sunglasses on, but since Blair's her best friend or whatever, I figure she's as freaked out as everyone.

Now I'm home, shaking, freezing cold because I'm still wet from the river, still have my suit on, and I'm standing under the blasting AC as mom drills with me with her interrogation.

Now she's racing around the room, tossing shit into her bag, snatching the keys off the counter.

"Where are you going?" I ask.

"To the *hospital*!"

"Want me to come—"

"No!" she snaps, which makes me flinch. "You need to just stay right here. Do not move!"

61

JANE

can't get her scream out of my mind.

And the sight of her being pulled to shore, blood leaking from her head. Her body motionless.

I was motionless, too. After hearing her scream, seeing her smack, headfirst, into the *tip* of the canoe, the boat jutting out from under her after she hit it—like a toy boat in a child's bath— while her body lolled into the river, blood spurting from the gash, my knees buckled. I felt like I was gonna be sick.

Like having a nightmare where you're chased but not able to run from the bad guy, I couldn't budge.

I looked back over to the boathouse, saw that the metal doors were cranked open just so. Enough room for the canoe to have made its way out.

And the ambulance, the cops, just everything, were all too much.

Tommy kept screaming, asking, "Is she gonna live?"

At least she was breathing.

But she wasn't moving.

Luke's face was so white, I thought for sure he would puke, but he kept it together. Drove us both home in his Camaro because no way I could drive Pa's truck with my hands quaking like they are.

And I know that, at any second, the phone is gonna ring with news. An update.

Please let her be alive, I quietly pray.

62

JACKSON

Jackson gorged himself on breadsticks and lasagna. His stomach is leaden; he needs a cup of coffee to help cut through all the starch.

After scraping his key in the lock, he opens the door to his hotel suite, finds the coffee maker.

As he's brewing a pot, he glances over, notices that the phone is blinking red.

Charleigh. Must be.

She can wait.

He pours himself a cup, tears open a package of creamer (it will have to do), and stirs until the liquid turns from ink to the color of sand.

Before he hit the Italian place for dinner, Jackson visited two gay bars he used to frequent back in the day. Asked the bartenders, the cocktail servers, *anyone*, if they'd heard of Ethan Swift.

No one had.

After nursing a Tom Collins at each, he left, feeling bummed.

Ethan Swift is an unusual name. It's not like Tom Johnson or Ryan Jones or something generic. It's as memorable as the man himself.

Yet Jackson can't fathom Ethan living this close to the gay bars while he was in Dallas and not sneaking out, visiting them.

Maybe he really is just a closet case, and, with a flush of pride—and okay, maybe it's not a flush of pride but the warmth from the wine at dinner, coupled with the hot coffee now—he thinks that maybe he *is* the only one who coaxed the real Ethan out. The thought of which also dashes him because that would mean they *did* indeed have a connection, or at least an attraction as electric as Jackson felt it was.

Sadness and shock spear his chest again, replaying the scene in his mind, the nasty, surprising way Ethan turned on him when he found out about his wife banging Alexander.

Again, a lump forms in Jackson's throat just thinking about having to tell *both* of these betrayals, these secrets to Charleigh. First, that he slept with the enemy—and worst of all, kept it from her—and secondly, and more horrifyingly, that her husband did, too.

The red light on the phone keeps blinking at him from across the room.

Piping-hot mug in hand, he plods over to it.

Presses it.

The front desk answers. "Mr. Ford?"

"Yes." Jackson sips at his coffee, stares out over Dallas.

"You have a message from a Charleigh Andersen. She said to call right away. That it was urgent."

Jackson sighs over his coffee. *Of course it's urgent. It's always urgent.*

"Thanks." He thuds the phone down into the receiver. He'll deal with Charleigh when he's ready.

63

CHARLEIGH

The tires on Charleigh's Jag mew as she screeches into the hospital parking lot.

Trembling, she twists the key, kills the ignition.

During the five-minute drive over here, she kept repeating, over and over in her head, *Please let this really be an accident. Please let Blair be okay.*

Still dressed in her swimsuit, she managed to at least throw on a cover-up, but she looks like a wreck, feels like one, too.

She shuffles into the ER, and the waiting room is clogged with people, faces she knows; everyone is there for Blair.

In the corner with Chip, Blair's father, she spies Kathleen, dressed demurely in a white tee and cotton shorts.

Charleigh looks down at her attire and feels naked, ashamed. But she knows that's not why shame is rushing over her skin right now. It's because of what all this might mean.

Fuck.

Kathleen looks up; Charleigh catches her eye, motions her over to the only corner that's not littered with folk.

"I came as soon as I heard. As soon as Nellie got home and told me—"

Tears brim in Kathleen's eyes. She shakes her head.

"Is she…?" Charleigh can't force herself to mutter the rest of the question out loud.

"She's still with us, thank God in heaven," Kathleen says, her voice trembling. "But it's *bad*."

Charleigh's throat turns to dust. "What *happened*? Nellie just said it was an accident, an awful one, and then I rushed out the door—"

"Apparently"—Kathleen's eyes whisk around the room as if she's about to tell something she's not supposed to—"Blair had just smoked some pot, and…she dove off the roof of the old boathouse. And the exact second she was about to hit the water, a loose canoe floated out, and she landed on that instead—"

"Oh, my God!" Charleigh sucks in a sharp, dramatic breath, covers her mouth with her hand in horror. Even though right now all she feels is relief. This *was* an accident. At least she thinks so. "That's *terrible*. What are the odds?"

"I know. Monica's in there with her right now. In the ICU. And," Kathleen adds, her voice wobbling again, "she's in a coma."

"A coma? God, that's awful! Poor Monica! I can't even imagine how she must be feeling!" Tears gush into Charleigh's eyes. Tears of empathy, of sadness, but also tears of relief. "Was there anybody by the canoe? How, I wonder, did it come undone?"

Kathleen's face screws up in confusion—mixed with a little suspicion. "Umm. I'm not sure? I think it's just one of those freak things—"

"Yeah, of course," Charleigh says quickly, hopefully covering her misstep. Thank God Kathleen's no genius.

"Her head injury is pretty severe, according to what the doctors told Chip."

Charleigh glances over at him and feels awful. His face is mottled red, his hands tunneled in the pockets of his golfing shorts.

"Do they think she'll make it?" Charleigh whispers.

"It's too soon to know. But they said there's hope. So we're all about to do a prayer chain."

That's Charleigh's cue to go.

At least she and Nellie are in the clear.

And obviously she will pray, in her own way, that Blair pulls through.

"I gotta get back home to Nellie. She was pretty shaken up over this." She leans in to hug Kathleen. "But call me the sec there's any update, okay?"

"I will." Kathleen rubs circles over Charleigh's back as if she's consoling a small child. Charleigh pries herself away, scurries out the door.

64

CHARLEIGH

Charleigh's entire body sags with relief when she pulls into her drive.

An unmoored canoe that drifted out, precisely at the wrong second. A freak accident. Nothing to do with her child, then.

She takes a moment to herself before opening the door. Exhales, regains composure.

Alexander's Wagoneer is still gone, and she's grateful. She's not in the mood to be peppered by questions from him, because she's certain he'll instantly have the same suspicions that she did about Nellie being involved. But she'll never admit that. The whole shock-and-denial game is too exhausting for her to deal with right now.

She needs to be a calm, solid, nurturing support for Nellie, who must still be so rattled.

She steps inside her grand foyer, sandaled heels clicking along the tiles, and cocks an ear up the staircase.

Running water. Nellie's in the shower.

Good, she can wash all that disturbing blood off her, distance herself from this completely.

Charleigh drifts into the kitchen, cracks open the fridge. Extracts an icy cold bottle of chardonnay. To mix a margarita right now seems too festive, so she's going for the more reserved choice.

She fills a glass to the lip, nearly slopping some on her wrist as she guides it down her throat, but God damn it, she *needs* every drop.

Poor Blair, and poor Monica.

She'll go back to the hospital later, after the church revival has died down. Clutching hands with other people and praying has always made her feel disoriented, claustrophobic. No, she'll support Monica quietly, privately, on her own. Maybe bring a nice bouquet of flowers.

She's halfway through her glass when she hears Nellie's footsteps on the stairs. The sound is discordant with the heavy mood; it almost sounds like she's skipping.

Nellie enters the kitchen in a robe, hair swathed on top of her head in a towel, skin pink from the shower. Her expression is neutral. "Well? How is she?"

"It's pretty serious. She's in a coma. I'm so sorry, honey." Charleigh sets her wineglass down, hops off the barstool, flutters over to Nellie. Reaches for her. But her daughter takes a step back.

"Just tell me the rest!" Nellie practically howls.

"So, the head injury she suffered is bad. Like I said, she's in a coma, but there is hope she'll pull through."

"Oh, thank God," Nellie sighs.

Again, Charleigh reaches out to hug her. This time she allows it, but her body is stiff as a mannequin's.

"I know you must be in shock, and I—" Charleigh's voice teeters; she's not a good counselor.

"I'm actually *starving*. I haven't had much all day. What've we got to eat around here?"

Charleigh hears herself nearly choke on her surprise. One of Nellie's oldest friends is lying in the hospital in a coma, and all she can think about is food? "Ummm…well, there's all that barbecue left over from the party—"

"Yuck, no—"

"Then there's some Hamburger Helper I could reheat?"

"Perfect." Nellie goes to the fridge, pulls out a beer.

"Hey—" Charleigh starts to protest. Stops herself. "Fine. I was only letting you drink the other day—"

"So you could get your way—"

"No, but—okay, whatever. But just the one."

Nellie pries the top off the bottle, downs half of it like a sailor.

As she watches her daughter, who's acting like everything is normal, unease crawls over Charleigh's skin; that same sense of foreboding she felt driving over to the hospital has returned. "You know you don't have to put on a face, play tough in front of me. Nellie, I know you and Blair had your differences, but—"

"Mom! Get off it! You know we're not even really friends, and she's been a cunt to me for years now. No, I don't want her to be hurt, and I truly hope she makes it out of the coma, *obviously*, but spare me the after-school-special bullshit, okay?"

Charleigh winces at Nellie's words. Surely she should still be upset. At least more than she's acting like. Just an hour ago, she was quaking in Charleigh's arms.

"I understand all that," she says through nearly clenched teeth, "but are you sure you're all right? I mean, what you witnessed was pretty traumatic, and you looked pretty, well, traumatized when you came home."

So why are you acting like a fucking psycho right now? Charleigh thinks, but doesn't say out loud.

Nellie rolls her eyes, unwraps the towel, letting her wet Medusa curls spiral down her face. "It's freaky, all right? I *am* freaked out by it. Fuck, Mom. I'm not a *monster*. But I kinda just want to push it out of my brain, you know?" She chugs the rest of her beer, clinks it down on the counter with a thud. "You gonna heat me up some dinner, or do I need to?"

Charleigh shrinks, spins around to the fridge, ducks inside. It *does* make sense for someone to want to try and push those images out of their mind. Nellie has a point. It makes rational sense. And sometimes, people disassociate when they have trauma. Lord knows she learned firsthand to do this living with her wretched parents. So that's all that's probably going on. But if it is, why does that sick feeling keep creeping over her?

As she slides the Tupperware of Hamburger Helper out, she

braves a question, not making eye contact as she asks it. "So, what all did you see?"

A sigh huffs out of Nellie. "Like, I didn't actually *see* the accident, okay? I was sitting on the shore, on the other side of the boathouse, kind of hanging away from everyone. Still pissed from last night."

For some reason, this makes Charleigh feel better. "Okay, good, honey, I'm so relieved you didn't actually have to witness it."

"I just saw the canoe drifting out, and Blair's body rolling off it, then all that blood." Nellie shivers. "So much blood, Mom." Her eyes look far away, distant.

Charleigh would go over and try to hug her again, but Nellie is actually opening up to her and she doesn't want to set her off. "Any idea how the dang thing got loose?"

At this, Nellie freezes; her face hardens, her eyes narrowed with suspicion. "No, Mom, why would *I* know anything about that?" Her tone is that of a violin string about to snap.

Hackles rise on the back of Charleigh's neck. Nellie sure got defensive in a hurry. "I'm just asking if you heard anyone talking about it. It's just such a freak thing—I don't know—" But Charleigh's voice peters out. She spoons some of the leftovers out onto a plate, then pops it into the microwave, keeping her back toward Nellie.

After a tense silence, Nellie finally responds: "No, nobody said anything really other than that it must've gotten loose somehow."

65

JANE

I t's nearly sunset, and we are all gathered on the dock. The air is heavy, dank; a gang of mosquitoes fogs over us, hovering.

We usually do Vespers on Sunday nights, but Pa called an emergency one so we could all pray.

Pray for Blair, who is now in a coma.

Thank God she's still alive, but her condition sounds serious. I feel sick to my stomach. One of the ladies called Mom a little while ago to fill her in. Mom asked her if we should come to the hospital, but she said the family wants to be alone for the evening.

We'll probably go tomorrow.

But right now, Pa is leading us all in prayer. "Dear Heavenly Father," he starts, his voice booming across the pond, "please lift Blair Chambers up in prayers. Lord hear our pleas. Place your loving, healing hands on this poor girl!" His voice shakes at the end, and tears roll down his face.

He looks—and sounds—drunk. His eyes red and glassy, skin clammy.

He continues with a Bible verse, and as he reads it, I look over at Julia, who is praying intensely, her eyelids fluttering, her lips moving without making a sound. Sometimes in revival tents, she'd stand up, start speaking in tongues—she can really lay it on thick, like she's doing right now—but I don't believe in all that bullshit, don't really believe Julia believes in it either.

Dad ends his prayer, opens his eyes, and starts in on a rambling sermon, slurring some of his words. First it's about healing, then about God's children, his eyes roving over our faces, his expression manic.

Oh, he's definitely drunk.

Mom is seated right next to him, sober as a nun, her face pinched with impatience. I'm sure she's ready for him to wrap this up; she's probably steaming in her long flowery dress, thinking about the pile of dishes she needs to wash in the sink.

She pats Pa on the wrist, a cue for him to call it a night.

He scowls at her. Then, his voice thundering, he shouts, "Oh, do I have a special verse to share with everyone!" He says this as if he's up on an actual pulpit, as if he has an actual congregation he's preaching to and not just me, baby Molly, Luke, Mom, and Julia.

"Listen to this one." His fingers nearly tear the tissue-thin pages as he prowls through it. "Proverbs 12:4." He stabs the page. "*A wife of noble character is her husband's crown, but a disgraceful wife is like decay in his bones.* That's a good one, isn't it, Abigail?"

He jabs her in the side with his elbow, laughs darkly.

Mom's face turns red; she just shakes her head.

"Shall I continue?" Pa asks, a sinister tone in his voice.

"That'll be enough, Ethan," Mom hisses at him. With that, she stands and pulls the skirt of her dress around her.

"Suit yourself!" he hoots at her as she stomps away.

Again, I wonder if he noticed she was missing with Nellie's dad at the party the other night.

Pa tosses his Bible aside, picks up his guitar. "I dunno, I could sing a gospel, but I wanna sing a happy song, a hopeful one, for… the poor girl." He's already forgotten her name.

As he strums, I recognize the opening notes to "Here Comes the Sun." I usually love it when Pa sings the Beatles—and I usually sing backup, harmonizing with him—but right now, I'm twitchy, overheated, and just want to be done with all this.

And I want some alone time with Luke. After what happened, I feel like a soda can that's been shaken up. I ache, right now, to be in Luke's strong arms, to be comforted.

But after what happened to Blair, we have to be even more careful that nobody knows about us.

I have to watch my ass. I have to stay one step ahead.

66

JACKSON

The hell have you been?" Charleigh's voice screeches in his ear. Jackson already regrets calling her. "I left word that it was urgent—"

"Sorry, I was *out*. Hit a few bars, treated myself to dinner—"

"Okay, okay, but listen. Things are *crazy* here." Charleigh sounds unsteady, unhinged.

For a panicked second, Jackson wonders if she's somehow found out about Abigail and Alexander. Because if she *has* heard it from someone else first—like Alexander—she'll *never* forgive Jackson for keeping it from her. He'll basically just have to act shocked, like it's the first time he's ever heard such a thing.

He palms his glass of water, swallows a mouthful, readies himself for his Oscar-winning performance. But then Charleigh says, "Blair Chambers is in a coma."

Record scratch. What the—

"Oh, dear God, what happened?" he asks, feeling terrible for being just a tad relieved that this isn't about Alexander's cheating.

"Diving accident. Out at the swimming hole—"

"But, like, *how?*"

"It was a freak thing." Charleigh lowers her voice almost to a whisper. "Apparently, a canoe somehow got loose and drifted out at the exact moment Blair dove off the roof of the boathouse—"

"Oh, my God." His hotel room spins, twirls. Jackson clutches at his stomach. "That's awful. What's the prognosis? And how's Monica?"

"She's a mess, I'm sure. I actually haven't seen her yet. Hospital lobby was a zoo. I'm going by there in the morning. Jackson, it's bad. But hopefully she'll make it—" Charleigh's voice cracks.

Jackson's mind spins.

A freak accident?

He doesn't say the quiet part out loud.

The part that the back of his mind is chewing on. Seeing Nellie, face tear-streaked, storming out of the woods the night of the party.

Charleigh telling Jackson later that night, after all the guests had left and it was just the two of them sipping champagne by the pool, that Blair had tumbled out of the woods with Luke, shirt on backward. That Nellie was upset.

Another thought chases that one. An even darker one. Jackson remembering when Charleigh first told him about Nellie's crush.

And how Luke might be dating Blair. *But if he is*, Charleigh had said, *I will find a way to fuck that up*.

"You still there?" Charleigh asks, jittery. He can picture her roaming around the kitchen, splashing wine into the bottom of a glass, chewing her nails.

"Yes, sorry, but good grief, that's so very terrible. And sickening—"

"I know," Charleigh says, her voice small and sad now.

Jackson silently admonishes himself for even entertaining the thought that his best friend could be capable of something so atrocious.

But Nellie…

"Well, keep me posted. I'm only hanging around here for another day or two. And I promise to call you back sooner next time. Love you."

"Love you, too."

67

JANE

wait until I hear Julia snoring before creaking down the ladder.

It's midnight. Pa and Mom should be asleep, and by this point, I'm desperate to see Luke. As I reach the floor, I can see that the light in their room is off. Good.

But the second I step out the front door, I can hear them, voices raised, bickering on the back porch. They're trying to be quiet, most likely so they won't wake us, so I have to strain to catch every other word.

"I didn't mean for you to actually"—Pa's even drunker now than he was earlier—"the man."

Dammit, I wanna get this, so I kick my shoes off, then crawl around to the side, as quietly as I can.

"Oh, and you're one to talk! Always running around, screwing God knows who!" Mom's voice is a razor, sharp and deadly.

"Am I not man enough for you anymore? Huh? Answer me!"

So Pa's not the only drone bee in this house. Mom's been fooling around, too. With Mr. Andersen. Or so it seems.

I place my hands along the wooden boards of the cabin like I'm scaling a high-rise, then risk a peek around the corner.

"What am I gonna do with you?" Pa's face is twisted up in pain. His words almost sound like a threat. But then he leans into Mom, takes her by the wrists, lifts her arms, plants them along the wall. Starts kissing her. Hard. And she's kissing him back.

I can't stand here watching them go at it anymore, so I skulk away, tiptoe down the length of the side porch.

I can't go to Luke's cabin now; I've lost the mojo for it. My head's spinning too much with Mom and Pa and what Mom may or may not have done with Nellie's dad.

Disgusted, I slither back inside before they catch me.

68

CHARLEIGH

t dawn, Charleigh rolls out of bed. She hasn't slept a wink. Bleary-eyed, she pads to the bathroom, tosses water on her face, brushes her teeth.

After a swift cup of Folgers, she slips out before Alexander and Nellie are awake.

She's desperate to see Monica, to see how Blair's doing, without any company from either of them.

When Alexander got home from the rifle range yesterday, she told him about the accident. As predicted, he played the whole shocked-denial game. But she could see it in his face—that pinch of concern that went beyond Blair's well-being—so she set about making dinner, busying herself in the kitchen.

Now she's making the short drive over to the hospital, taking deep breaths as she weaves through the tree-lined streets.

This morning, thank God, the lobby is empty. Empty, that is, of faces she recognizes.

But as she turns down the hall, her feet stutter, and her heartbeat bangs in her throat.

Standing outside Blair's room is a police officer, hat in hand. Her radio crackles softly by her side.

This is bad.

Charleigh wants to run screaming from the building, but she can't; she needs to find out what's going on.

She walks toward the room, the soles of her sandals tonguing the sanitized, polished floors. In her arm, the glass vase of white irises she picked up at the hospital's flower shop wobbles.

At the entrance, she stops, her eyes taking in the room.

Monica sits in a chair next to Blair's bed, her hand laced through her daughter's. Blair's eyes are closed, her head encased in a bandage so thick, she looks like an Egyptian mummy. Tubes snake from her arms, her chest; machines bleat all around them.

Chip's standing opposite the door, arms folded across his chest, leaning against the windowsill.

Next to Chip, seated in a chair, is Detective Roy Walker—a stout, middle-aged man with a healthy paunch—whom Charleigh recognizes because he's been on the police force for as long as she's been back in town. He's kind, warm, the type who always seems to be offering doughnuts in the break room at church (not that they go very often or anything), making house calls if there's a key locked inside a car. Pulling over to change a flat. That sort of thing. But today, he eyes Charleigh warily.

Great.

It's not like Nellie's ever been involved with the police, per se, but it's also not like everyone in town is unaware that she's a problem child.

But before she can mull over this too much, Monica's eyes meet hers, and Monica bursts into tears.

Charleigh rushes over to her, pulls her into a hug. "Oh, honey, I am so, so sorry. I just can't believe this happened!"

Monica's skinny frame quivers as Charleigh holds her. "I know, I know... My baby. What am I gonna do if—"

"We have to keep positive," Chip says, his voice leaden, sad. "Charleigh, that's what I keep tellin' her. Our Blair is a fighter; she's gonna make it. And just this morning, she opened her eyes."

A nurse sweeps in, lifts the vase from Charleigh, sets it on a cabinet.

"Chip is right," Charleigh says, fighting back her own tears. "Blair is tough and strong. She's gonna get through this!"

At this, Monica crumples into full-blown sobs. "I—I'm grateful you're here, but I don't think I'm up for visitors—"

"No, of course you're not, honey, but—" Charleigh fumbles. "I'll pop by later, okay?"

Chip follows Charleigh out. As they walk down the hall, he sighs. "I'm broken up, obviously, and in shock, but that woman in there will not recover if Blair doesn't pull through—"

"I'm so sorry. But she will, because she *has* to."

"We sure appreciate you comin' by, but we need some time right now. There's been all kind of people in and out, as you can imagine—"

"Don't say another word. I'll tell the others to give y'all some space." With that, Charleigh senses her opening. "What in the world are the cops doing there when you need some peace? That has to feel odd."

They've reached the lobby. Chip stops, digs his hands into his pockets, studies the floor.

Charleigh's insides twist and churn, a wet towel being wrung out.

"Because it's such a freak thing, and because, I guess, somebody noticed that the doors to the boathouse were open, so they're keeping an open mind about all possibilities."

"Good Lord, Chip," Charleigh says, adopting the softest tone she can manage. "What does that even mean?"

"It means," he says, his ruddy face turning solemn, "that maybe the police think this wasn't an accident at all—"

"But whoever in God's creation would ever—" Charleigh stops herself, literally bites her tongue.

"I don't know what to think. But when they brought her here in the ambulance, the police told us to call if she—" His voice splinters; he takes a second and swallows hard. "If she woke up. And this morning, she did, but it was brief. Opened her eyes, shut them again."

"I see," Charleigh manages to utter, mind whirring. "Well, good thing they're here, then." She squeezes him into a hug. "Take care. I'll be praying."

She shuttles out of the lobby, practically collapses in the parking lot on the way to her Jag.

Maybe the police think this wasn't an accident at all.

Charleigh ferries herself to her car, drives away. Her grip is slick on the wheel, as if she's just rubbed oil into her palms, and her heartbeat is still banging in her throat.

Jesus Christ.

But also...surely not.

Nellie may have done some shady shit in the past, yet putting someone in a coma? But then Charleigh's brain ticks back to the dollhouse Nellie set on fire, to poor Thor almost asphyxiating...

She turns down her leafy lane, readies herself to pummel Nellie with more questions. She'll do it stealthily, but still, she's got to get in front of this. If there is even any *this* to get in front of.

But as she wheels up her drive, she spies Nellie and Alexander climbing into the Wagoneer. She hops out, walks over to them. Nellie's door is still open.

"Where are you two headed?" she asks.

"Shooting range," Nellie says coolly.

Charleigh waits for Nellie to ask about Blair—she left them a note in the breakfast nook, saying that she was going to the hospital—but Nellie just stares at her blankly, impatiently.

"Well, I've got a little good news," Charleigh chirps. Nellie lifts an eyebrow. "About Blair."

Alexander leans over. "Good, let's hear it!"

"She woke up this morning. Just for a sec, but at least she opened her eyes. It's a good sign, I think? Monica was a wreck, so I didn't stay too long—"

"No, that's a *really* good sign, baby." Alexander winks at her.

Nellie whistles out a long sigh. "Oh, thank God. That's such a relief. She'll be okay, right, Mom?"

Charleigh can't tell if Nellie is relieved because Blair actually has a shot at recovering, *or if*, because she's gonna make it, Nellie can't be charged with *murder*.

She needs to inhale, exhale, *relax*.

"Yes, I really believe she will. She's tough as nails."

Alexander nods, places a hand on Nellie's shoulder.

Charleigh is about to close Nellie's door, let them go, but she pauses. "And the police were there today."

Nellie's features rearrange themselves from cool, detached, to puzzled.

"Why? What for?" Alexander quizzes her.

"Seems far-fetched to me, but they're looking into foul play. Said if Blair came to, to call them. But she only opened her eyes, closed them, so—"

"Dad, let's go," Nellie says, shutting the door. "I'm getting upset."

If Charleigh thought she'd get an ounce of relief from spilling this, from gauging Nellie's reaction, she was wrong.

Her insides begin churning again as she watches the Wagoneer disappear down the drive.

69

NELLIE

D ad turns off the highway onto the farm-to-market road that leads to the shooting range.

It's like a twenty-minute drive from our house; I've stayed silent the entire time, seething. Just being this close to Dad makes me wanna punch him in the face. I can't get what I saw the other night out of my head. Him slumped over Jane's mom, her smiling at me in that sick, evil way.

And now he's acting all concerned about *me* because of *Blair*.

"You okay, honey?"

I sniff, nod, then turn my face to the window, away from him.

"You can open up to me, you know, if you want to talk—"

I shake my head, comb my hair forward, like a shield between us.

Can I open up to you, Daddy? Obviously you really give a shit about me. And Mom. No, fuck you...

And Blair.

She's now suddenly become a saint.

Like, even though she's absent, lying in a coma in the hospital, somehow she's even *more* present. Getting even *more* attention.

God knows I've wished her dead many times, but for obvious reasons, I hope she makes it.

Dad pulls into the shooting range.

We're the only car in the parking lot.

Good.

Most people don't come out here in the middle of the week, during the day.

He grabs our guns out of the back; I carry the gear: our earmuffs, safety glasses.

Normally, I'd be excited to be out here with him—away from Mom, away from everything, just me and Dad out under the pines.

But at this moment, I can barely stand the sight of him.

"What'll it be today, shooter? Glocks or rifles?"

It's been a while since I've practiced on a Glock.

"Glock." It's the first word I've uttered to him.

The shooting range is a do-it-yourself operation. Dad strides the length of the lane, hangs our targets.

We then stand side by side and blast away.

I'm off my game today, my bullets barely striking the outline of the man on the paper target.

Dad, however, has hit the man in the chest, in the forehead.

I place the Glock down, shake my shooting arm out, roll my shoulders.

"Can't hit 'em all," Dad says, glancing over at me.

I don't know why, but this is the *wrong* thing for him to say to me. At the *wrong* time.

"Gimme a minute," I grunt.

He takes out a rag, starts cleaning his gun.

A rage so hot, it threatens to light me on fire comes over me. Dad *knows* I hate Jane, knows Mom hates Mrs. Swift, so how in the world could he have possibly betrayed us like this? What the actual *fuck*.

"I'm ready," I say, staring straight ahead.

We aim, shoot. I hit my targets like the sharpshooter I am, wiping out the man's brain with my bullets.

"Damn! That's my girl!" Dad hoots, sticks his hand up for a high five.

I ignore him.

"Again," I command.

It's time for fresh targets.

Dad walks up the lane, his boots crunching on the pine needles, cocky with his hot-shit swagger, cold as ice.

As he removes the old sheets and is tacking the new ones up, I raise my Glock, get *his* head in my line of sight.

And take the gun off safety.

70

JACKSON

t's so dark inside the bar, after the harsh afternoon sunlight, that Jackson has to blink away the sunspots in order to see.

He's at Leslie's, an upscale gay bar in lower Greenville, just next to Highland Park, where Ethan said he had most of his gigs.

At this hour, the place is still empty, just a slow trickle of pre–happy hour customers scattered at a few tables.

Jackson approaches the bar, plops down on a stool.

This was one of his regular hangouts when he lived here; a pang of sadness and nostalgia seep over him. He should just move back. Seriously. What the hell is he doing in Longview? Rotting away the best years of his life. He's saved enough so that he *could*, at least enough to rent something decent, but that would mean giving up on his long-held dream to move to San Francisco.

He can't think about all that now.

The handsome bartender glides over, torso a bundle of

muscles under a tight T-shirt. Damn, Jackson *misses* being around openly gay people so much—at least open in the sanctuary of a handful of establishments—and watches as the man wipes the bar off with a white towel, beams a gleaming smile at him.

"What'll it be?"

"Draft beer, please."

Seconds later, it arrives, starkly cold and frothy, so chilly that the beer makes the glass fog. Jackson takes a long, refreshing swig.

"That hittin' the spot?" the bartender asks, still grinning.

"Yes, in more ways than one. Used to live in Dallas, stuck in a small town now, so—"

The bartender scratches the back of his neck. "That's *rough*."

Jackson takes another pull, feels the beer loosening him up. "Hey, I wanted to ask, I'm, um—" He feels comfortable with this person for some reason, feels like he should shoot it to him straight. At the other bars, he just asked after Ethan, offering no explanation. "Just had my heart broken and was wondering if the heartbreaker ever frequents this place. Or frequented it. Woulda been a few months ago."

"Ahhh," the bartender says, blotting the top of the counter again with his rag, "that's rough, *too*. Sorry to hear it. Ask away!"

"His name is Ethan Swift. Probably close to my age. Handsome, like deadly handsome."

The bartender's eyes glimmer with mirth. "Go on; I'm intrigued."

"But also, kind of *different*. Like," Jackson starts, nips at his beer, steeling himself, "pretty sure he was in the closet. Wife, kids—"

"Ouch. But yeah, that's most of the clientele here—"

"And kind of a Bible thumper? Like totes a Bible with him? Dresses like he's from the 1800s—"

The smile on the bartender's face instantly vanishes; he hangs his head, gives it a long, slow shake. "I know *exactly* who you're talking about. But that's not his name. At least that's not what he called himself around here. Said his name was Charles. Never caught his last name."

71

CHARLEIGH

Charleigh walks laps around the kitchen island in a tight, agitated loop.

She can't sit still, can't settle her nerves, which are shattered.

This is like a nightmare she woke herself up from, but she knows she needs to get a goddamned grip, calm the hell down.

Just because the police were at the hospital doesn't mean that what happened to Blair is anything but an accident.

It certainly doesn't have to mean Nellie was involved in any way.

Her daughter is right: Blair has been downright nasty to Nellie—for years now—so why should Nellie pretend to be in a twist over it?

But still.

Charleigh doesn't know what to do with herself, with her body, how to calm herself down.

She hates that she's home alone right now, hates that Jackson's away.

She peers into the fridge—looking for what, she doesn't know—the thought of food making her belly ache even more.

"Calm *down*," she says out loud. Great, now she's talking to herself.

Her monologue is interrupted by someone knocking at the front door.

Blood whooshing through her temples, she practically runs to answer it.

Is it the police? Detective Walker?

Peering through the peephole, she exhales a frayed sigh.

It's Ethan Swift, hat in his hand, with Luke at his elbow, hands working through his glossy black hair. Grateful for the company, she cracks open the door.

"Hi!" she says with too much cheer.

"Afternoon, Ms. Charleigh," Ethan drawls. His skin glows in the sunlight, his mouth dangling open in a grin. "We were in the neighborhood, thought we'd stop by. See if we could come in, talk about the custom piece you and your husband were interested in."

Charleigh freezes. Even though she's happy they're here, relieved that her spiraling attention can be brought elsewhere, she's unsure about letting them in. Doesn't know if she's up for this kind of visit right now.

"Well, Alexander's out, at the rifle range with Nellie, so—"

"That's prolly for the best," Ethan mutters under his breath, so softly that she's not sure if she's heard him correctly.

If she has, what the hell does he mean? He's relieved Alexander's gone, or that Nellie is?

"Excuse me?" she demands.

"Nothing, I was just thinkin' out loud, that maybe it wasn't a good idea to pop in on you like this—" His eyes twinkle, and *did he just wink at her?*

"Oh, don't be silly! Come on in. Sorry, I'm feeling off today, with all this stuff that's happened—"

Ethan strides past her, Luke in tow. "It's tragic. We've been praying nonstop—"

"We have, too," Charleigh lies. "It's...*terrible*. Unthinkable."

The trio stands in the foyer; Charleigh studies Luke's face, searching for signs. *Of what?* The boy just looks bewildered and half his age today.

"Anyway, I was thinking," she says, her hands twisting into knots together, her adrenaline on overdrive, "I'd love a new sideboard for the den. It's the back room here that looks out over the yard, the pool."

Charleigh leads them down the hall. She thinks she can feel Ethan's eyes tracing her backside. She flicks her head over her shoulder, and yes, that's exactly what he's doing. This man is an impossible flirt, and she's positive Monica's spread her legs for him.

What is wrong with me? How can she even be having such thoughts with poor Monica at Blair's bedside at the hospital?

"Along this wall?" Ethan asks, tracing his finger over the light-splattered wall opposite the French doors.

"Exactly."

He nods quickly, gnaws on the side of his index finger. "I have just the perfect thing in mind. Lemme get back to my shop, sketch up a spec for you—"

"I'd like Jackson to weigh in, too, of course, and Alexander—"

She's not sure if she's imagined this, but did Ethan just roll his eyes? Surely not.

"Oh, of course! But I can visualize something *amazing* here. And no cost to you for me to draw up some plans, a quote. Then we can run it by your husband and Mr. Ford."

Luke hasn't uttered a word; he's kept his head down, gaze cast to the floor.

Charleigh can feel this little interlude wrapping up, and now she's desperate to keep them here. "Y'all want lemonade? A beer for you, Ethan?"

Ethan looks over to Luke. "Son?"

"Um, sure, that sounds nice. Thanks."

Charleigh shuffles into the kitchen, delighted to have something to do with her hands, her mind. They trickle in behind her.

"Nice kitchen!" Ethan beams, running his hands along the marble countertop. "My wife would kill for this."

Even though she *hates* his wife, his words make her sad. For *him*. She has never forgotten the hardscrabble life at the farm. The rickety cabinets in her childhood kitchen—roaches scurrying out, aluminum baking tins clanging together as she rummaged for food—the sad little sink with no dishwasher, her mother's hunched form over the cutting board, butchering a hog because they never had money to buy meat from the supermarket.

"Well, I do feel blessed and don't take it for granted!" she chirps, sounding like an entitled imbecile. She wants to fess up, tell Ethan that she, too, used to live out on the land, that her life hasn't always looked like a magazine spread, but she can't muster the energy to.

She cracks open a beer, passes it to him, scoots Luke's glass of lemonade across the countertop. Opens a beer for herself.

"Cheers!" Ethan says, tipping his bottle to hers, his eyes grazing her chest as he sips.

Charleigh swoons, feels the pinch of attraction, but represses it. Again, she's never felt the need to stray—or the desire to—but this man could seduce the panties off Mother Theresa.

She inwardly scolds herself again for thinking such ridiculous thoughts.

"Hope you don't mind, but I need to use the men's room," Ethan says.

"Oh, be my guest! There's one right there, but the one off the foyer is much nicer. And much cleaner."

As soon as Ethan exits, Charleigh turns her full attention to Luke. "How are you holding up?"

What a dumb thing to ask.

He sips at his drink, sets it down, hands wobbly. "I—well, it's pretty freaky, what happened and all. I just really hope she's gonna be okay—"

"Yes, of course you do!" Charleigh walks around the island,

folds him into a hug, needing one herself more than he probably does. He accepts it, his skinny frame poking into hers.

She unlatches herself, fixes him with her eyes. "I know you two were dating; I saw you together at the party. I'm *so* sorry. I went to the hospital, and they said they need their space, so that must be *really* hard on you, having to be away from her."

Luke takes a tiny, imperceptible step back, stares at the ground again. His feathered black hair falls over his eyes, and his face looks solemn.

"Must be tough to be *here* and not there," Charleigh quickly adds, trying to keep the line of conversation flowing.

"Well," Luke replies, shaking the hair out of his eyes, "she's not my girlfriend."

Charleigh's pulse thrums in her veins; she was not expecting him to say that. Sensing her opening, she lets words surge from her lips. "Oh! So who *is* that person you're seeing?" She knows she's walking a fine line here, that she's at risk of him shutting down at any moment, but she's pedal to the metal now, full bore.

If Nellie was behind Blair's accident, then she's got to stay ten feet ahead—no, a thousand feet ahead—of what she might do next. Charleigh's gotta try and hook Luke for Nellie.

"Hmmm?" she pesters.

He sighs, drags a hand through his hair, flicks his eyes up at hers. Biting the bottom of his lip, he says, "Oh, I'm not really seeing that other person either."

Boom. She leans in, lowers her voice in case Ethan is on his way back from the bathroom.

"Well!" She literally licks her lips. "What about Nellie, hm? I know you two like each other!"

Luke shifts his weight from one foot to the other, digs his hands in his pockets. He's squirming, his neck blooming with red streaks. "Like I said the other day, your daughter's cool, but—"

Charleigh wants to grab him by the shoulders, shake him, scold him, bark, *Hey, you little shit! Just take my goddamn daughter out! On a date! One date! What is the matter with you?*

Ethan's been gone long enough; he should've been back by now, unless, well, *eww*. But she doesn't have much time.

"Look. I know Nellie is *different*. You are, too. So, whaddya say? One date? Make a girl's day? Her month? Her whole year?" She inches even closer, goes in for the kill. "What'll it take? I know you're not in town for shits and giggles. I have *a lot* to offer."

As he fidgets, working the chain that runs from his belt loop to his wallet, Charleigh walks over to the counter to fetch her purse.

She slides out her wallet, snaps it open. Tugs out five one-hundred-dollar bills. "This is what I have on me."

Luke eyes the bills, gulps. "Ummm, I don't know how I feel about this—"

"I also have a checkbook. I can write you a check for more. Just one date," Charleigh presses.

He continues staring at the money, at her purse. She's got him.

But then he shakes his shaggy hair, scoffs. Throws his palms up, backs away. "Nothing against your daughter. Honestly, ma'am, and I could really use the cash, but...this...this is all... creepy and *gross*."

Charleigh whips out her checkbook. She can't risk fucking around here. "I will write you a check for five grand. For one date."

His lips part; he scratches the back of his neck, apparently reconsidering. "For just the one date?"

"Yes. But a *real* date. Flowers, wine—or whatever y'all drink—give her attention. And give her a chance. You might find out you like her."

"This is still creepy and gross. But yeah, I'll do it."

Charleigh scribbles out the check. Signs Alexander's name, which is something she does regularly. But especially now, just in case. If this ever gets out, Nellie won't be able to blame this on her. She gets *so* much less angry at Alexander.

She folds it, passes it over to him before he changes his mind. "And Luke, one last thing: You're not to tell a *soul* about this. And I mean *anybody*."

72

NELLIE

stand there, my fingers gripping the Glock, squinting at Dad's head.

Ever so slightly, I squeeze the trigger.

Though not all the way. I want to but can't make my fingers follow through.

As if he can sense me, Dad freezes, spins around, sticks his hands up as if I'm holding him at gunpoint, which, obviously, I am. His face warps into a contorted mask. "What the *fuck*, Nellie!"

I keep the Glock trained on him.

I can't help it; torturing him right now feels *so* good after what he did to Mom. To *us*.

He takes a step forward, hands still raised, face scrunched up like he's confused.

My heart is racing now, and my hands start to shake.

"Nellie!" he shouts. "Put the goddamn gun down! Have you

lost your mind?" His eyes are pleading and sad. And—best of all—scared shitless.

After a few long seconds, I lower my arm, set the gun on the shelf.

I rub my hands together, work out the soreness.

That's when Dad breaks into a run at me.

He grabs me by the shoulders, squeezes me, his eyes knifing me. "What the fuck was that?"

I twist out of his grip, start walking toward the car. "I could ask *you* the same thing."

"What?" he yells at my back.

"Just forget it," I spew over my shoulder.

Forget you.

The whole ride home Dad interrogates me. "What kind of stunt was that? Have you forgotten the basic rules of gun safety? Why the hell were you pointing a gun at me? Are you mad at me? Did I do something?" Blah, blah, fucking blah.

I stay silent, let him fidget, make him squirm.

He deserves every bit of feeling like this. I'm so enjoying pouting, sulking, making him guess. He *must* know I know.

But I don't want to confront him just yet. I'm still working on my plan for Dad, how I can best use this against him and for my own benefit. Hold it over his head for ransom? Wait to blurt it out when there are a lot of people around? It's too good.

I finally understand the expression *revenge is a dish best served cold*. While I'm usually the hotheaded one, I need to cool down, make sure the revenge I'm going to unleash on Dad will be the most punishing.

He's got it coming.

73

JACKSON

Jackson's vision begins to swirl. *Ethan Swift isn't Ethan Swift?*

The bartender's words ring in his head. *Said his name was Charles. Never caught his last name.*

Jackson has to make sure they are actually talking about *his* Ethan. "My name's Jackson by the way," he says, holding out his hand.

The bartender grips it, shakes it. "Troy."

"So, just to be sure we're talking about the same person, Charles, or whatever the hell his name is, was he a furniture maker?"

"Bingo. Among other things. *Many* other things."

"But why would he go by a different name? Maybe because he's in the closet, didn't want it to get out—"

At this, Troy cackles. "Ha! No. That's not it at all. It's because he was *trouble*, with a capital *T*. And left town as soon as he was found out."

Jackson lifts his beer, slams the rest of it. "What do you mean, exactly? What did he do?"

"That man," Troy says, "is a *thief*."

Jackson twirls his beer glass on his coaster.

"Lemme get you a refill—"

"Yes, please."

Troy pulls the lever of the draft, releasing pale-gold liquid. It sloshes in the glass after he slides it toward Jackson.

One more sip, then Jackson asks, "What do you mean? Like he held up the bar? Pickpocketed?"

Troy hangs his head, shakes it, grins. "Oh, if it were all that simple. No, higher level than that. His little business," he says, using rabbit ears, "is a front. Those high-end pieces of furniture? Sure, he makes them, sells them. But they're just a way to get into people's houses. *Rich* people. Like stealing jewels out of the panty drawer."

Everything Troy says tracks for Jackson. Ethan's charm, their need to move from town to town.

Holy shit.

"Wanna know the worst part? The vilest part? At least, to me, anyway?" Troy asks, leaning in, lowering his voice.

Jackson nods, not knowing if he *does*, in fact, want to hear the worst part.

"He'd come in here, seduce some of our wealthiest clientele— *and* our most closeted—gain access to their homes under the guise of making custom pieces, rob 'em blind, like I said, jewelry, that sort of thing. Then, if they caught on, he'd threaten to out them. Or worse."

Or worse.

He threatened to kill Jackson. He knows just what Troy means.

"You seem so nice, I'm sorry he got his hooks in you." Troy folds his arms across his chest, leans back against the bar. "And I understand how he did it. *Believe* me. He was the hottest thing that ever walked through here. *And* the most manipulative. I woulda hooked up with him myself, but the whole Bible thing? Freaked me out, honestly." He shakes as head as if he's swallowed something distasteful.

This makes Jackson chuckle, but all he really wants to do is die. And cry. He can't believe he was such a fool. "Did anyone ever report him to the police?"

"No! How could they? And out *themselves*? This man is a bona fide hustler, a grifter, and as soon as enough people put it together, started whispering, he hit the road."

Jackson's mind spins, the beer fizzing in his gut. He downs the rest of his glass. He'll need to stop after this one to safely make it back to the hotel, but whew, this is *a lot*. He wonders if Ethan's been brazen enough to steal from the Chambers yet. Or from Charleigh's house during the party. All those connections he made that night… The whole town is ripe for the picking.

Anger spears through Jackson as he relives Ethan shoving him down, threatening him, like he's disposable. Like he's nothing.

Well, Jackson will show him just whom he's fucking with.

74

JANE

t's dusk. The sun is hovering behind the pines, casting jagged shadows on the ground. I'm up at the vineyard, waiting for Luke.

We agreed earlier today to meet up here at sunset so we could be together. We can't risk making out in his shed, getting caught; it's too close to our cabin. To prying eyes.

We all just finished dinner, and I told everyone that I needed to get some space, do something with myself other than worry about Blair.

I *am* worried about Blair. Sick over it. But staying cooped up in the cabin with everyone won't help a thing.

I drag my basket to a fresh row, twist berries off the vine. The cicadas have started their nightly chorus, buzzing so loudly that I don't hear Luke until he's standing at the end of the row.

"Anybody see you?" I ask.

"I don't think so. I acted like I was going to the woodshed, then snuck around back. Walked behind the trees by the fence."

MAY COBB

Luke walks over to me, pulls me up. He kisses my neck, his lips moving down my arm until he's reached my wrist. I shiver. It's been a little while since we've been together; it feels so good.

I bring his hand up to my mouth, nibble on his fingers.

"God, I've missed you," he moans.

Now my mouth is on his, kissing him, his hands fumbling with my dress.

He breaks apart, drags a hand down my face. "You, Jane Swift, are amazing."

I grin up at him. My heart thumps against my rib cage.

"I have something to tell you. Some good news. No," he adds, flipping his bangs out of his eyes, "some *great* news. And, well, some bad news. What do you wanna hear first?"

My heart bangs even faster. What could he be talking about? "The great news first."

"We are going to New York. And we can leave as soon as you want." His eyes are serious, skittering over my face.

"Like, before I finish senior year?"

"Yes! You can finish there if you want. You're eighteen, so you're free."

"But, like, how?"

Luke tugs his chain wallet out of his pocket. Flips it open. Pinches out some bills. Five hundreds, which he fans out. "And this is just the first of it. I have five grand in the bank. Should clear by tomorrow."

My jaw drops; my mouth hangs open. I'm wondering if he's

robbed a store or something. Anxiety shoots through me. "Luke, how? Where did you get this?"

"Well, that's the bad news part." He combs a hand through his hair, exhales. "Ready?"

"I'm not sure."

"It's about Nellie."

Did he steal from her? From her house, at the party?

"I don't understand. What would this have to do with Nellie?" The sawing of the cicadas is so loud, I feel the need to shout at him. For this and other obvious reasons.

"Well, her mom paid me today. I know this is gonna sound crazy, but it's how we have the money to live our dream. It's enough to get us there, get our own place—"

"But paid you for *what*?"

"She wants me to take Nellie out on a date—"

"What?"

"Just one date. That's it. A few hours. Nothing more."

My head spins. I don't know what to think. This *is* crazy. And that woman is fucking insane! "Does Nellie know?"

"No! That's the thing. *No one* can know. I wasn't supposed to tell a soul. So keep it hush-hush."

I feel ill, thinking of him out with Nellie. "But you won't have to, like, touch her?"

"No. None of that. I just have to take her out. And then you and I will be free. We can leave next week, seriously."

I look through the woven vines, down at our little cabin. Think of Pa inside—I'll miss him for sure, and baby Molly—but when I think of Mom and Julia, well, fuck it, I quickly realize I can't get out of here fast enough. Can't miss this opportunity to be with Luke. In New York City! Together, without worrying who will know about us. Nobody will care! Nobody will be watching us, spying, judging.

"Say you're in!" Luke's eyes dance over my face; his hand clutches my wrist.

"Yes! But one date and that's it. And then we leave next week."

"God, this makes me so happy. I hate it here," Luke says, laughing.

"Not as much as I do!" I laugh back, my eyes filling with tears.

He tugs me into him, cradles me, starts kissing me again. My vision swims with stars.

He snakes his hands under my dress, thumbs down the top of my panties. It feels so good, it's almost excruciating—I could scream—but I chew the bottom of my lip instead, my hips moving against his hand. Luke is so delicate with me; I can't wait to finally go all the way with him. But I'll wait until we're in New York, in our own bed, safe. It'll be all the more special then.

"That feels so good," I purr in his ear.

"That's all I want to do, make you feel good."

His lips are on my neck again, grazing, his fingers moving over me so deliciously, I can't help it any longer—I let out a moan. "Don't stop."

A snapping branch jolts us both, causes Luke to pull away his hand, the sudden absence of which makes me want to cry.

My heart leaps in my throat. Who is out here with us?

Then I see her, at the end of the lane, scowling.

Mom.

"The hell do you think you're doing out here, young lady?" She's marching toward me, fists swinging by her side.

Luke steps away. "We were just—"

"You stay out of this," she hisses.

He jams his hands in his back pockets, but thank God, he doesn't budge.

Mom's shaking as she reaches for me, wrenches me close. "Answer me!" she practically screams.

Luke clears his throat, tries to step toward us, but Mom turns on him. "You get out of my sight. Right now! Go to your shed."

"Uh—"

"Now!" Mom snaps.

He ambles away, shooting me one last glance before he leaves.

"I did *not* raise you to be a whore!"

"Ha! You're one to talk!" I spew at her, thinking about her fight with Pa, the way she threw herself at Mr. Andersen in the store.

"What are you talking about?" she yells through clenched teeth, the bandanna on her head soaked in sweat. But there's recognition in her eyes, too.

"Oh, don't play coy, Mom. Not with me. I know what you've been doing with Mr. Andersen—" I don't even get the rest of my words out... Her palm strikes my cheek, swiftly, landing hard.

I stagger back a few feet.

"You don't know what you're talking about. And don't try to change the subject. I *saw* Luke's hands up your dress, saw what y'all were doing. You stay up in your loft, young lady; you are *grounded*."

"My ass, I'm grounded. You can't control me anymore. I'm old enough—" Another slap silences me. This one is much harder.

"It's for your own good. But you know what?" Mom tosses her hands up in the air, like a deranged person, and says, "What do I care? You're just like her. A *whore*."

She turns to leave, but I claw at her arm, even get a little skin under my nails. *Good.* "Who, Mom? Who are you talking about?" I screech back at her.

A venomous grin creeps across Mom's face; I've never seen her look uglier than she does in this moment. "Your *mother*."

My mother? What the hell is she talking about?

"What the hell are you talking about?" I repeat, this time out loud.

She scoffs, toes the ground, kicks up a clump of dirt. "She was a whore, too. You're *just* like her."

I feel like someone's grabbed me by the ankles, is dangling me upside down, shaking me. "You're a *liar*."

"Ha! I wish." She shakes her head slowly, that wicked grin still slithering across her face. "Jane, didn't you ever wonder why you don't look like me? Or your sister? Why, you know, you look—"

"Pretty?" I fire at her.

"No. *Sluttier. Dirty.*"

Dueling emotions tumble inside me. First, I feel like my whole world has been tilted on its side. *Who am I?* But also, there's elation. Liberation. This means I'm not the spawn of Mom. And the fact I've always felt like an outsider with her and Julia, now I get it. Now I understand why she's always despised me.

But if I'm not hers, then…whose am I?

"Is Pa my father?" My voice trembles as I ask this question. Please, please let her say yes.

"'Course. Only reason I kept you."

"Well, who is my real mother? And where is she?"

"I'm done with you for now. Go ask your good ol' pa."

75

CHARLEIGH

ours later, Charleigh still churns in the kitchen, halfway through a fresh pitcher of margaritas.

It's past eleven, and it's still so hot outside that the chill from the AC has fogged the windows. Nellie and Alexander are both upstairs; she's grateful for that, especially after the phone call she just took.

It was Kathleen. She'd just gotten home from the hospital. "Charleigh, things have gotten weird."

"Oh, no! What's going on? Is Blair doing worse, or what—"

"No, that's the thing," she said, lowering her voice. "She's better...and well..."

Panic rose in the back of Charleigh's throat like bile. "Spit it out already!" she shrieked.

"Well, she woke up about six this evening, so Chip called the cops. It's *such* good news because she managed to stay alert until they arrived. But then..." Her voice dwindled again to a whisper. "They asked her a few questions. I was standing right there, holding Monica, ya know, in case... Well, anyway, they asked her if she'd seen anything unusual before her accident—"

"*And?*" Charleigh squawked, cutting Kathleen off.

"She still can't talk, but she nodded."

Charleigh gulped, studied the contents of her glass, watched the margarita slushy slowly melt. "Well, what does that mean exactly?" Hysteria clutched at her chest.

"Well, whew, then they asked if anyone had done this *to* her and—"

Spit it out and quit pussyfootin' around, Charleigh wanted to scream.

She could picture Kathleen in her giant living room, massaging lotion into her perfect calves as she doled out this intel. Charleigh wanted to drive across town and throttle her.

"*And?*" she asked again, sharply.

"And she nodded to that, too. But then she closed her eyes, drifted back off."

Silence, thick as pancake batter, hung over the line.

Was Kathleen thinking the same thing Charleigh was? That Nellie had something to do with it? She couldn't ask her, obviously, but as the silence stretched, that's all Charleigh could think.

"That's so creepy, right? That someone might do something like that to Blair on purpose?"

Creepy *was one way to put it.* Demonic *was another.*

"Yes, of course. Poor thing. Sounds insane to me, though. Like, who would ever do such a thing?"

"I know! But anyway," Kathleen said, then exhaled. "Poor Monica and Chip. I just hope Blair pulls through. It's a good sign she's waking up more, but Monica nearly passed out when Blair answered the police like that."

"Absolutely. Listen, I gotta run," Charleigh said abruptly. "Pounding headache. Call me tomorrow if anything changes or if you hear anything else at all." She slammed the phone down in its cradle, then eyed the ceiling as if she could see through it, all the way to Nellie's room.

She walked over to the liquor cabinet, splattered a bunch of tequila into the bottom of the blender, tore open the can of frozen mix, dumped it in, and pressed Blend.

Now she's finished her second glass, the edges of her vision growing murkier.

If Alexander hadn't been acting so funny when they came home from the shooting range, she'd *maybe* finally want to have this conversation with him. But when he walked through the back door, he looked spooked, out of sorts, and Nellie pounded the stairs up to her room, slammed the door.

"What's going on?" Charleigh asked.

"Nothing! Why?" Alexander replied, his voice edged with nerves. He stuck his neck in the fridge, rooted around for leftovers.

"What's up Nellie's butt? Why'd she storm—" Charleigh tried again.

"Hell if I know," he snapped back.

Charleigh crossed the room, went over to him, tried to put

her arms around his neck, but he gently shrugged her off. "Not now," he said.

Stung, she retreated inside herself, stopped her line of questioning. Nellie probably acted like a gigantic asshole the whole time they were at the range, taking her teenage bullshit angst—or her rising guilt and fear over Blair's accident—out on poor Alexander.

Charleigh swirls her third drink around in her glass, takes in a tangy mouthful. Picks up the phone again, dials Jackson's hotel in Dallas. The line just rings and rings and rings. She hangs up without leaving a message.

76

NELLIE

Smoke from my clove cigarette swirls above my head, then wriggles out the window.

It's 2:00 a.m., and I'm in my room, smoking the rest of the pack Luke gave me, making the air in here wavy, hazy. Which makes me feel even tipsier than I really am, which is *very* tipsy. Me and Luke drank so much tonight. On our date. *Our date!* I had a date with Luke. Well, sort of.

I still can't believe it; that's why I'm still up, smoking, processing it.

Earlier today I was locked in my room, hiding from Mom, who is a freaking *mess* right now. I heard Blair woke up yesterday, and now there's this whole deal with the police and them thinking that what happened to Blair wasn't an accident.

Mom told me about it at breakfast, her crazy eyes burning holes into my face as she manically talked, like she was trying to get me to fess up without coming out and asking me directly.

God, she's so annoying.

I just rolled my eyes, grabbed my Pop-Tart, and stormed out of the room.

Then the phone rang, and it was Luke. Luke!

"Nellie! You have a call!" Mom shouted up the stairs. "It's that boy Luke!"

I felt like I'd heard her wrong. My hands shaking, I picked it up.

"So...you wanna hang out tonight or something?" His voice made my insides explode, my vision blurry.

"Yeah, sure," I said, trying to not sound too excited. I mean, we hadn't really talked since I caught him in the woods with Blair, so I didn't want to sound desperate. "And do what?"

"I dunno. I just thought with all this stuff going on with Blair, you might be stressed, need a break. So I could pick you up. We could go somewhere and drink. Just us?"

Just us.

And all the stuff going on with Blair... I wanted to ask, *Is she your girlfriend? Aren't you all twisted up?* But I bit my tongue. I didn't care about it right that second because he was asking me out!

I could hardly breathe. "Um, yeah, I guess that sounds cool."

"I'll pick you up at eight."

How would I wait that long?

When Luke got here, his hair was freshly washed and still damp at the ends. He was wearing the same ratty jeans he always does, but he'd put on what looked like a brand-new black T-shirt. He looked so hot, I nearly fainted at the front door. And then, from behind his back, he pulled out a small bouquet of wildflowers.

"Flowers, really?" I asked, kind of making fun of him because that's so not my thing. Or his, I would think.

He laughed at this. "Yeah, like, whatever—"

I snatched them and handed them to Mom, who was hovering behind us like a witch on a broomstick.

"I would say to be back by midnight," Mom said, speaking too loudly, embarrassing herself, and me, "but just enjoy yourselves!"

I rolled my eyes at her again before sliding into Luke's Camaro.

He popped in *Led Zeppelin IV*, lit us both a clove before we were out of the drive. I looked over at him. Even the way he smokes is sexy, the muscles on his neck flexing when he takes in a long, hard drag.

I felt the urge again to ask him about Blair, to just straight up get it off my chest, but I didn't want to ruin the moment, the night. I mean, he told me when I busted them together that it wasn't what it looked like, but I don't know. It sure looked like they were together to me.

He drove out to the edge of town, to the Circles.

Thank God, no one else was there.

He parked, killed the engine, but kept his stereo on.

From the back seat, he pulled out a six-pack of beer and a bottle of whiskey.

"Shots and beers? Sound good?" he asked, twisting open the whiskey.

"Hell yeah," I said, grinning at him.

After two shots, I decided it didn't really matter what he'd had going on with Blair. She's pathetic and in the hospital; he was out with *me*.

He called *me*, brought *me* flowers, picked *me* up.

I took a third shot, the liquor burning my throat, numbing my nerves.

Luke drummed in time to the music on his steering wheel, his eyes intense, fiery.

I sipped at my beer, the can already warm from the heat, took big drags off my smoke.

Luke then flipped down his visor, slid out a joint. "Yeah?" he asked me, waving it around.

"Fuck yeah."

This made him cackle. "I like you, Nellie Andersen. Mouth like a sailor, parties like one, too."

I smiled so hard, I felt like my face was gonna split.

"You really surprise me, ya know that?" He lit the jay; sparks flew off the tip, down into his lap. He sucked on it, passed it over to me.

"Oh yeah, how so?" I took a huge hit, one that sent me into a coughing fit. After that, my vision had a film over it, and all the muscles in my body were relaxed.

"You're not like the others. The other rich girls, I mean. They're more—"

"Prissy? Stuck-up little bitches?" I said, filling in the blanks.

He laughed. "Yeah, somethin' like that. It's like you don't

give a shit about what anybody thinks of you, and I really admire that."

"Oh, but I do give a shit—"

"You don't show it, though."

He took another drag off the joint, a huge one that sent smoke tumbling out of his mouth. "Why are you like this? I've seen your house, met your parents—"

"Oh my God, you mean my *mother*—"

"Yeah, she's a trip—"

"That's one way of puttin' it—"

"But you're, like, an *outsider*. Which tells me you're goin' places. So fuck this town and fuck these people in it and fuck what they think." He shook his glossy hair. "I want you to remember that," he said, his face looking sad all of a sudden.

He said it like this was our final night together, like I'd never see him again. "What do you mean? You goin' somewhere?"

He spewed out more smoke, shivered even though it was ninety degrees outside. "Yeah, someday. Not today, but—"

"Where?"

"Where would *you* wanna go, if you could pick?" he asked, turning in his seat to face me. It almost felt like he was asking me, *Where would you wanna go with me?* Now I keep turning it over in my mind, picking his words apart, and this is what I'm choosing to believe he was asking.

"Europe. My dad's family is from Sweden, and I love it there. It's so chill, less judgy than here—"

"You've been to Sweden?" His eyes lit up, danced all over me, dropping to the top of my tank top, which I purposefully wore because it shows off my cleavage.

"Yeah, for a whole summer. It's just," I said, then exhaled, tried to come up with the coolest words, "*different* than America. Especially different than *here*. Like, everyone swims naked there, and it's not this big deal; like, they don't have the same hang-ups there. So, yeah. You'd love it."

His face turned sad again. "I hope I can get there someday, then."

He rested his arm on the console, inches away from mine. I stared at his forearm, ripped with muscles from all his woodworking and stuff, and my stomach dropped. I moved my arm closer so that it was touching his; it was as if there were electricity moving between us.

We sat like that for a second, both stoned, staring out the front windshield. Then Luke opened two more beers for us.

"Cheers?" He knocked his can against mine.

"Cheers!"

"This is nice. Like, I don't even feel like I need to talk when I'm with you. I can just *be*."

I squirmed in my seat. I wanted to take both our beers, pitch them out the window, and climb on top of him.

Instead, I downed mine as fast as I could, crunched the can in my fist, tossed it out the window.

"Damn, girl!" Luke smiled in approval. Then copied me.

After his can went flying, I leaned over, put my hand on the back of his neck. His mouth dropped open, and his eyes were all over me again, checking out my tits, my face. My heart drilled in my chest. I felt like I might faint again.

Then I leaned over even more, put my lips on his.

Kissed him.

And he kissed me back. Slowly, deliciously.

I was delirious inside, like fireworks-popping delirious.

But then he pulled away, shook his head. "Nellie, I—I can't... I shouldn't have done that. I'm sorry, but—" His hands were balled in his lap.

What the fuck?

I wanted to grab him by the back of the neck again, continue making out. What did he mean he shouldn't have done that? It felt *so* good, so right.

"It's Blair, isn't it?" I asked, tears stinging my eyes.

He dragged a hand through his hair, sighed. "No, it's not Blair. Like I told you at your party, there's nothing between us. Even though she wants there to be."

"So what *is* it, then? And why bring me out here, just the two of us, if you didn't want to make out, be with me? Is there something wrong with me?"

"God, no. That's the problem. I *like* you. I meant it when I said that. But I'm already with someone else. I told you that before—"

"Yeah, but I assumed it was Blair. So, if it's not her, then who?"

He grabbed the bottle of whiskey, took a long sip. Then another. "Fuck. I'm not supposed to tell anyone. But I feel like I can trust you."

You can't, but I'll pretend like you can. I nodded.

"I'm with Jane. I'm in love with Jane."

I felt like I'd been stabbed. In the eye.

Fucking Jane Swift. Of course.

"Ugh." I couldn't help it; it just came out.

"What? Jane is awesome—"

"Then why are you out here with *me*?" I practically screeched.

Luke shook his head, licked his lips like he was trying to work out a problem. We were both wasted by this point; I felt like I had cotton balls jammed in my ears. And in my mouth.

His eyes were bloodshot when he turned and looked at me dead-on. "I just wanted to hang out with you, because I *do* like you. As a friend. But this *is* confusing to me. I just didn't expect to have, like, these kinds of feelings for you. But I am in love with Jane, and we shouldn't have kissed."

Any other normal girl would be sad at hearing this, but not me.

I am not normal.

Instead of hearing that he's in love with someone else, with that ho, *Jane*, all I could hear was that he had feelings for me. All I could feel was his lips kissing me back.

He drove me home soon after, his Camaro crawling slowly up the drive. "I hope this doesn't make things weird between us. I want to still be friends."

I cracked open the door, held it with my foot. "Of course. It's no big deal," I said in the breeziest way possible, like he was crazy for even thinking that. "Thanks for a fun night." I winked at him, then shut the door.

I can play it cool for now.

I know Luke really likes me. I *will* find a way to fuck things up with him and Jane.

Lighting up the last of the cloves he gave me, I suck in a lungful, hold it in, and let it burn.

JANE

uke and I can't get out of here fast enough. Like, I'd leave tomorrow if we could.

I know we're not gonna be ready *that* quickly, but we seriously need to leave in the next few days.

And never come back.

I'm up in the loft, watching Julia sleep, her chest rising and falling, her stringy hair pasted across her forehead. A mix of fury and pity wash over me. I still love my sister deeply, even though she can be a monster. And I know what drives her do to certain things is a lack of feeling loved. And that makes me so sad for her. But still, I know I *have* to get away from her.

I can't sleep, of course—not after what happened tonight— plus, I'm watching out the window, waiting to see Luke pull into the pasture.

Tonight's his date with Nellie. *Ugh!* Makes my stomach sick just thinking about it, but then I think about the cash in his wallet, the money in his bank account—our ticket to ride—and I try to push the sickening thoughts away.

We'll be out of here soon enough.

Earlier tonight, I couldn't just sit here, stewing, thinking about their date. And I couldn't stand to be around Mom and Pa for one second longer, so I held out my hand, told Pa to give me the fucking keys.

I've got him over a barrel right now—I can't believe he's been lying to me my entire life about who my real mother is—so he dug them out of his pocket and slapped them in my hand without even asking me where I was headed.

I took off toward the hospital to visit Blair, the first time I've gone to see her since the accident. Her family wanted space at first, but now that she's doing better, waking up, they're allowing more visitors.

And I just had to see how she's doing for myself.

But as I stepped into her room, I nearly tripped over my feet when I saw two police officers in there, their notepads open, standing near her bed, asking questions.

Her eyes flitted to me for a sec as I walked in; I waved at her as hot tears sprung to my eyes.

She looked *awful*, her head so wrapped in bandages that it looked like she was wearing a towel on her hair, fresh from the shower. Her face is so swollen, her eyes don't even look like hers.

"Thanks for coming by," her mom, Mrs. Chambers, said to me, giving me a side hug, rubbing my back like she was consoling *me*.

"Of course," I said meekly.

"She's doing better," Mrs. Chambers said in a soft voice, "but she's still unsteady. Cops are here because she woke up again."

My stomach was clenching like there was a tight fist in the center.

The cops?

"We're just trying to determine how much you saw. How much you know," the male cop said to Blair. "You said you saw someone, that someone did this to you—"

The room began to spin.

"Here's a list of letters. Can you spell the person's name out?"

I watched as Blair nodded, cast her glance toward me as if asking my permission.

She could barely lift her arm, so the policeman placed the laminated sheet right on the bed to make it easier for her. Blair's index finger moved across the page at an excruciatingly slow pace.

Then it stopped.

"Jay," the male cop said, and the female cop jotted that down.

My heart thumped so loudly in my chest, I was worried the whole room could hear it, gonging away.

Blair looked over at me again, and Monica glanced at me suspiciously.

"Okay, this is good, keep going," the male cop encouraged.

But Blair's arm sagged, and her eyelids fluttered.

"I think that's enough," Mrs. Chambers said, "for now. Jane, you were out there, who else out there has a name that starts with *j*?"

My face burned as all eyes in the room turned on me. I fumbled through the group of teens, and yep, I'm the only one whose name begins with *j*. "Welp, just me, I think, but obviously—"

Silence blanketed the room. Blair's various machines chirped and beeped.

"Like maybe she pointed to *j* because I'm here, because I came to see her, ya know?"

I was reaching, and it seemed like everyone in the room felt the same way.

"That's possible," the female cop said. *Thank God*. "Where were you, exactly, when the accident happened?" Her eyes were kind, but still, the question was anything *but*; I wanted to bolt from the room.

I did my best to explain that I wasn't anywhere near Blair, that I was hanging out in the water near the dock with Tommy.

"Did you see anything suspicious? Anything at all?"

My mind went back to the old boathouse and the door that was ajar. I mentioned that, that I'd never noticed it open before, but that other than that, no, nothing out of sorts.

"Well, could be like you said. She's on so much medication that she might've been excited to see you, so she went to the *j*."

Of course, I know, with a feeling of sickly dread, that Blair knew exactly what she was doing.

CHARLEIGH

J ackson's on his way home, thank God in heaven. Charleigh sighs to herself, cradling her first cup of Folgers.

She doesn't think her nerves will last another second without seeing him.

She called him again, late last night, waking him up, telling him all about the police and Nellie's date with Luke. Leaving out the part, though, where she quite generously bribed Luke to ask her daughter out.

"So can you please come the fuck home now? My whole system is on overdrive, and my partner is MIA."

"Yes! And I got what I needed here, so—"

"Ooooh, do tell! What's the lucky guy's name—"

"No, not that, but I have a lot to share, too. I'll head home first thing."

The sec she hung up with Jackson, the phone rang. She

figured it was him again, but then Kathleen's mousy voice squeaked across the line. "I just went and visited Monica and Blair, and, my God, this is getting stranger by the second!" She almost sounded excited, which grossed Charleigh out.

"Okay, what now?" Charleigh pinched the phone cord between her perfectly manicured nails.

"Well, the cops were there earlier and asked her to spell out the name of who she saw, who might've done this to her—"

Charleigh felt herself gulp, felt herself struggle to take a breath. With utter dread, she said, "Go on."

"They had this sheet with letters printed on it, and anyway, she pointed to the letter *j*. Which is crazy, right?"

Crazy, why? Charleigh thought. *Because she didn't go to the letter* n?

"I don't know. I don't know what that means" is all Charleigh could muster because her body was sagging with relief, a helium balloon with the air being let out of it.

"Well, that Jane girl was there, at the hospital visiting, and so they are thinking that's maybe why Blair chose the letter—like she's mixed up or something—because *obviously* she and Jane are friends, and Jane would never—"

"Nobody knows that! That Jane girl and her family are weird as hell. I've said it from the moment they hit town. So—"

"Well, nobody's really thinking that, but it *is* weird, isn't it? And poor Blair, that's all she could manage. She passed back out right after."

Charleigh was having a hard time focusing on Kathleen's

voice. It was as if the heavens had opened up and it was the day of rapture. "Huh? Yeah, whatever. Keep me posted." She dropped the phone on the receiver, then blew out a sizable exhale, a breath she'd been holding ever since Blair's accident.

Jane Swift.

So Nellie's not the only one who wasn't all that happy about Luke and Blair being in the woods together.

After Kathleen called, she waited up for Nellie to come home from her date, and by all accounts—not that Nellie spilled a word, but she looked cheery and springy on her feet when she waltzed through the front door—the date with Luke was a success.

"Seriously, you're waiting up for me? Get a life." Nellie huffed as she blew past her mother on her way up the stairs.

"Well, how was it?" Charleigh attempted.

"It was fine, Mom. Enough, I mean it. Leave me alone, okay!"

Her words were nasty, but there was a lightness to her voice; Charleigh heard Nellie humming to herself as she headed to her room.

Charleigh was so keyed up that even though it was the middle of the night and Alexander was dead asleep, snoring on his side of the bed, cradling a pillow—the sight of which always makes Charleigh's heart surge, so tender, so innocent looking—she peeled back the covers, started kissing the back of his neck.

He groaned, rolled over on his back, still asleep, hair mussed.

They hadn't had each other since—Charleigh's brain ticked

back to try to remember the last time, which is unusual for them—the morning before their party. She hadn't given it a second thought, but with this little update, she realized how hungry she'd been for him. Her body, not her mind, which has been spinning.

She climbed on top of him, kissing the top of his waistband before rolling it down.

He stirred then, rubbing her head while she continued her mission.

But as she was just getting started, Alexander shifted, pulling her off him.

"What is it? It's been a minute, and I—"

He sighed, slung his arm over his forehead, eyes aimed at the ceiling. Where he kept them. With his other hand, he began rubbing her back, though, slowly, softly. "Sorry, baby, I'm just too bushed. Early day tomorrow at the hunting lease."

Charleigh bristled. Alexander had *never* turned her down. But she hadn't exactly been focused on *him* lately or even paying attention to him at all. She'd been a mess and she knew it. She probably wouldn't want to sleep with her either, right now. But still. "Fine." She pouted.

At this, Alexander tugged her back onto his chest, started stroking her hair. "Rain check? And I promise I'll make it up to you, make it worth it."

Now Charleigh grips her coffee mug, sips. Feels like the weight of the world has been lifted off her shoulders. Maybe, just maybe,

Nellie's not mixed up in Blair's accident after all. And maybe it *was* just a freak thing. Maybe Jane's not even involved.

And maybe, just maybe, Charleigh's little plan to get Luke to fall for Nellie might have actually worked.

79

NELLIE

Mom thinks she's so smart, but really, she's *so* not. She's such a freaking idiot, it's almost funny.

She burst into my room this morning, carrying a plate of hot Pop-Tarts, grinning like a psycho. I could tell she wanted to dig more out of me about my date with Luke. As if *that's* happening. I'm not telling her shit.

"What do you want?" I asked, bunching my comforter around me.

"You don't have to always be so tacky, Nellie."

She traipsed across the room with the plate, placed it on my nightstand, then plopped down on the edge of my bed.

"I didn't get the chance to tell you this last night, because you ran up the stairs the sec you got home, but Monica called with an update about Blair."

"And?"

"Well, apparently, Blair was alert enough to point to the letter *j* on a sheet. When the police asked who did this to her."

Mom's ridiculous grin appeared again. "Isn't that just great news?"

Why? I wanted to shout. *Because you still think I'm the one who did this to Blair?*

"Could be that Jane girl? I mean, no one's saying that but…"

J, as in Jo. Nellie Jo. Blair's little nickname for me.

I'm not off the hook at all. Blair would honestly love nothing more than to lay this at my feet.

I eyed Mom, wanting to tell her, to throw her off her game, put her back to walking on eggshells, but I decided to wait. I was still basking in the glow from my date with Luke. It was *so* great that I didn't even have the energy to fuck with Mom, deal with getting her all keyed up again.

80

JANE

t's ten in the morning, already blistering hot, and I'm coated in sweat. I've been at it all morning in the barn, grooming Indy and mucking Cookie's stall, which I'm almost finished with.

I can't believe I'm leaving them both behind, the only downside to getting out of here. So the least I can do is make sure I've taken care of these last few things for them.

I stab the pitchfork into the ground, wipe my forehead with my shirt again.

We are leaving first thing in the morning.

When Luke got home last night, late, which I was so annoyed by, I told him our plan.

We can't stay here one second longer than we have to.

He was bombed, weaving on his feet; I drilled him about his date with Nellie and why the hell he was out so late with her.

"I promise, n-nothing happened," he hiccupped. "But I had

to make it a good time, worth all that money her crazy-ass mom gave me!"

I let him stagger off, pass out in his shed.

Whatever. We'll be gone and away from all this bullshit before the light of day tomorrow, before anybody else wakes up, notices we're gone.

"Morning, Sunshine." Pa stands at the opening of the barn, grinning at me sheepishly. "Wanna talk about it?"

"Not really," I say, not making eye contact. I grab the pitchfork again.

After Mom told me the truth, I was too burned up at Pa to even ask for the full story. So I've been punishing him, giving him the cold shoulder. But now I feel myself softening. This might be the last time I see him.

Or at least the last time for a while. Also, I do want to know the truth.

He takes a step forward. "I'm so sorry I kept it from you all this time. I just thought it'd be easier if you didn't know all that—"

"All *what*? Who is she, Pa? Didn't you think I deserved the chance to know her? To get to meet her? Especially with Mom acting like such an atrocious bitch to me all my life? You and I have always had a pact: Be straight with each other. And I've damn well kept up my end of the bargain. Acting as your front woman, putting myself out there—"

His honey-colored eyes scan my face, and dammit, they mist with tears. He walks over to me, lifts me in his arms. Then I start crying, too.

"You've been the best girl ever. The girl of my dreams, Sunshine, and I just never wanted to hurt you. I'm sorry I lied, kept it from you. But I thought it was for the best. For your own good."

He keeps clutching me, which makes me sob harder. I'm crying not just because my whole life has been a lie and I feel like I can't trust anything or anyone anymore, but also because I'm gonna *miss* him. And for a second, I'm not so sure: Do Luke and I really need to go through with this? Run off? I can't imagine a world without Pa in it. We're a team. Always have been.

But then I think of Blair, of the letter *j*, like a glowing neon sign hanging over this family.

I *know* if anyone had anything to do with it—if it wasn't just some crazy accident—then it was her.

Pearl Jameson's mangled body flashes across my mind again.

She was the popular rich-bitch queen bee of Highland Park, and like Blair, she had her eyes on Luke. Flirting with him, competing for him. Luke flirting back, playing along so we could keep our secret. To an outsider, it might appear that Luke and Pearl were a thing. It definitely did to Julia.

She couldn't stand it, would thrash around our room, mooning over Luke while tearing Pearl apart.

Then, one Friday night, while Pearl was driving alone, down a steep hill from White Rock Lake back to her house, her brakes went out, and she crashed, wrapping her shiny convertible Mercedes around a tree.

No one could prove a thing, but it seemed pretty clear that her brake lines had been cut.

I knew, of course, that Julia was behind it all.

We'd all been hanging out at the lake that night, drinking. Julia was there.

But...she wasn't at the boathouse when Blair hit her head. So, even though my gut has been sick with suspicion that she might've been behind this accident, too, how could she be involved, unless she snuck out there the night before, untied the canoe, and then it magically drifted out just as Blair was diving into the water?

She was riding Cookie that day, shopping.

Or was she?

Either way, and regardless of how hard it will be to leave Pa, we really do have to get the hell out of this town, away from all this. What if the police want to ask me some questions, keep me stranded here? Will I really turn on my sister? And what if someone finds out about the money and we lose it? No, we are leaving first thing, even if it hurts me to say bye to Pa, to Cookie, to Indy.

I pat Pa on the back, then pull away. "You owe it to me to tell me the truth." Now I stare him straight in the eye. "Who is my real mother, Pa?"

He whistles out a sigh, shakes his head. Then stares at me straight back. "I'm gonna level with you, but promise me this, that you'll never breath a word to anyone. And I mean *anyone*."

"Okaaay," I say, genuinely baffled at what it could be, and even more curious now than I was when Mom first told me.

"Her name was Marissa. She was gorgeous, just like you.

Same green eyes, same smile. Beautiful. And, I'm ashamed to admit this, but when your mom was pregnant with Julia, I fell in love with Marissa."

I nod, not blaming Pa one bit for cheating on Mom. My mind swirls with thoughts of this beautiful woman, my *real mother*, and where she might be and when I might be able to meet her. "Where does she live?"

Pa shakes his head. "I'm getting to all that. So, she was as pretty as a summer daisy, and I was smitten. And I'm not proud of this, but after Mom gave birth to Julia, we found out Marissa was pregnant. With *you*. I'd gotten her pregnant, and it was a mess."

"Okay, so what's her last name?"

"Smith. But that doesn't matter anymore—" Pa's face is sad now.

"What do you mean?"

"Because she's no longer with us, I'm sorry to say."

My head reels. "Cancer? She must not be very old."

"This is the part you can't tell anyone. Hear me?"

"Yes."

"I was gonna run off with her—that's how in love I was—start a family with her. I know it sounds terrible, but she was just like you. Same spirit, same brilliant mind, an artist. But then—"

"But then, what?"

"Your mom caught wind of our plan, stormed away in the middle of the night while I was sleeping. You had just been born; you were just a few weeks old. And—"

"And tell me!"

"And there was a horrible accident." Pa shakes his head, stares at the ground. "And your mom was there."

"An *accident*?" I shrill. "What, did she poison her? Take her out with one of her freaky potions?"

"God, no. It wasn't anything like that, anything premeditated. You have to understand, life was harder on the prairie. It was...*different*. Rougher. Like I said, it was an awful acci—"

A shadow sweeps across the barn floor.

Pa looks up.

Mom's standing at the entrance, scowling at us. I don't think she's heard us because she just got here, but it's enough to shut us up.

"Molly's crying. I need you to bounce her on your knee so I can get everyone's goddamn breakfast ready."

I need to hear the rest; waiting is going to be torture. And what does he mean, Mom was there? But I'll have to wait; I have no choice. Mom never uses the Lord's name in vain, and Pa has closed up like a clam.

"Talk later," he mouths to me before turning and trailing her into the cabin.

I jerk the pitchfork back out of the ground, start mucking again. What in the hell does he mean by *an awful accident*? I'll call him from New York, first chance I get, make him tell me *everything*.

After a half hour of this, I'm completely drenched in sweat. When the tines of the pitchfork strike something solid, I shift the pine needles around to see what it is.

A blue snorkel mask.

What the hell?

It's not like we've ever done much pool swimming or have a pool of our own, so we don't have gear like this.

And then it hits me, so crystal clear that it makes me shudder.

Julia *was* there the day of Blair's accident. Except no one saw her, because she swam underwater. Was hiding in the boathouse.

She must've tied Cookie up to a tree, out of sight, then swum her way down river.

No one saw her, that is, except for Blair.

JACKSON

A warm gust rakes over the lake, ruffling the glassy-still surface of the water, combing through Jackson's hair. He's back in Longview, sitting on the deck at the Boat House, taking his first sip of the night from a banana daiquiri. If he squints, he can pretend he's really in Cancun, overlooking the ocean as the sun faints over the horizon, tinting the sky with bands of lavender, nectarine.

He's waiting on Charleigh, of course, who is always late, but he's okay with her tardiness tonight. He *needs* to have some liquor running through his veins before he tells her all that he's got to say.

About Ethan. About Alexander and Abigail.

The daiquiri tastes like dessert, and before he knows it, he's already sucked down half of it through the long red straw.

Thankfully, the Boat House is nearly empty tonight. Garth Brooks is playing at the Oil Palace over in Tyler, so everyone must be at the concert because only a few tables are occupied on the large deck, giving Jackson and Charleigh plenty of much-needed privacy.

He's slurping the dregs of his cocktail when he sees her—tanned skin radiant against a canary-yellow sundress—teetering in high-heeled sandals from the parking lot down to the dock.

"Well, heeeey, stranger!" she yells, waving her hand, her cream-colored Gucci dangling from her thin arm.

He rises to hug her, and as they embrace, a knot forms in his throat, just thinking about how he's about to dash her whole sunny mood, shatter her very existence.

"We sticking to daiquiris or moving to margaritas?" She sits, flips over the laminated menu, scrutinizes it.

"Lady's choice!"

"'Ritas, then. I need tequila, and lots of it." She sinks a tortilla chip into the salsa bowl, dredges it. Between bites, she talks at a fast clip. "So I'm gonna need to hear what this mysterious trip to Dallas was all about! But first, whew, boy, do I have some tales to tell of my own!"

Of course you do, Jackson thinks. *And, of course, you need to go first*. He's anxious to get everything off his chest, *finally*, but also cognizant of the fact that it will perhaps land better after a pitcher of drinks.

"First things first," Charleigh says, whisking her straw around in her drink before taking a long pull, "Blair woke up again. And get this"—she sucks the top of her drink down in one snort—"*this* time when she woke up, she was able to point to the letter *j*, to let the cops know that was the first letter of the person's name who might've done this to her!"

Jackson takes a long pull himself, the tartness of the drink making his mouth pucker. "What does that even mean?"

Charleigh leans in, a mischievous grin spread across her face. "Well for one thing, it takes the heat off Nellie. Blair didn't point to the letter *n*. So"—she shakes her head, sucks more margarita down—"I'm thinking it might be that Jane girl, or maybe it was all just a mishap. A freak thing! Sometimes I'm so on guard for Nellie doing something horrible, but this time, it truly seems like I'm being paranoid."

Paranoid or possibly right on target, Jackson thinks.

"Well, that's good!" he offers. He's still not convinced Nellie wasn't somehow involved, but he's relieved that Charleigh can move on from that topic for the meantime. "I mean, obviously. And obviously it's good news that Blair is coming to."

"Yes, totally!" Charleigh says. "I mean, *of course*, that's the most important thing. Poor Monica—"

"I can't imagine."

Charleigh lifts the pitcher, refills their glasses with the pastel lime-colored slush. "And it gets better!" Charleigh shimmies in her chair. "So, I know I told you about Luke and Nellie and their little date. But what I didn't get to tell you—because you abandoned me—is that Ethan's drawing up plans to make a piece for the den! When they came over the other day, I told him I'd have to run it by you first, so he's drawing up a spec—"

"Well, that's actually what I wanted to talk to *you* about."

"Okay, in just a sec. But anyway, it's *so* great! I mean, it's not like we need another piece of goddamn furniture, but this way, Luke can be in the house even more. Around Nellie. I'll make sure of it. So—"

"I'm not sure you're gonna want to go through with that once you hear what I have to say." Jackson stares at Charleigh, whose pewter-blue eyes crinkle in confusion. But it's now or never.

"What are you talking about?"

He's just about to tell her when the server appears. "Having anything to eat?"

"Yeah, we always split the chicken fajita nachos. Sound good to you?" Charleigh asks Jackson.

"Yes, extra sour cream, please!"

He takes a fortifying pull off the 'rita, continues. "Well, this is *a lot*, so..."

"Out with it."

"Ethan's the reason I went to Dallas. And I found out some not-so-great things about him."

Her eyes darken with confusion even more. She stabs her drink over and over with her straw. "I don't understand."

"Okay, whew, hear me out." Jackson's heart is ticking in his chest like a time bomb. "I hit the gay bars there, like always, but I found out that Ethan Swift is a swindler. And that Ethan is not even his real name. His real name is Charles." Jackson sighs, then immediately chases that sigh with a deep inhale.

The sky throbs a gorgeous saffron as the sun finally vanishes;

Jackson gazes out over the water, wishing he could dive in, swim away from this very fucked-up but necessary conversation.

"Whoa." Charleigh dots margarita off her lips with her linen napkin. "Told you. I *always* knew something was off about that family."

"Yep, you were right, unfortunately."

She eyes him over her giant goblet. "But tell me the rest. What do you mean, Ethan was the reason for your trip?"

Jackson inhales forcefully, again, readies himself to spill it all.

82

JANE

The lights from about thirty lit candlesticks flicker against the night sky. All us teens are out at the Circles, holding a vigil for Blair.

Tommy wanted to do this; he rounded up the candles from the Methodist church where all the rich kids go, asked us all to come out here to pray, as a group, for Blair's full recovery.

I heard that she woke up today for the longest stretch yet. The police came back, but she only had the strength to point to the letter *j* again.

I keep waiting for a knock at the door. So Luke and I leaped at the chance to get out of the house tonight, come out here and pray. And drink. And smoke pot.

We are leaving first thing, still; my duffel's all packed, hidden in his shed.

I'm meeting him at four. He'll roll the Camaro as far from the house as possible before starting it so we don't wake anyone.

I can't wait. Cannot wait to get back on the highway, head across to Arkansas, where we'll sleep over. I can see us now, cruising down the road, listening to music, smoking, holding hands, dreaming.

I'm giddy just thinking about being in New York. Thinking about exploring the Village with Luke, our fingers laced together, me starting my own band, Luke getting serious with his poetry. And I'm not nervous or scared. My childhood hasn't been ideal by anybody's standards, but living a life of crime teaches you street smarts like nothing else. I'd dare someone to try and pickpocket me.

Thank God almighty Julia stayed home tonight.

If she knew this was the last night she'd see Luke, she'd have come out for sure, ruining everything, like she always has.

But since she's not here, I'm letting my guard down, hanging closer to Luke. Even standing in front of him, taking his arms and wrapping them around my chest for a sec.

I'm drunk. I've had two cups of Hunch Punch and am now working on my first beer. After today, I need it.

Luke is tipsy but not as wasted as me, and he smartly wriggles out of the embrace, careful to not let anyone see us. We are still supposed to be a secret. Not just to Julia, but to Nellie, and to everyone else as well.

And then I hear it. Hooves. Clip-clopping out of the parking lot. Through the wavy sticks of candlelight, I see Cookie. And riding Cookie, Julia.

Fuck me. She's made us, me and Luke. She knows. Now we

really *do* have to leave town. But not in the morning. Tonight. As soon as this is over.

Or Blair's not the only one who's gonna get hurt.

83

JACKSON

'm such a fool, Charleigh," Jackson says, his belly and veins swimming with the frozen drinks.

"What are you talking about?" She tilts her head to one side, reaches out, places a palm on his forearm.

"Ethan. I fell for him. Big time."

"Oh, honey! You're not a fool! I get it! he's such a looker. Hey, it's okay to have a crush, ya know?"

"Oh, no! This went way beyond the crush stage."

The server reappears, splits the rest of the pitcher between their glasses. "Y'all want another?"

"You bet," Charleigh answers, not breaking eye contact with Jackson. "What are you talking about—"

Fuck it. Here goes.

"A few weeks ago, hell, maybe it's been a month, I ran into him at Sullivan's, you know that little bar—"

"That little shithole, yes, go on—"

"And we hit it off. Like, really hit it off. I don't know how to describe it other than that. But we had this instant connection. I'm a designer, he's a custom woodworker, and there was *chemistry*."

Charleigh narrows her eyes; she's almost squinting, like she's trying to puzzle something out. After a minute, she finally replies, "And you never thought to tell *me* about it?"

"Well, you *hated* them from the jump, so…and I didn't know if anything was gonna happen between us. Like, really develop. So yeah, I'm sorry, but I kept it to myself."

A knife tip of anger burns in Jackson's chest. He knew she'd be pissed about this, about being kept in the dark, but my God, why does she always have to make every single thing about *her*?

She stirs her drink, pouts. Sucks the 'rita through the straw, her cheeks puckering from the force with which they're pulling. "Well, what *did* happen?"

"We hooked up!" Jackson says with a flare of pride in his voice over his conquest. Even though he despises Ethan Swift, or whatever the hell his real name is, he still feels the friction of attraction, still remembers how it felt being with Ethan. Not that he'd ever want to be with him again, even if Ethan came begging. As if.

"You *did*? Like, when? Where? How? And seriously, how the fuck did you keep this all from me?"

"It happened gradually. Remember that day you dragged me out to their land for that vagina revival? He came on to me then. But I'm such an idiot; he was never really into me. I know that now. He was using me," Jackson says, then lifts his glass, rakes a clump of slush into his mouth, "to get to people like you."

"I don't understand—"

"What I found out in Dallas is that's part of the scam. He hooks up with people like me, lonely gay men, and uses them to gain connections to rich people. Makes them furniture, yes, but also steals from them. Jewelry and whatnot."

"Shit, he was in the bathroom for a long time the other day at the house. I better check my stuff—"

"Yes, you'd better. But I'm a *mess*. I've been a wreck, and it's been killing me not being able to tell you about it. The one night we had together, out on his land, was unreal. Like, the man was on *fire*. But it felt more than just physical with him. Charleigh, I thought he was gonna leave his wife for me—" Jackson pauses, embarrassed, his throat tightening with emotion.

He can't help it; tears bloom and roll down his cheeks. He was in love and got played, got his heart ripped out. He blots his eyes with his napkin, looks up at Charleigh. He's expecting tenderness, compassion, but when he gazes into her eyes, he sees fury smoldering in them.

What a selfish fuck she can be. He's just poured his heart out to his best friend, and she's pissed that he kept this a secret from her.

He waits for her to rearrange her face into something normal, something human, but she keeps on glowering.

"Well, I don't even know what to say. First, you sleep with the *enemy*, behind *my* back, and then you keep it all from me."

Indignation rises in the back of Jackson's throat. He fights the urge to reach across the table, throttle her, chuck her in the lake.

But he knows his best friend is a drama queen, and he also knows he hasn't delivered the worst of it yet. So he takes in a steadying breath, then calmly says, "Well, I'm telling you now."

She rolls her eyes, lets out a dramatic sigh. "That whole time I was ragging on them to you? And you still hooked up with him? Kept it from me? I don't know, I feel betrayed."

Oh, sugar, you don't know how betrayed you've truly been.

Jackson takes all her punches in stride, struggles to remain unperturbed. But it's hard. She's being such a cold, unfeeling bitch. He was getting ready to tell her the worst of it, that Ethan laid hands on him, threatened to kill him if he said a word about them, but he suddenly feels oddly protective over himself, senses his walls coming up. What if Charleigh isn't sensitive about *that*? He'll never be able to stay friends with her.

"Why Dallas? Why'd you go there?"

"Because," he says, then takes another frosty sip. "He suddenly broke it off with me in a nasty way. And I needed to find out if Ethan was really gay or if I was just a one-off for him. I did *not* expect to learn that the man's a scam artist. So, obviously, he *won't* be going over to your house again."

"Obviously."

She sighs again, shakes her head. Her icy eyes flit over him as if he's been a bad boy and she's trying to decide what the best punishment for him will be.

And that's when the flip switches. He's had enough alcohol,

and his friend is acting atrociously, so he blurts it out before he loses steam. "That's not the very worst of all this."

"What could be worse than this?"

"That whole family is rotten. To the core." He reaches across the table and now puts *his* hand on her forearm. "I can't believe I have to be the one to tell you this, but Alexander is fucking Abigail."

Charleigh jerks her arm away from Jackson like she's been bitten by a snake. She recoils in her chair, eyes flaming now. "Jackson Lee Ford, what in the Sam hell are you talking about? Alexander would *never*. And he would *never* lower himself to touch that woman."

But Jackson detects the uncertainty behind her steely gaze, can practically see the gears turning in her mind.

"Answer me!" she nearly shouts, slamming her hands down on the table, causing the glasses to convulse.

The server, nearly to their table, pauses. Jackson nods for her to come on over with the nachos. He needs as many barriers between himself and Charleigh as possible.

"I am so sorry, but I saw them with my own two eyes."

Charleigh shrinks in front of him, her features folding into bewilderment.

A minute later, she mutters, "When. Where." As if her voice is disembodied.

"I told you that I hooked up with him on his land, right? We got it on one night in his pasture, up at their pond, behind the house. On the dock. And I went back out there one night looking for him, wanting a repeat, and that's when I saw them."

"Tell me *exactly* what you saw."

Jackson's throat burns. He doesn't want to get too graphic; he wants to spare Charleigh. Even though she's been awful to him tonight, she *is* his best friend, and he loves her, cares for her. He picks his words carefully. "It was hard to make them out at first—I assumed it was Abigail and Ethan there on the dock—so I got as close as I could. And that's when I saw it was Alexander."

Charleigh's hand flies to her throat; Jackson thinks she's gonna be sick right here.

Night has descended, and they are the only table left. All around them, bullfrogs croak their nightly song, sounding like deranged foghorns.

He wants to circle the table, hug her, but she looks so fragile, like she might shatter into pieces at the slightest touch.

Gently, he says, "I'm so sorry. I couldn't believe it when I saw him. We both know Alexander isn't like this. And I've been struggling with how to tell you, because, what if it was just a one-time slipup? But I felt like you needed to know the truth—"

"It's so fucked up," Charleigh says, shaking her head. Tsk-tsking.

"It really is."

"I don't mean what Alexander did. Yes, that's giantly fucked up. But what's really fucked up is you sitting here telling me about it."

Jackson's mouth goes dry. The words dry up themselves, too. He never expected this reaction from her.

The fury is back in her eyes, molten, simmering. "You didn't want to sit here with this, with your own pain, so you couldn't *wait* to drag me down with you. You were hurt, and you wanted me to be hurt, too."

Is she for real?

"That's not fair—that's *not* why I'm telling you! I'm telling you because it was killing me *not* telling you. Keeping it from you. I told you because I love you!" He's nearly yelling, he's so wound up.

She spears her drink with her straw, consumes the last of it. Wipes her mouth with the back of her hand. "We could've gone the rest of our lives and been fine. And now we'll *never* be fine again. *Why* did you have to tell me?" she shrieks.

She's acting like fucking Nellie. Throwing a tantrum. Shooting the messenger. Unbelievable.

Adrenaline pounds through Jackson's system; he's quaking. He's just about had his fill of her toxic bullshit. He can't just sit here and take her abuse anymore. He gets that she's demolished, but to take it out on him?

"Charleigh, I know you're—"

She cuts him off, her words a steel blade. "You could've *protected* me from this!"

He can't take it anymore.

He stands, the metal chair skittering behind him. If he stays here one second longer, their friendship will disintegrate; this time, it won't recover. He doesn't think he'll be able to sweep this one under the rug. "Call me when you've calmed the fuck down," he says over his shoulder. "When you've remembered who truly loves you."

"Fuck you, Jackson."

He turns away, marches across the deck, seething. There is so much more he could, and should, say to her, but he just can't. His face burning, and now with enough distance, he shout-whispers through clenched teeth: *"Fuck you forever, Charleigh Andersen, you enormously entitled bitch. Fuck you, fuck you, fuck you, fuck you for life."*

84

NELLIE

hate Jane Swift, cannot stand the sight of her.

Like just now. We are supposed to be out here at the Circles for a candlelight vigil for Blair, and she's marking her territory: Luke. Backing into him, pulling his arms around her, making sure that I, and everybody else, will know they're together.

How *pathetic*.

She looks so self-satisfied, so full of herself, I want to walk over and smack that smug look right off her face.

But then I see Luke peel himself off her, back away, and I remember our kiss the other night. Passionate. Firecrackers. Him telling me he *does* like me, but that he's confused.

Jane might win the immediate battle—she might hook up with him later tonight on the funny farm—but I'm gonna win the war.

Jane heads off toward the keg, is refilling her cup, when I move in for the kill. She's all alone; it's the perfect time to knock her down a notch, put her in her place.

Plus, I've been pounding the Hunch Punch since I got here, and I'm full of piss and vinegar, as my stupid mother would say, ready to unleash.

I start by snatching the hose from her midstream, filling *my* cup instead.

"Hey, I wasn't finished—"

"Oh, sorry! My bad!"

She narrows her eyes at me, crosses her arms in front of her chest. Thinks she's wounding me with her look.

"Just so ya know," I say under my breath, "Luke's really into *me*. He may be with you, like, officially, but he took *me* out the other night." A feeling of righteousness seeps over me. I know I'm not supposed to tell anyone about our little date, but I can't stand to sit by and not try to mess them up.

He's *mine*.

Jane huffs, bites the bottom of her lip. Looks up at me like she feels sorry for me.

"What? Why are you staring at me like that? It's true, he took me out. Everyone pities you, ya know. He just pities you and your freaky farm family. But he's *into* me."

Jane cackles in my face. "As if he'd be caught dead with you! God, you're *so* delusional, Nellie. Like he'd ever be into *you*. Get a life."

Rage bubbles up inside me. "He's going out with the pathetic farmer's daughter. You have *nothing*. Why would you think you could even compete with me and all I have to offer?"

"Go fuck yourself, Nellie Andersen. Because seriously? No one else would ever."

"Oh, Luke would. And will. We kissed the other night, can you believe it?"

Jane freezes; I've got her. I shouldn't have blurted that out, but fuck it and fuck her. Her face gets red, then redder, and she shakes her head again. But this time, she's not laughing. She's seething.

"Well, you're right," she says, her voice almost a whisper. "You do have more than me. More money. So much so that your mommy had to pay him to go out with you."

This nasty little bitch. Filthy slut.

"You're fucking lying and you know it." But even as I say the words, my mind reels. Did Mom actually do this? Oh, fuck, did she set the date up? Doubt creeps in, blotting my vision.

"You think *I'm* the one everyone pities? Everybody *hates* you, Nellie. Always have. We may have nothing, but you have everything, and your mommy still had to beg Luke to take you out. She had to bribe him."

Blood whooshes in my ears, pounds through my brain. I'm seeing red. I want to yank Jane down to the ground by her hair, beat her with my fists. This lying little whore bag.

But the truth settles over me like a fifty-pound bag of sand.

And everything clicks.

Luke and Mr. Swift were at the house the other day while I

was at the shooting range with Dad. Luke was *unattended* at the house with Mom.

And then he magically called, asked me out on a date.

How fucking stupid am I that I fell for it? But even knowing this, I also know that what we have is real. Not something Mom would have to pay for.

I'm shaking, standing here in front of Jane like a fucking loser as she smirks at me. As much as I want to beat the shit out of her, first I'm going to fuck up Mom.

Mom, the hideous bitch who is right now at the Boat House, drinking with Jackson.

It's five minutes down the road.

I'm hoping, for Mom's sake, that she'll convincingly tell me Jane's a liar, disprove all this. She fucking better.

85

NELLIE

y tires squeal as I peel out of the parking lot and screech onto the highway, punching the gas as hard as I can.

The top is down, and the wind has knocked the cherry off my cigarette, but I'm too consumed with hunting down Mom to care if it's burning a giant hole in the leather seats.

I flick it out the window, my breathing too shallow to smoke anyway.

I'm so angry, I'm seeing double and nearly hit a deer because I came up on it so fast.

Fucking *Mom*! If Jane's telling the truth, God help her.

I'm horrified, so fucking humiliated. I've never felt more ashamed.

Not just that Mom most likely paid Luke to take me on a freaking pity date, but that Jane knows about it. That Luke would tell her what a grotesque freak I am. And all that after I got in her face, insisting he likes me better. I'm a disgusting joke.

Tears burn my eyes; my throat feels like it's closing, so now I can barely breathe.

Why the fuck did Mom have to stick her nose into this? Why can't she stay the hell out of my life? I *know* in my heart of hearts that Luke and I are meant to be, that he really likes me. He must; I can feel it. Sure, it woulda taken me some time to pry him away from Jane, but I remember his lips on mine, know the way we are together, can hear him saying that he loves how we can just be together and not even feel like we have to talk. He woulda come around to me eventually, I know it, and now Mom has gone and royally screwed all that up.

Because now it will *always* be awkward between us.

And I'll continue to be the laughingstock of Longview. The ugly town loser.

I turn down the blacktop that leads to the Boat House, wind tangling my hair, my rage exploding.

I see Mom's Jag in the parking lot and jerk my car into the spot next to hers, so close that I almost smash it. God knows I want to.

I'm pounding down the walkway when I see her sitting alone at a table littered with empty drinks, half-eaten plates.

Jackson must be in the bathroom.

Good.

The rest of the place is empty.

I storm over to her.

"Nellie! What a surprise!"

I can't even look at her, I'm so mad. "Where's Jackson?"

"He took off. So it's just me. Have a seat—"

I stay standing, looking down on her. "No, Mother. I will *not* be having a seat. We need to talk. In private. Now!"

"But there's no one here. Sit down!"

The way she thinks she can order me around...

"There are waiters here. You come with me. Right now!" I growl.

She doesn't budge, just sits there, pats her hair, takes out her mirror, and reapplies her lipstick, looking coy.

"Get up before I make the biggest scene of my life!" I nearly shout.

"What's gotten into you? Is it Luke? What's going on?" As she stands, I yank her by the wrist, tug her along. "Nellie, what in the hell is the matter?"

I march her off the deck, up the walkway, and into the woods that separate the Boat House from the swimming hole.

We need to have this fight in private.

I drop her arm, let her flail for a second. "Mother. I'm going to ask you this once, and if you know what's good for you, you better tell me the truth."

But I can already see it in her eyes—she knows what's coming for her. I see her expression changing, shifting, as if she's angry at how I'm threatening her but already trying to cover her ass.

"Did you hire Luke to take me out on that date?"

Silence.

She studies the ground, traces a line in the dirt with the toe of her sandal. In the trees above us, doves coo. But Mom stays silent.

I grab her by the shoulders, shake her. "Tell me, God damn it, that it's not true!" My voice squeals in my ears. "Mom, Jane just told me that you *paid* Luke to take me out! Is it true?"

I want her to lie to me. She could; I would want to believe it. So badly. If she lied well enough, I could lie to myself, pretend that what just happened, didn't. This is what we do; we've been doing this shit all my life. I could look past it, forget about it. Call Jane the liar.

But Mom's still just standing there, eyes still glued to the ground. She can't even look at me.

I shake her harder.

"Ow, Nellie you are *hurting* me!" She throws my hands off her. She's stronger than she looks.

"Tell me!" I yell, blind fury making my head throb.

"Okay, okay, yes! I bribed him! But I did it to make you happy!"

"Happy? Mom, Luke *likes* me, or did like me. Before all this. Now, I'm sure, he's mortified! He woulda been mine eventually. *Why* do you always have to meddle?"

Mom takes a step back, shakes her head. Stares at the ground again.

When she looks up at me, she's smirking.

"Why do *I* always have to meddle?" She scoffs. "Are you *kidding* me? Ever since you were little, I've had to get involved, keep your strange ass in line, cover up for all your gross, embarrassing, demented behavior."

I'm shaking. This isn't one of her cover-up jobs; this is her trying to control everything, control *me*, and fucking it all up in the process.

I've been angry in my life, but never like this. I'm literally seeing red. Luke is the only boy I've ever truly loved, and we coulda been together, but she went and stuck her big ass in the middle of things, as always. *She's* the reason my whole pathetic life has always been such a horror show.

"You fucked this all up!" I shriek.

"Oh, please! First of all, he's a lowlife, Nellie, beneath us! Not fit to shine our shoes. Get a hold of yourself! But when I saw how much you were hurting over him and how twisted up you were, and then that mess with Blair—"

What the fuck?

"You think I had something to do with that? You fucking psycho! You're even more deranged than me!" I glare at her, go in for the kill. "But I guess, ya know, born trash, always trash—"

Her swift slap lands sharply and instantly stings. White-hot pain explodes across my cheek, my eyes brimming with tears at the shock of it.

"Nellie, I—" Mom's eyes grow wide, and she looks like she's horrified that she just struck me. She steps toward me, tries to reach out, but I smack her hand down.

"Luke and I have a *connection*. He and I woulda been together if you hadn't come in and screwed all this up."

Her momentary look of sympathy vanishes; now it looks like she's the one seeing red. "Give me a *break*, Nellie! That boy told me he was seeing someone else and wasn't interested in you. So I offered him five hundred dollars cash to take you out."

The blood drains from my face; I feel hollow, sick.

Then I hear Mom's hideous laugh, tiny but wicked. Self-satisfied. "And that wasn't enough for him. So I offered him a check for five thousand dollars. Only *then* would he touch you with a ten-foot pole."

That's all it takes. I slap her back, hard, across her snarky mouth.

"Ah!" She holds her hand to her face. "You ungrateful little bitch!"

The next thing I know, I'm all over her, tackling her to the ground, dirt dusting both of us in little clouds.

"Nellie, get off me! What do you think you're doing?"

I pin her wrists to the ground, shake her.

I feel like a mountain of shame has been dumped on me. How can I ever face Luke again? Or anyone? Mom's ruined it. Forever. Am I really so disgusting that she had to *pay* him to go out with me? And what the hell does Luke really even think about me? How could he go through with her crazy-ass plan? I'm so angry; I despise them both so much.

Ugh. There I was, like a reject, taunting Jane about how Luke really likes *me*, so full of myself, so sure, and now I'm just a giant loser. My mother and Luke have turned me into a joke. I'll always be a joke. Always have been, always will be. Just wait until the others hear; oh, they're gonna love this one.

I'm about to release her wrists, get the hell out of here, when Mom adds, "He feels sorry for you, Nellie. Pities you. You didn't *really* believe he liked you, did you? Have some dignity, damn it! Now stop this foolishness and get the fuck off me." She squirms, but that only makes me grip tighter.

"Nellie! Now!" She kicks, but I sit on her legs. "Do you have *any* idea what kind of mud pit I had to climb out of to build this life for us? For *you*? You've had your whole life handed to you on a platter, like an indulged, spoiled brat. You don't even realize what all I've given you. You ungrateful, clueless little twat, you don't even know the *half* of what I've done to help buffer your nothing little life."

That wicked smirk bleeds across her face again. She says the next part under her breath but loud enough that I can hear it: "Nobody ever had to pay someone to go on a date with me." I look at Mom, beneath me—perfect Mom, gorgeous Mom, never-had-to-worry-about-boys Mom, vicious-as-a-snake Mom—and I snap. I'm not even thinking anymore when it happens.

My hands wrap around her throat, squeezing. Shaking.

I feel like she and Luke just pulled down my panties in front of the whole town. I keep squeezing. Her legs kick and flail, but I sit on them harder. The memory comes flooding back of her laughing, drunk, asking Dad, *Are we sure she's even ours?* How assaulted I felt, how small and alone. How I cried myself to sleep until I could hardly breathe while they fucked and giggled in the other room. I squeeze even harder.

Her eyes fill with fear. "Nellie, stop—" but she can't finish her sentence because she's choking now. It feels *so* good to hurt her, so good to unleash my pain onto someone else.

It's only after she stops coughing that I realize I've taken it way too far.

86

NELLIE

om's dead. I killed her.

I couldn't stop myself.

And now it's too late.

I stand over her lifeless body; her mouth is still open, like she's in shock.

What the fuck have I done?

Fresh tears filling my eyes, I stagger, then start puking up my guts.

This didn't have to happen. Why did I do this? And what the fuck am I gonna do about it?

I walk to the edge of the woods, look down at the Boat House.

The inside lights are now turned off; the deck is empty.

Other than Mom's Jag and my bimmer, the parking lot is also empty.

I've gotta do something.

It's too far to the river. It'd take a mile of hiking to get there.

And I don't have a shovel on me, so I can't bury her.

I run down to the Boat House, stumbling around the deck, making sure the coast is really clear.

After I catch my breath, I calmly walk back up the hill, back to Mom in the woods, where I left her.

For a second I think about lifting her, putting her in the trunk. Dumping her on Dad's land. But that's so far away, and the thought of driving around with her makes me ill. And what if I get pulled over?

No.

The lake will have to do.

I take a deep breath, work up my nerve, and grab her by the ankles.

She's surprisingly easy to drag, especially downhill; the pine needles make her glide over the ground, smooth as glass.

Things get rocky only when I reach the boat ramp, which is concrete and much rougher.

But I tug on her ankles, then wade into the warm lake, where I pull her body, flipping it over before I push it all the way in.

The wind is gusting tonight, making the surface of the lake ripple.

Mom's body bobs but doesn't sink.

Why the fuck isn't she sinking?

I'm starting to panic. I've got to get rid of the body. It's water-logged now; it's not like I can drag her back out of there—she's already floating away, just not going under—so what the fuck am I supposed to do?

I need someone to help me.

Someone strong.

I race back to my car, slowly pull out onto the road. I can't risk driving like a maniac right now.

Please, please let Luke still be at the Circles, I pray to a god I don't believe in.

As I cruise down the highway, I light up a smoke, trying to calm the hell down.

I pull onto the shoulder and sigh: Luke's leaning against his Camaro, away from the crowd. Smoking a jay. *Fucker.*

I kill my headlights, park far away so that no one will notice me, then sneak along the tree line until I'm close to him.

"Hey!" I whisper-shout from the woods.

Luke twists around, spots me. Walks over. "Hey. What are you doing?"

"Shhhh. Listen, I'm in deep shit. And I need your help."

"Look, I heard you and Jane fighting and—I figured you'd never want to talk to me again—" He hangs his head, stares at his feet. I want to slap him out of this.

"Fuck all that right now. Listen," I hiss at him. I can use his guilt to my advantage. Use it to play him like he played me. "You gotta help me, okay? I'm going to leave, and when no one is looking, you're gonna drive away, too. If anyone sees you, tell them you're going to buy smokes and that you'll be back. Then meet me at the Boat House. The place by the swimming hole. In the parking lot. *Now.*"

"Okay—"

I turn and leave before he has the chance to change his mind.

Five minutes later, I'm standing back in the parking lot. The INXS song, "The Devil Inside," is playing on the radio in my car. I left the stereo on to help calm my nerves, and now this damn song is playing, but it's so alarmingly spot-on.

Then, over the music, I hear Luke's tires crunch on the gravel lot. I watch him as he slides out of his car, his body lean but strong, the bottom of his Bauhaus T-shirt creeping up, showing off his tanned abs.

"Does this mean you're not mad at me?" he asks.

"Um, yeah, sure, whatever," I say. "Look, I had a nasty fight with my mom, and things got really ugly, and welp—" I point to her body in the lake.

"Fuck, Nellie!"

This makes alarm bells ring loudly in my head. "I know! I know! But just help me! Whatever, make her body sink!"

Luke looks spooked, freaked out. "I'm sorry, Nellie. This is fucked up. I can't get mixed up in all this."

"Well," I reply, "you want to keep that five thousand dollars of blood money without anybody knowing about it?"

"Jesus Christ." Luke slides a hand through his hair, tugs on the ends. "Okay. Yes. Fine."

He walks a few steps forward, and I nod. "Just go have a look, then report back. I—I'm a wreck." Tears flood my face.

As soon as he's ten feet away, I do the only thing I know how to do, the thing I've been doing my entire life.

I run through the parking lot to the pay phone.

Pick up the phone, dial 911.

A calm voice says, "Nine-one-one, what's your emergency?"

My own voice shaky, I stammer, "S-something terrible has happened. At the Boat House, off Highway 259. There was a fight, a woman and a tall guy, someone got hurt. No, *killed*, and I'm terrified for my life. Can you send someone out here to help me?"

87

NELLIE

The woods shiver all around me; the hot breeze continues to gust. But, like the trees, I'm trembling.

After I called 911, I crept over to my bimmer, started the engine. Luke was at the water's edge by then, his back to me, so I eased it up the hill—headlights off—toward the swimming hole. Stashed it deep into the woods.

Now I'm hidden in a thick part of the forest, watching. Waiting.

Poor, stupid Luke is now wading into the water, knee-deep.

It doesn't take long.

Before I know it, I see red and blue lights strobing over the darkness as three cop cars race into the parking lot.

Perfect.

Their sirens squeal; Luke spins around. In their headlights, I can see his expression: first confused, then horrified.

He scans the area, as if looking for me. But, of course, he won't find me.

Blood pounds in my temples; I can't believe this is all happening, but fuck him, he shouldn't have made a fool of me.

I crouch on my knees, just in case, get my body behind the widest part of the tree trunk.

My breathing is so shallow, I feel like I'm gonna pass out. I want to get the hell out of here, but I need to see the rest.

The cops are on him, first talking to him. I see Luke raise his hand, point toward the parking lot. Fuck, he's telling them about me; I'm almost certain of it, even as I'm silently praying that he keeps his fucking mouth shut. But then, to my relief, they slap handcuffs on him, lead him through the gravel lot. Stash him in the back seat of a patrol car.

Good.

Very, very good.

I shrink even farther to the ground as I watch the line of cop cars drive past, their suspect in custody. Only once they're gone do I stand up, dust myself off.

No way I'm going down for this.

If they can't make a case against Luke, Daddy better watch his ass.

READING GROUP GUIDE

1. What do you think of Charleigh's parenting style? Do you believe Charleigh's actually trying to help Nellie, or is she only trying to maintain her image?

2. Should parents attempt to fix their children's problems for them? When might it be a good idea to step in, and when is it better for the children to handle themselves?

3. Charleigh didn't grow up wealthy, and her parents remain in a different economic class from her. How does this affect her? How might being in a different economic or social class from friends or loved ones affect those relationships?

4. How might your upbringing influence your parenting style and your relationship with your own children?

5. Is it wrong to be ashamed of the wealth your family has or doesn't have?

6. Did you obey your parents' rules when you were a teenager, or were you more rebellious? What do you believe made you behave in either way?

7. Were you one of the "popular kids" in school? If not, what did you think of them? Did you want to join them, or did you prefer your own group?

8. If your partner disrespects or hurts you in some way, is it right to do to them what they did to you? What might be a healthier way to communicate that you've been hurt?

9. The characters in this book aren't exactly models of good behavior. Why do you believe they act this way? Is it the extreme wealth, or is it something else?

10. Why do you believe Jackson considers Charleigh his best friend? Would you continue to be friends with Charleigh if she treated you as she treats Jackson?

11. How much do you believe children owe their parents? Should they always be grateful, or is there a limit?

12. Were you surprised by the end of the novel? Were you expecting something like this to happen, or did you have a different event/person in mind?

A CONVERSATION WITH THE AUTHOR

Where did the inspiration for this story come from?

Growing up in the 1980s, I was pretty obsessed with the *Little House on the Prairie* TV series. It's something I would watch with both my sisters (and perhaps because I'm the middle child, I related to the Laura Ingalls Wilder character the most?) and also at my grandparents' house. It had this captivating, multi-generational appeal.

Cut to a few years ago; one morning I was writing, ahem, procrastinating, on Twitter and I tweeted something to the effect of "Hey, wouldn't this make a great Netflix series: Little House on the Prairie but make it horror?" And my friend, the incredible thriller author Riley Sager tweeted back something to the effect that I must write this. And it kind of grew from there into it being set in the '80s in East Texas, less horror and more soapy, salacious thriller. Lastly, I've kind of fallen down the trad wife rabbit hole and wanted to incorporate elements of that here.

What kind of research did you need to do to make everything feel realistic?

I did revisit some of the episodes from *Little House*, but in the spirit of wanting to keep my novel its own thing, I didn't go back and binge-watch entire seasons or anything. It's more of a love letter to that show, told through the twisted lenses of the characters I like to write.

Did you have a favorite character or a favorite character to write?

Gosh, starting out, I would say my favorite character was Nellie! I loved being inside her unapologetically bold and devious mind! But as the novel came to life, I must say that Jackson became my favorite.

Most of the characters in this novel are pretty morally gray. What was it like to get in their heads?

I take this as high praise, lol! I'm always fascinated by characters whose moral compasses are skewed. In particular, I love peering behind the high-gloss curtain of the superrich and trying to view the world from that often-fraught point of view. What a pressure cooker!

What is your writing process like?

I write five days a week and sometimes on the weekend as well if I'm nearing a deadline. I love mornings best and find that I'm most productive before noon! I like to keep things simple:

hitting a thousand words a day and then thinking about the next day's chapters.

Do you have anything in mind for your next work?

I just started working on the sequel to *All the Little Houses* and couldn't be more thrilled to be back in this spicy, scandalous world!

ACKNOWLEDGMENTS

It truly takes a village to publish a book, and I'm so very grateful that I get to work with the very best village. First and foremost, massive thanks to my incredibly brilliant and truly wonderful editor, Shana Drehs. I'll never forget our magical first phone call, and how enthusiastically you said yes. Also, thank you for the spectacular title! Thank you to Dominique Raccah, fearless and wondrous leader of Sourcebooks, and to my whole Sourcebooks family: Cristina Arreola, Beth Sochacki, Molly Waxman, Jennifer Steinhagen, Valerie Pierce, Mickey Tirado, Gretchen Stelter, the Sourcebooks Library team, the creative/art department, the sales and marketing teams, and the lovely copy editors! I could not have landed in better hands!

Thank you, as always, to my phenomenal agent, Victoria Sanders, the very best of the best. I'm so lucky you're both my agent and my friend. Thanks, as always, for your unwavering faith and support. Writing a book can be a lonely journey, but thanks to my fabulous, longtime development editor, Benee Knauer, the journey is not only a lot less lonely but a helluva lot of fun. Thank you, B, for your incredible friendship and razor-sharp guidance. Huge thanks as well to the rest of the spectacular team at VSA—to Bernadette Baker-Baughman, Christine Kelder, and Diane Dickensheid—I'm so very grateful for your hard work behind the scenes on my behalf.

Enormous thanks to my amazing film/TV team: to Hilary Zaitz Michael, my magnificent agent, thank you for continuing to work miracles; thank you to my extraordinary manager, Jordan Cerf, I'm so very happy we've joined forces and can't wait to see what we'll cook up; and thanks as well to Darren and Julia for your incredible diligence.

Huge shout-out to my hunting wifey, Rebecca Cutter, for making the show that blew up the internet. I adore you for life. And big, Texas-sized thanks to everyone on team Hunting Wives!

Thank you to my fabulous friend Josh Sabarra for too many things to count.

My writing career wouldn't exist without the endless support of my family and friends, and a special thanks is owed to my incredibly loving & supportive parents, Liz and Charles, who cheer me on always. Massive thanks as well to my sisters, Beth and Susie, for EVERYTHING, and to my bestie and our fourth sister, Amy.

Huge thanks as well to my brother-in-law, Paul, and my nephews, Xavier and Logan. Thank you to Joni, Courtney, Buddy,

Marc, Kip, and Mac. And thanks to my husband's wonderful family and also my extended family—Keegan, Slade, Jess, and Trev, David and Clara, Dorthaan Kirk, and my East Coast family, T-Pa and Feeney.

A special thanks to Ron and Lolita, Valentina, and Anton.

I'm so grateful for the generous authors and friends who took time out to read this early, and offer blurbs, I owe you all margaritas: Laurie Elizabeth Flynn, Riley Sager, Jeneva Rose, Rachel Harrison, Lisa Jewell, Julie Clark, Vanessa Lillie, Karin Slaughter, and Elle Cosimano.

Thank you also to the rest of my author friends who I lean on mightily: Jesse Sutanto, Katie Gutierrez, A.J. Finn, Samantha Bailey, Eliza Jane Brazier, Gabino Iglesias, Ashley Winstead, Stephanie Wrobel, Hannah Morrissey, Rachel Koller Croft, Don Bentley, Tara Roy, Chandler Baker, Hank Phillippi Ryan, and so many, many more.

An enormous thanks to all the wonderful booksellers, reviewers, bloggers, bookstagrammers, and librarians who truly keep books alive—you are all literary heroes.

Bookstagrammers are such a vital part of social media and word-of-mouth and I can't thank the bookstagram fam enough for all your support! Special thanks to my dear friend, Abby Endler, for all the things, to Dennis Michel, I'm so grateful for you and for our longtime friendship, to Ashley Kritzer, Tonya Cornish, Agatha Andrews, Carrie Shields, Dallas Strawn (and the live DMs), Shelly Robinson, and to Gare Billings (ILYM).

A special shout-out to the wonderful Jordan Moblo for your incredible support and friendship, and a huge shout-out to Carey Calvert—you are every author's dream reader.

And saving the best and biggest thanks to my fabulous husband, Chuck, who loves to talk plot and publishing, and runs through everything with me with the same zeal he applies to his fantasy football team! I could not, and would not, want to do this without you. Love you and J so very much!

ABOUT THE AUTHOR

May Cobb is the award-winning author of five previous novels, including *The Hunting Wives*, soon to be a series on STARZ. Her essays have appeared in the *Washington Post*, *Good Housekeeping*, and *Texas Highways*. She lives in Austin with her family, where she has a love/hate relationship with the summer heat.